Onward
Silent Apostle

The Falklands 1982
- a hidden conflict.

George Deeming

 **New Generation Publishing**

Defender of the Realm's adversity,
I the faceless 'mid the crowd,
One thousand nine hundred and eleven (*)
From the rooftops clear and loud.

Lions to the slaughter of identity,
Pride of place for faithful and the coward,
Sleep of the mindless, mind of the sleepless,
Day by day flesh by the pound.

Through all matters with no pity,
None of the loyalty nor the proud,
Onward Silent Apostle, Onwards,
No escape but gagged and bound.

(*) Official Secrets Acts 1911 amended 1920.

Email George Deeming:
george.deeming1982@gmail.com

Website:
http://sites.google.com/site/georgedeeming1982

CONTENTS

ILLUSTRATIONS

Authors Notes

After I left the factory where I worked on secret projects on behalf of the Ministry of Defence, I made notes from memory and this book is based on those notes. It has to be stated that I feel uneasy in doing so, because of the necessary and obligatory prerequisite of not speaking and especially not writing about factory work, under the ever-present threat of thirty years in jail if you fell foul of the Official Secrets Act.

The book is a mixture of fact and fiction. While the basic facts are true, I have endeavoured not to exaggerate some of the stories for effect, nor to underplay the seriousness of other incidents, but despite this I am unable to guarantee the actual words used in dialogue during events that took place.

All the characters in the book are true, but names have changed to protect their privacy and that of their families and descendants. It may be possible for some individuals to recognise their character, because of projects named or events described, but as employees should not have discussed their work, I am confident that families and descendants will not be able to identify their relative. It is not part of my plan to give convincing pseudonyms, but neither do I intend to be cavalier with the lives of others and ultimately I have an obligation to protect the privacy of others.

As with WW2 there are many books and articles on the actual conflict, but this story is unique as it relates to the Falklands War at home. It is the equivalent of the Colditz Story. ESR inmates were free, but prisoners of silence until the end of their 30 year rule. Colditz inmates were prisoners and were freed at the end of the war after a maximum of 5 years. You the reader will have to decide which is worse for the state of mind of an individual. In both cases there is no escape but gagged and bound.

The names of places, streets and other identifying locations have been changed for the same reason. The actual factory gave no outward sign of the secrecy, which existed within, and the faded sign even suggested a factory of no particular importance.

At the present time, March 2012, the newly elected coalition government has chosen to decommission the aircraft carrier Ark Royal as part of spending cuts and to scrap the Harriers. The message this sends to the Junta of Argentina is open to debate; one can only hope that they do not invade as they did in similar circumstances thirty years ago after there were plans to sell off HMS Endurance to Brazil. With some irony I have learned whilst preparing this text that Brian Hanrahan has died age 61. Brian was the journalist who counted the Harriers out and counted them back during the Falklands conflict.

The same elected coalition government has warned us to expect to go through a tough period of belt tightening because of the severe economic recession. In addition there are threats to our health and well-being by terrorists and their suicide bombs, crime, superbugs, cyber attacks and I don't know what else.

In writing this, I was given a sharp reminder of the hardship of not being able to of talk about my work with my wife. It must be said that my parents, clearly did not sympathise nor understand the need for secrecy. If you work in a factory, a supermarket or a school, it is perfectly normal to talk about your employment when you get home from work. *We brought out a new design today* or *There was a special offer on corn flake's* or *We had several children out with chicken pox today.*

What do I talk about?

'I did a modification to the Sentinel lag lines today.' or *'Made good progress on the triple torpedo launcher design with MoD.'*

I think not!

Now my 30 years are up, I cannot help reflecting that I am having it easy by comparison, but it still seems strange talking about that which in 1982 could end with me being given a lengthy prison sentence. There have been one or two people who held a privileged position who should have known better, but chose to publish anyway despite the consequences. To say this infuriates me is not an exaggeration and the opinion I express about them is just that -opinion.

To emphasise the need to remain silent, and the distinct absence of contemporary written text in a true story albeit thirty years old, is the anecdote as related by my colleague Harry Fether about Gabby Hayes in an old black and white film. Try as I might, I am unable to remember the full text, nor am I able to trace the film, despite hours of research on the internet. I have included what I can remember of the narrative so I hope you can forgive me for what is missing

I hope you find the book enlightening and perhaps this story of a stormy period of my life may help to keep your own trials and tribulations in perspective.

*

It would probably be helpful to provide you with a bit of background detail about the political and cultural lie of the land in 1982.

Mark Thatcher son of British Prime Minister Margaret Thatcher, educated at Harrow School, where his nickname was *Thickie Mark*, decided to live up to his unofficial title by disappearing in the Sahara during the Paris-Dakar Rally, prompting a large scale search and he is found after six days.

Unemployment in the United Kingdom is recorded at over 3,000,000 for the first time since the 1930s.

French-Canadian Grand prix driver Gilles Villeneuve is killed during qualifying for the Belgian Grand Prix.

Laker Airways collapses, leaving 6,000 passengers stranded, with debts of £270 million.

The DeLorean Car factory in Belfast is put into receivership.

Her Majesty the Queen opens the Barbican Centre in London.

1982 saw the death of Arthur Lowe, Captain Mainwaring in *Dads Army,* Douglas Bader the Spitfire ace during WW2 and with some irony Kenneth More, the actor, who depicted Bader in the film *Reach for the sky*. Arthur Askey, comedian (born 1900), Marty Feldman, comedian and actor (born 1934) and Colin Chapman, automotive engineer (born 1928).

On the music scene, we were listening to *Golden Brown* by the Stranglers, *Ebony and Ivory* by Paul McCartney and Stevie Wonder, *Blue eyes* by Elton John. The England and Scottish football team both recorded songs for their participation in the World Cup. England went out on the second round, but Scotland, whose song was entitled *We have a dream* went out in the first round. Some dream! Later in the year Dexy's Midnight Runners recorded *Come on Eileen*, which reached number one in August.

For the people of the Falkland Islands in the South Atlantic, their lives were interrupted by the invasion by Argentina from 2 April to 4 June.

Amid a recession and high unemployment, Margaret Thatcher's popularity had gradually declined, though economic recovery and the 1982 Falklands War brought a resurgence of support and she was re-elected in 1983.

4 June - Falklands War ends as British forces reach the outskirts of Stanley after *yomping* across East Falkland from San Carlos Bay. They arrive to find the Argentine forces flying white flags of surrender. A formal surrender is agreed that day.

9 July - Michael Fagan breaks into Buckingham Palace and spends 10 minutes talking to the Queen until he is apprehended. Since it was then a civil matter rather than a criminal offence, Michael Fagan was not charged for trespassing in the Queen's bedroom. He was charged with theft of half bottle of wine, but the charges were dropped when he was committed for psychiatric evaluation. He spent the next six months in a mental hospital before being released. In June the previous month, a man with a knife burst into the forecourt of Buckingham Palace and in 1981 three German tourists camped in the grounds, believing it to be Hyde Park, laughingly describing it *We thought it a publish park,* as if every public park in London is surrounded by a twelve feet high brick with barbed wire at the top! It is the first time that private royal apartments have been penetrated since Queen Victoria's reign, although the Queen Mother disturbed an army deserter in her bathroom during the Second World War. 20 July - bombings. The Provisional IRA detonates two bombs in Hyde Park and Regents Park, central London, murdering 8 soldiers, wounding 47 people, and leading to the deaths of 7 horses. 21 July - HMS Hermes, the Royal Navy flagship during the Falklands War, returns home to Portsmouth to a hero's welcome.

11 October – Mary Rose, flagship of Henry VIII of England that sank off Portsmouth in 1545, is raised.

*

I offer my thanks to Don, Terry, Frank, Kathy, Pauline, Alan, Les, Ron, Bert, Eddie and Bas for their lasting friendship and endless humour. All of them are no longer with us.

Grateful thanks are due to author Lyn Carnaby, who, whilst on a well deserved holiday in Turkey, spared a great deal of her precious time to give me her undivided attention, coupled with candid criticism, inspiration and encouragement.

Finally I owe a debt of gratitude to Marcelo Pozzo, a survivor of the cruiser *ARA General Belgrano* and to Frank, a former crew member of nuclear submarine *HMS Conqueror*, who when I traced him worked in the far east. Both men went to great lengths to answer my endless questions and agreed their story could be told.

George Deeming
London, 2012

Prologue

The eyes staring intently through the lens could see wave crests of a grey sea out of focus, the wind whipping off the tips, sending spray into frenzy.

'Bearing?'

'Screws at two four nine.'

'In the right spot, but where is she?' He muttered quietly.

Then momentarily he glimpsed a dark grey shape, which gradually materialised into the silhouette of a cruiser on the horizon. He recognised it instantly from a number of photostats he had taken of *Janes Fighting Ships,* kept in his cabin.

The eyes moved briefly away from the eyepiece and blinked away beads of perspiration. He heard the loud voice of his Grandfather. 'No time like the present!' A voice so close by it make him physically jump. The boat was already at a high state of readiness, all five main bulkhead watertight doors shut and dogged. 'Make ready tubes forward. Mark eights, set for high speed, at ten feet depth.'

A sea of expectant faces and a wall of complete silence surrounded him.

'Range?' He whispered, caused by a nervous dry throat rather than by necessity.

'1,400 yards, true bearing two four nine, target speed moderate.' Came an instant reply.

'Down periscope.'

A gentle swish and the mechanism dropped.

The ships image remained in his head, as the *Jimmy* beside him repeated range and distance.

This was it.

Now it was real.

There were real people on the cruiser, real torpedoes, loaded and ready.

'Range?'

'Steady at 1,400 yards.'

'Left, five degrees rudder.'

'Stand by one.'

'Firing switch electrical malfunction!' A clear hushed voice.

The irony of a submarine costing umpteen million pounds and at the most critical moment, the failure of a twenty pound switch! 'Go to manual! Tell me when ready.'

There was moment of frantic activity behind, then silence resumed.

'Manual ready, Sir.' The familiar voice of the *Jimmy*, offering reassurance.

'Stand by one.'

'Fire one!'

'Fish away!'

'Stand by two.'

'Fire two!'

'Fish away!'

'Stand by three.'

'Target has moved to starboard!'

'Fire three.'

'Fish away!'

The torpedoes sped towards the target.

Seconds ticked away as each crew member held his breath.

This was the moment for which they had trained. A moment few believed they would encounter. Until now it had been a dress rehearsal for a performance that would never take place. At the moment of firing their lives would never be the same. Although they were not aware of it, they were now on the worlds centre stage. *Belgrano* had real people on board, with three high explosive torpedoes fast approaching.

Forty three seconds later, two torpedoes struck home in the bowels of *Belgrano*.

An announcement by the Skipper to the whole boat, combined with the sounds of explosions, brought great elation. But if the Argies knew they were close they would probably have helicopters up with anti submarine torpedoes. Best thing, move away as quietly but as fast as possible and perhaps play possum like some boats did during the war.

'Stand by for counter attack!'

The initial euphoria turned to both dismay and fear, when they were attacked with depth throwing hedgehog projectiles from both escorts. Trained they may have been, but none had ever experienced a counter attack. *Conqueror* went deep to 1,000 feet.

1

Drinking Team

Tower Hill in the depths of winter. A bitter ceaseless easterly wind, with nothing to blunt its sharpness, sped across the North Sea, thrashed the normally genteel waters of the estuary by Southend-on-Sea, hurtled up the River Thames, then swept around the Tower of London, onwards into the City of London. The deserted narrows streets and alleys funnelled the wind into a virtual wall of biting penetrating gusts. It battered shop signs and rattled office doors, setting off alarms, whose alerting sounds lost in the din, confused an overstretched Constabulary sent out to investigate.

The Roman Wall on Tower Hill over thirty feet tall and several feet thick, solid and imposing, easily resisted the onslaught, shielded its citizens, as it had for the past one thousand years. In the protection of its lee, two brave citizens walked about with ease, glancing upwards at the force of the gale, which carried leaves and debris over the top of the wall. As they moved off into the blackness the small square became deserted. A solitary male figure emerged through the portal of the underground system into the night air, hesitated momentarily before progressing through the gale, which raged beyond the protection of this small section of Roman Wall. A lamp swung gently above his head and once outside its miserly cone of illumination, the blackness coincided with his first encounter with the storm.

The streets were empty of pedestrians, as were the roads, quite an unusual occurrence, apart from an occasional hardy motorist chancing a potential hazardous journey, who passed slowly by with caution.

Due to a prolonged local power cut, the night was black with the absence of street lighting.

Thank God the underground system has an independent power supply, else I'd be stuck in a tunnel somewhere.

Once car headlights passed out of sight, total blackness returned. Darkness so intense, a procession of shadowy figures shuffling up the slope to the execution scaffold site, would not have seemed out of place. Ghosts drifted through the Tower Hill Memorial Merchant Navy to renew acquaintance of their fellows, unseen by human eyes, who had abandoned the highway in favour of remaining indoors. An eerie place, even in daylight, the execution site, reserved for prisoners of high importance and rank, including Sir Thomas More, stood impassive. Most prisoners were executed in front of a large audience and gave little privacy for those about to meet their maker. A few yards away, the imposing Merchant Marine Memorial and in a sunken garden, lists over 36,000 names of those poor souls lost during two World Wars with no known grave.

It was to this bleak spot, just within the boundary marker of the City of London, that there came, towards the end of January, a middle aged design draughtsman named George Deeming. As President, founder member of the *Fairlop Formation Drinking Team,* he had arranged a Thursday evening gathering in their favourite hostelry, the Golden Lion, a small pub nearest to The Tower of London, with the sole intention, according to the exaggerated romantic language of Donald, one of the team. 'To partake of a beverage or three'.

Aware of the ghosts that live on in this place of untold violence, George walked cautiously past the Tower Hill Memorial and the site of the execution block, buffeted by the gale the whole time. Once, the force of the wind carried him into the roadway, where he tripped and fell to the ground grazing the palms of both hands. Fortunately the highway was empty of traffic at this time. As he made his way towards the darkened building ahead, the lights suddenly came back on, bathing him in light. Blinking in the brightness and wincing from the pain in his hands, he pushed the door open to be met by peace and tranquillity within. He walked through the deserted bar to the back room. He found the three other members of the *FFDT* in the warmth of the snug, seated around a table by a cosy imitation, but totally realistic coal fire. The sound of a sash window rattling in its frame, and wind quietly whistling through a gap in the fire door, indicated a strong wind outside, without hinting at its ferocity.

The four men had known each other for over sixty years, in particular since an enforced but chance meeting on the morning the of first day of term during September 1948, where they endured initiation to the noisy intimidating chaos of Fairlop Infants School playground. From the first day, they sought each other for reassurance, unaware of their social differences, but fully conscious of the bond that held them together. The playground resembled a cauldron of humanity where size and aggression held more sway than manners or politeness. Bad behaviour and language overpowered the majority of quietly spoken children. The quartet experienced at first hand, the furious onslaught by some of the children from the appropriately named Midway Estate. Mentally they cowered, but were obliged to physically remain in the playground until a teacher appeared on the front steps to ring the bell for silence. Hearing this, the whole school, including the bullies, were forced to stand as still as statues. When the teacher was satisfied, they lined up in orderly fashion by class order then marched off and the four were able to seek refuge in the comparative safety of the classroom.

This reaction was not uncommon.

Fairlop catchment area encompassed three main residential areas. On the plain, at the foot of Claybury Hill Wood, an established middle class housing area, complete with a modest shopping area, a swimming pool, which should have been built to Olympic Standards, but was not, due to short sighted Council, and a recreation ground which boasted four football pitches and two cricket squares. On the crest and beyond, perched exclusive Chigwell village, an ancient rural community, first mentioned in the Doomsday Book. Midway between the two developments, half way up the hill, set back from the main road, an unattractive modern council estate. In its time, Claybury Hill Wood had seen many changes. Also mentioned in the Doomsday Book, but without feigned pride of its neighbour on the hill, it had remained unchanged for centuries. In Victorian times a few cottages sprung up along the highways and byways, a handful of hamlets scattered as far as Seven Ways Brook. When Essex County Council built Claybury Lunatic Asylum in 1883 on the western fringes of the wood, this extensive development had little impact on the small isolated communities, on the eastern side.

In between the wars, housing developoment gradually encroached eastwards from London, but Claybury Hill Wood remained largely untouched. The construction of an airfield known as RAF Station Fairlop, sealed the fate of the Wood, halting further development on the southern side. Designated as green belt, a swathe of open land extended south beyond Seven Ways Brook, as far as the dual carriageway arterial road to Essex. After the war the airfield became surplus to Air Ministry requirements, around the time an economic aggregate resource was discovered deep below ground level. Over a thirty year period, this aggregate was extracted and the resulting excavation in filled with household rubbish. This too prevented substantial development, but housing was desperately needed to ease the housing shortage. A single forty-acre field of no particular agricultural benefit, set in between the Wood and Fairlop, found itself under scrutiny form the Borough Council as a possible housing site.

The announcement to build such an estate, caused consternation and panic amongst existing residents, concerned about having common riff raff from the East-End of London, living in their midst. They mounted a well organised campaign aimed at placing pressure on the Borough Council to reject the proposal, came to no avail. Despite the protest, the plans were approved and in no time buildings sprung up on former farmland, then were occupied. The estate quickly acquired the name of *The Middern*, such was the local hostility aimed towards its residents, who were in the main from solid, honest working stock, bombed out during the war. To these fine people, who endured years of bombing and hardship, then continued to reside in decayed Victorian accommodation or temporary prefabs for years after the end of the war, the prospect of a new house at Claybury, surrounded by idyllic countryside, resembled a move to paradise. There were a few notorious families though, who chose to live up to their presumed reputation, and until the estate gradually eased itself into the resemblance of a community, caused considerable disturbance everywhere, including the school playground. Children more used to playing in the rough and ready areas of the East End, surrounded by bombsites, found renewed energy when it came to playing on a level playground. They were inclined to steal food and personal items from their better off contemporaries, without stealth or subtlety, the playground offering them up to an hour of opportunity. Bullying came as second nature and a gang of thick set boys from the estate picked on any individual souls not able to fend for themselves.

The four stayed together for defence and by this combination were usually able to ward off potential bullies and thieves. The journey to and from school made them vulnerable to attack because the gang usually went about together. More than once George was kicked and punched on a walk to school. The other three suffered similarly.

The friendship continued, despite separation when two passed the eleven plus examination, and left for grammar school pastures new. The four remained firm friends, because they kept in contact throughout their time of adolescence, and became known as the *Fairlop Four*. They enjoyed varying levels of employment, from an apprentice toolmaker and Royal Navy diver, to an actor and a trainee bank manager. Later, after each went through a period of courting, then became engaged, they awarded themselves the grand name of *The Fairlop Formation Drinking Team*. The quartet were unlikely friends because of their differing lifestyles, but the variety of personalities mixed as easily as whisky did with soda.

George Deeming, a slim six footer keen on athletics, a Senior Design Draughtsman at ESR, an established military hardware company to the east of London. He acted as the catalyst that held the four together, and arranged the get togethers and by so doing claimed the illustrious and unique title of *Founder, President*. George, the first to marry, lived in the suburbs, with two children, first worked with ESR, straight from school as an apprentice toolmaker. Long hours of arduous manual labour working for a pittance in a large noisy factory workshop with 150 other men and a handful of women who worked in the office. This experience set him up for future life because all aspects of working life, hours, pay and holiday entitlement improved with the passing years. Nearing the end of his apprenticeship he moved to the draughting office and after an initial period of uncertainty took to it like a duck to water. He left when he was twenty one and took up contract draughting for five years mainly in London and suburbs, to gain experience. After he married he returned to ESR as a draughtsman and provided the defence contracts continued, planned to remain there until he retired. The MoD's decision to place contracts elsewhere put paid to these plans and over a period of three year there were two major redundancy phases. With a substantial mortgage, a wife and two children George decided to call it a day. Plans were proposed to move part of the factory to the west country, and ESR asked for volunteers. George considered his options and chose to stay in London. On impulse he responded to an advertisement, in a local newspaper seeking suitable and experienced applicants for the post of assistant artist, able to produce sketches, artwork and illustrations. The publishing house situated close to Bow Flyover in east London, produced a wide range of quality artwork for a variety of clients. Applicants should provide examples of their work and be able to justify their suitability for the post. Providing examples of his work at ESR was impossible, so George asked a friend who worked for an engineering firm if he could *borrow* some blank layout sheets, which he did. Armed with these blanks George drew what were in effect fake component drawings in Orthographic Projection. He found he was on a sort list of three with two posts on offer, but on the day of interview one candidate dropped out.

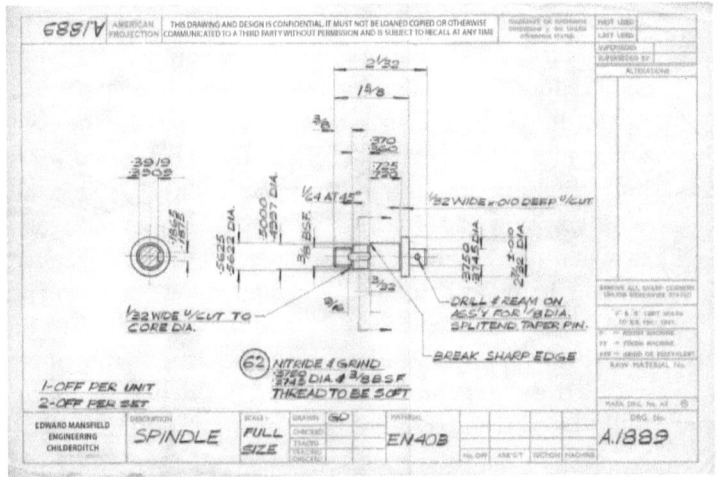

The fake drawing (the author).

With the threat of redundancy, two years out of three, alternative employment was sought. Examples of recent work were required to be presented at an interview. Working within the Official Secrets Act made this impossible so George had to resort to subterfuge.

A friend borrowed some blank layout sheets, which were drawn up - in effect a totally fake drawing and component, but they were an actual example of work.

He took with him his collection of fake drawings together with oil paintings and Indian ink drawings, completed before his marriage. They were favourably received. The interview went well and he was offered a post, which he accepted. There was some risk attached to whether he was suitable for the task, but fate favoured him and he landed on both feet.

Fate decreed that he made a wise decision as within a year, the ESR closed and moved to a sister plant on the outskirts of Bath. Many employees, because of family commitments and young children chose not to move and a great many of his former colleagues were made redundant, some with serious consequences.

Martin Hillier, also a six footer, but of the sun tanned muscular species, a former fly half, served for a short time in the Royal Navy as a Diver, when he travelled the world. Martin had made some grand plans for when he retired from the navy. He and colleagues planned to go into partnership and dive onto wrecks known to contain gold or substantial exotic cargo to be sold to the highest bidder. With the profit from their first private expedition he was confident his group would be offered lucrative sponsorship for other dives.

These grandiose plans were scuppered when he sustained injury, which forced him to retire back to civvie street. Martin had been on a rescue mission attempting to free trapped passengers within a sinking ferry in Hong King Harbour after a collision. During the rescue attempt his arm became trapped in lifting gear cables and he severely injured an elbow. When he came out of hospital the navy decided he could no longer dive with safety and pensioned him off. He now worked as a plaster technician in a London hospital.

Ray Smith, the third six footer, with a sharp almost chiselled nose, *makes me streamlined,* Ray always claimed. A fanatical follower of Charlton Athletic Football Club, one of the pair who passed the eleven plus. From humble beginnings, working as first as a junior clerk, then trainee bank manager in a high street branch of a well known establishment, Ray progressed speedily onwards and upwards. A combination of hard work, qualifications and by his admission, more than a fair share of opportunity and good fortune.

Ray was now a senior partner in a Merchant Bank within the square mile, but chose to describe himself with fake modesty as a *Big Noise in the City*. He often paid for the whole evening session including a slap up meal in an expensive restaurant if he enjoyed a good period of trading. Shortly after the group resumed their friendship, Ray offered to set up investment funds for the trio. They all now enjoyed financial benefit from what was jokingly referred to as *Ray's insider trading*!

The last of the quartet was Donald Poole, known as *DP*. In contrast, *DP* a thin, pale skinned sickly looking five foot sixer, with not the slightest interest in anything that resembled physical activity either as a participant or spectator, also passed the eleven plus and went to the same exclusive grammar school as Ray. *DP* tended to disregard academic studies and veered towards drama, in particular character acting. He was inclined to brush aside a reasonable standard of dress and always wore grubby jeans, shirts in the lumberjack style and equally grubby suede shoes. Before he left school *DP* joined an Amateur Dramatic Society and eased into a successful and occasionally volatile clique. Eventually a talent scout, or whatever, but definitely someone in an influential position within the theatrical world, saw *DP* on stage and invited him to join a local repertory company. He was an immediate success and within the year another talent scout spotted him and he joined a west end repertory company. He travelled the country on tour with them and along the way met his first wife Elaine. She was apparently heading towards a successful acting career and had resisted offers of a Hollywood film contract, preferring to remain within England. She was tragically killed in a messy car accident caused by a drunken driver. *DP* did not reveal the circumstances but he successfully sued the driver and went into semi retirement. To the amazement of everyone he remarried a member of the company after a very short period of mourning.

*

For years the *FFDT* gradually drifted apart, Martin went off with the navy, and the remainder married one by one, and settled down with a new wife, in the case of Donald, two wives. Then by chance, George met Ray in a bar and they found they lived and worked within ten miles of the city. The renewed friendship, prompted George to contact the others, and had since met regularly each month. This search for his friends proved to be time consuming, George did not know of Martins accident and subsequent retirement and *DP* no longer lived in his original marital home. He persevered and located them all within a few months.

*

Donald, the first to notice his arrival, rose to shake his hand with his aggravating limp grip, moved swiftly to the bar to order another round. George immediately detected the distinct smell of body odour and noticed Donald's badly creased red lumberjack shirt and frayed, dirty jeans.

'Good evening George, your timing is impeccable, as per usual.'

George grimaced at the feigned Sloan Square accent, which Donald could turn on and off at the blink of an eye. He wondered whether they were going to be treated to an animated conversation, between Ian Paisley and Brian Clough, after Donald had lubricated his throat with a few more pints. Donald clamoured onto the bar top, both feet off the floor, hanging on with both elbows whilst he peered around a wall trying to locate a barman. 'We have been sitting here like lemons for absolute aeons in the dark, including the odd ice age.' He complained over his shoulder whilst waving to an out of sight barman. 'We had negative bar staff when the lights were out and we have been gasping for another pint.'

With the brief greeting formalities over, George moved to stand in front of the fire, rubbing his hands with gusto, in an endeavour to rid his fingers of the cold. A clean cut barman complete with waistcoat and red bow tie appeared and with ease quickly poured out four pints.

Donald, having successfully located a barman and placed his order, came over and handed over a pint. The trio looked at George, awaiting his reaction. George turned and accepted the drink, then stared lovingly at the glass, then gulped a mouthful with relish.

'Ah, Spitfire! My favourite! He closed his eyes then gasped with ecstasy as he recognised the taste. 'What a brilliant name for a Battle of Britain commemorative brew!'

Tradition intact, the trio relaxed as Donald handed a pint to each man.

Martin responded immediately even before he sipped his beer he needed so desperately. 'Rubbish! Don't pull that stunt with me George, it doesn't work! Any alcoholic liquid is your favourite!'

'That's not true. I don't like gin, vodka or sherry!'' George laughed, hesitated before taking a second gulp, then sat down at the table. In doing so he caught something with an elbow and knocked a book off the edge. He bent down to retrieve it, and inspected the cover. He looked at a hardback copy of memoirs written by a former Assistant Director of MI5.

'Huh!' He snorted with obvious disapproval, immediately placing the book, title down, on the table. He wiped his hands on his handkerchief as if to rid his fingers of the taint of corruption that exists after touching such a book. 'The man should not have put pen to paper.'

'What makes you say that?' Ray asked innocently, knowing in advance from past experience the way the following conversation was likely to proceed. He deliberately chose to offer a challenge. 'You should buy it, it's a bloody good read, plus you might learn something about real official secrets!'

'Huh!' George repeated. 'I don't read rubbish!'

The trio waited for a verbal reaction to the claim made by Ray. This fake conflict had happened before. Although they knew that George worked on sensitive projects for the Ministry of Defence, they did not know any details, nor did they suspect that his hardware had been used publicly nine years previously. George had often defended some controversial aspects of defence, but unbeknown to them was hampered by being forced into silence, because of restrictions placed upon him by the Official Secrets Act. There had been many an argument when his circumstances forced him into making general comments or stating his opinion only, and not participate fully as he dearly wished.

When my thirty years are up, I'll show this bunch of clowns. He often thought.

'Why huh, George.' Ray challenged. 'Explain if you will.'

George glanced across the table and took a deep breath. The onlookers knew from past experience that George was going to express some firm views, as he generally did on matters of defence. They sat back in their chairs fully prepared to listen and learn. The differences of opinion, if there were any, could be left until after he had finished talking.

George glanced down at the book still on the table, shook his head, then looked up at the three in turn before speaking. ' In my opinion, publication of these memoirs by a former assistant director of MI5, clearly broke a freely given vow of silence by this individual.' He paused for a reaction, but the listeners remained quiet. He took a deep breath before continuing. 'He chose to publish his memoirs in a former colonial outpost on the other side of the world, conveniently distant from the long arm of the law. Had the man been sincere about revealing details of the many activities in which he participated or which took place under his nose, he should have done the decent thing and made his disclosures on home ground. Rather then that, he crouched behind, and remained in the shadow of a lawycr. The weakest part of the publication is the period covered was so outdated, it can be classified, no pun intended, as ancient history. The motive for publication must therefore be sensationalism, prompted by profit! Not as is claimed to reveal these disputed events apparently approved by the establishment.'

George felt surprised, perhaps disappointed, that there had been no reaction to his controversial views, decided to continue. 'I hypothesise that the said assistant director, knowing full well that the publication of such controversial material, would cause embarrassment to his former masters. Surely, if one joins a select exclusive club which pays well, kept a wolf, or perhaps even a bear from the door, then paid a good pension at the conclusion of your membership, what possible motive could provide the drive to affect the current membership?'

Donald interrupted. 'A bear George? What do you mean?'

'He means the Russians, idiot!' Ray retorted immediately, sounding cross at Donald's apparent ignorance. 'Pay attention man and don't interrupt.'

George resumed talking. 'This club however, does not resemble for instance, a golf club, for the reason for joining obliges a strict code of conduct with serious implications for the many, rather than a mere dress or green code for a few. There could also not be much opportunity to relax in the comfort of the nineteenth hole, for by the time a player completed a round, another had taken his or her place. This particular aspect annoys me for I do not enjoy the luxury of a nineteenth hole but have to remain isolated outside and fend for myself.'

His audience remained impassive, but still attentive. George found it odd that his reasoning was considered to be acceptable, even though the four held diverse views on politics and state violence. Even when his ramblings were considered unacceptable they always gave him opportunity to express his opinions. Ray and Donald in particular considered the defence budget an obscenity when there millions of starving people throughout the world. George argued that the hordes of starving would exist whether or not a defence budget existed, as the probable cause was the consequences of a corrupt government or ministers. Neither man would accept that defence projects kept many employed and occasionally improved civil activities as a direct result of military requirements.

*

During the Falklands War of 1982, both became outspoken, and held the view that the issue of sovereignty, a smoke screen which enabled their guru Margaret Thatcher, to flex her military muscles. When the Belgrano was sunk in the early days of the war, with a loss of over 300 lives, only added weight to their argument. DP said. 'Protecting a few sad Falkland islanders and lots of sheep is a waste of taxpayers money!'

Ray took delight in attempting to taunt George into retaliation by saying. 'It's an act of murder George, so don't try and defend it.'

George could not and did not.

However when the Sheffield, followed by Ardent, Sir Lancelot, Sir Galahad, Coventry, Atlantic Conveyor and Fearless were attacked or lost at a cost of many lives, first reduced them to silence and then to admit that they had spoken in haste. George in a permanent state of shock throughout the war was forced into silence for a totally different reason.

*

'The assistant Director claims that during training, he was informed that MI5 operated on the basis of the 11th Commandment, *Thou shall not get caught*. He should have been advised of the existence of an unwritten but nevertheless obligatory 12th Commandment, *Thou shall not tell,* but he clearly had no intention of complying, choosing instead to be selective over his obligations. Central to his publication, runs a theme, which suggests that a mole existed within MI5 for many years and that the mole was in fact the Director General himself. Perhaps the author, who made claim to the over exaggerated title of *a catcher of spies*, was in reality *a hunter of moles*. In either scenario he has failed miserably.'

'How do you know all this, if you have no knowledge of it, as you claim?' Ray asked, pleased that he had seen through George's ploy of hiding behind his precious Official Secrets Act. His challenge was accompanied by a characteristic rise of an eyebrow in order to emphasise his reasoning.

George took a deep breath before replying and the intense discussion continued for ages.

*

A decade passed and the *FFDT* were drinking in the same hostelry. Over the years they had tried a variety of meeting places, but for a number of valid reasons found them to be unsuitable. The premier reason lay with the last two words of the group's name -*Drinking Team*. The beer was most important. George still preferred Spitfire and the *Golden Lion*, sold the brew at a lower price than many competitors. Further more, music did not feature there, which allowed talking to continue without interruption. Also to be both fashionable and healthy, drinkers could sup in a non-smoking atmosphere.

Ray had purchased another book, which he deliberately brought with him, and left it in full view, knowing that George would react. In the same snug, George stood on his soapbox with a captive, but attentive audience.

'In order to even the score or perhaps comply with the edict of equal opportunities, another director of MI5, this time a woman, whom I have given the nickname *The Housewife*, has followed suit. I know this is rather derogatory, but she too has published her memoirs whilst still within the period of time, in security terms, when silence is deemed to be golden. The real motives of *The Housewife* can only be guessed at, but she too enjoyed the privilege of full membership to an exclusive club, with substantial pay and generous pension, she chose to cock a snoop at her masters after she retired.' George shook his head in apparent amazement. 'I wonder why she chose to join the club in the first instance? It has been claimed in the popular press, that prior to publication, her former employers vetted her text. In which case, her disclosures too, fall into the category of relatively harmless and ancient history. It is common knowledge that her book has won her few friends in Whitehall. Frankly I am amazed she was allowed to get away with it!'

His audience sat quietly and patiently listening, as George went through a process of reasoning. 'Recently there has been some startling revelations made by a Soviet defector, who claims to have fallen for *The Housewife*. Initially the former KGB Colonel did not disclose his feelings of ardour for his interrogator. Once uncorked, his passion for the former MI5 chief's curves and green eyes was more suited to a Russian romantic novel than the KGB Manual. As head of the Counter Espionage Team, *The Housewife* was entrusted with extracting detailed intelligence from the Colonel, regarding Soviet spies in Britain. The number of Soviet Embassy *Officials* expelled shortly afterwards, are measure of her success. In the long hours during which *The Housewife* debriefed and questioned the Colonel, there was one secret, which she somehow failed to unearth. For someone who, by the very nature of her employment should achieve a high competency in observation, how could she have failed to notice the adoring glances of her undeclared admirer?'

George paused for breath and to shake his head again with amazement and annoyance in equal quantities.

'Perhaps *The spy who loved me*, could be an alternative title for her publication. *The Housewife* took the helm years after the retirement of *the catcher of spies* also described by me as *the Hunter of Moles*. I would ask you to consider the appointments, which existed in between the two. With a diversion by the infamous published duo, perhaps one of this unknown select group was the true mole, that is if one existed in the first instance? A possible explanation for the disclosures made in their respective publications, is that these claims acted as a spoof, or cover for other activities yet to be revealed. Only time will tell, for the truth will emerge eventually.'

With the trio still attentive, George continued. 'Others have broken their vow of silence, one a most uncivil servant within the Ministry of Defence; another using the relative safety of Parliamentary Privilege within the House of Commons, or from abroad. Either way these people should be despised for breaking a trust. I have had to keep quiet, so should others with equal responsibility. It has been frustrating. I too have a tale to tell, but my obligations prevent it from being told.'

Ray interrupted at this point with impeccable timing.

'If they have managed to do it, why can't you?' Rays eyes flicked towards George, momentarily onto the trio, than back to George, as if trying to detect a reaction. He thoroughly enjoyed being controversial and forcing people to defend themselves. George's answer must have been a disappointment.

'That would make me as bad as them.' George retorted. He visibly cringed at the outrageous suggestion. *Jesus, what did this lot take me for? How can I justify writing about my work when the object of the exercise is to keep silent for thirty years!*

'Surely someone with your talent, could tell his story without being explicit?'

For the first time in his life, Donald made a suggestion that made sense. Usually he thought at a tangent to the others, which tended him to remain a listener, until he chose make a minor contribution. Often his out of sync remarks caused the conversation to become side tracked, which George found annoying for DP's comments usually served no useful purpose and generally spoiled the subject under discussion. This remark however gave George a kernel of a static idea, as yet without momentum. He would need time to gather his thoughts then make a reasoned assessment.

Donald detected a flash of enthusiasm, so he offered encouragement.

'Go on George give it a try.'

George shook his head, but inside his mind was whirring. *Could it be done, telling the truth, but not giving secrets away?*

'Telling the truth in the presence of your masters can be painful, if not costly, if they take away your freedom. I'm supposed to keep silent over such matters.'

Ray chose his moment to rejoin the discussion. 'You are beginning to sound like a disciple, George.'

George turned to glance in his direction as if trying to make his mind up over Ray's motives, in making such a provocative remark. George suspected that Ray often acted as Devils advocate, stimulating conversation and debate towards those inclined to remain on neutral ground.

'No you are quite wrong Ray. Disciples follow, I want to be original.'

From behind came an exasperated groan from Martin.

'Puhlease God, give me strength!' He protested, peering upwards in as if to appeal to the Almighty. 'Strike him dumb with a bolt of lightning! Anything to stop him preaching again.'

'I suggest you go up market then, George. Go on promote yourself! Become an apostle and lead from the front.'

'A silent apostle? What an thoroughly excellent idea.' Martin sounded annoyed, quite unusual for him. 'Oh, sweet bliss, that would suit me down to the ground. I thought we came here to drink!'

Ray took little notice of this outburst and started quietly singing to the tune of *Onward Christian Soldier*. 'Onward silent Apostle, Marching off to war...'

The comments made before the heavy drinking began, gave George serious food for thought. Ray and his substituted words ruined the 6565 metre of the hymn, *Onward Christian Soldiers*, published by Sabine Baring Gould in 1864, but his syllables, which interrupted the rhythm, somehow made sense. Was it conceivable for him to write about his work, without incurring the wrath of his former masters?

*

He made tentative notes. Retrieved his old typewriter from the loft, but had second thoughts when he saw its condition and enquired about the purchase of a new ribbon. Without success for an outdated model, George eventually gave up and replaced it back in the loft. His son Steve owned a rarely used computer. George went off to search Steve's bedroom and within minutes discovered the PC lurking under the bed, amongst discarded trainers, comics and assorted trivia associated with a lively teenager. The worst item was hardened curled up remnants of a half eaten marmite sandwich with a thick layer of mould on the crust! He rescued the monitor, the screen covered in finger marks, and the CPU from an uncertain death from being smothered by a disgusting grubby pair of worn out jeans. He endured a minute of violent sneezing, as both were covered in a thin grey coating of dust. He took the unit, monitor and keyboard downstairs to the study, gave them a thorough clean and carefully removed all trace of dust and debris. He plugged the wires hopefully in the right sockets and turned on the power. To his surprise it booted up and after a minute, found himself looking at rows of meaningless icons on a blue desktop screen. A white coloured arrow, which responded to mouse movement waited with patience. Where was the word processor programme? He looked in an array of meaningless directories and folders, but eventually found the icon and double clicked. The word processor opened to the gentle sound of whirring. He looked down at the keyboard and made a cautious start attempting to type with two fingers. Within minutes he could foresee a lengthy process of overcoming his lack of typing skills, quite apart from writing a worthy document.

*

Could it later be claimed that he was doing the same thing as *The catcher of spies* or *The Housewife*? That being the case he would be obliged to defend any such accusation. Although he would tell the truth, for every word he committed to paper or saved to disc must be true, he refused to break the Official Secrets Act, and would not consider doing so. The only time George would reveal what he did on behalf of the MoD would be on the day after his *Thirty Year Rule* had expired, and not a moment before. He was not prepared even to reveal the date of this momentous event, for that in itself, could to a trained eye, communicate a great deal of information. It could have already expired, but this would be a negative step. He had already criticised others about dealing with ancient history!

He and his former colleagues at ESR had dealt with secrets of substance, the divulgence of which would have a significant impact on the security of the projects manufactured there. Not all employees at ESR saw their project in situ, but they knew, or could establish, range, depth, sensitivity, frequency, speed and other operational details, which combined with intelligence obtained elsewhere, would be useful to a potential enemy.

He had not tinkered with telephones and the tapping of conversations, nor placed microphones in the walls of key or strategic buildings. If he excluded the time when he was asked help track down the maker of obscene telephone calls, made on a private exchange, that claim was true. Neither did he deal with defectors from the KGB, but rather worked at the cutting edge of the technology of the time, knowing that the defence of the realm may depend on the Sentinel project functioning as it was supposed to do. The lives of British sailors would be placed at risk if it did not perform as required, and of equal significance, lives of Soviet sailors placed at risk if it did.

There could be no compromise.

Lives and perhaps freedom of friends and fellow countrymen would be lost if the equipment did not function. Lives and perhaps freedom of an enemy to the state would be lost if it did.

A catch 22 situation, except there could be no catch.

It must work.

He had to stand up and be counted, without revealing that his body had moved from a sitting position.

It could be painful.

Early one morning George found sleep elusive, so was laying in bed at five o'clock in the morning listening to a hand sized portable radio, with the speaker pressed against an ear. His wife Carole lay asleep, a barely discernible movement of the duvet, the only sign of her presence. He could scarcely believe what he heard. Why had the situation been allowed to develop into an armed conflict? No one enters Britain or a British Territory bearing a sword. A valid passport is usually the only requirement. But someone had entered British Territory, bearing a sword and everyone had to face up to the consequences of their actions. So far it had been a bloodless coup, at least on the British side. Nothing short of a miracle could prevent outbreak of hostilities, fought between the youth of two nations, on disputed territory 8,000 miles away in the South Atlantic. There were leaders of two great nations, one a woman democratically elected, the other a male dictator. Both determined to declare war for totally different causes.

The Americans, always ready and willing to interfere with world events, nominated a broker of peace, whose motives were questionable, because everyone suspected he was there to ensure that, if hostilities worsened, the interests of the United States were not prejudiced. He bore the unfortunate surname of Haig, a name that haunts Britain and most of the Commonwealth to this day. His task seemed doomed to failure even before it commenced.

George listened over a period of weeks as the situation deteriorated, then after the landings at San Carlos, the announcer described the latest turn of events and spoke of military gains and losses together with the latest released casualty figures, during what had developed into an armed conflict. Eventually he was able to wake up in time to catch the first news report of the day without setting his alarm, and kept his fingers crossed about there being no casualties.

Imagine the reaction of George arriving home from work to view the same conflict on television. During the vivid news report he saw actual visual proof that his equipment had worked, and way down across a vast ocean, young men as enemies were killed as a consequence, and he was forced to suffer in silence.

The Sentinel project had been specifically designed to be used in waters of the northern hemisphere against a Soviet enemy, definitely not Argentina nor in the waters of the South Atlantic.

The conflict was shown nightly on television, dissected and debated by those who claimed to be experts, in all its horror and glory, and he sat still almost without breathing. He dare not speak else his emotions would give him away, and he had to exercise care whenever his projects were spoken of, or shown on television. The journalists concentrated on the glory. To dwell on the horror served little purpose for the general public eating their tea, whilst watching the six o'clock news. The stark reality of horror must be left to those involved directly. It was personal to them and to George sitting safe and warm at home, their horror was not his concern.

Except that in some cases it was.

Although his project was not mentioned directly, he gleaned from even from vague reporting, often conflicting, that his work, in the words of a journalist, had been used in anger. The fact was, he knew that it had been used quietly and deliberately with concern only about success. Anger or failure was not part of the equation.

The price of freedom and that of silence does not come cheaply. Ultimately there is a price to pay. There is no option to avoid the demand of payment in full.

There existed a mental version of the grim reaper, named the harvester of sovereignty and privilege, from which escape was impossible.

There was much more to official secrets and security than spies, moles and defectors. A relatively small number of people have worked on completely unpublished projects. Mostly these are anonymous people, passed in the street without a second glance, who have made a significant impact on the freedom others have enjoyed and even more are enjoying as this text is being read. Far more perhaps than those who broke cover to reveal that which they previously promised not to tell.

For the families of service personnel living at home in the United Kingdom during the Falklands War of 1982, a knock on a front door or a ring of the front door bell could mean tragedy. Everyone with a service background knows that if a padre comes to your door, it means there had been an injury. If two padres come to your door, it means there has been a death. If during this period many footsteps were heard walking on the front path, followed by a tap on the door, or a ring of the bell, a heart missed a beat. The tortuous walk to the front door, knowing that absolute horror waited just the other side of the familiar woodwork, seemed to resemble running a marathon. The woman would feel absolute dread and exhaustion even before she touched the handle and nervously opened the door, with her heart beating like a drum inside her head, to confront her fears.

If it was one, she gave an audible sigh of relief, for it meant an injury. Her loved one was at least alive, hopefully not with a serious injury or a loss of limb. Many families, not all, were spared this agony, because of a number of people like George. He did his job without personal risk it is true, but, his perseverance along that of colleagues ensured that if the hardware was used, it did precisely what it was designed to do, and worked. Even more than that, the hardware worked exceptionally well, occasionally in conditions, which went far beyond its intended capability. There exists to this very day, quite a significant number of souls who owe their very existence to the success of these same unpublished projects, simply because they are alive to tell the tale.

No catcher of small burrowing insectivorous animals, a housewife, a particular civil servant or a gullible Member of Parliament, can claim that.

2

Threes

It is traditional to accept that the best things come in threes.

In his early childhood there was the nursery rhyme *Three blind mice*. They chased about and terrorised the wife of a farmer, then suffered immediate savage retribution when she cut off their tails with a carving knife. A surprisingly violent rhyme for young children, accepted as being normal behaviour for an anonymous female adult, who showed extreme cruelty towards animals for no apparent reason. In his experience most adult women and girls, in particular his Mum and sisters, were guaranteed to utter a scream then ran away in the presence of a single rodent. To encounter three simultaneous without vision was a rarity.

Much later in life he discovered that the *farmers wife* was a reference to the daughter of King Henry VIII, Queen Mary I. A staunch catholic and persecutor of Protestants, she was so called because of the impressive estates she and her husband, King Philip of Spain, possessed. The *three blind mice* were three noblemen who adhered to the Protestant faith convicted of plotting against the Queen. She did not have them dismembered, but she did have them burnt at the stake.

The last of his childhood trinity, *Infants, Junior and Senior*. Three stages of schooling, through which all children had to pass, before progressing towards the distant and mystic life of a grown up. The junior school held little mystery for George, being as it was on the floor above the Infants School. Hearing the word Senior though, made George visibly cringe at the thought of it. Rumours of bullying by teaching staff, who put pupils through intense physical training, abounded around the playground, and George dreaded getting old. He just wanted to stay where he was quite prepared to endure the bullies from the estate. He later discovered that the stories were false, put about by rumour mongers hell bent on putting fear into the minds of the innocent.

During adolescence there was an infamous military trio in the form of Tom, Dick and Harry, three tunnels dug by prisoners of war of Stalag Luft III, a Luftwaffe run prisoner-of-war camp during World War II that housed captured air force personnel, then situated in the German Province of Lower Silesia near the town of Sagan, now Żagań in Poland, 100 miles (160 km) southeast of Berlin. The site was selected because it would be difficult to escape using tunnels. However, the camp is best known for two famous prisoner escapes that took place there by tunnelling, which were depicted in the films The Great Escape (1963) and The Wooden Horse (1950), and the books by former prisoners Paul Brickhill and Eric Williams from which these films were adapted.

The prison camp had a number of design features that made escape extremely difficult. The digging of escape tunnels, in particular, was discouraged by several factors. Firstly, the barracks housing the prisoners were raised several inches off the ground to make it easier for guards to detect any tunnelling activity. Secondly the camp itself had been constructed on land with very sandy and unstable subsoil. The sand was bright yellow, so it could easily be detected if anyone dumped it on the surface (which consisted of grey dust), or even just had some of it on their clothing. In addition, the loose, unconsolidated sand meant the structural integrity of a tunnel would be very poor. A third defence against tunnelling was the placement of seismograph microphones around the perimeter of the camp, which were expected to detect any sounds of digging just below the surface.*Harry* was finally ready in March 1944, but the American prisoners, some of whom had worked on the tunnel *Tom*, had been moved to another compound seven months earlier. No American prisoners of war actually participated in the great escape, but in typical fashion, Hollywood modified facts to show Americans as heroes.

The night of the Great Escape was planned for 24th March 1944, a moonless night. Lots were drawn for the 200 places and maps, papers and disguises were completed. All allotted escapees took up positions in hut 104. It was planned that the escapees would leave the camp in stages. Everyone was very nervous and tense, a situation that was made worse by the discovery that the tunnel was around 10 feet short of the woods. This meant that the tunnel exit was on the path of a perimeter guard. By the time a decision had been agreed on how to signal when the coast was clear, it was around 10pm. Men panicking in the tunnel caused further delays. By 4a.m. it was clear that it would be impossible for all 200 men to escape and the decision was made to close the tunnel at 5a.m. At around 4.45a.m. a single shot was heard at the tunnel exit.

A guard on the perimeter had easily discovered the tunnel.

76 men escaped through the tunnel. Of the remainder, those that were found waiting their turn in hut 104 were sent to the solitary confinement cells. Of those who escaped, 3 made it home to the UK, 23 were recaptured and sent back to Sagan. Hitler personally ordered the execution of the other 50 men.

The abandoned tunnel *Harry* exists to this day. Its history is hidden there, because the Germans never discovered it and it probably still contains contraband and escape material placed there by prisoners.

Every child became familiar with *Gold, Frankincense and Myrrh*, three mystical components of the Nativity. Lastly there were *The Three Degrees*, Fayette Pinkley, Sheila Ferguson and Valerie Holiday, an American soul vocal group formed in 1963. George fell in love with them from the moment he first saw them on television.

*

Sitting in front of his PC, George had entered a new world complete with its unique international language, USB stick, spacing, page number, toolbars, bullets, headers and footers, justify, indent, undo, ctrl+z, cut, copy, flag for follow up, formatting pallet, find and replace. At first very little made sense.

*

The acceptance that all the best things come in threes is probably due to ancient history and the Christian religion. God the Father, God the son and the Holy Ghost.

A Holy Trinity.

Until the factory was demolished, ESR followed this trend.

A visitor entering via the tree lined but otherwise scruffy Upper Drive, through the outer security doors, came under intense scrutiny of alert uniformed security staff in their control room on the right hand side. No further access was possible until they were satisfied with the identity of the visitor, who would be escorted to the appropriate destination by one of the security staff or collected by a secretary. On the opposite side

behind a plain green door, the telephone exchange
where George spent a few uncomfortable but totally
absorbing hours, whilst attempting to trace the person
making obscene telephone calls.

ESR Factory layout (the author)

**The factory layout during the time of the Falkland War,
included to guide the reader of events which took place.**

Ten feet further on, a major junction.

A three way split to a trinity of industry.

Ahead, a spartan and partitioned corridor painted a
dreary yellow colour, which led to the drawing office
and beyond the entrance to the workshop and to the left
the front office. To the right the Chemi-lab and an
alternative corridor by a circuitous route to the Drawing
office. The left turn down a darkened corridor passed
by the pay telephones and the workshop toilets where
George's friend Tim Gabriel ended his life. Employees

were not allowed to use the firms telephones for private calls, instead they had to ask their section head for permission to leave the office and use the pay telephone. Reminiscent of being at school and having to put a hand up in order to ask permission from the teacher to go and use the toilet!

A smart varnished oak door led to the front office, the home of technical authors, personnel, purchasing and the petty cash office, including the lovely Julie, a tall shapely blond technical writer, who wore short skirts or revealing hotpants during the summer. When George presented himself at security on his first day, he had been collected by Julie, then a trainee and had the pleasure of being shown around the works by her and had to concentrate on paying attention to the personal tour and not allow his eyes to be distracted. It would be considered unusual for any drawing office staff to enter the front office apart from visiting the petty cash office from time to time. Everyone spoke in hushed voices, the office ambience resembling that of a church. With a large number of women in the office, there was always a fragrance of alluring perfumes, alternating with cooking smells drifting down from the staff restaurant and works canteen on the mezzanine floor. The mouth watering aroma of fresh bread wafted down when bread was baked each morning. This tempting smell pervaded every corner of the front office beckoning you towards the canteen. Despite strict restrictions on staff movements, this did not apply to those going to buy bread sold at discount each morning at 11 a.m. prompt. At the far end past the lines of desks, a heavy sound insulated door, led to the workshops and assembly area. Those who worked in the front office considered themselves to be the elite and as such entitled to be both isolated and insulated from the remainder of the factory. The workshop itself contained a variety of light engineering lathes, milling machines, surface grinders, drilling machines and a single medium sized jig borer. This jig borer was so sensitive it had foundations separate from that of the factory. In the early days, a heavy lorry passing by on the main road twenty feet away caused the tool bit to vibrate and ruin hours of work. So essential was the defence contract to the safety of the realm, so critical was the tolerance on some machine parts, ESR was able to place considerable pressure on the council to keep the road in good repair.

The business had changed beyond recognition, and expanded to the size of a village since the original modest premises of the Hayne Brothers who formed a company with the grand name of Executive Sound Radio, hence ESR, making wireless sets in a small garage to side of the family house nearby in Manor Park. Originally a single factory in Regents Lane suited their needs as the business expanded to make the executive radios. When after the war, there was need for further expansion, they purchased a large redundant site at Upper Drive, comprised three business units, a plumbers merchant, a veneer specialist and a woodworking machine shop. Between the factories and the main road to Essex, stood a large car park, in the middle of which stood the Directors suite. The three factories had been badly converted and as a result the single factory was a mishmash of winding corridors and cubby holes, which connected the spacious areas of the assembly area and workshop to the drawing office. In this area came mixture of smells from machine oil, soldering and cigarette smoke, combined with a variety of sounds, from machinery and the manufacturing processes.

Further down beyond a small partition lay the main assembly area. Here the electrical circuit boards of the

Sentinel Project were constructed and assembled, always a busy place, the drone and whirring sounds of machining and other activities, to the extent that there was an inclination to speak in a loud voice so as to be heard. Above lay a continuation of mezzanine floor, which contained progress chasers and production engineers. To the back lay an area out of bounds to most workers. The highly sensitive mock up for the Sentinel Project was an actual size replica of a submarine interior, always manned by security. Within the secure area stood a hatch ring through which all components were required to able to pass, being the same size as the forward loading hatch on a nuclear submarine. The mock up was accurate down to the finest detail including companionways, replication of lighting conditions and other features peculiar to the submarine. It was useful to be able to view the project *in situ* and this brought to light many unexpected problems, including that of access within such a confined space, especially when modifications were to be carried out on board, even those carried out during a refit. The main console George worked on regularly, had within its non-reflective black painted interior, a series of mirrors, which were used to project sonar images, enabling the signal from a potential target to be photographed and used for interpretation purposes. These mirrors were like no other he had seen. They were very expensive to produce and were made by a specialised company. They were irregular in shape and reflected over 95 percent of available light. More than once George caught sight of his reflection in one of the mirrors and each time banged his head as he reacted to the view!

The way to the drawing office went past a small section, which specialised in precision grinding and engraving. The supervisor in charge was a small, partially bald, pale skinned, sickly looking individual with the unfortunate name of Archie Andrews. Perhaps his parents had a bizarre sense of humour. He had ears that protruded naturally, made worse by wearing cumbersome hearing aids on both ears. They looked extremely uncomfortable, making George feel grateful he did not have to wear such devices. Archie was married with two children, both with normal hearing, despite that he and his wife were dumb and profoundly deaf. For reasons that remain obscure and back in the depths of time, Archie went by the nickname of *Dummy*, which surprisingly was not meant to be derogatory, but rather a good example of humour combined with determination of the human spirit. It may have been that Archie acquired his nickname after *Archie Andrews,* a dummy created and used by the ventriloquist Peter Brough in the 1950's radio show *Educating Archie*. Archie the supervisor was a popular character mainly because of his sheer strength of character and ability to overcome his affliction. George and Archie's paths did not cross except occasionally and each time George experienced difficulty in understanding him. To those who dealt with him on a daily basis this was not a problem and communication was apparently easy. George was once walking past with an engineer when a strange noise came from one side. It was Archie attracting the attention of George's companion. He did not wish to mock the afflicted but the following conversation is typical of how communication seemed impossible but with understanding and tolerance was achievable by the most unlikely of characters. The engineer who walked over was named Terence Upjohn from Walthamstow, not renown for subtly or tolerance. He apparently understood.

*

Even as he typed the actual conversation, George wondered whether its inclusion would be misunderstood.

*

'Uh bli-ugh oh lk. Uh lk ph luc ugh aga agh, oh ugh!' Dummy said with concentration.

Terry turned to face Dummy so he could lip read. 'Why not?' He asked.

'Uh lk ph luc ime ugh ugu!'

'Don't worry, Dummy.' Terry replied at once. 'Just bring your holiday photographs up to my office at lunchtime and we can look at them there. I'll soon sort them out for you. If they're not any good I'll go with you to the chemists shop.'

'Uh lk ph wil ugh ay me. E lk ph luc ugh oon agh!'

'He won't say anything to you. We shall both be in our lunch hour so take no notice of him and don't worry. It will be fine!'

'Uh ugh-ugu oh'

'Good, I'll see you just after one o'clock then.'

*

A wireman, originally from South Africa, occupied the last workspace by the swing door, which led to the drawing office. He went by the name of Tiann Schutte who hailed from Centurion, a small suburb on the southern outskirts of Pretoria. Tiann held extreme views about nationality and race, making some fellow employees wonder how he qualified for working on sensitive projects, and hoped the security screening was effective. His work, intricate at times, required skill and patience, characteristics definitely not within Tiann's usual temperament. All wiring looms had to be placed within the units so as not to interfere with normal usage and abide with strict guidelines, colour coded for identification purposes and able to be removed from a unit *in situ* on the submarine, in the event of replacement, repair or update. Having located the components to be wired within a unit, the looms were mass produced using great hardwood boards with pins and codes and the looms assembled up from there. Sometimes these loom boards were twenty feet long or more and extended over gangways and the assembly area, which often caused arguments with those who worked nearby. Tiann was short tempered, thoroughly enjoyed disagreements, bitterly resented any form of authority, inclined to be corpulent, at least three or four stones overweight, with thick stubs for fingers. The description, *nasty piece of work* fitted Tiann with precision.

A few feet further on and the drawing office was accessed through a pair of large, transparent heavy cumbersome industrial swing doors.

The layout of the drawing office was by its very nature, regimental. At the workshop end were the clerical staff desks and the cloakroom. Each Draughtsman, Draughtswoman and Tracer had use of a drawing board with a parallel motion and a large pull out sloping reference table, which incorporated underneath a lockable draw and storage facility. They were good quality units made from pressed metal coated with a grey coloured hardwearing enamel finish. Each identical unit consisted of a drawing board on one side and a blueprint reference table on the other. These units were placed back to back in rows of two with an aisle wide enough for two people to pass. Then two additional rows of drawing boards and desks before the next aisle, followed but yet another further two rows of stations.

Reinforced high security filing cabinets were everywhere, usually by the desk of each section leader. A strict instruction was given to every member of staff that drawings or documents designated *Restricted* or *Confidential* and above were not to be left unattended or left on a desk overnight. Security was known to regularly inspect individual desks to check whether an employee complied with this prominent directive. They were required to be placed within a nominated cabinet. These cabinets had to be ready to be locked up fifteen minutes before the home bell. Each evening keeping to a strict rota, two senior members of staff checked each cabinet was secure, before the Chief Draughtsman locked the keys in a wall mounted safe.

A half-partitioned gangway separated a side row of desks from the print room and the filing room, whilst of the other side was a large brick wall, which separated the drawing office from the Chemi-Lab. Along the length of this wall a series of half glazed partitioned management offices, from the Chief and Assistant Engineer down to the Chief and Assistant Draughtsman.

Above the print and filing room the mezzanine floor extended from the above the workshop which were the offices of project engineers. These offices were accessed by an iron staircase, which stood at the far end of the drawing office and in full view of Ron Waud, section leader of the dunking sonar project. He sat in line with the staircase able to view the underwear of all females going upstairs, especially if he ducked his head down low. For Ron at least, one of the advantages of women wearing short skirts, fashionable at the time.

George found it amazing that that the attempt to combine a factory from a trinity of totally unconnected trades, a plumbers merchant, a veneer specialist and a woodworking machine shop, was quite unsuitable, considering the strict requirements of a modern electronics factory producing state of the art sonar equipment for the MoD.

3

Daniel Tailor

How can you describe Daniel Tailor, the senior engineer on the Sentinel Project? Definitely a one off, the mould broken immediately after he was born. This sentiment will be repeated time and time again before this tale is complete. In the factory where George worked, moulds of several extraordinary and exceptional characters must have been broken at birth.

Daniel was aged late twenties to early thirties. It was not possible to be more specific in an attempt to estimate, for he appeared to be rather sensitive on the subject. As a consequence no one knew his date of birth. Blatant open hostility or a blunt response, which left you in no doubt as to his attitude and sensitivity, met any inquiry or comment regarding his age. Daniel had blue eyes, jet black hair, always slightly unkempt, most likely to represent an intentional trait of non-conformity. He stood well over six foot six, with broad shoulders, which made him appear top heavy. When he strode through the drawing office with a distinctive and exaggerated swaggering gait, he resembled a cross between a sailor, recently back on shore after months at sea and a seasoned rugby player with a permanent knee injury. Daniel always wore an immaculate black jacket decorated with unusual gold buttons bearing the coat of arms of the Corporation of London. His father celebrated forty years with the Corporation and was presented with this exclusive set of buttons during a celebratory dinner held at the Guildhall. He passed away the following day before he could use them. In his memory Daniel wore that same jacket throughout the time George knew him.

With an easy manner, quick to smile and always prepared to crack a retort, especially if deliberate or provocative verbal abuse came his way. Daniel, prone to worry, could often be seen frowning whenever trying to solve a problem. To the annoyance of everyone, especially sub-contractors and the Chief Engineer, he possessed a photographic memory, able to recall faces, and agreements made in meetings or on the telephone in minute detail, weeks, often months later. He became renown for remaining calm no matter the provocation. Any display of emotion, a limited edition personal trait, an event to be savoured. His tendency to calmness confused an adversary during disputes, as many a contractor or senior manager, hell bent on diverting blame onto others, quickly discovered. He was honest in the extreme and expected others to act accordingly. He always carried a medium sized diary, which he regularly kept up to date, in a style resembling that of a calligrapher using a fountain pen. His diary was the envy of everyone who knew him.

*

It was a warm humid Thursday evening in August, the night before Daniel's meticulously planned house move from Romford, on the eastern edge of London's urban sprawl, to further northwards out to rural Helions Bumpstead, still in Essex, but very close to the leafy climes of the Suffolk countryside. Daniels mother had been killed in a road accident in Southern France two years before, and his subsequent inheritance, a combination of him being an only child and of selling two properties in France and England, left him with a tidy sum. Suspicious of banks and a declared ignorance of stocks and shares, channelled his thoughts into a decision to invest in property. After a lengthy search,

Daniel and his wife June found their ideal home. They were both looking forward to the move, having purchased a rambling 17th century four bedroom country house in the heart of the village. To Daniels delight, the house stood across the road from an ancient Coaching Inn called the *Three Horse Shoes*. The village had an active social life, revealed during a single visit when they took his mother-in-law out for Sunday lunch. When Daniel mentioned to the publican their intention to buy the house opposite, the reaction he received guaranteed full participation with the merest of formalities. He looked forward with anticipation to the weekly pub quiz, monthly dances and twice yearly beer festival. The landlord organised a day long pub crawl during the summer visiting local villages, always well attended as the crawl used a luxurious coach.

The house stood in its own extensive mature grounds, rambling walled rose garden, Victorian style vegetable plot and a small plum and apple orchard. Daniel knew very little about gardening and positively looked forward to the prospect of tending his plants and trees with great enthusiasm. This property was quite a contrast to their relatively compact three bedroom terraced house, situated on a busy main road, by a roundabout, adjacent to a major accident and emergency hospital and within walking distance of Romford Town Centre. Their postage stamp sized garden backed onto a shopping centre service road, ensured there was very little actual peace and quiet. Yes, Daniel was looking forward to the move. The only snag the prospect of a 50 mile each way drive to and from work each day. This could prove interesting especially during the winter months.

June, heavily pregnant, about to drop her first sprog at any moment, busy upstairs packing clothing into chests supplied by the removal company. She was assisted by her mother, Daniel's mother-in-law, known to those who worked with him at the factory, as *MDL*, short for Madalane, who was of course, it is alleged, a reformed prostitute! Daniel thought his mother-in-law to have suffered an even worse fate by assuming the role of a reformed prude! Fellow workers remained unsure whether he joked about his mother-in-law or was serious with his comments.

MDL was fussing about all and sundry, chattering the whole time, mainly about things trivial. Daniel, downstairs in the kitchen surrounded by cutlery, first wrapped each item with newspaper, then packed it piece by piece into a purpose built packing chest with drawers. He could overhear her irritating voice drifting down from upstairs. After many hours hard work, the end finally seemed in sight. The kitchen utensils were safely packed away in packing cases and placed on the work surface ready for the removal men in the morning. It left only for the cutlery to be packed and he could justify going to bed. He felt exhausted and longed for his bed. He realised from the tone of the clipped responses of his wife, that she too was finding the pointless chatting rather tedious. He knew from bitter experience that he could do very little to get his wife out of her predicament unless he chose to risk declaring world war three, by going to her rescue. A manoeuvre of this type would be easily detected and provoke the *MDL* into instantaneous stroppy defensive mode, the rescue attempt making her presume her presence was unwanted. This did have an element of truth in it, at least from his prospective. In all fairness she was being a great help to June, who months ago had been ordered by her doctor not to lift anything heavier than The Times newspaper. This caused problems in the early days, as June tended to forget and underestimate the seriousness of her condition. Daniel was forced to constantly remind her of the doctor's instructions.

This was her third pregnancy. The other two had been terminated naturally within twelve weeks and each miscarriage left her both physically and emotionally drained. On the outside Daniel remained philosophical about it.

'Can't let the poor mare off that lightly.' He once proclaimed, quite openly with a casual shrug of the shoulders, during an impromptu session of banter prior to a section meeting. 'I've got to keep up with tradition and ring the bell like the rest of my brothers! There's no way I'm going to be the odd one out. I'll just have to keep shagging away until I ring the bell! Someone's got to do it!'

No one knew what he really felt. It is quite possible joking disguised his true feelings.

Most of the heavy packing had already been completed over the weekend. Having taken time off work, he was relishing the opportunity of staying at home during the week, rather than live out of a suitcase in his usual somewhat seedy hotel close to the naval dockyard at Barrow in Furness. This way of life had been a novelty at first, but as the weeks transformed into months, then proceeded to top the year mark, the novelty had worn off and exposed the way of life for what it was, rather tedious and tending to be monotonous, especially during the evening. His counterparts at the dockyard not renown for being sociable with outsiders exploded the myth of friendly northerners. As far as Daniel was concerned it was a rumour put about to impress gullible southerners!

Each evening after he arrived back from the dockyard, he spent an hour keeping his day diary up to date, keeping extensive notes on the days events ready to be typed up by one of the secretaries when he returned to ESR. This was not obligatory but he knew from bitter experience that if things went wrong, and occasionally there had been disputes over the sequence of events and agreements made. His contemporaneous notes always included the precise reason for the failure and the identity of the individual, either the person or the company. Some engineers were not so attentive and subsequently endured an arduous time resolving disputes, a situation Daniel was keen to avoid.

Washed and shaved he ventured out into town to seek sustenance, trying to vary his diet and eat healthily. Going down the pub every night was definitely not his scene, especially the rough establishments he saw close to the dockyard. He would not venture in these even with an armed escort. When he returned from town, he telephoned June, listened to the radio for an hour so, then went to bed.

The work gave him a great deal of professional satisfaction as he had the opportunity of seeing the top secret Sentinel Project *in situ,* on board a nuclear submarine, much to the envy of a good deal of folk at the ESR Marine factory at Manor Park. The penalty to pay for what he described as *mynomadic way of life* was not seeing his wife during the week, although he did speak with her every evening. He travelled home early on Friday afternoon, and then spent a few tantalising nocturnal hours catching up with his wife in a sexual way. Simultaneous with his frantic sexual activity, despite his mental and physical exhaustion, he was expected to catch up with odd jobs like mowing the lawn, and socialising with his assortment of friends. Just as he felt relaxed and becoming used to the company, he had to endure a tearful goodbye from June, early on each Sunday afternoon, recently made all the worse by her condition. As a direct consequence of

61

this he had to rely on the *MDL* to keep a watching, and in her case, an interfering brief whilst he was away.

He had made good time and progressed onto his final task, that of packing his pride and joy, a professional knife block, rather an unusual culinary item to be found in England during the seventies, he bought from a Swedish businessman who also stayed regularly at the Osborne Hotel in Barrow. He removed the largest knife from its slot whilst he considered the best way for them to travel. Should he take them out and wrap them individually or leave them in the wood and risk the sharp edges being damaged during the journey? He ran his finger along the edge of the wide blade examining the exceptionally sharp cutting edge. No, he would wrap them individually, as he did not relish the thought of causing unnecessary damage to his prized possession.

The peace was disturbed by sudden loud knocking on the front door, which echoed throughout the house and startled him to the extent he nearly cut his finger. He glanced down expecting to see blood oozing from a cut but saw instead a small notch in his skin. Surprised by his good fortune, Daniel then changed his gaze to his watch. He pressed a button to view the time displayed on his latest LED electronic timepiece, a purchase inspired by the introduction scenes to a popular TV programme *Kojak*, a New York detective played by Tele Salvalas. He viewed *10:26* in small red characters. 'Who could it possibly be at this time of night?'

Whoever stood outside did so with impatience, for the knocker was used with great enthusiasm again. The loud reverberation echoed through the house. From upstairs, a predictable overreaction from the *MDL*, ever keen to poke her nose into things that did not concern her.

'Are you still down there, Daniel?'

'Jesus!' Spoken under his breath with noticeable venom over the stupidity of *MDL*. 'Course I'm here, where else would I be, you stupid old bat, you spoke to me only five or ten minutes ago!'

'Daniel?'

Out loud, he said. 'I'll get it!'

He slowly ambled down the hall still inspecting his knife, and as he approached the front door cast his eyes on a former object of his affection.

His door.

Not their door or Junes door.

Definitely *his* magnificent front door.

It was a great shame having to leave it behind really, for he was rather fond of his handiwork, the result of hours and hours of hard work, not forgetting a considerable amount of money. Shortly after they moved in six years ago, he quickly became subjected to some grief from June about renewing the existing door, as it looked jaded, the faded paintwork cracked and worn, in dire need of restoration and considerable TLC. The state of interior decoration was, in the main, remarkable, given that the previous owner, a frail seventy five year old widow had not decorated for years. The front door though looked in a sorry state, made the frontage appear scruffy and prompted early comments from June. He originally considered getting it dipped to remove accumulated layers of paint, and then restore it back to its former glory. But he had heard some horrendous tales about joints becoming weakened by such an extreme process, that he eventually decided against it. Instead he purchased a modern hardwood door in traditional style from a local timber merchant-cum-carpenter. This had immediate advantage, as he was easily able to persuade the craftsman to modify a standard partially glazed door to be able to include the stained glass from his original door. After several weeks of a hard and sustained delicate operation removing the fragile glass and its leading from the old door, but still maintaining security, the new door was eventually hung onto the frame with four impressive heavy duty brass hinges, all accompanied by appropriate approval noises from his wife. So distracted was he by his handiwork and those nagging regrets about the move, he opened the door almost casually without any regard to vigilance.

'Mister Daniel Taylor?' An official sounding male voice enquired immediately from the doorstep, the moment the door opened.

Giving this man with such an authoritative voice his immediate attention, he looked upon a heavily built individual wearing a scruffy black overcoat proffering a card, which upon cursory inspection turned out to be a police warrant card.

'I am he.' A frown appeared momentarily on his forehead, puzzled by the inquiry.

He noticed someone hovering behind the first policeman, in semi-darkness just within the range of the porch light. He leant to one side and saw a uniformed constable with anxious look on his face. The constable peered downwards and spotted the large bladed knife from the knife block that Daniel still held in his hand. The man stiffened in anticipation of an imminent attack, and immediately pulled back his colleague by the arm, who until this moment had not noticed the weapon.

'There'll be no need for that!' He exclaimed gruffly, immediately searching for his truncheon.

Seeing such frantic movement concerned Daniel, as the constable appeared to be extremely agitated for no apparent reason. He was still puzzled why they had asked for him by name and why the first policeman stepped backwards. Then he realised that he still held a large kitchen knife in his hand. Slowly and carefully he took a step backwards as he turned the knife around to hold it by the blade and offered the handle to the detective. The man reached out to take it and once in his grasp, this relaxed the constable, who pushed his truncheon back into the trouser pocket, deliberately leaving the leather strap protruding outside his uniform. The detective turned and handed the knife to the constable.

'You've caught me at a bad time, for I'm still packing.' He proffered by means of explanation, concerned that by carrying a knife to open the door it could be interpreted as a threat. 'We are moving house tomorrow, so I'm afraid you will have to come back. It's not very convenient now and its getting very late.'

'You don't seem to understand Sir.' The detective said approaching close so as to hold Daniel tightly by the arm. 'You *are* Mister Daniel Taylor?'

'I have already stated that I am he.' Daniel replied. He objected to being held in this fashion without good reason and made to pull away but the detective held his arm most firmly. Daniel glared at the policeman now standing very close. A frown appeared on the detectives face and he suddenly looked serious. 'In that case I have to inform you that you are under arrest.'

It was Daniel's turn to react and those thirteen words stopped him in his stride. Up to now he had remained calm and being at home in total control of the situation. Those few words had the effect of not only sweeping the carpet from under his feet, it also included instant removal of the floorboards and the supporting joists. Without such support he felt himself at once sinking down at frightening speed into an abyss. Quite in keeping with his character, he frowned again.

'Arrest?' He asked with his astonishment clearly sounding in his raised tone. Even in these few seconds there was no apparent reason why his behaviour warranted attention from the constabulary. 'What possible reason can you have to arrest me? I am a law abiding citizen.'

Anyone who knew Daniel would agree with this statement. He always drove in a sedate manner and kept to the speed limit, had never had an accident, renewed his tax disc well before the end of the month and had never been in trouble with the law, the police in particular. Most of his colleagues had points for speeding and a few involved in accidents. One of the engineers had been caught speeding so often he managed to lose his licence.

'Several counts of aggravated burglary.' Came a quick response. 'You are quite a slippery customer and you were very nearly caught in the act on your last escapade. Only, lady luck played into your hands and you managed to escape.' Daniel detected sarcasm in the tone and began to feel light headed for he could not even begin to imagine where this doorstep meeting would lead. The detective continued his narrative. 'You gave our colleagues in Kent the slip because of their carelessness, but now you are well and truly apprehended with absolutely no chance of escape. The Metropolitan Police will see to that!'

Daniel knew that this was no longer a joke, but retained enough control to realise that to resist would make things considerably worse, if that were possible. The fact that he had approached police holding a knife could complicate things but that would have to wait. His immediate concern was for June and what affect this would have on her condition.

'Where will you be taking me?' He asked. 'I can't just leave. I shall need to tell my wife where I am going. She's nine months pregnant you know and about to drop it at any time, plus we move house tomorrow morning at nine o'clock sharp!'

The detective smiled at these comments and made to come into the house. Once all three men were inside, the constable closed the door behind him and the detective released his grip on Daniel's arm. The three men stood at the bottom of the stairs in the small hallway, which seemed suddenly crowded.

'Who is it Daniel?' June's voice asked from the first floor with puzzlement sounding in her tone, regarding the identity of such a late visitor. A pair of female legs could be seen standing on the upper landing. 'Why have they called so late?'

'It's the police, Madam.' The detective answered politely, peering upward, but still not being able to view the speaker or her condition. "Perhaps you would kindly come down here Madam, as your husband is under arrest!'

'Oh, yes of course he is!' June laughed, and sounding both relaxed and cheerful, as if this occurred on a regular basis. 'How silly of me, why didn't I realise!'

'It's not a joke June, I am under arrest!'

'Don't be a rotter, taunting me with your silly jokes. Stop messing about and tell me the truth. You know full well that I can't keep coming up and down these stairs in my condition! '

There was no response as the three men continued to peer upwards.

Because of the silence combined with no reply, her tone of voice changed to that of concern. 'Daniel, you are joking aren't you? Who is down there with you?'

'You'd better come down here Madam.' The detective said in a kindly voice, peering upwards but still not being able to see the speaker standing at the top of the stairs. 'I am a detective from Romford Police Station with a warrant for the arrest of your husband.'

The legs moved to the top step and slowly and laboriously came down one stair at a time. The detective could now see a pregnant woman and gestured for Daniel to assist. June slowly negotiated the last few stairs with his assistance and stood looking apprehensive as she watched the detective withdrew his warrant card for her to view.

A uniformed constable holding a large kitchen knife in his hand stood by the front door.

'What are you doing with my husbands knife?' She asked, as she briefly peered down at the warrant card.

'Why Madam this was taken from your husband as we made the arrest!'

'You did not take it from me.' Daniel protested. 'You know full well that I handed it over when I realised I still held it in my hands.'

'What on earth were you doing with it Daniel?' June demanded with a distinct angry tone in her voice. 'You do not answer the front door with that knife in your hand surely? You sometimes amaze me with your antics!'

'I was packing, the same as you!'

'Are you all right dear?' A predictable plaintive bleat from the *MDL* still upstairs.

'Jesus wept!' Daniel uttered with a shake of the head. 'One stupid remark after another.'

June virtually collapsed onto the bottom stair and started to cry. 'Why is my husband under arrest?' She asked in between sobs.

Daniel placed an arm on her shoulder but June immediately pushed it away.

'I have a warrant from the Kent Police for the arrest of a Daniel Taylor who resides at this address. This Daniel Taylor is the chief suspect in a series of aggravated burglaries.' The detective replied at once. 'We will be taking him to Romford Police Station overnight and early tomorrow morning the Kent Police will come and hold him for questioning with regard to said burglaries.'

'This cannot be happening to me.' June sobbed, taking great gulps of air. 'What on earth have you been up to?'

'Nothing!' Daniel insisted. 'What do you take me for?'

'Sounds to me you must have been up to something. They can't arrest you without due cause.'

The detective sensed a domestic situation was developing and thought it better they should leave, and soon. He turned to face Daniel. 'Sorry Sir, it's about time we left. It is late and there is still much to do.' He said trying to sound firm but gentle. 'Go and get yourself a coat, there's a good chap.'

Being described as a good chap did not go down very well in Daniel's book so he protested. 'Don't patronise me!' He said firmly. 'Just speak to me properly.'

He turned and went up the stairs two at a time, disappeared from view and returned moments later holding a paperback and a black leather jacket draped over his arm. En-route he passed the *MDL* who sat on the bed, wisely not making a comment whilst he remained in the room.

'What shall I do about the move, Daniel?' June still seated on the bottom stair, enquired in a trembling voice, as she watched her husband, the tears streaming down her face. 'Should I cancel the move or wait for you to return? I couldn't possibly manage it without you being here.'

'No, don't cancel, go ahead and move as planned. You could telephone Phil and Jack and see if they can come over to help.' Daniel replied trying to sound confident. June's brothers were a lazy pair of sods but they might be persuaded to help. 'I won't be there too long, for there is not a case for me to answer. I expect to be back shortly when they realise their mistake.'

The detective shook his head. 'I think it may be some time before you return.' He advised. 'I am not familiar with all aspects of the case, but the Kent Police claim to have substantial proof of your involvement so you will appear in court early next week and I expect they will ask for you to be remanded until your case is heard.'

'I have not been to Kent for years! I must have been about twelve the last time I visited!' Daniel protested. 'So how could I have committed burglary?'

'They all say that!' The constable said, speaking for the first time since entering the house. "Every man jack is innocent right up to the moment they are presented with evidence.'

'Oh, Daniel what is happening to us?' June sobbed.

The detective persisted with his request to get away soon. He still felt anxious about leaving before the situation deteriorated and suspected that to delay would only prolong the agony for them all. 'Sir, we really must go.' He insisted.

June stood up and grabbed hold of Daniel in a desperate embrace, sobbing the whole time. The constable held Daniel by the arm, then gently but firmly pulled him away. Daniel tried to resist but the constable showed determination and maintained a firm grip.

'What shall I do Daniel?' June sobbed still clinging onto his hand.

'Telephone Henry and tell him I am going to Romford Police Station. He'll know what to do, he may even offer to help if you ask him.' He replied over his shoulder, then turned to the detective. 'Where am I being taken to in Kent?'

'Not for me to say, Sir.' The detective replied deliberately evading the question, but detecting a look of hostility in Daniel's eyes, chose to be more forthcoming. 'I am really not familiar with the procedures of the Kent Constabulary, so you could end up anywhere in the County. You could be taken to their headquarters in Maidstone, Canterbury or even to Whitstable itself where the burglaries took place. I really have no idea, and that's the truth.'

To the amazement of Daniel, the constable then retrieved a set of handcuffs from a pocket and with practised ease swiftly placed over his right wrist and the constables' left, before he had a chance to protest. 'Don't worry Sir.' He assured with a wry grin on his face. 'This is standard procedure. We do it to both the innocent and the guilty without prejudice!'

In complete silence trying to look over his shoulder at June, a dismal creature still seated on the bottom stair, Daniel was led away from the house and into a waiting police car, ready with the engine running. Daniel became immediately aware that utmost care had to be taken at this time to ensure the handcuffs that joined them did not injure the wrist of either man. The constable noticed this and wondered whether the prisoner had done this manoeuvre previously. This observation gave him encouragement that the Kent Police had the right man, even though this suspect did not seem like the sort of burglar he normally encountered.

Even before the police car slowly drew away, Daniel began to wonder how much time would elapse before he saw June again. Once seated comfortably and no risk of escape or injury to the wrist of captor and captive with the car on the move, the atmosphere relaxed.

'Sorry to have sounded so formal, Sir.' The detective apologised, speaking over his shoulder from the front passenger seat. 'But we are simply expediting a Warrant on behalf of the Kent Police, beyond that we have no further involvement. We are not given opportunity to examine their evidence, to establish whether or not the Warrant is justified. From our point of view we run all the risks and the Kent Police will have all the glory when your case comes to court.'

'You had me worried Sir, when you answered the door with a knife.' The constable chatted, sitting beside him in the darkness still holding him firmly by the arm. 'I thought we were in for a rough time with you. I don't mind admitting it.'

'I think I have already explained that we are packing up to move.' Daniel replied with some impatience, for he did not feel inclined to talk, turning to look at the constable and seeing his face spasmodically in the rhythmic glow of street lights as they sped past. 'I did not know who was at the door and most certainly did not know I would be confronted with police armed with a warrant for my arrest.'

It went quiet in the car as the driver negotiated the five roundabouts skirting the shopping centre. They were designed to keep the traffic at a reasonable speed, but Daniel knew from bitter experience that many drivers viewed these congestion aids as a challenge to their driving skill. Late at night many drove at high speed from roundabout to roundabout with a screech of tyres, accompanied by great acceleration and hard braking, fouling the air with fumes in the process. So bad was it when the air was calm, you could almost taste it, even in the back garden away from the main road. As from tomorrow he hoped the air would be more pleasant, but first he had to survive being inside a living nightmare with no apparent means of escape.

Within minutes they reached the outskirts of the town centre, the familiar shops rushing by, then the driver slowed and turned the car off the main road into a darkened alley and into a floodlit yard. An assortment of Police and other vehicles were scattered about in random fashion. One parked in the corner caught his eye being as it was a badly damaged car with the driver's door and its bonnet missing. The front off side wing had been partially torn off and the punctured tyre and front wheel hanging at an unusual angle. The constable noticed Daniel glancing at the damaged car.

"Month or two ago one of our lads on a chase following some bank robbers when they chose to have an argument with a barrier on the A127 and went through the windscreen on impact.' He explained. 'The driver is still poorly in hospital, and not likely to last.'

Daniel so distracted climbed out still being firmly held by the detective, despite the handcuffs and led firmly up a short flight of steps to a door where the detective pushed an illuminated button. There followed the sound of a metallic click and the door partially opened. He was led into the police station and down a corridor, past a row of cells, a medical room and one containing a camera and an identification frame. In the empty charge room a uniformed sergeant stood in anticipation, watching their approach from behind a counter, which stretched across the room. He looked a man of experience, and resembled a father-like figure, authoritative but approachable. Daniel began to feel light headed again. This affair was getting to him and he hoped his nightmare would end soon so he could go back to June and the impending move.

*

*On the face it typing is easy. A simple matter of tapping
keys in the same order as words are spelt with a space
in between each word and a full stop at the completion
of each sentence. George could only type with two
fingers. Encouraged by his wife Carole, he attempted to
use more, but instead typed gibberish. He suffered not
so much as from a dyslectic brain as from dyslectic
fingers, which often typed 'hte' instead of 'the' on the
page.*

*

'Who have we got here, Dick?' He asked, studying
Daniel with a shrewd eye as he awaited a reply. In turn
Daniel determined not to be intimidated, inspected the
Sergeant.

'Mister Daniel Taylor, wanted on warrant by Kent
Constabulary, Sarge.' The detective answered, noticing
his prisoner and his sergeant eyeing each other with
obvious suspicion and resentment.

'Oh yes, we have been expecting him.' The Sergeant
replied, taking his eyes away from Daniel momentarily,
before reaching for a file on a shelf behind him, which
he opened and selected a particular sheet. 'Did he give
you any trouble?'

'No I did not!' Daniel retorted immediately. He
resented the uncomfortable feeling of penetrating eyes
upon his person and felt angry at being spoken about,
but otherwise ignored. 'What sort of a bloke do you
think I am?'

'Oh, we have a lively 'un here and a clever dick to
boot!' The Sergeant commented to no one in particular,
giving a knowing smile as he maintained his stare into
Daniels face. During his long career, this man had seen
it all. Nothing could surprise him. He stood with arms

akimbo as he looked at Daniel in the eye as he attempted to size him up. 'So you did give my officers some trouble then?'

'No I did not!' Daniel countered.

'Except for answering the door with this knife, that is true Sarge!' The detective remarked, revealing the wide bladed kitchen knife for the first time.

The Sergeant stiffened when he saw it, and stepped back in mock horror. 'Have you searched him?' He demanded, sounding stern and glaring at both his officers.

'No, for there is no need, really.' The constable replied. 'He is moving house tomorrow and we caught him packing up the kitchen utensils, that all. He gave it up immediately once he realised it was in his hand. I don't think there was any intention to use it.'

Hearing this Daniel relaxed as at last someone was on his side and telling the truth.

'Maybe so, but give him a frisk anyway.' He insisted with a shake of his head. 'Better to be safe than sorry.'

The constable patted his jacket and trouser pockets, then ran his hands up both sleeves and trouser legs. He found nothing to concern him. He then grabbed the paperback away to inspect it closely. Satisfied, he handed it back. When he had finished the Sergeant spoke, as he referred to an official looking paper, which lay on the counter before him.

'Will you confirm that you are Mister Daniel Taylor from 229 Waterloo Road, Romford, Essex?' He asked, without looking upwards, then held up the document for Daniel to inspect.

Daniel glanced down at the file and read the Warrant from the Kent Police, upside down.

'I am he.' He confirmed. 'But my name is spelt T-a-i-l-o-r, not the way you have it spelt it on your Warrant.'

'I will make a note.' The Sergeant promised, without making any alteration despite holding a pen in his hand. From the depths of the police station came sounds of a woman attempting to sing a song in a loud voice echoing around the bare walls, out of tune and obviously drunk. The overloud noise interrupted the proceedings. The Sergeant stopped speaking and looked in the general direction of the cells waiting for the singing to stop. He had no intention of straining his voice by having to shout over tuneless singing.

'You neeeeed loooove!'

A pause.

The sergeant took a deep breath as if to speak but the singing resumed.

'Lovely loooove!'

Another pause whilst she took breath.

'My darling loooove!'

A faint sound of shouting, a loud bang of a fist on a door, followed by a male voice complaining. 'Shut up you old cow!'

'Quite agree.' The Sergeant mouthed.

'You neeeed loooooove!'

From close to, the constable's voice. 'Is that Loony Lucia, Sarge?'

'It is.' Sarge confirmed sounding bored by the affair.

'She's started a bit early, it's only Thursday today.'

'I know but she won a considerable sum of money on the gee gees. Didn't even know she could write, though you don't need much for a betting slip. The Sergeant answered. 'Quite a bit by all accounts, for she bought all the drinks for her cronies at the Plough this lunchtime and she still had over eight hundred quid on her when she was arrested outside the pub.'

'Bloody Hell, it'll mean more trouble once she gets going tomorrow.'

'Maybe, maybe not.' The Sergeant replied with a slight shake of his head. 'She's yet to go home and tell her hubby about it. It won't last long once he gets his greedy mitts on it! That's of course Loony Lucia lets him have it.'

The trio laughed heartily at the prospect of untold grief for Loony Lucia, once she sobered up and returned home to face her husband. The laughter was short lived when the detective commented. 'Will probably mean we will have to go and clear up the mess. You know what they usually do to each other when those two fight.'

The sergeant then referred to his notes and continued with Daniel's case. 'As I was saying before I was rudely interrupted, I have here a signed warrant from the Kent Constabulary for your arrest. You will remain here overnight and tomorrow morning an escort will arrive to take you to Whitstable. You will be given a drink when my paperwork is up to date, most probably within the hour.' He glanced up at the clock. 'You have missed tea but I can arrange a spot of supper for around ten, after shift change. Are you on any medication?'

'No. I am not.' Daniel felt his head spinning and wished the nightmare to end so he could go home and await the removal men.

'Good. In that case, have you any requests before you are locked up for the night?'

'You neeeeed loooove!'

'Yes. I have.' Daniel replied, trying to remain calm, when he realised a nightmare did not exist. This was reality. Calmness was a difficult state to achieve along with the prospect of being locked up in the near vicinity of a drunken woman. He knew nothing of burglaries in Kent and did not know much about Whitstable, except he recalled it being along the coast from Herne Bay. He certainly had not visited the town since he was about twelve, but already knew it would be pointless to protest. His main concern, June and the pending move on the next day, now likely to be very much complicated by his enforced absence. 'My wife is nine months pregnant and we are due to move house tomorrow morning. I would like to telephone her to enquire of her condition. I would also like to telephone my boss to inform him of my arrest.'

'Looooove is all around!'

'The direct use of a telephone by yourself is denied, because of the serious nature of your arrest.' The Sergeant replied, immediately taking notes. 'I will personally telephone your good lady to advise her over your concern for her welfare and inform her of your situation at the same time.'

'Thanks.' Said without enthusiasm. 'So much for the rights of prisoners.'

'You *DO* have rights sonny!' The Sergeant retorted not looking up from writing on a note pad. 'But at *MY* discretion only. Due to the violent nature of this case, you will be fed and watered, but nothing else.'

He looked up when he had completed writing a short note on a pad lying on the desk for that purpose. 'I admit to being puzzled why you need to speak with your boss, as against, for example, your solicitor, but that is your choice. I am not inclined to allow you to speak with him direct either, given the factors of the case. What do you do for living Mister Tailor?'

This question planted seeds of doubt in his mind for the first time. His involvement with the sensitive Sentinel Project for the Ministry of Defence required him to inform the Chief Engineer, Henry Reade immediately in certain circumstances, to ensure the security and integrity of the project was maintained at all times. The substantial list he knew virtually by heart. Being offered a bribe or other inducement by a contractor or other interested party or parties, which included evening or other prolonged entertainment and food other than a light meal. Being followed, both suspected or in reality. Propositioned by a person or persons claiming or suspected to work at a certain bookshop in the parade of shops opposite the factory, or at the infamous garage next to the Red Cow Public House in Ilford. It was common knowledge at ESR, KGB agents operated out of both locations. KGB, abbreviation for *Komitet Gosudarstvennoy Bezopasnosti* or Committee for State Security, a most sinister organisation. A list that included being arrested by the police, except for a motoring offence. On the face of it, the Sergeant could not be blamed for being puzzled why he asked to speak to Henry but in any event he would not reveal his true occupation.

'I am an engineer.' He replied, being deliberately vague about his job title. 'If I am going to be away longer than a few days, and your detective has already indicated this is likely to be the case, I need to inform my boss so my post can be covered. There is an important deadline to keep, and meetings to attend. My prolonged absence must not be allowed to delay the contract.'

It sounded plausible enough he thought, but would the Sergeant agree to telephone? There appeared to be more to it than met the eye with this affair and included violence of some sort.

The Sergeant glanced up, pen poised above the notepad. 'Where are you employed Mister Tailor?'

Daniels brain cells worked overtime. He tried to recall the procedure, if one existed, about revealing the name of the factory to officialdom. During the last census, there had been nervous representations made to management by cautious employees regarding the identification of ESR Marine on the census returns. Eventually a written mandate was issued that for security purposes the word *'Marine'* was to be omitted in the section headed Name and address of employer. Daniel decided to treat this as a similar situation as the census, considering that to identify the name, *'Marine'* to a third party was a sensitive matter, so he issued a private and unpublished silent mandate of his own. 'ESR, Upper Drive, Manor Park, London.'

'Is that the place where they make torpedoes?' The Sergeant asked, immediately shaking Daniel to his bones.

'Where have you heard that?' Daniel demanded, trying to appear casual on the outside. Inwardly his stomach churned and he felt sick. He felt the colour drain from his face. If the sergeant noticed his change of state he did not comment.

'Oh, don't get me wrong, Mister Tailor.' The sergeant replied looking up from his writing looking directly into Daniel's face, for once sounding benevolent. 'I have no insider information, but I recall there was an article about ESR in the local paper about a year or so ago.' He sat up now looking into space, scratching his head with a frown upon his face as he tried to remember. 'Isn't that the place built up from a workshop garage by the Hayne brothers? I think there was a picture in the paper taken during the war showing one of them on the roof of the Main Plant, firing a machine gun at a low flying German fighter.'

Daniel relaxed, recalling the article. When it was published it caused a ripple of both concern and annoyance amongst the engineers at the plant. ESR Marine was a subsidiary of ESR and they often felt infuriated by lack of responsibility shown by the directors who leaked certain unrestricted facts to the local press in order to get free publicity for the company. How the Ministry of Defence tolerated this naïve approach was unknown, but it did little to those whose main priority was maintaining secrecy of certain projects. What was the sense in announcing in the press that ESR Marine had obtained the contract for this torpedo or that Naval Sonar equipment when the spouses and families of all employees had virtually no knowledge of their loved ones work? Some were badly affected, judging by the complaints made by the team at the plant. One set of parents having read the article, then demanded to know what their precious son did at work, being offended because the offspring would not reveal any details had pestered one junior individual in the drawing office at length.

'We're your parents?' They both apparently proclaimed. 'Why can't you tell us? Don't you trust us?'

Even when the offspring explained the severe restrictions of the Official Secrets Act and the far reaching consequences if one fell foul of the MoD, like thirty years in jail, fell on deaf ears. Nevertheless life at the factory went on despite outside influences and the security surrounding the Sentinel Project remained intact.

'I work at ESR.' Daniel repeated.

'Not on torpedoes then?'

'I have no comment.' Daniel replied without emotion.

The sergeant duly noted the uninformative response and much to Daniels relief chose to change to subject.

'Write down the name of your wife and your boss together with their telephone numbers please, and I will do as you request.'

Daniel duly complied, after which he was led down a dimly lit corridor. He felt relief that the loud singing from the drunken woman had stopped. The Sergeant stopped by the first opened door and removed the handcuffs. He turned to Daniel, now fully occupied in rubbing his wrists. 'I need your watch, tie, shoe laces and belt, Daniel.' He said quietly.

Daniel felt like screaming at this latest insult but knew it would not further his cause, so he removed the items without comment and handed them over. The Sergeant occupied himself by chalking *Tailor* -spelt correctly, in scruffy writing on a small blackboard beside the door. Daniel walked into the sparsely furnished cell as behind him the Sergeant placed a key in the lock and checked it functioned correctly. 'I will sort my paperwork out, telephone your wife and boss, then arrange a hot drink for you. Try not to get too depressed, I am sure everything will turn out fine.' He assured, sounding almost pleasant before shutting and locking the door that sent echoes around the cell.

The cell was like no other room he had seen. His footsteps echoed around, the sound of the slightest movement amplified considerably. A room about ten feet by twelve. Bare walls, bricked from floor to ceiling, painted with gloss a bland colour of grey. A concrete bed with a single blanket and a thin foam mattress. The final insult screened by a stud wall, a grubby porcelain toilet bowl without a seat. Even the cistern was mounted elsewhere. A short length of sisal string, only about six inches long poking through a hole rough cut in concrete, represented the means by which to flush the toilet. He was in the cell less than a minute and he felt depressed beyond his wildest dreams. He sat down on the bed fully intending to pass the time by reading his book but as soon as he opened it he had already lost interest so he lay down on the blanket and closed his eyes. He fell into an uneasy sleep. Almost at once, or so it seemed, the sound of a key being turned in the lock, woke him.

A constable stood in the doorway, holding a tray on which was placed a steaming mug of tea. 'Hello Mate.' He greeted. 'I put two sugars in, but have not stirred it yet in case you don't take sugar. That okay?'

'Thanks.' Daniel replied getting up to take it, hoping for some human contact.

'I'm locking up now, so I will see you tomorrow morning. Knock if you have any probs, but try not to eh? Sweet dreams!'

'Thanks.'

'Oh by the way, are you on medication?'

Daniel shook his head.

The constable turned and locked the door, leaving Daniel on his own once again.

He drank the tea, then lay down and looked at his book but found it difficult to concentrate. Sometime later he fell asleep and when he awoke the light had been switched off. It was quiet with a faint sound of traffic on the main road, but otherwise still. He drifted off to sleep again.

When he awoke, feeling refreshed though with a stiff neck and aching legs, a faint glimmer of light ventured through the fanlight high up in the wall above the bed, and he could hear the faint sounds of sparrows chirping. He made to glance at his watch then remembered it had been taken from him. Today was the day of the house move and he wondered how June would hold out. He felt sick to his stomach at not being able to take part and the feeling of helplessness overcame him to the extent that tears welled up in his eyes, one thing he had not done since childhood. He happened to glance at the door. The notable absence of a door handle depressed him further and the tears fell freely until he slowly regained control of his feelings He sat on the edge of the bed, head down listening to the faint sounds of freedom outside of his temporary prison. Time passed slowly until he heard sounds much closer from the other side of the door. Keys rattled in the lock and the door opened to reveal a different young constable holding a large metal tray.

'Breakfast time, Mate.' The officer revealed as he laid the tray on the floor by the door, then locked up and left without speaking further. Daniel gazed down at an average standard serving of fried eggs, bacon and mushrooms. The highlight on the plate being a doorstep sized chunk of farmhouse loaf with lashings of butter. The sight of the meal cheered his spirits considerably. Afterwards he sat about more or less in a dream gazing at the wall opposite without any desire to read. He had trouble keeping himself awake. It would be so easy to sleep but he resisted the urge and watched as a spider wandered apparently aimlessly around the wall, traversed it until it reached a corner, then headed straight down to the stone floor, and crawled away from him to eventually disappear towards freedom through a small gap beneath the door.

After an age the keys rattled in the door, but this time a different sergeant to the one of the previous day, came through the door accompanied by two officers whose uniforms were slightly different. One was about the same age as him, the other probably nearing retirement. 'Morning Mister Tailor!' The sergeant greeted cheerfully. 'Did you sleep well?'

'Not too bad thanks.' Daniel replied, grateful for some human company.

The Sergeant looked around for signs of the tray. 'I see you've had breakfast, so I am going to hand you over to these two Officers from the Kent Constabulary, who will be acting as your escort.'

'Okay.' Daniel replied without enthusiasm, feeling detached from reality. 'Where am I going?'

' I have no idea.' The Sergeant replied glancing at the constable nearest him.

'We've been told to take him to the Nick at Whitstable.' Came a grumpy answer from the younger one. 'Why we have to travel all this bleeding way by train is beyond me. We should have come by car for a serious case like this.'

'Well you asked a question, and now you have an answer.' The Sergeant replied with more than a note of cynicism sounding in his voice, before turning to face the speaker. 'I take it you've not been to charm school yet sonny, or don't you blokes from the Kent police enjoy such luxuries, out in the sticks!'

There was no response to this obvious insult. Which brought a grin to Daniels face. One of the Kent constables reached for handcuffs and placed them on Daniel's wrist. To his surprise the older Officer made sure they were not over tight. 'Do they feel comfortable?' He asked, checking the gap between the metal and the flesh.

Daniel moved this wrist and found they were not too tight. 'Yes, they're fine thanks.' He replied trying to sound friendly. If he was to travel with these two clowns to Whitstable, he may as well try and be amiable so he did not have a bad time. He was led through the station to the yard and climbed into the back of a waiting police car, remembering to exercise care with the handcuffs. It was noticeable that on the long drive to London Bridge Station, nobody in the car spoke a word.

At the Railway Station unusually crowded for a Sunday, he felt conspicuous of his handcuffs and could sense the eyes of other passengers when they glimpsed his plight. He felt like shouting out *I'm innocent, this is wrongful arrest!* but suspected his two escorts would not take too kindly to this approach. Their train had only five minutes before it departed from platform three and with some relief they walked along a deserted platform climbed into an empty compartment away from prying eyes of the public. Here his handcuffs were removed, accompanied by an open threat by the officer who had yet to attend charm school. 'If you make one move to get away, I will not hesitate to use my truncheon! You have led my shift and me a fair dance by your slippery antics and we are all a mite pissed off, I can tell you!'

Daniel thought about proclaiming his innocence then had second thoughts. 'I'll give you no trouble, you have my word on that.'

'You'd better take heed young fellow me lad!' The other escort warned, speaking for the first time. 'You have caused us a great deal of grief and it will take only the slightest excuse and there are few people out there who will give you a good hiding, which includes us two. So no antics or else there will be instant retribution.'

Daniel chose not to answer, so he sat down by the window and peered out through dirty glass in dire need of a clean. The train moved slowly out of the station and progressed through south London and by degrees moved to north Kent, where after passing though Dartford, it became noticeably rural. He ignored his escort and they in turn reciprocated. At Faversham Station the younger one spoke the moment the train left the station. The sudden sound of a voice close to, made Daniel jump noticeably 'Give us your hand.' He demanded in an aggressive tone. 'Chances are you may get jumpy now we're nearly there. Time to get you handcuffed, so there's absolutely no chance of your escaping again.'

By the time the train slowly drew into Whitstable station five minutes later, Daniel and his escorts were standing by the door waiting for the train to come to a standstill. The elder constable opened the door, alighted first and helped Daniel down onto the platform. Daniel held his right arm back and avoided injury to his wrist and the left arm of his captor. A young couple and two small children, a boy and a girl, in the next carriage alighted also, who after a cursory glance generally took little notice of his predicament, except for the small boy who insisted on staring. Even as his father led him towards the unattended ticket barrier, the boy continued to stare, turning his head almost right behind him. If Daniel tried to imitate this, the strain imposed on his neck would require a prolonged stay in hospital with a serious injury, instead of the police station! He felt irritated by this and just as the boy walked through the ticket barrier, Daniel could not resist but to poke his tongue out!

The boy responded immediately and yelled out in apparent anger, in order to complain to his father, who by this time had abandoned his attempt to drag the boy along and had disappeared from view beyond the barrier. A second later the father reappeared from the pavement to investigate the claim made by his son.

He saw only Daniel handcuffed to his escort. Daniel ignored the father, and the escort, who knew nothing of the incident, strode on. For his trouble the boy received a heavy slap around the ear. Harsh punishment perhaps, but in Daniel's opinion well deserved! The boy stood crying continuing to stare. Daniel repeated the movement of his tongue, which caused the boy to cry louder. The father returned a second time, slapped the boys backside and dragged him off, crying, but still looking over his shoulder. It must have been frustrating for the boy to see an adult acting in an offensive way, and when he complained received a punishment from his father.

'Serves the little beggar right!' Daniel said under his breath, smiling at the boy ahead.

'What?' His escort asked.

'Sorry, I just coughed.' Daniel lied, fully satisfied with his successful retaliation, which cheered him considerably and caused a pleasant diversion from his present plight.

Directly outside in the station yard, a police car awaited them. The young driver glared at him. Daniel noticed this but chose to ignore the stare as he climbed aboard concentrating instead of trying to avoid banging his head simultaneous with not overstretching his handcuffed arm, or that of the younger constable.

'Nice to be back, intit mate.' The driver said in a noticeable Scottish accent, grinning all over his face, studying Daniel via the rear view mirror.

'As I have not been here since I was twelve, no it is not nice, not that it has anything to do with you!' He retaliated, surprised by his reaction to a simple comment. He had an uneasy feeling he could be in for a rough ride, but what the heck? May as well go down fighting, and show them he did not intend to be intimidated. 'Just concentrate on your driving and keep your nose out of things that do not concern you!'

'Cheeky bastard!' The driver retorted and made to get out of the car.

'Don't be stupid, Ian, he's just winding you up!'

'I'll wind the bastard up make no mistake about it!'

'Get back into the car, Ian and take us to the nick, you can give him a tap there if y'want!'

'Good idea mate, thanks.' Ian said as he climbed back into the driving seat, now less aggressive. He had not quite finished though. 'I'd advise you to keep shstum pal, otherwise you'll get more than a tap, and that's a promise!'

Daniel shrugged his shoulders in defiance.

'You'd do better to say and do nothing until we are under the gaze of our Station Sergeant.' The older one cautioned. 'There'll be plenty of opportunities for you to fall down the stairs at the station, believe me!'

'I will give you some advice, as you have been kind enough to offer me some.' Daniel said quietly. 'I have no idea what this is all about. I have not visited Whitstable since childhood and do not take it kindly that I am being treated in this way. I will not give any trouble unless I am provoked, and believe me I feel very provoked at this precise moment.'

'Maybe, but I would strongly advise silence.'

'Ok, comments noted.'

The engine fired into life and they set off. Whitstable is a small town with the feel of a village and one, which gives the impression of being in a time warp, reluctant to change, and it appeared that nothing had changed much since his last visit. Every shop, mainly in private hands and not part of a national chain, looked cared for and each gave the appearance of being modestly successful. When Daniel, even from the back seat, managed to glimpse the painted sign for the Three Keys Inn, it seemed like instant replay childhood. He felt immediately transported back to the sunny carefree days of 1954, when aged nine he and his family first stayed at Mrs Browns, by coincidence above the drapers shop, still there by the railway bridge passed under moments before. There had been elaborate plans to spend a two week holiday with his Uncle Arthur, Aunt Ellen and cousin Linda the previous year, but in January 1953 the whole of the south-east of England, including Whitstable, were subjected to severe flooding. Instead he, his Mum, Dad and brother Steve went to Folkestone. After initial disappointment, the bed and breakfast chosen by Dad more than lived up to expectations for it overlooked a railway track along which, the *Golden Arrow*, the pride of the Southern Railway, passed regularly on its way to Folkestone Harbour. The infamous seven made it to Whitstable the following year. Fortunately the main street, Harbour Street, which runs parallel to the sea, is about fifteen feet above sea level at high tide and is the only reason the main town of Whitstable remained above the flood water. Access to the sea from Mrs Browns was via a side road off Harbour Street containing a small cinema where Daniel remembered seeing *Ivanhoe* there. Moving towards the sea, the road dropped the best part of ten or twelve feet before the lines of terraced houses. The third house boasted a hand painted sign on the wall between the ground floor and first floor windows *Flood water level - 1953*, way above Daniel's head at the time. The way to the sea seemed magical, a narrow lane adjacent to the railway line, then across open ground with a timeless smell of sea and damp vegetation wafting the senses of the nearness of sea and sand. On the waterfront, splendid views across the sweep of the bay towards Sheerness and further away on the horizon, Southend on Sea. An ideal spot to witness daily glorious sunsets. Behind the modest pebble beach, fishermen's black tarred stores, old sail lofts and picturesque weather boarded cottages, part of another era. As a bonus when the tide retreated, a bank of shingle known locally as *The Street* became exposed, said to have been built by the Romans so they could gain access to the sea at low tide. It mattered not who constructed it, more important, a small boy had access to it and able to marvel at starfish found along its length.

The driver slowed to allow a young woman, wearing a short skirt, which left little to the imagination, pushing a pram across a zebra crossing.

'Look at the tits on that!' The driver commented, the lust clearly sounding in his voice.

Daniel paid little attention being preoccupied by the sight of the Three Keys Inn, the scene of a series of family misdemeanours. His Uncle Arthur, Mums youngest brother, enjoyed a pint or two every day, whereas his Dad was tea total. Every evening during their stay, after his cousin Linda was put to bed at around eight o'clock, Dad and Uncle Arthur wandered off to The Three Keys Inn. Being the eldest Daniel was allowed to go with them. The public bar boasted a piano and Dad was apparently persuaded to play. In those days it was customary to buy the pianist a pint every now and again in appreciation for the entertainment. Consequently the piano became crowded with glasses of beer. Dad was content to drink orange juice, but Uncle Arthur not wanting to let good Kent ale go to waste, obligingly drunk the it on Dad's behalf. Daniel watched the antics from the safety of a side door, conveniently left open because of the warm weather. He was kept stocked up with crisps and an assortment of drinks by the same kind folk who bought beer for the pianist. Within a couple of hours Uncle Arthur became decidedly pickled and when the time came to return home he had to be assisted, quite incapable of standing unaided. The following evening at closing time, the antics of Dad carrying Uncle Arthur home came to the attention of a local bobby, and for a moment Daniel began to wonder whether Uncle Arthur would be arrested. When Dad told the constable that Uncle Arthur had been a Japanese Prisoner of War, the officer shown considerable sympathy, even gave Dad a hand. It is not too difficult to imagine the effect on the domestic scene when a constable escorted home a drunken husband and father! The outcome of the subsequent inquiry by Mum and Aunt Ellen, which

Daniel felt must have taken place, he never discovered, but he had the impression Dad was punished as much as his Uncle! This did not prevent them from going down The Three Keys Inn on several occasions throughout the holiday, but after the incident with the Police, Uncle Arthur became careful to disguise his drunken state, apart from snoring in bed, which everyone in the house heard!

The driver decided to deviate from the route to the police station, for he turned off into a residential area, mainly well kept bungalows, each with lovingly mown lawns and well tended flowerbeds. Even Daniel felt compelled to look. The driver noticed this at once. 'I thought this would wake you up, for this is your territory.'

'What makes you think that?' Daniel asked almost casually, continuing to peer out of the window.

The driver slowed. 'You did that one and the one next door.' He said pointing out of the open window. 'Plus those two over the road.'

'Oh, did I?' Daniel wondered casually, trying to work out the connection between him and the burglaries, and why the police seemed so positive he was the villain, when in reality he had never visited this part of Whitstable prior to today. He knew little about the criminal justice system apart from the obvious, but knew that for him to be arrested and treated in this manner, there must be justification, possibly with evidence in the possession of the police. Would a magistrate be permitted to issue a warrant without evidence? If he had not been here, there was no possibility they could have evidence of this nature, was there?

'Yes you bloody well did!' The driver exploded and he braked hard bringing the car to an abrupt stop.

'You shouldn't be doing this Ian!' The older constable advised.

'Mabee, mabee not.' The driver retorted. 'But I'm going to do it anyway, so you can put that in your pipe and smoke it! This evil bastard first beat up two elderly residents for no good reason, then he jumped on the old lady and broke both legs. The sight of that poor lassie in hospital with two eyes beaten black and blue made me feel sick. Or had you forgotten old man?'

'No, I have not forgotten as well you know. We have all been affected by the plight of those two old folk, and the unpleasant antics of this joker, but you are wrong to get emotionally involved. Let the process of law take its course, that's all I'm saying.'

'Bloody Hell, you English have no balls!' The driver exclaimed thumping the steering wheel. 'It knew it was a mistake coming down here to you southern softies! I should have stayed in bonny Scotland!'

Daniel wisely refrained from making any obvious comments regarding this observation. He had an uneasy feeling in the pit of his stomach that he was going to be in for a hard time, if Police thought he was the one responsible for inflicting severe violence and injuries on two elderly victims. By the sound of it there was more than one case of aggravated burglary. His main concern was the process by which the police thought he was the perpetrator.

The driver though did take heed of the comments and advice offered by his senior colleague, for he turned the car around at the next side road and headed back towards the High Street. He drove slowly through the almost deserted shopping area and arrived at the Police Station. The elder constable escorted Daniel firmly and quickly into the relative safety of the charge room. Here Daniel came under the piercing gaze of a corpulent Station Sergeant, resplendent with three magnificent chevrons and a crown above. Daniel felt relieved, given the previous threats, that he made it to the desk Sergeant in one piece.

'Mister Taylor, nice to have you back on our patch with us at last!' He greeted with a smile but without apparent malice. 'You led us a merry dance but we nabbed you in the end.'

Daniel refrained from reacting.

'Oh. Lost our tongue have we? Being locked up overnight has damped your spirits, I can tell.' He said with more than a hint of sarcasm, accompanied by a large grin on his equally large face before turning to speak to his escort. 'Take him along to cell number three. We'll let him stew there for a while until the CID arrive.'

'I would like to telephone my wife and to have a drink, please.' Daniel asked politely.

'Denied!'

'Be reasonable. My wife is nine months pregnant!'

'Still denied! You should have thought of that before getting violent with senior citizens in my town. Now get him out of my sight, before I do something we will both regret!'

For the second time in twenty-four hours Daniel found himself locked up in a bare cell, and despite being warm and sunny outside, here it was cold and dim, only a faint light penetrated through a small window high above his head. As the door closed he knew his plight to be real, substantial but misleading evidence surely in the hands of police. His whole life disappeared in the blink of an eye. Nothing left but all the time in the world to contemplate what June was going through at home or rather in between homes. With a lowered head feeling totally depressed, he resigned himself to a long wait, knowing that judging by the hostile reception he had received, that the CID would not be in any hurry to deal with his case.

He must have dozed off, for the door being opened woke him. Another constable stood in the doorway, who beckoned without speaking. Daniel followed wearily because of his aching limbs, wondering what would be happening this time. He followed the constable up a short flight of stairs and was ushered into an interview room. Seated at a table were two detectives surrounded by files and assorted papers. Both stood as he entered. The taller man, probably the senior of the two, invited him to be seated by indicating a chair in front of the table. The two men sat only when he sat. The men waited as if weighing him up. The senior man reeked of tobacco, his nicotine fingers evidence of a smoking habit. He was considerably overweight with a fat beer belly protruding over the top of his suit trousers. His jacket was peppered by dandruff about the shoulders, quite unusual because the man had thinned light brown coloured hair showing signs of balding about the crown. The other detective, twenty years or so younger, a non smoker with a full head of hair, but already showing signs of physical inactivity, his almost bulging cheeks, a giveaway sign of either overeating, a bad diet, combined with a lack of exercise, or all three.

The senior spoke. 'Will you remain with us Jim?' He asked. 'This rooster may give some trouble, if his past form is to go by.'

'I have no past form, so don't make slanderous statements.' Daniel demanded, then noticing that his outburst caused both detectives to hesitate, continued. 'I refuse to answer any of your questions until I have been given the opportunity to make a telephone call to my wife and to be offered some refreshment. I have no idea of the precise time but know it has been several hours since breakfast.'

'We may be here for some time, then if that is your opinion.' The senior detective replied. 'I am Detective Sergeant Hill in charge of this case. I should point out to you, that you have a number of serious charges to answer, which include several counts of aggravated burglary and a serious assault. I am in no mood to negotiate prisoner rights or any other bullshit delaying tactics you may put to us. I intend to get answers from you, the sooner the better for both of us. We can sp…'

'I am not answering any questions until my reasonable request has been granted.' Daniel interrupted. He stood up which caused apprehension to the two still seated men. 'I want to return to my cell until my demands are met fully'.

To his dismay this caused no reaction other than the men were now paying full attention, watching him intently. The constable stood nearby, at the ready for any sudden movement. 'You can stand or be seated it makes no difference. I have an investigation to carry out and intend to continue as of now.'

'You are Mister Daniel Taylor of 229 Waterloo Road, Romford, Essex?' The junior detective spoke for the first time.

'I am of that name and as of yesterday, that address.' Daniel replied at once, but continuing to remain standing. 'I saw your warrant yesterday, and suspect that you have my name spelt incorrectly. Today without me, my pregnant wife has probably moved to a new house in Helions Bumpstead.'

'How do you spell your name then?'

'T-a-i-l-o-r.'

The junior detective sorted through his papers and chose one. This he inspected carefully then looked up.

'He's right Sarge!' He said to his sergeant, sounding surprised.

The elder detective shrugged his shoulders. 'Makes not a scrap difference. Daniel Taylor or Daniel Tailor, the spelling is of little consequence.'

Daniel stood whilst the two men, who ignored his presence entirely, discussed the case without revealing a single clue as to the evidence, which they surely possessed. After a minute or two he decided to intervene. 'I would like to make a telephone call to my wife and to have a drink.' He said quietly.

The two men stopped their conversation and looked up, then at each other.

'Request denied.' The older detective said. 'Are you going to co-operate now?'

'No! Not until my request is met.'

'In that case you can return to your cell and contemplate your situation.' He leant over to speak to the uniformed officer behind him. 'Take him back to the cells Jim. We'll go for lunch now and will be back in an hour or so.'

The constable held Daniels arm and led him back to the cell.

Seated on the bench his parched throat made it difficult for him to swallow. He was in an impossible position and he could see no let up unless he could find a way out of the impasse. He paced up and down trying to make some sense of his predicament but could not. He may have to compromise and go along with the charade in order to find out how June was progressing and to get some refreshment. Then he had an idea. He walked around the wall to the toilet, an unexpected source of water. One look though at the disgusting state of the bowl, grubby above the water level and badly stained below it, made him immediately abandon the idea. So desperate was he that he even tried to get his hand through the small aperture through which a length of chain protruded, to try and see if he could reach the cistern the other side of the wall. He groped about and thought he was succeeding until he managed to get his hand well and truly stuck. He panicked and set about freeing his hand succeeded within a few minutes. His hand came out with the skin very red where it had scraped on the concrete aperture, so he abandoned this idea too. Resigned to the fact that he was doomed, he sat and waited for the two men to return from lunch.

Eventually someone arrived and unlocked the door. A different constable stood before him, who like his other colleague refrained from speaking and gestured with his hand. Daniel knew where to go and walked ahead of the constable to the small interview room. As before, the two men, senior and junior sat at the table but rose and did not sit until he was seated.

'I have decided to co-operate with your enquiries.' He offered, hoping for some positive reaction. There was no obvious sign, which disappointed him.' I am sure I will not be of much use to your enquiries, for until today I have not visited this town since about 1955.'

There followed a moment of silence until the senior man spoke. The unexpected sound of his voice made Daniel jump.

'Where were you on Monday 21st February?'

'That was over six months ago, I really have no idea.'

'If you want a drink, you will have to try won't you?'

'Okay.' Daniel replied thoughtfully, and he tried to recall. Around the first or second week in February he had placed a deposit on the house in Helions Bumpstead and after being offered advice from the estate agent took a week off work to redecorate the lounge. He went on a course sometime in late February but could not be positive about the date unless he referred to his diary. 'For the past few months I have spent my working week away from home. Around that time I did have some time off work in mid February then went off on a three or four day course at Bath, but without my diary could not swear to it.'

'What do you do for a living Mister Tailor?'

'I'm an engineer.' The first alarm bell ran inside his head.

'And you spend time away from home?'

'Yes.'

'Where precisely?'

'For the past year or so, at Barrow in Furness.' An answer accompanied by more alarm bells ringing internally. 'I stay there from late Sunday afternoon until midday on Friday and come home at weekends.'

Where's Barrow in Furness exactly? Sounds a long way away.'

'Its in Cumbria across Morecombe Bay from Morecombe in Lancashire.'

'How do you travel back and forth? By car?'

'No by train.'

'Do you own a car?'

'Yes.'

'Make and registration number, Mark 3 Ford Cortina, YPU 367F?'

' Yes. How do....'

'Insured with Eagle Star?'

'Yes, but....'

'Do you have a brother named Ian, who has recently married, emigrated to Canada and with his wife named......' Here he paused to refer to a file on the table before him, thumbing through it until he found the correct paper which he gave a momentarily glance. Even seeing it upside down, Daniel recognised it as a letter from his brother sent to him months ago. How on earth did this come into the possession of the police?

'... wife named Caroline, who works as a stewardess for Air Canada?'

'Yes, but how do you know .....?'

'Your solicitors are Sedgewick and Porter of High Street, Epping, Essex?'

'Yes, but....'

'Your Grandmother, Joy King died last year and left you a sum of money.'

'She did, but....'

You bank at the National Westminster Bank in Ilford.'

'I do, but....'

The questions then came quick and fast, the two men between them not giving him adequate time to answer properly as if trying to catch him out. He tried to slow them down without success. The two detectives acted as a pair, went through a pre-planned pattern and were very skilful in their method of interrogating him. Daniel knew that they had must have gone through this procedure many times before.

'Where were you on Sunday 5th March this year?'

'Probably at home in the morning then in the afternoon travelling north by train.' He felt confident that this was the case, so answered without hesitation.

'So you would have been away for your birthday the following day?'

This remark was a bolt from the blue. How on earth did these two clowns know that? He was visibly shaken and began to feel very apprehensive to the extent that he would have fainted had he been standing. Seeing his reaction the atmosphere changed at once.

The senior detective stared at him intently then spoke very quietly. 'I put it to you that you have been leading us a merry dance like you were when we nearly caught you two weeks ago.' Daniel sensed that he was very angry, when a frown appeared on his forehead and his face turned a touch on the red side. Tiny beads of perspiration appeared as if by magic on his forehead. 'I put it to you that on the 23rd of February, the 1st of March and the 5th of March you were in fact resident here in Whitstable committing burglaries at 25 Barrow Road, 13 and 15 Harbour Lane, during which time you were disturbed and in order to make your escape, set about the elderly occupants with a heavy object! On the last occasion you beat both occupants senseless and then deliberately broke the woman's legs. She is ninety three years old and as a result of your handiwork spent four painful weeks in hospital and is still incapacitated to this day!'

Daniel felt as if he lived in a tall building whose foundations had been built on clay and a breeze caused it to collapse like a pile of stones. He had only a single answer and knew before he spoke that his reply would most probably cause extreme anger. The chances of a drink and the opportunity to telephone June seems as remote as when he had first arrived. 'I have already told you that I have not visited Whitstable since 1955, so you must be mistaken in thinking that I wa....'

Angry before, the older detective exploded and stood up suddenly in a fashion not normally associated with someone of his size and age. An outstretched arm grabbed Daniel by the shirt below the throat and if the younger detective assisted by the constable standing behind had not intervened and pleaded with their colleague to let go, he would have strangled on the spot.

Daniel collapsed onto the back of his chair gasping for breath and the detective acted in a similar fashion, looking decidedly ill. The younger of the two leant

101

forward on the desk, and spoke to Daniel in a calm manner, as he listened in horror hearing the revelations.

'We are confident we have arrested the correct suspect for the following reasons. Our suspect who is known by the name Daniel Tailor shares both his name and birthday with you. He also once resided at 229 Waterloo Road Romford, same as you. The registration of his car, a Mark 3 Ford Cortina, registration YPU 367F, a vehicle insured with Eagle Star, also by coincidence same as you. He has a brother named Ian who resides in Canada whose wife named Caroline works as an air hostess, same as your brother. His solicitor is the same person as your solicitor with his office in Epping. Give me one good reason why we should not have arrested you?'

'I can give you several, since you have asked.' Daniel replied, seeing an immediate reaction from the senior detective. He sat upright with a look of menace on his face. Daniel hesitated for he knew in advance there could well be a reprisal for his next statement. 'Firstly I told you several times that I have not visited Whitstable since I was about twelve years old, but that is of little importance. What is important is that I am positive that my diary will substantiate my claim that I could not have been here on the three dates you have previously mentioned. I am also confident that your evidence is either fake or obtained by dubious means, although I cannot begin to imagine at this time, either how, when, why or by whom.'

The two men remained passive and showed little emotion. Of more significance the senior man sat head down studying papers on the desk before him. They had now turned full circle and no nearer a solution to their enquiries that had commenced much earlier in the day. The junior turned to face the senior. 'We are not making any progress, so I suggest we adjourn now and tomorrow we can make further enquiries, starting perhaps with Mister Tailors employer. Do you agree?'

The senior nodded.

'Tell us who your employer is?

ESR in Manor Park, London E12. My boss is Henry Reade whose telephone number is....'

'We already have the telephone number of your boss, but there had been no answer, so we will see you tomorrow morning then Mister Tailor.'

With these words Daniel was led down to the cells, thinking on the way he was wise not to repeat his request of a drink and to make a telephone call. After the cell door closed and the footsteps faded away, he had a short nap until keys in the lock awaked him. The door swung open. Before him stood another constable who carried a tray, dinner, some sort of beef stew, a piping hot mug of tea, with apples and custard for dessert. Afterwards he felt able to concentrate enough read his book until the light went out and he fell into fitful and disturbed sleep. He awoke at dawn as the first trace of a new day penetrated his cell through the small window above his head.

Breakfast arrived shortly, more hot tea and scrambled eggs on toast, which he ate with relish. Afterwards read some of his book then, he hung about feeling bored for ages until keys were heard in the lock and once again he was escorted upstairs. He had no idea of the time, but thought it must be quite early on Monday morning. He sat down facing the same two detectives. Junior was the first to speak.

'We have contacted your wife who has successfully moved into your new house. Apparently there were no significant problems and she sends you her love. As for Mister Reade we are reliably informed that he is away on business so there will be a short delay until he can view your diary to confirm or otherwise your whereabouts on the days in question.'

'Thanks.' Daniel replied, feeling relieved that June had moved in one piece. She was probably still lumbered with *MDL*, but he supposed she was slightly better of with her than without her presence. As for Henry, Daniel's brain refused to function and he was unable to recall where Henry had gone. He hoped it was not too long a trip.

'There is little point in continuing our line of questioning until your Chief Engineer returns from his trip. We shall only go round in circles like we did yesterday.' Junior continued. 'Instead we shall use the time to get confirmation from you that the documents in our possession are genuine. Do you agree to this?'

Daniel nodded.

The detective laid out a number of original documents encased in a polythene folder for him to inspect. 'May I pick then up?' Daniel asked.

The detective nodded.

The first document was an out of date insurance certificate for his car. He cast his mind back to the near past. His insurance expired on the last day of February, and he recalled telephoning his broker to try and find a cheaper premium. He had been on a value engineering course at Bath at the time and had discussed the higher premium with fellow students, which had prompted him to contact his broker in London. He noticed that the insurance certificate had been neatly folded to a quarter size and the corners were badly creased, whereas he always folded his documents in half only and. There was little doubt regarding its authenticity but how had the police obtained it? Perhaps he should ask.

'How and where did you obtain this document?'

A simple question, which required a simple answer.

Senior spoke for the first time, for once sounding calm, quite a contrast to his performance yesterday. 'That document together with all the documents before you, were found in the flat you rented down by the Harbour here at Whitstable, and before you ask, here is a signed copy of the tenancy agreement found on the said premises.' He handed over another apparently original document also encased in a polythene folder.

Daniel inspected a printed agreement between Kent Estates and a Daniel Tailor, spelt correctly, regarding the tenancy of a fully furnished first floor flat for a period on six months. The untidy signature was not his, but he could not reasonably expect the police to have noticed this. He looked carefully at each document in turn trying to reason how they came to be in the hands of the police. The documents consisted of a birthday card still in it envelope, letters from his brother with news of Caroline and her promotion to Senior Hostess with Air Canada, letters from his solicitor regarding to sale of his house and a number of documents relating to his car. One letter in particular was dated 13 March, and in all probability he had read on the train.

During his time at Barrow in Furness he had usually taken all his mail with him and dealt with most of it on the train on the way up. One of the advantages of travelling first class was that he usually had a fair bit of space to spread out. How he disposed of any unwanted correspondence was any ones guess. Try as he might, he knew the documents and letters to be genuine, but to establish how they had found their way into a flat in Kent presented him with quite a problem. He could finally appreciate why the two men sitting on the other side of the desk were convinced into thinking he was their suspect. Quite a few questions but with little prospect of finding the answers. He took a series of deep breaths before he spoke.

'They are genuine documents.' Daniel admitted finally, noting the relief on the faces of Senior and Junior. 'The only snag is that I have not been to Whitstable since I was about twelve and can only surmise that someone has obtained these from somewhere, I have no idea how, and passed themselves off as me. There can be no other explanation. I am positive that my diary will confirm my whereabouts for the two dates in question. That is all I am able to say on this matter until I have the opportunity to refer to my diary.'

The two men considered his answer for some minutes before giving a reply. Junior was the first to speak. 'I think we have made some progress and agree that your diary will allow our investigations to proceed further. You are still our chief suspect and will have to remain in our custody until the contents of your diary are known to us.' Daniel had the impression that he was thinking on his feet and held a hand up and counted the items off on his fingers as he spoke. 'I admit I do not understand, assuming you are telling us the truth, how someone has acquired these papers over a period of several months and then used them to adopt your identity. If this is the case it explains fully why you are insistent regarding your innocence. It remains for us to....'

Behind, Daniel heard faint sounds of the door opening, interrupting junior in full flow. Daniel turned his head. A male face appeared briefly to look at Daniel's face. In an instant the face retreated out of sight.

'I would appreciate an urgent word with you both.' A male voice said from behind the partly opened door.

'Does it have to be now, Mick?' Senior demanded. 'As you can well see, we are conducting an interview with a suspect.'

'I would advise you to stop until you have heard what I have to say.'

'Say it now.'

'I don't think that is advisable, come out here so we can discuss it.'

'Say it now!' Senior repeated with a raised voice.

'Okay, if that's the way you want it, but don't blame me of the consequences.' Came a curt reply. 'That's not the suspect I saw making his escape on the shop front roofs. Just for starters he was thick set with light coloured hair, not black like your suspect. You have arrested the wrong man!'

These few words had a noticeable impact on those in the room. The two detectives rushed outside and closed the door. Daniel felt elated, which gave him hope of a triumphant return home. Outside in the corridor came faints sounds of a heated discussion, which Daniel only heard occasional words. He quickly deduced that the informant was the only witness who had seen the actual subject on the evening when the real burglar, alias Daniel Tailor, made his escape. In the considered opinion of the policeman named Mick, the person in the interview room was not the suspect seen to make his escape. There followed a period of comparative silence during which Daniel could hear mumbles but not distinguish a single word. Finally the door opened and in walked Senior and Junior. Considering the bad news, which had recently been given to them, both men were smiling, which Daniel found surprising. They walked around the table and sat down. Senior spoke very pleasantly. 'Mister Tailor, as you have just heard, it would appear that you have been correct all along. We have made a regrettable but understandable mistake. My colleague who has seen our real suspect has confirmed you are not the person we have been seeking. I have sent for some refreshments and will be issuing you with a railway warrant by which means you can travel home.'

Daniel shook his head. 'You can stick your tea up your arse!' He said with venom. 'I want to see the Senior Officer now and require the use of a telephone. A travel warrant is not acceptable. Given the inconvenience and my treatment since I arrived yesterday, denial of food and drink and the need to telephone my pregnant wife, I demand to travel home by car immediately after I have made my telephone calls.'

Senior nodded to Junior who stood up and left the room. 'I can only repeat my apology Mister Tailor.' He said quietly. 'We applied for a warrant in good faith and given the unusual circumstances of this disturbing case, felt we were dealing with a dangerous criminal and acted accordingly.'

The interview room suddenly became crowded and the tea arrived simultaneous with a Superintendent resplendent in his distinctive and faultless uniform adorned with the silver braid of office. He breezed up to Daniel hand extended with the intent to shake that of Daniel. Daniel deliberately held his hands down. 'Mister Tailor!' He greeted cheerfully, with what Daniel took to be feigned cheerfulness. 'I understand there is a regretful case of mistaken identity. How can I assist?'

During the period of quiet, Daniel had composed himself to the extent that he knew he how held the upper ground and fully intended to take advantage of this sudden change of fortune.

'You are?' He demanded.

Superintendent Heathfield'

'I was brought here yesterday under arrest which has subsequently proved to be unjustified.' Daniel said just loud enough to be heard above the ambient noise in the room. 'I have been denied basic rights such as food and refreshments and have been intimidated without due cause by two of your lesser clowns in this second rate circus. I have now been informed that I am free to go and will be issued with a railway travel warrant, which under the circumstances is unacceptable.'

'Mister Tailor.' The Superintendent interrupted. 'My officers have conducted this case in the belief tha..'

'Further to this injustice.' Daniel interrupted, now in a raised voice. 'I inform you that I shall be suing the Kent Police for wrongful arrest. I demand to be taken home now by car without delay. My wife is due to give birth at any time and...'

'Mister Tailor!' It was the turn of the Superintendent to interrupt. 'To save you further inconvenience I have already authorised a car to take you home immediately. It should arrive within the next few minutes.'

'Good!' Daniel replied. 'I would like some paper and to borrow a pen.'

'Certainly.'

Daniel now armed with pen and paper asked each officer in turn for their name and rank, writing furiously. Coffee, tea and orange juice together with a plate of sandwiches appeared on the table before him and he tucked in with relish now his shoulders no longer had the weight of arrest bearing down on them. He then made a quick telephone call to June, surprisingly calm considering the recent chain of events, and learned that he was not yet a father.

A limousine arrived within ten minutes, apparently the official vehicle of the Superintendent and drove him back to Helions Bumpstead. The police chauffeur, totally unaware of the circumstances surrounding the Monday afternoon dash through the countryside, chatted away and the journey though northern Kent and the lanes of Essex was quite pleasant. On the outskirts of Haverhill, they managed to get lost, all because Daniel now showing signs of relief did not pay full attention.

His arrival home was emotional, even the *MDL* seemed pleased to see him and did her utmost to keep out of their way. He telephoned Henry at home, now back from his business trip, to be told that the Kent Constabulary were not forthcoming when he telephoned and had not been able to speak with anyone who admitted being familiar with the case. Daniel gave a resume of events and Henry admitted being very concerned by the accumulated collection of original documents and admitted he was intrigued how they came into the hands of the police. When Daniel mentioned that he intended to sue the police, Henry was not impressed, saying that the MoD may feel that their project compromised, but Daniel cast this opinion aside. Henry ended the conversation by saying that Daniel was to take further time off and return to work only when he felt able to and when Junes condition stabilised. Daniel came off the line slightly put out by Henry's attitude to the episode.

Things happened rather quickly

Three days later, an hour after Daniel put the *MDL* on the train home at Chelmsford, June felt the first twinges of childbirth and went into immediate labour and give birth to a healthy bouncing baby boy in the ambulance whilst on the way to hospital. Reeling from relief, Daniel arrived home after a rather traumatic time. Within a minute of arriving home, he received a call from Superintendent Heathfield from Kent Police with the news that the actual burglar had been caught and that all charges against Daniel were dropped. Daniel took the opportunity to inform the

Superintendent that this changed little and he fully intended to speak with his solicitor with the intention to sue police. The Senior Officer was not too impressed to hear this and attempted to persuade Daniel to do otherwise.

'I should point that it can be very stressful undertaking to sue police and the cross examination by solicitors is not a pleasant experience. Its very similar experience to a major court case.'

'What do I care?' Daniel responded with no intention of being charitable. ' If your clowns had their way I would have been charged and made an appearance in a real court and most likely sent to prison. No I have avoided that and am quite prepared to do whatever is necessary to gain compensation. Good afternoon.'

He replaced the receiver feeling very pleased with himself.

When the dust settled and everything seemed normal with the baby, June arrived back home and easily established a routine with their new son, Daniel went back to work leaving the *MDL* in charge. He endured a series of interviews with senior management, during which the circumstances of his arrest were dissected in great detail with the intention of establishing how he had been compromised. The Chief engineer was disturbed by Daniels insistence that he proposed to sue police, because he feared the MoD might come to the decision that ESR security had been compromised and place the lucrative contract elsewhere. In the event the first event took place and the second did not. Daniel enlisted the services of a solicitor who specialised in wrongful arrest and successfully negotiated a satisfactory monetary settlement of £100 per hour throughout the time he remained under arrest. The Sentinel Project remained at

ESR until its completion months later, followed by the contract for series of major modifications, which followed extensive sea trials conducted on board a nuclear submarine.

The truth of the mistaken identity saga did not emerge until months later. Daniel stayed regularly at the Osborne Hotel, Barrow in Furness, and innocently discarded most of his unwanted mail in the rubbish bin in his bedroom. An unscrupulous cleaner at the hotel collected all manner of documents and over the coming months acquired quite a collection until he could easily pass as Daniel Tailor. The cleaner left to move to Whitstable and there conducted series of burglaries some involving some disturbing acts of violence. The police, prompted by the extreme violence gave the case top priority and gradually the net closed in on the perpetuator. He was almost caught a few days before Daniel was arrested. The villain rented a flat above a fishing tackle shop down by the harbour. As the Police came in through the door at the back, the burglar escaped via a front window, climbed a wall then made his way across a series of shop fronts and jumped off at the end and thence into the alley to that side and disappeared into the night. Along the way he was accidentally spied by a policeman passing by in a panda car unaware of the raid going on from the rear and saw a blond man on the shop front roof. Some days later the officer learned of the raid and hearing that a hostile suspect protesting his innocence was in custody, decided to conduct a identity parade of his own making.

There was a moral to all this and lessons to be learned. It was that from that moment on, every letter, bill, junk mail and unsolicited mail had the address torn off and disposed of separately. Daniel remained determined that an event of this nature could not repeat itself. Others at the factory took note of a hard-earned lesson and acted similarly. In the Manor Park area, sales of paper shredders increased.

Nevertheless life at the factory went on, despite outside influences and security surrounding the Sentinel Project remained intact.

4

Harry Fether

Harry Fether, another of the colourful characters whose mould was broken after his birth.Married to Sylvia with no children, they resided in Hornchurch near to Roneo Corner, in a terraced house with a narrow strip of land, named locally as *the alley*, used by the neighbours as a wide pedestrian access, which allegedly belonged to the Council. On the far side of the narrow strip of land, a small stream named the River Rum. When Harry and his neighbours heard of a proposal to build a new hospital, they all extended their gardens to include *the alley* and hastily planted shrubs and in some cases extended an existing allotment garden and gradually removed all traces of the concrete to disguise the lands former use. The council process included an extensive period of public consultation, during which Harry and land stealing neighbours took part in the process, but deliberately kept protests low key so as not to create waves and so draw attention to their misdemeanour. The plan worked, for two years after *the alley* had been removed, work commenced on the hospital. The land on the other side of the now fenced alley, the river, was first turned into a culvert, then developed as part of a hospice up to the new fence, so the disturbance after completion was minimal and *the alley* now officially acknowledged as part of gardens.

Clean cut features and smartly dressed, a legacy of his time in the forces. Harry always wore a Harris Tweed sports jacket with front pleated black trousers with creases so sharp you could almost cut a finger and highly polished black Oxford brogues. Clean shaven, he took pride in his appearance, hair carefully groomed with a merest sign of ageing with grey hair on the temples, in his view it made him appear distinguished.

He usually had an answer to anything and everybody and it was rare for anyone to get the last word. George managed it once only.

*

One afternoon, during a moment of great mirth, Harry had been on top form and feigning annoyance grabbed a roll of drawings and hit George round the face.

'Two can play at this.' George thought, and frowned at the same moment he poked a finger towards Harry. 'That's it!' He threatened, thrusting his fully loaded finger towards his intended victim. 'That is the last time you hit me around the face...'

Harry was not impressed by this outburst and hit George again.

'You don't take any notice, but I advise you that you do.' He said sternly, glaring at Harry without blinking. 'If there is any more of this violence you will pay for it!'

This stopped Harry dead in his tracks, unsure whether to laugh or otherwise. By now those in adjacent desks were watching and listening, thoroughly enjoying every moment.

'Hit me again at your peril.' George said, and seeing Harry stiffen, added. 'You WILL pay!'

Harry threatened again with the roll of drawings, but did not hit George.

Over the coming weeks this occurrence was mentioned several times. Out of Harry's sight, George had placed a plastic cup with less than a quarter inch of water in the bottom. He intended to throw it in Harry's face should he get hit again.

The joke went on for weeks and George began to suspect that Harry had forgotten his threat. Every week much to the delight of those who knew of it, he refilled, the plastic cup with clean water.

Then one afternoon when they came back from a leaving do at the Greengage pub, everyone relaxed, Harry called out Georges name. Similarly relaxed George stood up and turned to face Harry.

Quick as flash, Harry hit George around the face with a roll of drawings.

This was the moment for which he had planned. Without taking his eyes off Harry, George reached down for the cup, and threw the microscopic amount of water in Harry's face.

'I warned you that you would pay and you took no notice!'

Harry stood silent with water dripping of his face.

Everyone was laughing, eventually Harry grinned, but did not speak.

*

Harry was one of two in the drawing office who were called up for National Service, Basil Morley being the other one. What he did, where he was posted and which unit or regiment he served, remained a mystery. Harry did his initial training at Bulshort Camp on Salisbury Plain, which suggested the army, and it quickly became renamed by the inmates as Bullshit Camp! Harry claimed the predictable army bullshit existed, saluting everything that moved and painting everything, which did not. The hut Corporal by the name of Harris, most of the time without the H, was spelt B-A-S-T-A-R-D. Each man suffered hell, but Harry survived, just, and kept his head down so not to get picked on. As the end of their training period approached they all looked forward to a weekend off. Corporal *Bastard* Harris however had other ideas. Minutes before the hut were due to set off towards the main gate with their passes, he walked into the hut grinning, carrying a small cloth bag.

'Where do you think you lot are going?' He demanded, still grinning, looking at each man in turn.

Harry felt like saying something sarcastic, but thought better of it. 'Weekend leave Corporal.' He answered.

The Corporal looked at Harry, then shook his head. 'You lot are a complete shower, and I have a job for you to do first.' He stretched the bag open and emptied the contents onto the nearest bed. They could see twelve very grubby empty .303 bullet cases. 'Leave is cancelled until noon tomorrow. By then I want these all highly polished with a dandelion in each.'

He about turned and left, saying over his shoulder. 'See you tomorrow at noon, prompt!'

Not much point arguing, so they set to making a determined effort in on the shell cases so shiny you could see your face in them. Every man took part, and after three hours good progress had been made, but there was much work to be done, especially as most cases had been deliberately scratched and every one had to be polished out. It became apparent also that the small groove separating the primer from the brass case would be scrutinised closely. Harry suggested someone donate a tooth brush and they set to giving each groove a good enthusiastic brushing with Brasso, followed by careful attention with a cloth covered matchstick to polish the groove sides.

After breakfast, the cleaning resumed. Harry disappeared for ten minutes and when he returned was very cross. He burst in through the outer door. The eleven energetic polishers all looked around. 'Do you know what that bastard 'Arris has done?' He demanded angrily.

Most shook their heads.

'By stopping us going on leave before noon means we cannot go home because the last London bound train goes from Grateley at 1152! In effect we are stuck here for the weekend.'

The whole hut stopped work and moaned.

Don't waste your time, we are stuck with it. But..' Here he emphasised the last word. 'I fully intend to get our own back. Get on with the polishing and leave the rest to me, but be patient.'

By half past eleven the polishing had been completed and twelve polished cases each with a daffodil inserted were on display on the table. At precisely noon, the door burst open and in came Corporal *Bastard* Harris, and began examining each individual cases on the table. Finally he turned around, smiling. 'Well gentlemen you have excelled yourselves. I am most impressed. You can all leave now. See you on Monday morning. Make sure you are in camp by six a.m.'

After he had gone, some challenged Harry about his train theory. He put up with for a while, then said. 'Bastard 'Arris was far too casual, he knows we can't get home.'

There were even more protests, until Harry had had enough. 'All right, all right clever dicks, see if you can get a train home. I'm not wasting my time so I'm off to the pub.'

They all strolled over to the main gate and presented their passes. Outside eight went right towards the train station and three turned left and with Harry went to the pub. About an hour later the others arrived at the pub, the looks on their faces more than suggesting that Harry had been correct.

*

Generations of those called up for National Service and stationed for training at Bulshort Camp on Salisbury Plain, quickly discovered that only one in six trains stopped at Grateley during the week, only two on Saturday and none on Sunday. This was very frustrating as every train stopped at Salisbury twelve miles down the track and of more significance sixteen miles further away from Bulshort Camp. Those with a weekend pass were supposed to return by 6 am on Monday, but the majority caught the last train on Sunday to arrive back at camp around midnight, if they were able to get a lift from Salisbury.

Some wags discovered that a milk train went through Grateley station at around 4 am but did not stop there, so it became common practice to pull the communication cord when the Black Swan Public House came into view, then jump off at the station and disappear into the night taking advantage of the resulting chaos.

As time passed some sympathetic engine drivers used to slow to a crawl at the station and so it would have continued forever, but one early morning a squaddie with a bellyful of beer jumped off, somehow tripped on the platform, fell under the train and was killed. The authorities were most displeased, but from that time every milk train stopped at the station.

*

True to his word, Harry made plans to get even with the Corporal. Two weeks later at the completion of their training the hut planned to have a passing out party and they contrived to invite Corporal Harris. Harry had a friend who was an accomplished chemist, supplied Harry with a liquid concoction to achieve their objective. On the appointed evening the party started and early on the corporal made an appearance in full dress uniform. He accepted a pint of local ale, which also contained the tasteless, but lethal liquid. The party appeared to be lively, a false impression intended to impress the victim. It seemed to work because the corporal, with gentle encouragement downed two more pints.

Nothing happened.

The corporal seemed as unaffected after four pints as he did after only one. Then without warning he turned into an incoherent lump of jelly without any limb control.

Harry leapt into action and with others dragged the virtually unconscious corporal outside to the flagpole, where the lanyard was passed through both sleeves and they started hauling his body skywards. Harry had brought some of the chemical liquid with him and forced fed some of the liquid down the throat of the victim, then without ceremony usually associated with the flagpole he was hauled up a few feet and unveiled without undue formality. The unfortunate corporal was not quite out, for he continued to struggle with an unseen opponent, and was heard to utter.

'Leave me alone!'

A short pause.

'Leave me alone won't you!'

Always immediately obedient in response to orders from the corporal, the hut, with sweet revenge undertaken, returned to the hut and carried on with the party, but not before Harry repeated the agreed sequence of events which would ensure their part in the revenge would remain undetected. Harry crept away for a while and disposed of his concoction and container in a remote place, which ensured they would not be discovered. The party ended shortly after the booze ran out. They all crept into their beds in a drunken state and Harry, at least, waited for the balloon to go up, which surely it must.

At dawn there was a great deal of noise from outside the hut. Harry heard shouting, realised the game was up and thought it wise to go back to sleep. He too had consumed a great deal of beer so it was not too difficult a task and he quickly dropped off to sleep again. Some time later, it was not known how much later, Sergeant Bennett burst into the hut and demanded their full attention. The hut occupants slowly roused themselves and they stood yawning at the foot of their bed. The Sergeant walked along the line glaring at each man in turn. 'So you had a party last night to which you invited Corporal Harris.' He said to no one in particular. He suddenly turned to glare at one man without warning. In a raised intimidating voice, he demanded of Private Milgrove, the least offensive of the hut. 'What time did Corporal Harris leave?'

Ray thought of his answer for a millisecond, then said. 'I think around ten o'clock, Sarge.'

'Think, Sarge! What sort of answer is that?'

'We were having a party Sarge.' Ray replied, in a raised voice. 'I don't clock watch at the best of times!'

The Sergeant about turned and spoke to the man on the other side of the hut.

'What time did Corporal Harris leave?'

Johnson did not think before he spoke. 'I reckon ten is about right, Sarge.' He answered.

'Fether! What time did Corporal Harris leave?' The Sergeant did not turn around.

This caught Harry by surprise, and the first feeling of doubt crept into his mind. How should he answer? He quickly decided to stick rigidly to the agreed plan. 'I think the Corporal left at around ten. I seem to recall he was going on to another function.'

'Where?'

'Don't think he mentioned it, Sarge.'

'You lot are as slippery as a bunch of eels!' He yelled. 'How can you say he left at ten, if one of you does not watch the clock, another just reckons and surprise, surprise, Fether you are equally evasive.'

'What has happened t.........?' Harry asked.

'You know Fether!'

'No Sarge, I don't. Corporal Harris arrived around eight and left around ten.'

'Corporal Harris ended up suspended from the flag pole all night and was discovered this morning at first light. No doubt you heard the noise?'

No one answered.

'I can't prove you did it, but I will search for evidence and if I find you were involved, you will end up in the glasshouse. That is all.' The Sergeant then turned and stormed out of the hut. There the matter was dropped. The Corporal did not enter the hut again and within days the hut went on to their individual postings.

Harry's eventual postings remained a mystery and over time he told a series of stories, none of which offered any clues to where he went or with what unit. He carefully avoided all conversation regarding his army number, which every squaddie knew by heart. He spoke of being in Aden on a train, stationary at a stop in the desert negotiating with natives swopping a blanket for cigarettes with the blanket tied firmly to a fixture on the carriage. He often related another tale of being in port, thought to be either Hong Kong or Singapore. He and six randy and alcohol starved oppos arrived in port after their long sea voyage and headed straight towards the nearest bar. The six men sat at a table and called for prostitutes and beer. Both arrived quickly, the beer was placed on the table, the female arrivals went under the table, became fully preoccupied with an individual serviceman and within minutes were fully paid up by satisfied customers and on their way to other clients.

*

One story Harry related accompanied by full animation, concerned a trip to an Army Live Firing Range on the Isle of Purbeck for a days shooting. They all thought it was going to be a relaxed day out by the coast. As soon as they alighted from the coach, it became apparent that they were in for a hard time. The sergeant instructor raved and ranted the whole day while they learned about weapon training, rifle care and cleaning, ending with range safety. It went on hour after hour in brilliant warm sunshine and they did not manage to get onto the range until after a short break for lunch.

On the range each man was given ten rounds and under the watchful eyes of an instructor, they fired their rounds. Afterwards they went through checking the targets with better than expected results.

The peace was disturbed by the arrival of two American style coaches. A great deal of shouted ensued when the coaches stopped and to amazement of them all, the windows were lowered on the side facing the targets, and in the space of a few seconds, the equivalent of ten rounds were fired by men on board. The silence when the firing ceased was almost deafening. The windows were closed and the lorries sped off. The American contingent spent about a minute on the range instead of the British Army time of all day!

To all those who heard this tale were under no illusion that Harry did not hold Americans in high esteem!

*

Along the way he became a skilled watch and clock repairer, a skill he continued in civvy street and within ESR ran a quiet personal business, which he called Harry's Horology. Harry was always the romantic. He also knew about locks and up the time of the thefts in the drawing office, boasted he could pick any lock and occasionally in a relaxed atmosphere like during a Christmas party would picks locks for bets. He usually won.

He had a marked fondness for women of ample proportions, chocolate and television – in that order! Every woman who came in contact with Harry was scrutinised closely and delicately interrogated with carefully constructed sentences and deliberately aimed comments to check for their sexual experience and to establish whether they were sexually active. If Harry established that they were experienced *AND* sexually active, this sent him into a controlled frenzy, a contradiction of terminology, but with great glee he would dissect every clue in great detail.

George recalled when Harry had occasion to speak to June, a technical writer, well endowed and recently married, when she delivered a spares schedule, which needed explanation. She borrowed a chair and sat down beside Harry, whom George could see became quite excited. Her demeanour telegraphed innocence to Harry, so he mentioned a male body part, which sported a blue vein, describing the dorsal veins of an erect male copulatory organ. George, listening intently, without appearing to, at least that is what he hoped, detected that June knew exactly what Harry referred to, outwardly participated in the sexual badinage, but skilfully sidestepped giving the answer Harry sought.

Logic suggested that Harry would be frustrated by lack of progress. Instead, the opposite was achieved.

Harry became animated, almost frantic with his mistakenly presumed objective.

At lunchtime, Harry resumed his excitement trying to imagine being with the young lady, undressed and in a double bed. 'They all like a good fugging!' He claimed, adopting a claimed American slang expression instead of the usual Anglo–Saxon equivalent. If he had problem with an engineer on a technical matter, which he did regularly, Harry would terminate the conversation with the expression, 'Go fug yourself!'

'All you have to do is find the key to get inside their knickers or get them to take them off! But, they all enjoy a good fugging session, George, believe me.' In his excitement Harry grabbed hold of Georges arm. 'June can be persuaded to drop 'em, so I will have to go to work on her.'

George attempted to point out that being newly married and already participating in passionate sexual activity with her husband, she was most unlikely to do anything sexual with Harry, mainly because she was fully satisfied.

Harry remained unimpressed. 'They can never get enough cock, George.' He insisted. 'I shall have to keep on trying.'

Harry, despite trying very hard, did not succeed with June.

He did succeed elsewhere though.

What puzzled George was why Harry continually sought sexual satisfaction outside of his marriage to Sylvia, who he claimed was very enthusiastic for close bodily and sexual contact.

One Thursday afternoon, Harry suddenly exclaimed. 'Great night tonight George!' He boasted. 'Its Question of Sport first, then Softly Softly, followed by Sex with Sylvia!'

The first time he heard this George was puzzled. Question of sport was a popular quiz programme hosted by David Coleman, with captains, former Liverpool footballer, Emlyn Hughes and Welsh rugby hero, Gareth Edwards.

Softly Softly equally popular, was a police drama series, which centred around the work of regional crime squads in the fictional region of Wyvern, supposedly in the Bristol and Chepstow areas of England. The main characters were Stratford Johns who played Detective Chief Inspector Charles Barlow and Frank Windsor who played Detective Inspector John Watt. George thought it odd that both men used towns as part of their stage names as if it gave them credence. Harry's favourite character, played by Terence Rigby, was dog handler P.C. Snow, always accompanied by his dog Inky.

George had not heard of a television or radio programme called Sex with Sylvia, so he asked. 'Never heard of that one Harry. What channel is Sex with Sylvia on?'

'What television programme? Channel? What are you going on about?'

'You mentioned Question of sport, which I have heard of, as I have Softly Softly. I watch both. But not Sex with Sylvia. I've never heard of it. '

Harry drew his head down and peered at George as if he were mad. 'Sex with Sylvia is not a programme you silly sod. It's sex with Sylvia, my wife. You know. She usually feels randy on Thursday. I don't know why, but she does. Must be my manly body and charm.' Here Harry gave a big grin. 'But that does not happen with you, does it?'

Georges wife, was equally enthusiastic in matters sexual, but thought it wise not to contradict Harry, so he said. 'You're right Harry, as usual. It does not happen to me.'

Status quo maintained, Harry worked away with an air of satisfaction. If Thursdays were significant, this applied to other days and evenings also.

Harry was a great creature of habit.

Monday evenings were normally free because Sylvia went to Hornchurch Conservation Group meetings. Tuesday lunchtime was always the day for *Fish and Tators* in the fish restaurant on the other side of the main road.

*

A small, lively and jovial Scot, by the name of Archie and his German wife ran the aptly named Archie's Fish Bar. Archie served in the Tank Regiment during World War two as a driver and had escaped serious injury at El Alemain when his tank received a direct hit and exploded. Somehow Archie had scrambled from the burning tank and although the incident was mentioned occasionally, he refused pointblank to elaborate on his escape. Understandably Archie was not particularly fond of Germans, so it was a mystery how he first met his wife, fell in love and remained happily married. Part of her charm was she was a stunner and with an ample bosom which must have contributed to the attraction.

Rebekka, whose name was shortened to Bekka by Archie, was a lively character, with a wicked sense of humour and the merest trace of an accent. Bekka took charge of all matters financial in the business, if claims made by Archie were true. In the fish bar she took charge of the till. If it were quiet and just Harry and George in the fish bar, Archie would joke with his wife. He once called her. 'The Hun at the till!

Bekka found this most amusing, then spoke in an exaggerated German accent. 'If I amza Hun, you are

127

Jock zaScot za lousy tank driver! Vouldn't put you in charge of a pram!'

Both remarks, the cause of great merriment between them.

On one occasion Harry and George arrived when things were busy with some lively children from the school nearby.

'I'll have plaice and chips please Bekka.' Harry said in a raised voice above the din.

'Did you enjoy your holiday, Harry?' Bekka asked.

'Don't go away for another two weeks yet.'

'You went to Cornwall.' Bekka insisted.

'No, I'm off to the broads again in two weeks.'

'How was Cornwall?'

Harry said to Bekka, still looking at him, with a vague expression on her face. 'Do you not have Plaice?'

'Could you say that again?'

'Do you not have Plaice?'

'Do I not have plaice?' Bekka repeated, then appeared to be puzzled. 'No, I do not have plaice, but I'll check with Archie.'

'Have you got time delay hearing today, Bekka? '

'I could have sworn you went to Cornwall.'

At this point Harry gave up and went down to Archie. 'Do you have any Plaice?'

'No, but I'll cook you some skate instead.'

'Thanks.' He then went back to the Hun at the till.

'We don't have Plaice today. I'll get Archie to cook some Skate. You'll like that.'

Harry had had enough. He handed over some money, took the change and sat down. The meal was eaten in silence.

*

Wednesday lunchtime was the day for a meal in the staff canteen, Wednesday evening was set aside by Harry for Hornchurch stamp club. Thursday lunchtime a trip to Nans Pantry for a traditional meal of beef or lamb, accompanied by close inspection of the mature waitresses who were always smartly dressed in black skirts and blouses with white collars and cuffs. Here Harry excelled himself by chatting up every waitress, causing embarrassment to George, being just that bit younger. The restaurant was luxurious, but jaded, a reminder of past times. Small round tables with weighted table cloths each with silver topped cruets. It was claimed that the founder of Nans Pantry had travelled on the Queen Mary. He was so enthralled by the splendour of the ship that he commissioned top designers and craftsmen to turn a dilapidated furniture store into an elegant pantry in a land-locked location of Manor Park. Harry and George sat surrounded by huge curved windows, elegant wood panelling and ornate mirrors, so they could almost imagine they were aboard a luxury liner. Nans Pantry would today be considered to be old fashioned, but to George and Harry was ideal and meals not expensive.

The menus were typed and on one visit there appeared an item typed as *BA Kewell teat!* George quickly identified the pudding as Bakewell tart, despite the typing errors, but to Harry the mention of a female body part too good to ignore.

Nans Pantry was always followed by a visit to Chapman's Radio Shop by the traffic lights to check on the availability of Rita, the well built owner for a sexual liaison after work on Friday. The radio shop was privately owned and run by Rita and her husband, but anyone could be excused for finding this puzzling, for the husband was seldom there. In modern day parlance she was a golf widow. Harry had taken advantage of this situation and quickly seduced the attractive, and has to be said vulnerable woman, who immediately succumbed to Harry's advances. Over the months Rita confided that she suspected her husband had a mistress but could not leave her because she was the actual owner of the shop. On her part the Rita felt insecure and lacked confidence and combined with her religious beliefs would not consider divorce. She claimed to be a strict catholic, but if only half the claims made by Harry during their Friday evening frolics were true, to be a fly on the wall during confession would be most revealing and some would say exciting.

Rita, or Reet, as Harry called her, became devious to ensure she and her Friday evening lovemaking session were safe from spousal interruption, and she would telephone a friend who lived nearby to the home of the mistress on the outskirts of Colchester and the friend promised she would also advise if hubby left early. This early warning system ensured at least an hours notice.

George could detect the attraction of Rita. With auburn hair and sexy eyes tending to be bulbous. She wore purple or blue tightfitting silk tops and a thin bra, which left little to the imagination. Her nipple shapes were in full view and Harry boasted that he could get her aroused simply by licking or sucking them. Their favourite sexual position was mutual oral sex, or soixante-neuf, sixty nine in English, but which Harry, always frustratingly different, chose to call it thirty four and a half multiplied by two!

Harry also had a long standing affair with an allegedly attractive next door neighbour. A single mum aged twenty five, who initially Harry suspected her other half was in prison. The affair continued for months whilst Sylvia was at her Conservation meetings. Harry's suspicions proved to be correct for around two years later the husband, without warning, suddenly appeared back on the scene, which compelled Harry to keep well away from the house next door. Harry appeared to be more relieved than annoyed.

'Young Deeming, you don't appreciate just how lucky I was.' He revealed. 'Christ! I don't appreciate it myself! The bastard came back on a Sunday. If he had come back the next day he would have caught me at with his missus. He's a big bastard and nasty with it!'

The regular subject of sex next door was not mentioned for months.

One Tuesday morning Harry seemed much more cheerful than was usual. When George commented, Harry spoke in a whisper. 'Had bit of luck young Deeming.' He confided, rubbing his hands with glee. 'Matey next door has managed to get himself killed.'

That's not very nice.'

'Perhaps not, but Reet is not bothered, for he was a pain in the arse.' Harry continued. 'He went on another bank raid, which went wrong and during a police chase the car overturned and caught fire. Reet has this smart arsed solicitor and she is suing police due to the death of her husband. Crazy world init. Best thing, I'm back on the job!'

He laughed at his own joke.

In between *Fish and tators*, Nans pantry, the staff canteen and Chapman's Radio shop, weather permitting, they used to go for a walk. Harry, ever the romantic gave each walk a name. The long country walk, as the name suggests consisted of a longish walk along a street of terraced houses then across a railway via a footbridge then into fields where the highlight was a walk along the top of around forty tanks traps, a legacy from world war two. It was childish perhaps, but satisfying, enhanced by the risk of injury, especially if you slipped after the two foot jump in between each one. Harry managed to slip once, when he put a nasty scrape down the entire length of his right shin. This wound turned septic and necessitated several visits to outpatients at the local hospital. The other walk was named short country, and was undertaken if time was short or the likelihood of rain. Whenever or wherever they walked for around twenty minutes, Harry held a one sided farting competition. George was invited to take part or at least offer a challenge, but he was not in the same league. George concluded Harry must suffer from a stomach complaint. On the long country walk, once out of earshot of people, Harry would chant. 'One! Two! Three! Four! Unroll slowly, head up last.' A remnant from his national service training days. Every precise syllable pronounced staccato fashion in time with an exaggerated marching style.

Another aspect of Harry's personality was revealed when he admitted he has worked on Concorde prior to moving to ESR. No amount of cajoling persuaded Harry to reveal what aspect of Concorde he worked on and he remained tight lipped. He admitted he had a valuable scale model of Concorde, but because his insistent of being deliberately unconventional, he had thrown away the box, and by doing so reduced its value considerable. He also let slip that he collected model cars and other vehicles and in order to remain consistent, threw away all boxes and in some cases had repainted some of the models so his collection was unique.

Because of the need to know process common within ESR, most of the time George had no idea what projects Harry worked on, despite the fact they were good friends, worked within six feet or so across the aisle and often, weather permitting, went for long walks at lunchtime.

During a quiet period of the Sentinel project contract, George worked on a triple torpedo launcher to be fitted on type 42 frigates. It was based upon an American design, modified, improved and updated to fire a variety of British designed torpedos. To complicate matters the Mod specified it to be designed using metric units. Over a six month period, George worked on the older Sentinel Project in imperial units in the morning and after lunchtime the new torpedo launcher project using metric system. This took some getting used to but George took only a short period to adapt from one system to another.

One afternoon Harry appeared by George's desk, and during the process of offering a piece of chocolate, noticed the drawing on the reference table. Unusual for him, Harry frowned. 'Is that a triple torpedo launcher George?' He asked.

George nodded.

'A new project?'

'It was, yes.'

'Fug it! In Metric?'

'Yes. What is this, twenty questions?'

'Oh fugging hell!'

'What are you going on about now?'

'How long have you been working on this?'

'About six months or so.'

'Fuck it, George! We have a problem.'

Harry swore so there must be a genuine problem. By now George was totally confused, and getting worried by the minute, not understanding where this conversation would lead. He looked up from the drawing. 'Harry I don't really understand.'

Harry turned and retrieved a drawing from his desk. With it in front of him George could see Harry's distinct precise writing style. He glanced down at a drawing showing a casting more or less Y shaped with equal curved surfaces, the ideal shape to hold together three torpedo launchers one above two others.

'Bastards!' George exclaimed.

'You know what this means?'

'We're in the shit!'

Harry grimaced, then nodded. 'We will have to come clean with *Child by name.*'

'Will cause some trouble.'

'There be even more trouble if my castings don't fit your tubes, George.' Harry peered at Georges drawing. 'They don't fit even now.'

'Are they trying to keep things hushed up?'

'No idea, but we must tell them.'

'Will have to be careful.'

'Of course.'

'Let me think about it for a while.'

They did not have a chance for *Child by name* chose this moment to wander by and glanced at the drawings on the desk. He understood at once and frowned. 'You'd better come with me, and bring those with you.'

In the office he sat down. 'Close the door and sit down. When they did, he asked. 'What are you two up to?

'Nothing. We acci...' Harry replied.

Child by name interrupted. 'Have you been comparing notes? You are not supposed to you know.'

'Certainly not!' Harry replied in a raised voice. 'Just happen to notice that we are working on two components that fit together, only they won't for they are different sizes.'

'Show me.' *Child by name* insisted. The two drawings were placed on the desk and studied closely. He looked up appearing very serious, then asked. 'Who put you on the project George?'

'Ed Littleboy.' George replied with reservations.

'How long ago?'

'Six months or so.'

'You Harry?'

'Ken.'

'Six months?'

'No, much less. About three weeks'

'You are not supposed to talk about your projects. Security is paramount. You sho...'

It was Harry's turn to interrupt. 'We didn't. We had discovered that we were working on parts, which fitted one to another, about a minute before you came along.'

'Pull the other one. You two walk at lunchtimes, you must talk about it.'

'No, why should we? You group leaders must talk about projects when Eddie Smythe has his soirees.'

'We do not talk about work..'

'Neither do we!'

Child by name realised he had just lost the argument, but remained defiant. 'You will have to carry on. I can't interfere wi......'

George now decided to make a point, if nothing else to back up Harry's case. 'You have to do something. These parts do not fit and we have already wasted a few weeks, and likely to waste considerably more. The MoD will definitely not approve, so make it official.'

Child by name frowned and cradled his head in his hands. 'This is going to be tricky. Keep it under wraps for now and I will go and see Mister Barrett.'

They returned to their desks and two hours later were summoned to meet in *Lumpy Bumps* office. Ken, Ed and *Child by name* were already there.

Lumpy Bumps spoke first. 'Harry please explain how you and George discovered the tube and separator casting were the same project.'

'Quite by chance. I happened to be at George's desk when he was working on his torpedo tube drawing. Ken had told me that my casting was the separator on a

triple torpedo launcher required for a modification.'
Ken appeared to be decidedly uncomfortable. "I did ask
for information of the tubes and he told me they had not
been created yet. Different contract apparently.'

"Technically it is.' *Lumpy Bumps* agreed. ' But, due
to your discovery, accidentally or no, we......'

'How dare you doubt our story!' George felt so
incensed, he interrupted. 'Harry and I can be accused of
many things, but being liars is not one of them.'

' Calm down George.' *Lumpy Bumps* replied with a
smile. 'It was just an unfortunate choice of words on
my part. You have my full apology. I would not accuse
you and Harry of lying under any circumstances. We
all know from past events that you are both
trustworthy. But now we know that different aspects
are being worked on, we will have to create a new
section so you can coordinate the design.'

This caused a reaction from both Ed and Ken, who
became animated and agitated in equal proportions
until *Lumpy bumps* made them stop. George and Harry
were asked to leave at this point, so they did, glad to be
free of internal politics.

Within a week they were working in the new section
under Ken. This did not stop George from working on
other Sentinel project obligations and Harry from
working his other, previously worked on projects.

As George predicted, the consequences of not
drawing the attention of their seniors of working
independently would have been disastrous had the
MoD learned of the unfortunate situation. Within
weeks two others joined the section and the new
draughtsmen, Rex Willcox and Bert Frost, initially
aided progress. George had heard of Berts alleged
inclination to being lazy and uncooperative. Rex
proved to be a worthy member of the section but Bert

quickly reverted to his usual self and within a few weeks went back to his previous occupation.

The American design was crude when compared to the new specification insisted by the MoD. A variety of torpedoes were to be fired from the triple launcher from the old Mk44 to the latest Mk23 and included a requirement for the Mk24, as yet completely unknown animal and this placed strain on how the tube design was formed. Also one addition was the need for the operator to know when a tube was loaded and its temperature. George was given this task and came up with a slow moving damped spring loaded lever incorporating a heat sensor, which did not extend fully until the propeller housing had passed by.

When George revealed his design to the section leader it was greeted by ridicule. When Harry saw the design he laughed until he cried. George was heartbroken, but did not overreact as he had complete faith with his idea. The others disagreed as they were convinced the propeller housing would destroy the lever at it passed by at speed. There was some relevance as the torpedo sent on its way by compressed air would be travelling quite fast when it left the launcher. There was an uneasy standoff. Towards the end of the month the section received the first of several visits from Pat Byrne, a Senior Design Engineer attached to MoD. There were many technical problems associated with the torpedo tube manufacture, which eventually necessitated the contractor coming down from Newcastle.

After a lengthy early morning meeting during which George nearly dozed off, Ken eventually raised the subject of Georges design. He made it obvious he did not approve.

Pat, however was not impressed by Kens comments. 'I will be the judge of the design.' He insisted. 'It is not your place to predict my approval or no.'

He studied the drawings as Ken glared at the back of his head. Eventually he looked up at George smiling. 'Quite an interesting design, George.' He said. 'What prevents the propeller housing giving it a hefty clout as it goes by?'

'The lever is damped by a vacuum so it should it not be a problem.' George responded.

'Huh!' Ken said under his breath

'I am inclined to agree that it may not work, but get one made and we will see, but otherwise I am most impressed by the original, and has to be said unusual design. Very clever incorporating the heat sensor as well'

George was ecstatic and set to work finding someone to make his sensor. He had dealt with a one man engineering firm in Chadwell Heath who specialised in small engineering runs. Within a couple, of weeks they came up with a prototype, which was quickly put under test in the workshop. After a slight modification, which involved some minor machining, it worked as George anticipated. Pat Byrne was summoned up from Bath and saw the sensor put through its paces and seemed impressed. The trial was ridiculously simple. The sensor was held in place on a bench and a six feet piece of timber with an extended slot cut to replicate the torpedo propeller casing, pulled along. When the simulated housing passed above the sensor it moved a fraction as the slot passed by and was gently pushed down by the wood representing the propeller housing. The process was speeded up with a satisfactory result. The prototype was taken back to Bath for evaluation and weeks later received approval from the MoD boffins. George felt his esteem had moved up a notch within the section and had definitely scored points over Ken, the hostile Section leader.

Ultimately the sensor design functioned normally and turned out to be the least controversial aspect of the project. The manufacturer in Newcastle had difficulty with the ram, which acted both as mandrel and mould for the barrels, which were made of a special resin.

*

After the Falkland War, when Prince Andrew came home, one of the frigates, which had a triple torpedo launcher as part of its armourment, visited the Pool of London. The Prince escorted his mother, Her Majesty Queen Elizabeth II on a guided tour. Being a mischievous individual, the tour went past a primed triple torpedo tube, which was activated by the Prince as the royal party went by. Everyone reacted to the escape of the compressed air, much to the delight of Prince Andrew and the crew, who were in on the joke.

*

With the closure of ESR, Harry was not one of those who chose to move to Wincanton. Probably a bad move on his part as he went through a lengthy almost semi-permanent period of severe depression. George by this time had moved to the studio at Bow and made an effort to maintain contact with Harry. Each occasion he telephoned Harry at home, although friendly, there was no inclination on Harry's part to agree a meet. It left George with the impression that Harry withdrew in himself. The former friends did meet occasionally and Harry seemed to be his usual self, but kept George at arms length. George attempted to meet Harry in Hornchurch at the weekend but he failed each time.

Harry withdrew into his self induced shell, probably due to a feeling of rejection by ESR that why should he, someone with so much talent and has to be said, comprehensive engineering skill and experience, be passed over or ignored, when lesser mortals almost fell into jobs they did not deserve.

A classic case is that of George Spicer, one of the senior section leaders, known as *Nutmeg,* who considered himself to be a cut above everyone. He strutted around in a fashion resembling someone who deservedly enjoyed a reputation of superiority. He had a level of incompetence, easily disguised by his public school accent and by the fact he could think quickly when in front of those with influence, managers and directors and the like. When dealing with men like Harry, who could easily detect his lack of knowledge, no concept of design procedures, or of more importance, the amount of time certain tasks took to complete, the deception was quickly detected. Harry walked rings around *Nutmeg,* who must have felt a distinct level of inferiority, plus an uneasy feeling with the reality of disadvantage.

Nutmeg applied for a senior post of departmental head in a major ESR establishment in the west country on the outskirts of Bristol. To the surprise of everyone, including perhaps, *Nutmeg* himself, he was appointed. Harry was openly furious. 'How can a useless pile of shite get a job like that? He can barely tie his boot laces, let alone manage a department.'

Nutmeg handed in his notice, then a general drawing office snub commenced. The traditional farewell collection and card signing was not supported, and it became common knowledge that *Lumpy Bumps* and *Child by name* were obliged to give an over generous donation in order to hide the blatant rejection statement made by *Nutmegs* colleagues. For those who attended the drink up at the Greengage Public House, it was an embarrassment.

Nutmeg headed west and he was quickly forgotten. Months past and rumours began to circulate via the ESR bush telegraph. The first rumour down the wire said that Nutmeg had been injured in a serious car crash. There were some predictable 'couldn't care less' comments from Harry. They sounded comical but were anything but. Then, an engineer came up to London on a course and revealed the true story. Nutmeg had been involved in a serious car crash but the injured party was a young girl hit by his car. Accidents do happen, but Nutmegs problems were just unfolding. First he had been drinking then it was revealed he was not insured, due the fact his wife forgot to post the insurance renewal. The girl died of her injuries, and *Nutmeg* was sent to prison. ESR quickly gave him the sack and it was alleged that before he came out of prison his wife left him and last they heard *Nutmeg* lived in a hostel for the homeless in Bristol.

As the years passed, Harry and George drifted apart, contact made only by holiday postcards during the summer and notes sent with Christmas cards. George regretted this as he and Harry enjoyed a typical male friendship during the time at ESR.

He arrived home one weekday and opened the usual assorted mail, bills, junk mail and a handwritten envelope. One such letter knocked him sideways. It was a handwritten letter from Sylvia passing on the dreadful news that Harry had passed away.

George's overriding remembrance of Harry was his manic sense of humour. In *Only fools and horses* series, Boycey the dodgey car dealer relates a tale of and investigation into the elders of Peckham. He refers to golden haired maidens dancing around a maypole and the affect when the Trotter family arrived in a stolen

Zephyr. The maidens were all up the duff and the Earl of Peckham sold some hooky armour.

Harry had his personal version of an anecdote told with great animation and exaggerated movement. The way the tale was told never varied.

Imagine an alehouse or perhaps a religious building on the Yukon or Alaskan goldfields as seen in a black and white film. Men are seated at tables singing with great enthusiasm: 'Cigarettes whusky and wild wild women, they'll drive you crazy, they'll drive you insane!' time after time. Gabby Hayes then interrupted the proceeding by shouting in a husky gravelly voice in an American accent. 'Play temptation will ya!'

In response the master of ceremonies stood up and said. 'My friend we don't play that sort of music here............'

'Play temptation will ya!'

My friend, I am afraid we don't play that sort of music here............'

'Okay then, show us your muscles!'

Unfortunately due to the passing of time, I am unable recall the whole tale.

5

Missile head and Dunking Sonar

This chapter could be named the unknown and the known. The most frustrating aspect of the need to know basis, meant that occasionally projects worked on remain a permanent mystery. The project known to me as SP2 is one such instance. Try as I did, I have not been able to establish what weapon this project was used on. It was in my care for a period when the Sentinel project was quiet and I had to visit a small insignificant lab on the top floor, beyond the progress chasers.

A single engineer worked on the project and he resembled Harry Worth the bumbling comedian of the 1960's and 70's. This engineer whose name, I regret I cannot recall, looked like Harry Worth, the suggestion came most probably from Harry Fether, who used to lean up against a partition and lift one leg and an arm. Harry Worth did this at the beginning of each television episode, to the extent it became his signature. If this were a shop window it would seem that both legs were off the ground.

SP2 was small enough to fit in the palm of a hand and appeared to be made of clear plastic type material. I say appeared deliberately, because I was never allowed to handle the warhead without wearing protective gloves. Even this description of apparent material is debatable, as the SP2 was theheat seeker of a short-range, air-to-air missile carried allegedly by unknown aircraft, thought to be a Harrier, and by its size must be similar to a sidewinder missile. Because of the need for complete security, the material schedule was kept separate and George never had a sighting of it.

Dunking Sonar (the author)

A Sea King (HAS Mk5 ASW version built by Westland), at Farnborough Air Show c1988, flying with a dunking sonar.

The dunking sonar was used publicly before the Falklands conflict during 1969 in an attempt to establish the existence of the Loch Ness monster. The results were inconclusive.

Its use during the Falklands War are not so well known.

The modifications arrived in the form of a MoD drawing, which had to be redrawn to the ESR standard format, and consisted of minor changes to dimensions. Why these modifications were needed is anyone's guess. We were never informed. As I have stated I have been unable to identify the missile, to which SP2 was attached. If you know of it, I would be glad to hear of it.

In contrast the ESR type dunking sonar is well known to me.

The bathythermograph unit was amazing, as it was lowered from a Sea King helicopter. The main internal body frame consisted of a single intricate casting, designed to ensure strength using a minimum of material. During manufacture it was quite normal for a frustrated machinist, probably the senior jig borer to wander off the shop floor with a request to find the dimension from one aspect to another. The five sheet drawings were of a tablecloth proportion so to investigate meant taking over a large section of drawing office space.

The frame was protected from the elements by an equally intricate case, which used specialised seals to keep seawater out. In the early stage of the project these seals were a problem were inclined to leak, and the project engineer Bob Virgo nearly had a nervous breakdown. His mental condition became apparent when the seal manufacturer paid a visit and Bob took them out to lunch at Nans Pantry. George had been with them all morning but because of niggling ESR petty cash restrictions, he was unable to lunch with them. Instead he and Harry went on their own and sat at an adjacent table. Throughout the whole time at lunch Bobs left leg bounced up and down, almost a tremble, as if playing an unheard rhythm on an invisible drum kit. The meeting was friendly than expected because much progress had been made and George anticipated that the leak problem was resolved. Up to this point, when assembling the case to the bathythermograph, the fitter placed a dry seal in the precisely machined groove and using a spanner severely tightened the nuts. After the meeting the fitter placed a seal lightly coated with a special lubricant in the form of apaste and did the nuts up as much as possible by hand, then finally tighten the nuts with a spanner to around a half turn to a specified torque. The leaks stopped.

Modifying the units mounted on board the Sea King were a nightmare because each case was so tightly packed with components. George once had to fit a single capacitor to the display unit, which when in use was mounted aboard the helicopter and spent a few uncomfortable days with the unit on the floor trying to locate sufficient space. In the end he designed a mounting post so the component was raised clear of wiring and other components, but was forced to fit a shroud to avoid a short circuit with the outer casing. At first Bob Virgo did not approve, but was eventually forced to concede it was the only solution, short of a major redesign.

The dunking sonar was used publicly before the Falklands conflict during the spring and summer of 1969 when a television company and a national newspaper decided to investigate whether the Loch Ness monster existed. A number of interested parties took part using various types of sonar from shore based equipment to one aboard a submarine and the ESR dunking sonar suspended from a stationery vessel in the middle of the Loch. Birmingham University used digital sonar developed by them. Their fixed beam sonar depended for results on targets moving through it. It is likely that the noise of boats and propellers as well as disturbance underwater may have served to frighten the *targets* off instead of upwards as had been hoped. Vickers Ltd and RW Eastlaugh and teams participated with varying types of equipment used, from a Marconi Depth sounder and Seascribe depth finder.

The results were surprising and in Georges view did not prove the existence of a monster or otherwise. Two major manufactures experimented with their sonar aboard a submarine which produced positive results, as were the experiment carried out by Birmingham University with their sonar.

However in September when the ESR Dunking sonar was used, there were no significant results. The sonars were operated from Temple Pier in Urquhart Bay and due to nightly coverage with no unexplained targets observed, it had a depressing effect on the attitude of the general public. ESR sonar used such a powerful audible sonar frequency, the loud *pinging* echoed up and down the loch.

A probable hoax occurred at this time when a large bone was found in Loch Ness, and only added to the confusion. Then there were some short but fascinating sequences on 33mm film of wakes shot at considerable range, which happened on five separate occasions. The scale and pattern ruled out fish and boats. It was suggested that subterranean tremors caused them, but it is difficult to imagine one at 600 feet below the surface, which causes such a phenomenon of a circular pattern of ripples 6 inches high and calm water stretching for half a mile, as if coming from a point in the centre, close to the surface. But with no solid object detected to explain, it was not conclusive. Unfortunately given such contrasting and contradicting results, the probability whether a monster existed is not recorded.

After 1982 the days of the ESR dunking sonar were numbered and came about because of political wrangling between the Indians, the French and the Royal Navy. The Indians favoured a French system, but the British were not agreeable to put the French radar on the Seaking nor were the French agreeable to fit the British radar in the Super Puma.

6

Lead up to the Falklands

George reasoned that The Falklands War was the direct result of political incompetence and a series of miscalculations. At least that is how he viewed it. Many pundits blamed a succession of British Governments for their failure to resolve the status of sovereignty of the Falklands, then justified their arguments around the presumption that war was inevitable.

But history is rarely that simple.

The key to the conflict was the remote island of South Georgia, lying in the South Atlantic around 800 miles south east of the Falkland Islands. The first person to sight South Georgia may have been Antoine De La Roche sailing from Peru to London in 1675. Blown off course in bad weather whilst rounding Cape Horn, he spotted a mountainous island with deeply indented bays and spent two weeks sheltering in a bay at the south eastern end. The weather was awful and he could not land. Supporters of the Argentine claim to the Falklands and South Georgia, believe that he had sighted Beauchene Islands 800 miles further west. However this island is relatively flat with a smooth coastline giving little credence to this theory.

The first known person to land was Captain James Cook RN, aboard *HMS Resolution* who landed at Possession Bay in January 1775, to map part of the coastline. Cooks party discovered Tussock Grass, Wild Burnet, a teeming bird and seal population, but no trees.

The ships logs states: *'....I landed in three different places, displayed our colours and took possession of the Country in His Majesty's name under a discharge of small arms.'*

This was the first claim to any islands in the Antarctic, even though Captain Cook did not appear to be very taken with South Georgia, describing the inner parts of the islands as: *' savage and horrible.'*

Ever patriotic he named the islands *'The Isle of Georgia'*, after King George.

The mention that the island teemed with seals soon attracted seal expeditions, which saw the rapid exploitation of Fur Seals. The Seal population soon declined and attention was drawn to elephant seals and the trade collapsed around 1830. The British occupied the islands and administered it from 1833 and had consistently rejected Argentina's claims.

The sovereignty issue had therefore been an on going dispute for over 150 years and had not resulted in war until 1982.

Why 1982?

Why after 150 years of non-violence did Argentina decide that force was the answer? Why did the military Junta believe they could accomplish what previous politicians had failed to achieve?

George conceded that peaceful negotiations had achieved little, as Britain dragged her feet and prevented any acceptable solution, or one that determined whether the Islands would ever be returned to Argentina. The Junta made plans to invade the Falklands between April and October 1982 for sound tactical and strategic reasons.

It was essential for an invasion to take place before March 1983, the 150th anniversary of the seizure, should the British or the Falkland Islanders choose to celebrate the event. In the Southern Hemisphere, the period from July to October are winter months, which the Junta hoped would forestall Britain's ability to

149

respond quickly. With rough winter weather to deal with, British aircraft would experience difficulty in supporting the disembarkation of troops on the islands. The Junta also made an enlightened presumption that by July 1982, *HMS Endurance*, a Royal Navy patrol and research ship, the only military vessel protecting the Islands, would have been retired. They declared that: '*Argentina will resolve what to them is a most and long standing territorial dispute, but to Great Brian is a distant and almost forgotten remnant of empire.*'

Finally, of more significance, by that time the Argentines should have taken delivery of large quantities of weapons previously purchased from France, in particular five Exocet missiles.

Unfortunately for them the chaos of its internal political situation forced the Junta to move its invasion plans forward to April 1982. Within a year of seizing power with a military coup, they were faced with rocketing inflation, and there had been violent demonstrations in Buenos Aires. They sought a diversion from their troubles. Then the Junta were presented with the impetuous to bring the Malvinas issue to the fore, in the form of an enterprising Argentinean businessman named Constantino Davidsoff.

In 1979, Davidsoff, with a businessman's eye for a money making opportunity, purchased a derelict whaling slaughterhouse, and made a contract with a Scottish company to salvage decaying whaling equipment and valuable scrap metal, at several locations around the island of South Georgia. He sought permission from the British Authorities to use *HMS Endurance*, to the haul the metal away. Not without surprise his request was immediately denied.

On the face of it, a sound business proposition.

In a hospitable part of the globe, yes, but South Georgia, 800 miles from the Falklands, was accessible only by using Antarctic going ships.

Two years passed.

He then hired a number of scrap metal workers and set sail for South Georgia, arriving at Leith on 19th March, and commenced operations, without first observing the usual formalities of reporting to the islands Magistrate, the base commander of the British Arctic Survey, located down the coast at King Edwards Point, near Grytviken. When the British Antarctic Survey team reached Leith they found workmen ashore flying an Argentinian flag, and reported the incident to Sir Rex Hunt the Governor 800 miles away in Stanley. He gave orders that the Argentineans must seek proper authorisation from the Magistrate and take down the flag. This they refused to do.

There followed two weeks of frantic diplomatic activity in an effort to resolve the incursion. As negotiations continued, *HMS Endurance*, on orders from Fleet Headquarters at Northwood, on the outskirts of Greater London, had arrived at South Georgia. There was no attempt made to remove the scrap metal workers. The Junta, however had already dispatched an icebreaker enroute to South Georgia, and upon arrival 100 Marines went ashore. From a carefully dug observation post above the landing site, the British Antarctic Survey men kept watch. Two days later an Argentine force landed on the Falklands and Port Stanley was captured. The same morning, the Argentine Marines who had re-embarked onto the icebreaker, arrived off Grytviken and called upon the Magistrate to surrender. He passed control of the islands over to Lieutenant Mills, as the first of the Marines landed near King Edwards Point.

151

A vastly superior Argentine force, including two warships and helicopters attacked his small party of marines. After putting up stiff resistance, shooting down a helicopter and severely damaging a warship using an anti-tank missile, Lieutenant Mills was forced to surrender in order to prevent loss of life.

By coincidence, 200 years earlier a Marine by the name of Corporal Mills, aboard *HMS Resolution*, participated in a display of firepower when the island was claimed for Great Britain.

For the first time in over two hundred years, a Union flag no longer flew over South Georgia. The Marines and British Antarctic Survey staff were captured and repatriated to the UK.

The Argentine occupation of the island was short lived. Four warships, *HMS Endurance, HMS Antrim, HMS Belfast* and *HMS Plymouth* led an attack on the island three weeks later. The SAS came to action for the first time to set up an observation post on the island. The first attempt, on 22 April, finished as a disaster. The party was dropped by helicopter onto the Fortuna Glacier and quickly realised to stay there meant certain death. The weather was so bad that they would have died of exposure within hours and an immediate recall was requested. The extraction cost two Wessex helicopters both of which crashed in appalling weather. A piece of brilliant of flying on the part of a third pilot in a severely overlaid on helicopter, nicknamed *Humphrey*, in blind flying conditions, led to the rescue every single man. In reality this meant 17 people on a helicopter designed to carry only five. Undeterred the SAS eventually landed on the island by boat. They observed the Argentina Argentine garrison at Grytviken comprising of about 100 Marines and the crew of the submarine *Santa Fe* that was in harbour delivering supplies. A British force made up of the SBS, the SAS and the Royal Marines attacked the base after being landed by helicopter with support from the Royal Navy. This led to the destruction of an Argentine submarine, *TheSanta Fe* and surrender of all Argentine Forces on the island.

*

It was late and George having difficulty concentrating decided to pack up for the night. Without paying full attention, he exited the programme without saving and lost two hours work. He resorted to plan B and referred to his notes, but simply could not reassemble the chapter, so he had to restart from scratch. This forced him to exercise care and disciplined himself into saving files regularly to minimise losing work.

*

Driving east past the Golden Lion Public House on Tower Hill in 1982 during the rush hour, the traffic was busy and congested but somehow lacked aggression. The term 'rush hour' was misleading, for in many parts of London even then, the volume of traffic, constant throughout the working day, eased only for a short period of time towards evening, before night revellers descended in droves back into the city.

To travel to the ESR factory ten miles away in Manor Park during the morning rush hour and avoid spending excess time in queues at busy junctions and traffic lights was an acquired art for one particular driver and his important passenger. Consider if you will, Michael Hayne, joint owner of ESR, being chauffeur driven to work in his Rolls Royce from his fine home in an exclusive part of Chelsea. He travelled along Chelsea Embankment and Millbank, passing by the Tate gallery to the Houses of Parliament, along the sweeping tree lined avenue of Victoria Embankment and along Upper Thames Street as far as the Tower of London. At this historic junction, close to the favourite watering hole of the *Fairlop Formation Drinking Team*, the ancient site of execution and the impressive Merchant Navy Memorial, the driver in such a vehicle had little alternative but to take the less adventurous route. To risk taking such a prestigious limousine through the narrow streets of east London as a short cut would be foolhardy. A much safer option to avoid all chances of conflict with other ordinary road users was to take the unsurprising route along Whitechapel Road. The Chauffeur would have been on a defensive driving course so he was easily able to keep his passenger safe from undesirables bent on either attack or kidnap. He had been properly taught, until it became second nature to keep a watchful eye on surrounding vehicles and to vary the route so as to avoid a detectable pattern, but travelling east had a limiting effect of the choice of available routes. He would drive over the flyover at Bow Church and via Stratford and Forest Gate, and once through Manor Park town centre, along wide main roads to the factory in Upper Drive.

Although the pace at that time appeared to be relatively calm, there prevailed enough hold ups and official delays to frustrate the calmest of drivers. How many drivers have waited for no good reason at traffic lights when there is no other traffic in sight? There was a temptation to go through a red light without fear of causing an accident but there was every possibility that one of the alert boys in blue would witness the misdemeanour, and then take great delight in reporting the incident.

For those not in a hurry, or for those with a noticeable gap in their knowledge of short cuts, travelling half a mile north to Whitechapel Road would be less adventurous, but they were less likely to get lost. The area of Whitechapel is steeped in history mainly because of the much publicised murderous deeds of the infamous Jack the Ripper and in more modern times those of the Kray twins. It is ignored that thousands of cheerful law-abiding folk with an individual kind of humour and wit, have worked and resided here for generations. George knew or met many such folk who were born or brought up there before the Second World War, and they all had one thing in common.

I come from Whitechapel! Born and bred in Brady Street! They would boast with genuine pride. George wondered how many folk would consider making that bold statement these days?

He found Whitechapel folk as fascinating as they were cheerful. They lived in what is now considered to be appalling damp and dingy overcrowded housing conditions, poor food, no heating, and few luxuries associated with modern living. They owned little apart from clothes. Front doors were not locked, mainly because most did not possess a lock. Nothing that resembles the self inflicted fortresses that exist these days, some with wrought iron defensive gates protecting front doors. Burglary and crime were comparatively rare simply because there was not much worth stealing. These Whitechapel folk appreciated their change of lifestyle as most, achieved much due to hard work, and progressed to a better standard of living.

Not that those travelling by road would concern themselves with such historic social distractions, being totally preoccupied with getting to their destination in one piece, without conflict and on time.

A typical journey for a driver commuting east would be to travel along the Highway, a long straight road that runs north of the docks more or less half a mile parallel to the River Thames. The first dock, St. Katherines, was virtually adjacent to Tower Bridge. Half a mile further along was Wapping Docks followed shortly by the smallest, Shadwell Dock. This area was typical inasmuch that the Port of London showed signs of diminishing month by month. Clear political symptoms were warning that within a short period of time the Port of London was going to disappear without trace. A former hub of great industrial maritime strivings, full of nautical merchant history, the once busy neighbourhood of Wapping was under threat by a political body bent on major redevelopment of the entire London Docklands. It should come as no great surprise that the local authorities on both sides of the River were in the main run by Labour controlled councils, whilst the government of the day was very extreme Conservative. Local politicians were often at loggerheads with an aggressive Tory Government, especially when it came to investment plans for east London. The Greater London Council regularly fell foul of the two seats of power on the other side of Westminster Bridge, namely Parliament and the Tory controlled Westminster Council. This great conflict and differing of political opinions would eventually see the abolition of local government for London in March 1986, the combined opposing antics of Ken Livingstone, the leader of the Greater London Council and Maggie Thatcher, the Prime Minister, ensured its demise. Plans were underway to create a business centre able to compete with the City and the great financial institutions in Europe, to transform or convert suitable properties into architect designed suites and penthouses for anyone with money. The locally born and bred were in the main ignored, not intended to be part of the redevelopment equation, simply because they were not able to afford luxuries like expensive designer flats or apartments. In fact many could not afford luxuries in any form, especially if cigarettes and alcohol were discounted.

At the major junction where the main thoroughfare offered encouragement to a traveller to venture down to the Rotherhithe Road Tunnel under the River Thames enroute to south London, the short cut went via a minor road to the left. This road ran parallel to a railway line high above on a magnificently arched embankment for over a quarter of a mile, until the two features parted company. A right turn brought you into Bow Road. This wide and tree-lined ancient carriageway built by the Romans travels in a straight line through the postal code of E3 as far as Bow Church.

St Mary's Bow, sometimes called Stratford Church, was erected around the year 1311 on an island site in the midst of the Kings High Way, by licence from Bishop Baldock, who was then the Episcopal Lord of Stepney Manor. Today it still stands with a roadway either side of it and is often confused with the church associated with Bow Bells, not helped by the fact that a pub facing the church on the southern side is named the Bow Bells. It was badly damaged by incessant bombing during the Second World War. The statue of William Gladstone, one of several prime ministers who served during the reign of Queen Victoria was erected in front of the church in 1882. The statue stands facing the east going traffic with an outstretched right hand pointing downwards. A typical Victorian pose perhaps, but any knowledgeable local will take great delight to explain that the statue is pointing to the location of the Gents toilets conveniently placed underground! William Bryant of Bryant and May's match factory nearby paid for the cost of erecting the statue. In keeping with making the east end of London, a playground for anyone with money, the now redundant factory has since been turned into luxury flats complete with

157

uniformed concierge, underground parking and inevitable security cameras.

Bearing left at the roundabout underneath the flyover, the road goes northwards again, this time onto a three-lane dual carriageway, which leads to Hackney Marshes. When the road divides by Victoria Park, bear right and enter a short tunnel, which leads onto the marshes themselves. Each Sunday morning during the season, hundreds of footballers battle it out with other amateur local teams on countless football pitches. Here once existed the rubbish tips of Edwardian London and is why the open space has survived virtually intact. Then you have to negotiate through the narrow but mainly straight roads of Leyton, with the parked cars on both sides of the road, as far as Leytonstone, where the main road out of east London is reached. It was then easy to travel through fast moving traffic on a modern dual carriageway until half a mile beyond Wanstead Flats, you turn right at traffic lights at the Greengage Public House. The large factory and office complex was the grubby and anonymous two storey building on your left hand side. It was deliberately understated, not wishing to publicise the secret activity within. A plain sign had the initials 'ESR' painted in faded light blue plain letters, on a pale yellow background.

On the other side of the road from the main ESR factory, the chauffeur, with practise precision delivered his passenger, Michael Hayne, safely on time to commence work by eight thirty in his the grand oak panelled office.

Work on the Sentinel project continued at ESR. With the prospect of war looming with Argentina, an event considered to be unthinkable, a serious mood existed throughout the factory. At odd moments the latest political developments were discussed openly until one of the section leaders choose to interrupt. A sense of urgency prevailed, which placed everyone on edge especially to those who were working on the projects most likely to be used in earnest for the first time. Exercises to test the equipment *in situ*, held regularly under peacetime conditions were one thing. They knew that the equipment would function correctly, with specialist engineers on hand throughout the time spent at sea, should a fault occur. These exercises had resulted in a series of modifications, but they were tried and tested locally under false conditions. How they would function in the cold and treacherous seas of the South Atlantic without spares or backup, out of touch with engineers with the skill to solve any problems and technical failures, was matter of conjecture. An air of quiet optimism came to the surface occasionally but an undercurrent of anxiousness was obvious even to the most casual of observers. For now it remained a game, the stark reality and horror resulting from political failure, still in the future.

*

Around the same period walking along the main road at Port Stanley, the capital of the Falklands Islands would literally be a hostile place. The islands suddenly appear strange and foreign. The buildings were as British as you could get, all the signs were in English, but some were hidden beneath crude alien replacements written in a foreign tongue. The first noticeable difference was the traffic, all military, driving on the right. The second was that there was not a Union Flag in sight, being replaced by a blue-white–blue banded version. The main street had a long line of armoured vehicles parked there. There was pile upon pile of assorted ammunition littered all over town. The mere presence of military personnel and equipment most inhabitants found intimidating, especially as large bands of aggressive soldiers, armed to the teeth, entered homes at the slightest whim to check on the inhabitants. Less obvious but nonetheless significant was that Port Stanley, the capital of the Falklands Islands, had been renamed as Puerto Argentino capital of the Malvinas. The new masters of the Malvinas took great delight to make a formal announcement over the radio.

For a variety of reasons, a succession of British Governments largely ignored the diplomatic sabre rattling of the Argentineans over a number of years. It was not until a small group of scrap metal workers arrived on South Georgia, ostensibly there to dismantle old whaling stations, but who chose instead to raise an Argentinean flag, that red lights began flashing in the corridors of power in Whitehall and beyond. By now these warning lights were already too late. When a force of Argentinean Marines landed on South Georgia, the local Falkland Island Broadcasting Station, taking advice of the Governor Sir Rex Hunt, made an announcement to expect an invasion, but when it did a couple of days later, it took everyone by surprise. If it were possible to be in the vicinity of Government House on the evening of the landing, it would have possible to listen to the invasion advancing. Certainly the Governor Rex Hunt his staff and an assortment of visitors resident in the building were able to do so, with predictable misgivings.

Naval Party 8901, a small contingent of Royal Marines were sent to deal with incursions of Argentine nationalist individuals, quite suited to the task of dealing with these eccentric folk. Everyone knew that the Marines were only a *trip-wire* in the event of a full scale invasion. Once in Stanley however, the invaders had in fact taken everyone by surprise despite the state of emergency, and during their initial advance were allegedly under strict orders not to harm civilians or if

160

at all possible, British soldiers. When the invasion occurred the Marines prepared to fight to the death.

The invaders had been ordered to use blanks and stun grenades, but this did not adequately explain fully why the buildings in which the soldiers were thought to use as their billet, became subjected to severe machine gun fire. All of the return fire this activity provoked was most certainly live, and several Argentineans soldiers were killed, some within Government House itself. Rex Hunt expressed a determination not to surrender to those who had the audacity to trespass on British territory, but in truth he had little option. Throughout the hours of darkness in the early hours, voices with a noticeable Spanish accent could be heard calling for Rex Hunt to be reasonable, as were some of the not so polite replies from the Marines!

When the surrender came, Rex Hunt suitably defiant, donned his full ceremonial Governors uniform including his sword and plumed hat, then, ignoring diplomatic niceties, refused to shake the hand with the Argentinean Officer. The accepted and desired hierarchies of Governor Rex Hunt together with prominent community figures were instructed to leave after the surrender. They had been forcibly removed to the airport and flown to Uruguay, together with the small Marines force of Naval Party 8901.

Despite the determined fight put up by the Marines, killing some of their number, the invaders tried to be pleasant, at first. The pleasantries were not to last for any length of time. The local radio was used to issue instructions about driving on the right and that all acts of disrespect or interference with official Argentinean signs would result in severe punishment being administered. Most soldiers were polite in the early days after invasion and even paid for any service or food they required but with Argentinean currency. All means of radio transmitters and transceivers, quite commonplace in the Islands, were confiscated, but the ever resourceful population kept in touch and passed on military information via the primitive telephone network, which for some obscure reason, the Argentineans chose to overlook. The Islanders were forced to accept the unwanted visitors, but kept in touch with news of the task force by listening to the BBC World Service. The service, openly with its usual frankness, also informed the Argentineans of the current situation. Indeed the day after *Belgrano* was sunk and an air attack made on one of the pickets protecting the Task Force, The BBC World service, without apparent censorship announced to the pilots who launched the Exocet missiles, the sinking of *HMS Sheffield*. Being a firm believer of *the need to know* basis, George was amazed that the normally reliable BBC World Service acted irresponsibly and handed on a plate such damning information to an enemy on the success of the air strike. Far better to make the Argentineans think *HMS Sheffield* was still afloat. He was also amazed that the government permitted and tolerated such an announcement to be made.

Then early one morning, the airfield near to Puerto Argentino, came under attack from an unseen Vulcan bomber, which managed to cause some damage the runway surface. The accompanying noises of the explosion were a warning of coming events. Shortly afterwards, all the Harriers of the Task Force attacked the airfield killing several airmen and inflicting severe damage to aircraft and assorted buildings. The Harriers were seen to come in low from the sea at incredible speed. The water and earth literally boiled with cannon fire then followed the loud report from their bombs on the airfield. It was over in a little more than ten seconds, one long roar and blast of ear splitting sounds, then absolute silence with a great pall of smoke hanging over the airfield which took hours to disperse. The occupying Garrison woke up to the fact that war is not a game and their previous generous mood soured and the conscripts took revenge by picking on the vulnerable local population. Soldiers began rounding up some part of the civilian population at bayonet point, with the intention of imprisoning them in the Cinema, but were released only after timely intervention by a senior officer.

The invaders became nervous and jumpy, peering anxiously skywards at the slightest sound of an aircraft, including those of their own side. A futile act, for the approach of Harriers could not be heard. Their presence was detectable only after they bombed the targets allocated and on their way back to the carriers. It is not far short of a miracle that Argentinean aircraft were not fired upon by their own side.

A similar reaction spread rapidly through the civilian population who dreaded as much Harrier attacks as those from the Argentineans themselves. Each raid brought on more fear especially when the Navy bombarded Stanley from far out to sea. The islanders, feeling exceedingly vulnerable, huddled in whatever makeshift shelter they had hastily constructed and generally kept themselves out of sight, praying for the attacks and bombing to stop.

When news of the sinking of *Belgrano* and the subsequent heavy loss of life, filtered through the telephone network, or heard through the BBC World Service, the islanders generally feared for their lives. They considered that the garrison would either seek revenge by killing them or hold them hostage, or should the anticipated landings take place, used as a human shield. The population could only pray and keep its head down so as to remain out of sight, hoping the invaders would be so preoccupied and forget about them. If reluctant contact was made, they tried to do absolutely nothing to provoke the enemy.

The Argentineans then introduced a night curfew and the islanders respected it totally. With good reason, for the inexperienced and untrained soldiers already nervous and jittery because of the raids, tended to fire upon any chink of light, indeed they overreacted and wasted round after round firing at anything which moved, including any washing flapping in the breeze. As a consequence, islanders had their sleep disturbed on most nights, only to find at daybreak that their sheets hung out the night before, now had a series of bullet holes in them. White flags became a common sight in the town and some islanders resorted to proffering white flags in daylight, if they were forced, albeit reluctantly, to show themselves.

*

In 1982, the 10,650 ton cumbersome warship was already aged. But with 15.6-inch long range guns and modern Sea Cat anti aircraft missiles of British origin, she was believed to be a serious threat to the task force, in particular to the aircraft carriers *Invincible* and *Hermes*. She had recently been in the company of an aircraft carrier named the *25 de Mayo*, a deadly combination despite their poor state of repair. However *Belgrano's* escorts, now two destroyers were thought to be armed with Exocet, helicopters and sonar. They were behaving as if they were planning an attack to the Task Force, still six hours sailing away. The loss of an aircraft carrier would have meant untold disaster, the end of the blockade of the islands and possibly postponement or abandonment of the planned invasion of the Falklands.

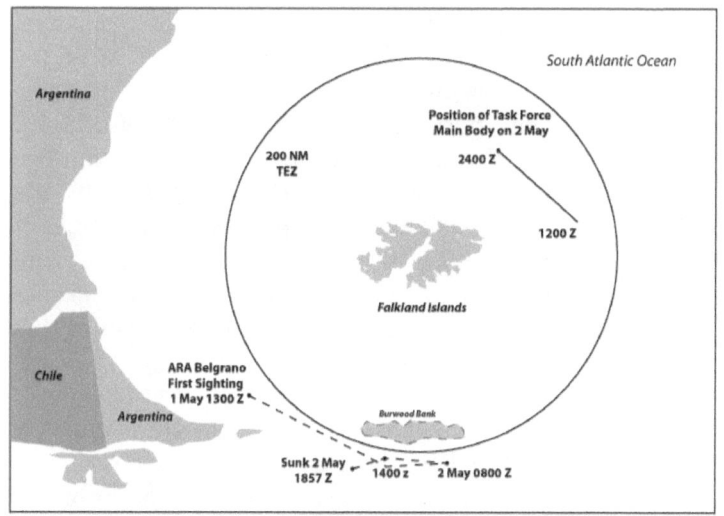

Total Exclusion Zone (TEZ) around Falklands
(the author)

Those intent on mischief made mileage on whether the Belgrano was within the Total Exclusion Zone and whether she was sailing away or towards the Task Force. In reality its direction was of no importance.

The TEZ had no military significance other than to give warning to the enemy and its creation did not imply that ships outside the zone would be safe from attack, disregarding their heading.

Unfortunately, for the Argentineans in particular, news of the cruiser sailing from Ushuaia, Argentina's most southernmost port, was passed to the British by the Chilean authorities, which gave adequate time for one of the nuclear submarines to position herself ready to intercept.

The C-4 Cruiser, *A.R.A Gral Belgrano*, formerly the *USS Phoenix*, laid down in 1938, a survivor of Pearl

165

Harbor, had been renamed in 1955 in tribute to General Altar Belgrano. He was a revolutionary, hero of the Argentinean War of Independence, creator of the blue and white and blue horizontal banded national flag of Argentina. *Belgrano* was going about her legitimate war function of trying to first locate and then hit the task force. She was old and as such totally incapable of taking any kind of hit, despite modernisation with torpedo bulges fitted beneath the waterline. She was not taking even the simplest anti-submarine measures, but she formed part of an aggressive act by the Argentineans. The accusation that she was outside of the total exclusion zone and as such safe from attack, is a diversion. The Total Exclusion Zone has no legal or military significance and was undefined. The Belgrano was sunk outside the 200-nautical-mile (370 km) total exclusion zone around the Falklands. However, exclusion zones are historically declared for the benefit of neutral vessels during war, under international law, the heading and location of a belligerent naval vessel has no bearing on its status.

It should be noted that the only group who made an effort to draw the exclusion zone on a map during the conflict were those on board *Conqueror*.

Officials and ministers have always insisted that, far from heading home, The *Belgrano* was sailing west to a point outside the Total exclusion Zone, from which it was to attach the Task Force. In addition, the captain of the *Belgrano*, Hector Bonzo, has since testified that the *Belgrano's* decision to sail away from the Task Force on the morning of 2 May was only a temporary manoeuvre. 'Our mission wasn't just to cruise around on patrol but to attack.' Captain Bonzo made a startling revelation during a television interview in 1994. 'When they gave us the authorisation to use our weapons, if necessary, we had to be prepared to attack. Our people were completely trained. I would say we were anxious to pull the trigger.'

The Argentine government has also agreed that the *Belgrano* was to be used aggressively.

Those in the Task Force were feeling uncomfortable and vulnerable as the war zone loomed. Every hour took them a few miles nearer their destiny. They had no airborne cover and were in unknown territory. Unlike the Argentinean grass roots, they believed in what they were doing, and were about to acted correctly in the face of unprovoked aggression.

The British, especially the English do not like to go to war. This fact does not stand up to initial scrutiny if past skirmishes are considered, Waterloo, Trafalgar, The Zulu Wars, first and second Boer Wars, first and second World Wars, Korea, Malaya and now the possibility of war with Argentina on the inhospitable and remote Falklands Islands. The ideal, of not wanting to fight does not preclude the will to succeed. What can be said without fear of contradiction is that the English and the British may not relish the idea of fighting, but if forced to they are generally bloody good at it. Traditionally the English are a seafaring nation and until the end of the Second World War possessed a navy to be reckoned with. A force, which by its very composition, training and equipment, anticipated fighting a Soviet enemy in the Northern Hemisphere. So why were they in the Sought Atlantic facing the prospect of waging war with a former friendly nation famous for its Fray Bentos Corn Beef? A flippant remark perhaps, but during Word War II, all the grain for British use came from Argentina, and George relished Fray Bentos, which disappeared from supermarket shelves literally overnight. The answer lies with politicians, who, closely on the heels of religion are usually the main cause of all wars and conflicts.

167

With the Americans conveniently sitting on the fence being *even handed*, a political term for looking after your own interests over all others, the flamboyant Maggie Thatcher steered her nation into war. George considered that she did not do much wrong. The only item he had a great deal in coming to terms with, -why publicise your intentions to a potential enemy? The Argentineans had in the region of eight weeks notice and could do a great deal to prepare for the arrival of the Task Force, when, definitely not if, political negotiations broke down.

On the other hand, the British had eight weeks in which to substitute the well-practised strategy of going into war with the old enemy, with adopting new tactics for the new, but without adequate opportunity of a worthwhile dress rehearsal.

Conditions on *Hermes*, an elderly aircraft carrier due for retirement at any time, was cold, uncomfortable, overcrowded and packed with stores and personnel. The decision had already been made that they were not going to risk losing people if they were torpedoed. The two British Carriers were the key to success. Take either away and the operation was doomed to failure, or at least the cause of delay. Therefore every man lived high up on the ship away from the waterline, sharing cabins and bunks. Sleep became an irrelevance. They found a space someone had vacated and rested where they could. Not all ships could do this, including *Belgrano*, but where they were able, every British ship adopted some form of life preserving action to prevent unnecessary loss of life. On *Belgrano*, conditions were equally cold and uncomfortable and at least a third of the 1093 crew were inexperienced and not fully trained. This is the way of second rate dictatorships who lure their young men into battle without adequate preparation.

*

Around this time, it has been claimed that the Americans offered the use of one of their aircraft carriers. How this was received is not recorded for public information.

What is certain is that if a *USS Whatever* had gone down south, there would have been disastrous consequences.

Can you see an F16 being serviced on the flight deck as Harriers were?

George thought not.

Can you see all the crew sleeping above the waterline, as on both British Aircraft Carriers and the rest of the fleet?

George thought not.

The Americans favour comfort before the reality of battle conditions and would have suffered casualties in direct proportion to the number of purple hearts awarded. Their military hardware is not capable of functioning in extreme conditions. It has been known to fail in extreme heat and George felt confident it would have failed in extreme cold.

*

Three weeks earlier, at Faslane Base, 25 miles north west of Glasgow, orders were given out of the blue, for *HMS Conqueror* to prepare for a fast departure, but Ken and Andy did not immediately associate this with the Falklands. There was some talk about some scrap metal merchants on a rocky island, called South Georgia, but no one had access to an atlas, and as geography was not a strong point for either of them, they were not unduly worried. Andy had been on *Conx* for five years, and joined as a Part III, an unqualified submariner. Although he had been through extensive submarine training, he had not yet earned his dolphins or qualified on the respective areas he would eventually be responsible for, as a watch keeper. Andy came under the wing of Ken. Despite Ken having a grumpy disposition for most of the time, he helped Andy qualify as a full submariner due to his experience and superb knowledge of the *Conx*, a nickname given by many of the crew of *Conqueror*. Similarly another submarine called *Superb*, as is the way of Navy parlance, became known as *Super B*, and another, *Valiant* had such a chequered technical career, and it was occasionally known as *The Valium*! Spending so much in each others company the pair became known as the 'terrible twins' in the *'back afties'*, a term given to those who were working in the machinery spaces and manoeuvring room and the machinery control area.

However suspicions were aroused when the order for a fast departure became allied to another ordering the *Conx* to be false decked. Tinned food was to be laid down in passageways and anywhere else it could be stored to provide extra food for the patrol. They also took on a full war load of torpedoes, slightly unusual perhaps, but not so much for the *Conx*, which was also a special fit boat at that time.

As things gradually deteriorated down south, Ken and Andy realised that the South Atlantic was to be their destination. Suddenly they had access to any stores they needed or were able to carry back to the boat. The storekeepers at Faslane Base became amiable overnight, a most uncharacteristic trait and a far cry from their usual demeanour! Making most of the opportunity, Ken and Andy rummaged around the stores and found all manner of kit, which could be useful. Ken even penetrated the realm of the notorious O ring seal storekeeper, and relieved him of a full set of seals for *back afties* use. The storekeeper remained surprisingly cheerful throughout the unexpected raid on his precious domain!

No Part III's were to be carried as crew down to the Falklands. They were not allowed to operate on their own, and would have ended up as passengers and double up on watch positions. With a full war load, they were put ashore to make way for more qualified people. The departure of all Part III's coincided with arrival of a group of Special Boat Squadron (SBS). The SBS, whilst being amongst the elite and the most famous of Special Forces teams, remain by necessity a regiment shrouded in secrecy. This unannounced arrival of an assortment of rowdy, well kitted out band of ruffians confirmed the suspicions of Andy and Ken and gave advance warning of busy times ahead.

On the *Conx* there was only beds for 100, so as a rule the Part III's slept on racks fitted over the torpedo themselves, in the *Fore ends*. Further more there was only escape gear for so many, but with the Part III's off the boat, ensured all crew would have use of escape gear. Many Part III's were thoroughly pissed off and rightly so, and made their feelings very apparent, but that is the way of things.The SBS with hardly a word of complaint resigned themselves to sleeping on the racks previously occupied by Part III's.

It was a time of great effort and there was much work to be done if the boat was to put to sea on time. When the *Conx* slipped it's mooring and sailed without fuss out into the Glare Loch then into the Clyde, it was almost an anti climax after the frantic activity of the past few days.

A few of the SBS were given a guided tour and in the *back afts* kept referring to the *Conx* as a ship. Ken, not renown for subtly nor politeness, explained with an amazing amount of patience that in time long past when submarines were in their infancy, submarines were referred to as *submarine boats*. Being a mouthful it became shortened to boats and had been known by that name since.

The next day, without warning, the *Jimmy*, a 1st Lieutenant who had the attack teams under his control, called the boat into *Action Stations*. The attack teams consisted of weapons engineering; the sound room crew, consisting of 3 ratings plus a senior; the weapons control team, whose task was to load and launch torpedoes, and also operate the plot. They had to ensure that all relevant information from the sound room and the scopes were combined to give an accurate assessment of the targets range and direction so a *firing solution* could be given.

Andy and Ken and the team went into automated mode and *shut* the watertight bulkhead doors. They were never *closed* for it was easier to hear the word *shut* in a noisy area. On this first *Action Stations* in the manoeuvring room the four SBS, caught off guard, appeared to be uneasy in such unfamiliar and suddenly crowded surroundings.

With the boat suddenly silent, one of the SBS, a dour Scot, piped up. 'Is this a good time to start a Ceilidh?

'What the fuck's that?' Ken demanded.

'A social event with traditional singing and dancing!'

'No it fucking well isn't, you bloody idiot!' Ken replied from his station. 'Just put a sock in it!'

The *back afties* were kept busy and being the first time, the SBS were for once totally out of their depth, and contrived to get in the way.

In the control room the Captain formally took control of the *Conx*, relieving the Officer of the Watch (OOW) by saying. 'I have the boat.'

The OOW gave the skipper the state of the boat, depth, speed, course, state of propulsion machinery, revolutions and the state of the Reactor. He also said when the slop drain and sewage tanks had last been pumped, plus any information that might affect the readiness of the boat. Seated in front of the OOW was a fore and aft man in position, who remained under direct control of the OOW, who relayed any orders from the Skipper. Nearby stood a technical officer, manning the ships console. This panel, on the starboard side of the control room was used for flooding and pumping tanks to keep trim as well as for blowing tanks to surface or opening the main ballast tank vents to dive the boat. At the back of the control room was the navigation table area and the officer designated as the navigator or *Navvy* had two or three ratings to assist with plotting the precise position of the boat during an action.

In the fore ends the Weapons Chief had up to six ratings under his control to *prepping* the tubes ready for launch and reporting back their state of readiness. In the back afts, in the manoeuvring room and machinery spaces, twenty men plus the engineering officer were closed up. 11 in the Manoeuvring room, 4 in the main machinery space and 4 in the turbine generator and switchboard area. Today on this first *action stations* the SBS were looking very uneasy.

Once everyone was closed up at *action stations*, each space reported back to the control room via the *Jimmy* who relayed this to the Skipper. The Captain was responsible for the attack, getting information from those around him. The *Jimmy* constantly monitored the state of the boat and reported any problems. This allowed the Skipper to concentrate on the action. The Skipper also ordered the raising and lowering of the periscopes to the required depth and behind him a rating called out relative bearings when given a *take that* or *at that* order came from the Skipper, so he did not have to look away from the periscopes. The periscopes were judiciously raised and lowered as they could be spotted by the enemy if put up too high or for too long. Often an order was given to *raise the scopes for an all round look*, this meant raising the scopes and going through 360 degrees and lowering them quickly again. If the Skipper knew the relative bearing of a vessel he would raise the scope on that bearing in order to minimise the time the periscope remained exposed.

The crew not closed up and not on watch in the control room hung around in an area adjacent to the *Tunnel*. This area was known as *Grumpy Corner* on the *Conx*. The *Tunnel* was a steel passageway lined with lead and other shielding material that allowed the *Back afties* access to and from the machinery room spaces by going over the Reactor itself. The crew often referred to the Reactor compartment as the *Pot*.

After stand down the SBS started to wander off, but Ken was not going to let them get away with anything. 'You may be the SBS, but do you have to get in the bloody way?' Ken commented. 'If this was for real, we would all be buggered with you fucking great useless lumps of shite wanting to dance all over the place!'

The SBS showing restraint and a good deal of discretion sensibly chose not to retaliate.

Today's *action stations* was just to get the crew back into a proper working state, and to emphasise to the SBS the importance of keeping out of the way. Long before the *Conx* reached its destination, *action station* caused little problems for the SBS who learned quickly by staying put and remaining silent.

The *Conx* and its new visitors gradually settled into a sea going routine. When off watch the crew slept, ate and watched videos. They could smoke and drink, unless at a closed up state. The exceptions were the fore

174

ends, for obvious reasons, the machinery spaces used for cleaning the boat atmosphere, making oxygen and the battery compartment area.

The Ship Office was tiny, just room enough for two crew members to sit and work. One of these would be the Office Writer, a junior rating who also acted as Captains secretary. On watch he was a planesman. The other occupant was the Coxswain, who was also one of the planesman at *action stations*. The Coxswain acted as the boat policeman, responsible for discipline, considered being the senior of senior ratings. The Coxswain on *Conx* was held in great regard by both upper and lower decks (Officers and NCO's), as he had spent much time in boats in order to qualify as Coxswain.

On two deck, adjacent to the Ship Office and the hatch leading to the Fore ends was a small cupboard designated as the boats canteen. From there, crew purchased cigarettes, tobacco, chocolate and sweets known in the Royal Navy as *nutty*.

Everyone took a turn on watch, even chefs and the wardroom stewards. If they were not asleep in the galley or wardroom they operated as planesmen. The front ends operated 4 hours on, 8 hours off, however in some spaces it would be 6 hours on, 6 off. In the back aft, Ken and Andy and their mates operated at 4 hours on, 8 off. If equipment went wrong or in need of attention, then the next on watch would be called to fix it, so if the situation was bad, crew off watch had only a short time in their bunk.

There were two bunk spaces on 2 Deck, one for junior ratings and one for Petty and Chief Petty Officers and senior ratings. Each bunk were about two feet wide and less than six feet long, with headroom of around two feet six inches. The only privacy was a small curtain, which could be drawn across the bunk space. Each crew member had a small locker to stow personal effects and uniform. During normal conditions the bunk space lights were never on, as the crew would be off watch sleeping, but each bunk had a reading lamp.

To pass the time in between practice *attack* and practice *action stations*, someone came up with the idea of a sponsored slim, and a few enthusiastic crew members suddenly became experts on calories, much to the amusement of others who could not give a damn about slimming and were more interested in eating. As the *Conx* sailed south, the call into *action stations* became routine, as did many practice *attack* runs. In any case everyone thought the war would be over by the time they arrived, and took the routine in their stride. The SBS though were taking it seriously as if they had some insider information and kept well out of the way. The war for the crew on *Conx* would commence when the SBS were dropped off at their rendezvous site on a desolate part of the islands, and the *Conx* set off around the Falklands on constant lookout for Argentinean warships.

On the third day, south of the Falkands, the boat went into *action stations*. Sonar, known back at ESR as the Sentinel Project, had detected what turned out to be *Belgrano* and escorts, identified using photostat copies of the relevant pages from Janes Fighting Ships.

Conx did not use active sonar, instead relied upon passive sonar. The huge sonar array on the bow, above six torpedo tubes, could be operated in active or passive mode. In active mode, generated sound pulses were sent out, then the returning echo revealed both range and bearing of the target. However the enemy would immediately hear the boat pinging, alerting them to the presence of a submarine. Instead the array was used as a rather large pair of ears to hear the enemy ships, but this gave bearing only and no range. Passive sonar provides a great deal of information from the target ship, which can be analysed giving indication of speed and other ship machinery noises. This is known as a ships signature and all ships have a unique sound identity. In order to get the range the *Conx* was fitted with a towed array, a long cable, which had sonar transponders on the tail. It effectively provided a long base line, which allowed triangulation of a sound source, hence the ability to calculate its range.

The *Conx* shadowed the vessels keeping their mast tops on the horizon. On one occasion there were four vessels being refuelled, viewed through the periscope. This cat-and-mouse situation continued whilst the vessels remained outside the total exclusion zone until orders were received to attack. Communication with Northwood in London proved difficult as *Conx* had an ageing radio system and the Southern Hemisphere was notorious for making communication with the Northern Hemisphere as difficult as possible. There were considerations given to change the rules of engagement making an attack politically acceptable, and this also took time.

For three days they shadowed the cruiser and its escorts as they zig-zagged westwards and eastwards along the southern edge of the Total Exclusion Zone. For three days a constant watch was kept and regular reports sent to the Task Force Commander, then twenty four hours before going into action the routine changed to one of that of a higher state of readiness.

The timing of the change was significant as it coincided with intense military activity around the Falkland Islands. Before dawn two RAF Vulcan Bombers, another piece of military kit months away from retirement after 25 years service, set off from Ascension, a tiny volcanic island in the middle of nowhere. Their destination was the single runway at Stanley Airport. That they succeeded was in itself a wonder given that one of the two Vulcan's returned to base with technical problems shortly after take off. The lone Vulcan travelled south, refuelled by an amazing series of tankers, a process called an air bridge, whose timings and navigation had to be accurate if the single aircraft in their care was to stay aloft and complete its mission.

At about 0400 on Saturday 1 May, the single RAF Vulcan successfully bombed Stanley Airport, followed an hour later by every Harrier in the Task Force, which sent shock waves throughout the garrison stationed there. Later in the day under cover of a bombardment from three naval ships, SAS and SBS squadrons landed on East and West Falklands. The Argentineans were active too, for the Task Force came under attack from air raids soon after. During the late afternoon British Sea King helicopters using equipment made at ESR, detected and attacked an Argentinean submarine.

The conflict had entered a critical phase, for the threat from other Argentineans units was increasing by the hour. It was decided at an impromptu War Cabinet assembled at Chequers that such was the gravity of the situation, it was necessary to take immediate action to foil the impending attack. The War Cabinet decided to attack the units closest to the Total Exclusion Zone, which included *Belgrano*.

Imagine it is dark and you have no night vision. You hear the enemy creeping towards you. For some reason he sneaks away. Then he comes back. It is your one chance to catch him.

This is the reason why the *Belgrano* was sunk.

It was war.

Of course there was sadness at the number of Argentinean sailors killed and wounded.

No one, including George, wanted that.

*

Isolation of life below the waves is heightened by the fact that radio waves, radar, infra red and a host of other mediums of communication, do not travel well, if at all in sea water. Visible light suffers a similar fate. Sound on the other hand, travels about four and a half times faster than it does in air, about 3,500 mph, compared to 750mph. Sounds can be heard over tens of miles.

Submarine warfare is always carried out in total darkness, is cold, essentially silent and mainly an invisible affair, in which those above and below water employ weapons of utmost technological sophistication. In submarine warfare the science of sound is thus the one overriding factor of technical innovation and concern. Modern nuclear powered submarines run fast, silent, are capable of running deep and equipped with long range guided weapons, which give an enemy little or no warning of impending attack. Patrols are lonely, long and for the main part, independent because of the difficulties of communicating underwater. Hunted by a large range of aircraft and helicopters, surface ships and other submarines, they can be tracked down by a large range of computer controlled sensors and can be destroyed by a range of very unpleasant weapons. If a submarine is detected and hit, submariners have little or no chance of survival. Submariners live in a cramped metallic environment, which imposes considerable physiological strain even when not under of threat of attack. Deprived of natural sunlight for months at a time and the obvious division between night and day when on patrol, the crew of a submarine need to draw upon considerable inner resources to main mental stability. During the long journey south, many of the crew of *HMS Conqueror* used the sponsored slim, as a diversion from reality whilst simultaneously practising for an attack they all hoped would not happen. Highlight of the week was the receiving of the *familygram,* a short message of forty words from family and friends, which for reasons of security cannot be replied to. A familygram is a simple form which a family fills in their love one's name, details, their service number so it gets through to them, and then it's a series of 40 boxes divided up five words wide, and you get to send them 40 words a week. The first two are always taken up with his rank and name, so you end up with 38 words to tell them what's gone on. You can try and run words together but then they become nonsensical and the Navy get wind of it and they don't like that, so you really are at your 38 words. Post that off and somebody at Faslane types it up and it gets sent off like the old-fashioned telegram-type things, on a piece of paper, no grammar, no commas or anything like that, it's literally just spelt across in a sticker-tape strip-type thing. And that turns up the appropriate locker on the submarine once a week in a brown envelope and they open it up and that's their communication for the week. It can only be a matter of conjecture the effect these messages had on family and crew alike, at such a traumatic time.

Anti submarine warfare (ASW) revolves around use of sonar, both passive and active, but is not the overriding factor for a submarine commander. To complicate the deadly game of ASW is the fact that the sea has a complex structure, which is in a permanent state of flux. This seemingly flimsy structure, without obvious strength, can destroy all manner of human activity on shore and at sea. A structure with its difference in temperature, pressure, salinity, weather effects, currents and marine life, makes any interpretation of acoustic information extremely difficult. In addition to refraction, reflection and corruption of an acoustic signal, assuming one can he heard above a cacophony of marine noises, the processing unit must even operate against the noise generated by the submarine itself.

For all its large bulk a nuclear submarine (SSN) requires delicate control mechanisms when navigating close to the sea bed, or following the layers of hot or cold water to avoid detection by sonar.

The rough and stormy conditions in the South Atlantic would have tended to mask any target with high levels of background noise. This natural degrading of sonar performance acted as an aid to the enemy whilst increasing the risk of submarines detection. Conditions around the Falkland Islands reduced anti submarine operations to a level of a war fought almost blindfold, with the accompanying scope for blunders and pressures on all combatants. Due to a quirk of nature, whales regrettably have similar shapes and acoustic signatures as submarines and it is certain that a number of ASW attacks were against these harmless mammals. It is certain also that these attacks would have been duly noted by the Commander of any Argentinean submarine in the area and give warning of the consequences of mounting attack against such a formidable and alert enemy.

*

When the crew were called into *action stations*, at 3pm on 2 May, the boat was brought into an ultra quiet state, with all fans and air conditioning shut down to reduce the potential for noise. Everyone was careful not to make any loud noise, movement around the boat was restricted and there was no smoking, eating or drinking. Those not closed up or next on watch, sat around the mess decks, one for senior and one for junior ranks, waiting for whatever occurred. Most were trying to read or occupy their minds until something happened. Back aft, the Propulsion Panel operator was using a passive hydrophone to listen to the screw to ensure cavitation did not take place as speed increased. Cavitation is the popping noise generated when bubbles of air collapse, caused by the propeller speed increasing too fast, which would be heard aboard the *Belgrano*, assuming a sonar operator was on duty.

The *Belgrano* was approaching the shallow water of Burwood Bank, considered too shallow for *Conx* to enter with any safety and increase the risk of being detected. In shallow water the *Conx* would be unable to retain full manoeuvrability, so essential under attack conditions. In those circumstances, there existed a serious possibility that the *Conx* could lose the Cruiser at a particularly crucial time and place the Task Force at considerable risk.

The War Cabinet made the decision to attack the *Belgrano* being the vessel closest to the Total Exclusion Zone. The *Belgrano* and her escort continued to take a random zig-zag course, still apparently unaware of the presence of an enemy submarine. Within five minutes of the decision signal reaching the *Conx* and deciphered, the torpedo tubes were loaded and ready to fire. The Captain decided to use old Mk 8 Torpedos instead of the latest *Tigerfish* wire guided Torpedos. The Mk 8's could be set to a shallow ceiling, which meant they would easily penetrate the hull whereas *Tigerfish* were really an anti-submarine weapon, designed to be use at depth and not in shallow water.

The atmosphere on board was tense, yet each individual went about his duties professionally as various orders were given to prepare for the attack.

An hour later the order was given to fire and after the last minute problem of a faulty firing switch had been resolved, three torpedos sped away towards the *Belgrano*. Seconds ticked away as each crew member held their breath. This was the moment for which they had been trained. A moment few believed, they would encounter. Until the moment of firing it had been training, a dress rehearsal for a performance that would never take place. At the moment of firing, their lives would never be the same again. They were on the worlds centre stage, the *Belgrano* had real people on board, with three high-explosive torpedos fast approaching.

Two enormous explosions were heard, then felt.

The Skipper announced from the periscope that he could see several flashes of orange flame, whereupon the control room crew erupted in cheers when they realised the torpedos had struck home.

'Rig the boat for depth charge attack!'

Conqueror turned and dived deep, shuddering to the sound of several explosions believing they were under attack from the escorts dropping depth charges. It was later established that although both escorts retaliated with depth throwing hedgehog projectiles, the sounds were mainly explosions coming from exploding boilers and ammunition aboard the *Belgrano*. The crew were no longer cheering. Trained they may have been, but no-one had ever experienced a counter attack.

For an hour the submarine moved away from the scene to allow an aerial to be raised in order to inform base what had taken place. The crew were scared but remained under control. Thinking that the submarine was still being hunted they carried out evasive manoeuvres.

*

The first torpedo hit the cruiser on the port bow fifteen feet below the water line, the explosion killing instantly ten men who were off duty in their quarters. The bow section collapsed almost to the front of 'A' turret, allowing tons of freezing sea water to pour inside the cruiser. Seconds later a second torpedo struck the Cruiser towards the stern in the vicinity of the aft machinery room, wrecking the steering gear and causing many deaths to those men off duty, either asleep in bunks or in the canteen. Damage control, if it existed in the first place, had little effect. The fact that about a third of the crew were raw recruits could only increase casualties. The explosion sent a wave of heat through the open doors. It lasted only a few seconds and reduced the ship to silence, apart from the shouts and screams of the wounded.

On a properly organised modern warship, the paint used to protect metal work from corrosion is designed to resist fire, all gangways and passageways are kept clear. Watertight doors are kept shut except when they are being used for access. The *Belgrano*, was not modern nor properly organised, the crude paint work cracked and peeling. All manner of items cluttered the passageways and watertight doors left constantly open. After the initial impact and explosion, a great searing wave of heat spread past these watertight doors, which should have been secured in a shut position. Many of the crew who survived the explosion, now found themselves being burnt alive. Stores and other items scattered about the floor, hindered their way of escape and many seamen were injured by broken glass, presumably from broken bottles of soft drinks or similar, stored there.

Then came smoke. Thick, black, choking smoke from the seats of three major fires that prevented many unwounded crew members from making an escape. All internal and external communications were lost in the explosions, so no clear instructions could be given to those still able to make an escape. Because of an inadequate number of medics, the wounded wandered about with little prospect of assistance. With a gaping hole in the bow, the seawater poured into the heart of the cruiser through open doors and hatches. This had the effect of making *The Belgrano* list about fifteen degrees within a matter of minutes and only added to the confusion for the conscripts.

*

One such conscript, named Marcelo, Conscript Class 62, a stretcher bearer and a fireman in charge of damage control, was enjoying a brief moment of siesta before supper, in his sparse quarters situated between the engine room and the stern. Captain Hector Bonzo, ensured that *Belgrano*, deliberately remained outside of the Total Exclusion Zone and because an attack was not anticipated, the crew were relaxed and not at full readiness. The time was 1600 hours and despite the bad weather anticipated with the arrival of a cold front and a falling barometer, it was already causing the ship to buck and roll. Marcelo contemplated the prospect of eight hours rest before going back on duty at midnight. He clambered into his cot, wrapped his single blanket around his body to keep as much of the cold out as possible, before he closed his eyes and allowed himself to gently relax and fall asleep. When the first torpedo struck the cruiser, being towards the bow, the explosion felt like another heavy sea and did not disturb his slumbers. The second torpedo exploded close by seconds later and the impact caused him to bang his head on the upper bunk before throwing him out of his cot. A moment later a searing ball of flame came down the passageway at breakneck speed. Marcelo crouched in a corner, his hands clasped firmly over his head. The heat resembled that from a furnace, enveloped him from head to feet and he began to scream. With his eyes firmly shut, he saw his life flashing past his mind, as a sequence as snapshots of noteworthy events during his short life; his first day at school, the first time he learned to ride a bike; the first time he kissed his childhood sweetheart. The colours were vivid as his life passed literally before his eyes.

Marcelo prepared to die.

The ball of flame passed by, and in the ensuing silence, Marcelo found that he was very much alive, but felt little discomfort initially and thought himself to be uninjured, totally unaware at this stage of his severe burns. His training urged him to carry out his duties of damage control and he slowly made his way to his post. Along the way he passed other conscripts, not so badly injured, emerging from what safety they had found. An officer saw his plight and urged him to leave immediately and make his way on deck. He expected to see much damage but everywhere looked in order. He also expected to see everything in shambles but felt amazed by the way crew emerging from lower decks went about in a calm manner. He saw a pile of blackened bodies caught in a moment of time on a companionway as they had made their escape. He found one of his friends, badly burnt, slumped by an open hatchway, doomed not to remain for long on this earth. The skin on his face, his hands and arms were red raw, his eyes appeared to be almost popping out. He must have inhaled hot smoke, for he showed signs of severe difficulty with breathing.

Marcelo Pozzo (courtesy Marcelo Pozzo)

Marcelo at home in Buenos Aires with his Belgrano collection.
He suffered 25% burns, 1st, 2nd and 3rd degree. His treatment was as painful as it was effective for he did not need skin grafts. Marcelo has made a full recovery and shows a remarkable resilience given his wounds.

'What happened?' Marcelo asked. His first impression had been that an Exocet missile had hit *Belgrano*.

His friend looked surprised at being asked such a ridiculous question.

'We have been torpedoed, you arsehole!' He croaked virtually in a whisper before he passed away and his head gently fell to one side. Marcelo noticed a pool of blood on the floor and looked around for the person with wounds. To his horror he established that he had severe cuts to his feet where he had walked on broken glass. It was customary to keep bulky stores in the companionway to ease the cramped quarters. As the ship began to list, the contents of bottles smashed in the explosion mixed with his blood making psychedelic patterns that swished gently away towards a sump. He inspected the wounds to his feet despite the urgency of others to keep moving. His socks had virtually disintegrated leaving shredded remnants of elastic and material on his ankles only, leaving his feet and toes bare. The skin on his legs hung in shreds as far up to his knees and his right arm totally burnt up to the sleeve of his uniform. On his right arm he had a nasty looking blister from his wrist to little finger. Strangely enough he still felt no pain. Perhaps the cold caused a delayed reaction but he suspected from his medical training that only long spell in hospital, would ensure these severe wounds stood any chance to heal. First he had to find safety and possibly prepare to evacuate from the ship, as it appeared to him that the cruiser was gradually sinking. A situation he considered would never occur. No one thinks that their ship would be sunk, but he knew that he must now prepare for that eventuality and if he were to survive, he must act accordingly.

The ship seemed strangely quiet, the gentle vibration of the engines and other machinery that brings a ship alive, strangely absent. More crew, in the main not so badly injured as he, appeared, urged haste in getting to his life raft station. There was no sign of panic as everyone went about quietly with a sense of urgency and the officers could be heard shouting commands, as without electricity there was no speaker system. On the way he passed through the infirmary where orderlies were struggling to get patients off the bed and towards safety. Two men were known to have had appendicitis and were unable to walk unaided. Being a ship of considerable length, to reach his life raft station Number 63, he knew would take a long time with the deck at such an unnatural angle, and so many of the crew scrambling in the one direction, meeting with others heading in the opposite direction in near darkness. Those who still had strength, were not carrying or escorting the wounded, or were officers, disregarded those around them and made passage through the melee of men.

Someone draped a poncho blanket around his shoulders, and another found some ill-fitting shoes, which eased the discomfort of his bleeding feet. He struggled past damage control crews who were still at their posts operating manual pumps in a vain attempt to keep the cruiser afloat. Others were assessing damage and he saw one crew busy shoring up a bulkhead. The list had now increased to almost 25 degrees, and making his way towards the stern became virtually impossible. Still those behind heading the same way urged him onwards, whilst those in front tried to pull him along. Progress was only possible by walking at an uncomfortable angle as to use the bulwarks for support whilst just being able to walk on the angled deck. Climbing through yet another open watertight door he spied a pile of sea jackets, so he grabbed one as he passed by and put it over his shoulders.

When he eventually clambered up onto the open deck, he saw to his horror Life Raft Number 63 was not where it was supposed to be. Marcelo assumed the explosion had forcibly moved it from its position. An officer appeared who gave the order to abandon ship before clambering into the nearest raft, already filled with a small number of other senior officers. There were several rafts already inflated and in the sea. Marcelo climbed onto a partially submerged ventilation shaft and by this means was able to climb down onto the nearest raft without getting his body wet. He looked back towards the ship, now badly listing with the crew having to jump into the sea in order to gain the protection of a raft and saw his raft hanging in shreds over the side, the number 63 clearly visible. Men were jumping into the sea with panic, desperate to reach a raft. By these means a total of eleven men sheltered in his raft, in the main without injury other than minor cuts and wounds, but who had been forced to jump into the sea, which as darkness approached was at a temperature of two degrees above freezing. The wind chill factor further reduced the temperature to nearer minus twenty degrees centigrade, with a sea increasing by the minute. The raft was still moored to the cruiser, which was sinking fast. Eventually the mooring rope was cut by mutual consent and the wind carried them gently away from the Cruiser, formerly their home and shelter from the bad weather. Through a small porthole the keel bottom of *Belgrano* could be seen before it gradually slipped into the sea stern first beneath the waves. Many rafts still moored to the cruiser or close by, were caught up by the suction, overturned or sunk.

With the loss of the cruiser there were a total of seventy rafts drifting each with many occupants in the first stages of freezing to death. After dark the wind began to rise and with the sea with gusts at 60 mph and waves sometimes up to 20 feet high. The crew was tossed about as if on a trampoline and with such harsh treatment some rafts already damaged by the explosion of the torpedo, began to let in water and became generally unserviceable. Men were forced to change rafts to one without damage and as a consequence some became overcrowded with up to thirty men contained within. The raft, in which Marcelo huddled, still had the original number of eleven, but a few men had already died. An observer going from raft to raft would have great difficulty in telling the difference between the dead and the living. Many were suffering from terrible burns, because no one had been wearing anti flash masks or gloves, as was common practice with the Task Force. In such terrible weather conditions, life rafts offer scant protection and a few blew over in the wind with the loss of all those on board.

How the survivors were finally rescued remains difficult to establish after all these years. It is possible perhaps, that two destroyers who fled after the attack returned after dark and picked up survivors using searchlights. Later during a concerted effort by two armed tugs, *Alfrerez Sobral* and *Commodoro Somellera* were searching for survivors when a single Sea King Helicopter from Hermes flew in the vicinity. The crew had seen a few brightly coloured rafts at some distance near to the horizon, which they suspected were from *Belgrano*. The tugs were around ninety miles inside the Total Exclusion Zone but the rule of the sea decreed that whilst on a rescue mission they were best left alone. One made the mistake of firing on the Sea King and this foolish act changed everything. The pilot summoned two Lynx helicopters from the nearest frigates, and armed with Sea Skua anti-ship missiles sunk the *Commodoro Somellera* and badly damaged the *Alfrerez Sobral,* with her captain and seven crew killed.

Marcelo in his raft fared badly as they could not properly close the portholes and freezing sea water poured in, so there was always an inch of two of water swirling about despite a constant effort to bale out. The temperature plummeted to below zero during the storm that raged during the hours of darkness, the raft and its passengers tossed about like peas by the turbulent sea. To add to their already discomforted situation several men in the raft became sea sick. Marcelo was amongst the first to succumb to seasickness and aided by a sympathetic crewman he was first sick in the hood of his sea jacket and when full, emptied through a porthole, then washed in sea water before he felt sick again, and the miserable process repeated time after time. By degrees the sea jacket became totally wet through and became unusable. To make matters worse, if that were possible, his scabby flesh stuck to anything which remained in contact with it for anything longer than a minute or two, with bleeding the consequence of moving out of contact. His helper found some cloth resembling a bandage and wrapped his wounds in to prevent further discomfort.

The dance that the sea forced the raft to endure was impressive. They went upwards on the crest of a wave with empty feeling in the stomach, then following a short pause, the raft plunged into the depths at a stomach churning speed, with a painful crash as it reached the lower water surface. And so it went on for hour after relentless hour. A leading seaman in the raft made them all move their fingers and toes to avoid getting trench foot, and when they became quiet, made them all clap their hands whilst singing patriotic songs at the top of their voices. The morale of the raft increased despite the effort it took out of each man to sing and clap with such enthusiasm. At dawn the weather eased and around one o'clock in the afternoon they were spotted by a passing aeroplane on maritime patrol, which gave a wiggle of its wings in response to the flares sent up. It is perhaps ironic that the flares used, had instructions in English! With the calming sea they could see other rafts within a quarter of a mile of their position, some tied together in groups, which had also survived the night. The initial enthusiasm of an anticipated rescue abated because they were not rescued until the following night by the armed tug *ARA Fransisco deGurruchag,* formerly the *USS Luiseno ATF 156,* an Abnaki Class Fleet ocean going tug, launched in 1945 and purchased from the Americans in the late 1970's.

*

When Marcelo arrived at Ushuaia he was taken to the Naval Hospital for treatment and was later flown to the Naval Base at Puerto Belgrano, where two days later he saw his parents looking though his room window. The other crew who were not wounded were taken to a hangar within Puerto Belgrano and the press were not permitted, nor were relatives and family. They felt disillusioned and angry that their masters had decided to abandon them.

*

By contrast, when *Conqueror* arrived home HM Naval Base Clyde at Faslane, 25 miles north west of Glasgow, flying the skull and crossbones in keeping with tradition, The Minister of Defence, Michael Heseltine went on board via tug before *Conx* entered the Gare Loch. The press and TV cameras were everywhere, but within Faslane, only immediate family were allowed on the jetty. A relief watch went on board immediately to allow most of those on watch to come up and meet their families. It was an extremely emotional time.

The skull and crossbones of the *Conx* was once on show at the National Naval Museum, Greenwich. It carries a dagger, as *Conx* took a group of SBS down south, plus a red bar for the *Belgrano*. This was the first time in over fifty years that skull and crossbones had been seen flying from the fin of a submarine.

*

The sinking of *Belgrano*, controversial in some quarters, enjoys the dubious honour of being the first and to date the only vessel sunk by a nuclear submarine. When news of the sinking reached the ESR factory, it was greeted by a prolonged silence.

HMS Conqueror (Courtesy Plymouth Herald)

HMS Conqueror (Conx) on 4 July 1982 returning to the Clyde Submarine base amid controversy over sinking of Belgrano. The Jolly Roger on the tower carries an atomic symbol (the first to be flown on a nuclear submarine) as well as a symbol denoting a sunken warship and a dagger for special ops. The Royal Navy tradition is to fly a Jolly Roger when returning to port after a kill at sea. The symbols used was not standard, normally a red bar indicated a warship sunk. Conx used a silhouette of a warship in white bunting. Crossed torpedoes were used instead of cross bones behind the skull.

Conx was built in 1971, carried a crew of more than 100 during the conflict and commanded by Commander Christopher Wreford-Brown.

7

Thefts

The theft of a one pound note belonging to Ed Littleboy, stolen from a wallet in his coat pocket hanging in the cloakroom, caused a ripple of concern amongst the cloak room users.

The cloakroom was in full view of the office.

Firstly, how was it possible for the money to be taken without anyone noticing?

Secondly who could possibly be the thief?

In those days of innocence, everyone appeared genuinely shocked by such a dastardly act and went through an impromptu investigation with the sole intent of finding a satisfactory solution to whether a one pound note ever existed in his wallet. Having established beyond reasonable doubt that it had, then the discussion then progressed onto by which means caused the one pound note to disappear. Everyone refused point bank range to accept that a thief stalked the drawing office cloakroom. George did not take part in the lengthy debate, but gleaned from the periphery, the debaters concluded that The Little Boy must have been mistaken, and either did not have a one pound note on his person or had spent it on his way to work without taking due notice. Ed Littleboy appeared to George as being generally meticulous in the way he conducted himself, including monetary affairs, so he formed the opinion that if he said that a one pound note had been taken, it was most likely true. Ed Littleboy was one of those men who enjoyed power over others and picked on anybody he considered being out of his private club or being socially beneath him. To show his contempt, George retaliated by calling him *The Little*

Boy, occasionally to his face. In reality this contempt was harsh, as Ed Littleboy had been taken prisoner during the first Battle of El Alamein in July 1942 and spent his time as a POW in a camp near Berlin. George justified this by the intolerable attitude of *The Little Boy* towards his staff.

The male cloakroom was situated at one end of the drawing office in full view of everyone. The nearest person, Bert Weaver, one of the section clerks, would be able to see all comings and goings from the cloakroom, without turning his head. Bert was inclined to be nosy and at the slightest opportunity generally poked his nose into other folk's affairs. Virtually every time George spoke to him, mostly about work matters and mentioned the name of a colleague, Bert would volunteer some obscure and generally personal or private fact about them, one not in common circulation. If anyone could catch the thief, Bert could be considered to be a safe each way bet. With the door left open he would even be able to catch anyone in the cloakroom with a hand in a coat pocket and still continue with his generally mundane clerical duties. All draughtsmen started and finished work at the same time, so there would normally be no need for anyone to be in the room at any other time, apart from the minutes leading up to the start time of eight thirty, during the lunch period and when everyone went home at five o'clock. There were exceptions of course and invariably someone forgot to take his cigarettes or lighter with him or perhaps a pen, but otherwise the cloakroom remained unoccupied during working hours. There were no hard and fast rules. The door was not kept locked, nor should it be, and users had access to their belongings at all times. In the big scheme of things, one did not reasonably expect to be robbed by a colleague, especially from within the depths of such a security minded establishment.

But in the way of human nature, there existed someone who could not resist temptation by resolving a temporary money shortage problem at the expense of a fellow worker. Up to the time of the first theft, George considered that a good, healthy, safe and friendly environment existed in the office. But the loss of that single one pound note left a nasty taste in the mouth.

The debate meanwhile, continued.

The Little Boy became subjected to some in depth questioning from those Section Leaders close to him, as to whether he could be absolutely positive that he had a one pound note in his wallet on that particular day. Having established that he thought he had a one pound note when he left home that morning, the questioning moved onto whether he could be absolutely certain that it had been taken? Could he have purchased some cigarettes from the local shop by the bus stop on the way to work, for instance? Ed Littleboy racked his brains under a hail of questions, which only caused him to cast doubts over his original claim that he had lost some money.

It is fair a reaction.

Does everyone know to the nearest penny how much cash they have in their pockets? The thief would be better off to take small change for its disappearance would be far harder to detect. But George suspected that the light fingered individual wanted a fast and simple resolution to his problem and he simply could not overcome his impatience about having a distinct lack of funds.

The incident was generally forgotten until a few days later, a second theft from the cloakroom was reported. This time the stakes had been increased, as a five pound note stolen from a junior member of staff who could ill afford to lose such a sum of money. Those in his section resolved the problem by an impromptu whip round and his five pounds became reinstated. The identity of the thief remained a mystery, especially when it became apparent that the theft occurred on a day of a general check up at a local hospital for Bert Weaver and noticeable by his absence.

Those at that end of the office now appointed Bert Weaver as unofficial cloakroom watcher. During the coming weeks there were several thefts from the cloakroom without anyone being seen in the vicinity or acting suspiciously. Most men, including George, were forced to take their wallet and small change with them, to keep it in a safe place, most probably like George, in their personal lockable facility. A few more decided not to use the cloakroom at all and placed their coats on the back of their chairs.

The thefts continued and moved onto a new phase.

The thief still had a cash flow problem by all accounts, for he persisted with his evil deeds, made all the easier by coats and occasionally a wallet being in full view on the back of a chair. During a period of months there were several men who lost money, usually a single one pound or one pound note from their coat pocket, all hung on the back of a chair, in general view and as such thought to be safe. On one occasion the thief hit the jackpot by stealing twenty pounds in one go. The situation had become serious and he had to be caught and quickly. George knew from experience that it would not be easy to catch him red-handed and obtain proof at the same time that the person caught had been solely to blame for all the thefts. There remained the distinct possibility that more than one person could be responsible for the now increasing number of thefts. During this period an unusually high number of folk left for pastures new, including about five retirements and a fair turnover of contract draughtsmen, so his theory that more than one thief could have been active during that time, retained some credence.

Employment at this time went through the period of high demand for draughting personnel. Defence contracts abounded everywhere including the ill-fated TSR project. At some time of our life, we have all complained about government expenditure, which invariably includes the vast millions spent of defence. It is a matter of opinion and conjecture whether this expenditure is justified, given the perceived threat from the Russians, thought to be the most likely adversary. One direct benefit from this expenditure is that unemployment is kept at a low level, and the economy is boosted with money in constant circulation. High employment is accompanied by relatively high spending so the whole community, including shopkeepers and local businesses benefit from defence spending, even though they do not participate directly. If the decision is made to close a local factory, the local economy suffers as a consequence. Another but less obvious benefit is that skills progress and pass from one generation to the next and as technology improves, many offshoots generally contribute to the well being of mankind. For example one offshoot from the space race between the Russians and the Americans to get a man on the moon was that a simple LED calculator became accepted and gradually replaced slide rules and in time logarithm tables in use since the Second World War. Even the LED watch owned by Daniel Tailor came as a direct result of the space race.

Other offshoots in the form of new materials and practices owe their origins to the necessities of defence. One system brought into being at this time had the unlikely name of *interchangeability*, but one, which described its function with incredible accuracy. It is not necessary to describe its complicated function except to say that the sizes of holes and slots in, for example, panels supplied by a variety of suppliers, as would occur during the time of war, guaranteed that each mating part fitted together with unlikely tolerances being applied. Defence systems can also be sold abroad, a lucrative business, which does a great deal to offset the balance of payments. There is fierce competition from manufacturers throughout the world and care has to be exercised to sell defence systems only to those countries considered to be friendly.

In 1982, Exocet missiles sold by the French to Argentina years previously almost proved catastrophic to the British Task Force in the Falklands War. This only proves how much care should be taken to avoid placing allies in embarrassing situations.

The possibility of that unlikely conflict remained in the future.

In the near vicinity of the ESR factory, many small businesses existed, mainly privately owned shops, which, to a greater or lesser degree, relied on the factory for custom. The newsagent by the bus stop sold all manner of items from newspapers and cigarettes to sweets and other sundries. The local café and the fish and chip shop always had ESR employees frequent their establishment at lunchtime. Wag Bonnets cycle shop, a bank, the Greengage public house and the Thorns Tavern all entertained ESR employees. The local café directly opposite the factory gates, run by three generations of a lively Italian family, which served an excellent variety of home cooked food, ceased trading within a few months of the main factory closing down, showing their reliance on a fairly large factory population close at hand.

During this period there was a good deal of staff turnover, which proved a stumbling block in George's private mission to identify the thief. The thefts continued from the cloakroom, with some poor souls being the loser more than once. George had mixed feelings, for had he been a victim, he would have taken preventative measures to frustrate further loss. These options went from placing a mousetrap in his coat pocket deliberately left in the cloakroom, to taking his wallet with him. This was however both unnecessary as it was inconvenient.

George established who used the cloakroom and to see if they sat anywhere near a victim who lost money taken from a coat pocket hung on a chair, a direct consequence of taking preventative measures as a result of the cloakroom thefts. The thefts from the cloakroom appeared to be random as about three quarters of cloakroom users lost money at some stage. They sat in all parts of the office, and in all probability, their location, as random as the thefts in varying amounts. Whereas thefts from coats hung on the backs of chairs were concentrated in the half of the office away from the cloakroom. There had to be some logic in this and George racked his brains over several lunchtimes attempting to find the solution.

This he knew could not be easy even before he tried. The best method was to use lateral thinking and solve it by less direct means. He first had to establish the motive of the thief to steal money from his colleagues.

Could there be any animosity or jealousy between two or more people, and the thefts purpose, to disguise a plan of revenge?

The answer most probably no. The office appeared to be stable with no obvious outsiders or extremists. Most of the office population were, like George, extreme moderates.

Was it to deprive a victim of his cash?
The answer most probably yes.
Was a victim chosen for a particular reason?
The answer most probably no.
Was a victim chosen at random?
The answer most probably yes.
Could the thief have an expensive drink problem?
The answer most probably no.

The drinking, which took place, appeared to be social and concentrated around Friday lunchtimes. It would be unusual for drinking to take place on any other day of the week except for special occasions such as a birthday or a leaving do. Despite it being a relatively large office, it was a balanced community who met socially at every opportunity, so he felt positive that if anyone had a drink problem this would have made itself apparent to someone. Someone like Bert Weaver, who was renown to be quick at noticing any unusual behaviour or habits, would have a field day, should a controversy be apparent.

Could the thief have a serious gambling problem?

As far as he knew no one showed any interest in horse racing, except for the sweepstake organised by Nan Lambert each year for the Derby and the Grand National, so that compulsive tendency could easily be eliminated.

The answer surely had to be that the person had a money problem of a relatively minor nature and felt compelled, either by greed or necessity, to obtain money by the easiest method possible. The person must be quite desperate or at least perceived his situation to be desperate, as the consequence of getting caught would be dire and ultimately end by getting the sack, and even a criminal record.

George tried to identify anyone with a money problem.

In all the years he worked there, no one ever asked him to borrow money, and trying to establish who had a money problem proved to be difficult if not impossible. The only source of open and public monetary discontent was the card school, who played solo whist each lunchtime at a penny per point. The card school comprised of four individuals who in any other circumstances would not tolerate each other.

The first member Alan Kippin, known to all as *Kipper*, a freckled faced, pipe smoking, well spoken and extremely young looking forty year old, educated at a private school, which he used to regularly boast. *Kipper* pronounced 'Year' as Yerr', and probably, to the envy of all, owned the best car of everyone, a new Sunbeam Talbot, except that is for the Rover Continental limousine owned by *Lumpy Bumps* the Chief Draughtsman. Always very smartly dressed, his only failing was on cold mornings he resorted to wearing a faded brown sweater, with severely worn elbows. The drawing office had been previously a warehouse and converted into an office with the minimum of expense and comprised a high ceiling at least thirty feet high, with an unlined roof of corrugated material, alternating with glass panels. It was always cold in winter and very hot in summer. Most folk had an old sweater to wear first thing in the morning until the office warmed. Whenever it rained, or worse hailed, the office always became very noisy to the extent that using a telephone had to be abandoned until the inclement weather had passed.

Kipper took his card playing very seriously and entertained the drawing office staff with noisy outbursts whenever one of the others misread the cards, to prevent a call being successful. He possessed a photographic memory, which allowed him to predict the hands held by each person.

The second member, John Ferguson. A dour Scot renowned for having an abrupt manner with all and sundry. He chain-smoked Capstan Full Strength cigarettes and considered himself to be an expert whist player. Judging by the intensive discussion that took place after each contentious hand, the other three often disputed this. He always wore a white shirt, brown tie and a lightweight green sweater, no matter the temperature, and neither felt the cold nor the heat. If someone commented on his unsuitable clothing, the remark always caused John to shrug his shoulders without further comment. John had a bad habit, inasmuch he would stand whilst smoking and study a particular person for several minutes. George often caught him staring in the general direction of the female tracers who wore short skirts in keeping with the fashion of the time and inadvertently exposed acres of leg encased in stockings. Even George had noticed this. Although not inclined to participate in blatant lechery, he had noticed one particular well endowed tracer, allowed her short skirt to ride up and expose white leg flesh above silk black stockings.

Then came Richard Dickinson, a well liked section leader known to all as Dick, quietly spoken but otherwise a determined man, whose hands shook incessantly. He used to spill his tea every day and spent more time clearing up than actually drinking the refreshment! He claimed to own a one hundred and seventy six thousandth share of the George Cross awarded to the Island of Malta during the Second World War. In the Thorns Tavern pub for a leaving do, George found he was sitting next to Dick and took the opportunity to ask him why his hands shook so much.

The answer came as a surprise.

In 1942, Dick had been in the RAF in charge of an anti aircraft gun crew manning the air defences of Luqa

Airfield. The airfield came under daily attack from the Germans and the Italians intent on bringing the gallant Island to its knees. In April that year the attacks became heavy, to the extent that the raiders, who usually attacked in waves, blended into one so as to the make the bombing appear to be continuous. One day Dick who had not slept for nearly twenty four hours, due to the persistent air raids, came off duty and retired to his billet where he fell into a deep sleep despite the air raids continuing. Even when the billet received a direct hit did not wake him and he was rescued from the rubble still in a deep sleep. Once he realised what he had survived it made him feel decidedly uneasy about his lot. Later that same afternoon he went back on duty and before he could reach his post, he was forced to crouch in a trench next to an anti aircraft battery on the perimeter, whilst another wave of Stukas bombed the airfield. He looked up and directly above saw to his horror a Stuka almost in a vertical position, commencing its bombing run. Transfixed, he watched as the screaming Stuka came incredibly low and dropped its deadly bomb. Dick saw the bomb head towards him, powerless except to watch.

He prepared to die.

The trench in which he crouched became subjected to a direct hit and for the second time within six hours had to be dragged from a ruin completely unharmed. The body can only take so much punishment and for Dick this proved to be his breaking point. His hands started to shake the following day and had shaken ever since.

*

With the experience of typing a few thousand words, Georges typing accuracy improved. His fingers often ached from the exercise and if he sat for too long, hunched over the keyboard, his back chose the period of inactivity to take revenge and kept him awake at night.

*

Last, but by no means least of the quartet, George Spicer, one of the senior section leaders, known to all as *Nutmeg*, despite his disapproval of the nickname. *Nutmeg* considered himself to be a cut above everyone and strutted around in a fashion reminiscent of The Little Boy. Even his brand of cigarette named *Passing Cloud* enjoyed a certain reputation of superiority, for they were oval shaped.

Nutmeg always smartly dressed, wore a blue blazer and light blue trousers, and sported highly polished black shoes. The heels of these shoes were capped with metal inserts called *blakeys* and *Nutmeg* tapped round the drawing office, to the annoyance of everyone.

The card school assembled every lunchtime at the desk of Dick, commencing at one o'clock sharp to play with intense enthusiasm, becoming annoyed if any one of their number were late or played foolishly. Every point, worth a mere single penny, became fiercely fought over and it always became an animated occasion. *Kipper* was nominated treasurer and kept account of the days play. His accounting system, whatever that consisted of, always disputed and noisily discussed. Annual leave and sickness presented the remaining three with a problem, for a substitute had to be found if they were to continue their daily ritual. Some poor soul roped in temporarily, immediately came under scrutiny if he did not play properly. George recalled one such occasion when a poor soul, another section clerk, came under such pressure and threats because he did not play in accordance with the unwritten rules of the card school, he abandoned his attempt to try and play with the trio within five minutes! Occasionally a suitable substitute could not be found so one member played with two hands which always ended up with an argument. Those trying to read or relax sometimes complained about the noise with a predictable reaction from the quartet.

Every few weeks, usually on the last Friday of the month, *Kipper* totalled up the scores and there followed a farce as each man tried to recoup his winnings and to check whether the others had paid their dues in full. George noticed that John Ferguson, the dour Scot, paid with reluctance and on more than one occasion claimed not to have any money and promised to pay the following week. George knew that more than once he had to be pressured to hand over his money, as he had still not paid up by the end of the following month.

He once overheard *Kipper* and Ferguson talking as they passed by his board.

'When are you going to pay up, then?' *Kipper* demanded. 'It's only fifteen and six!'

'When I have some cash!' Came an abrupt reply. 'I do have more important debts to pay as well!'

Money was stolen that afternoon and George saw Ferguson paying money to *Kipper* the following morning.

As the monthly card school bill came to a pound or two maximum, this did seem to be adequate justification for stealing from colleagues. For a couple of lunchtimes and at odd moments, he concentrated on this John Ferguson, to see if there could be some relevance or connection between his apparent card school money problems and the thefts. For weeks he failed to come to any positive conclusions. In the end he went through the drawing office personnel determined to get a short list of subjects. Within a few minutes of starting on this project George hit his first problem.

His first subject was Eddie Locke, a passionate though eccentric Section Leader with an unusual mop of jet black hair, who definitely had no vices and George spent a few milli-seconds with his morals under a mental microscope. His second subject was an unmarried female tracer named Carol, so named as her birthday fell on Christmas Day. She too was showed signs of eccentricity, for instance, by always sitting frowning with her chin supported by an upturned palm. This habit must have been going on for years to the extent that her front teeth were not straight but inclined inwards. Ultimately she fell under the same category of Eddie Locke, so she too became quickly eliminated.

To serve as an example of his difficult task, he considered the circumstances of his third subject and his dilemma in trying to identify the thief will be understood, bearing in mind that he still had to vet another sixty potential suspects. His third subject went by the name of Basil Morley, a tall quietly spoken bachelor known as *Bas*. He towered above those already over six feet tall, including George. His desk, right outside to the office of *Child by name* made him prone to interruption by many visitors to the office, all enquiring about the whereabouts of the assistant Chief Draughtsman. *Bas* enjoyed a hobby of radio controlled model aeroplanes and most weekends, especially during fine weather, could be seen on Wanstead Flats, once part of Epping Forest, now a haven of open space in the east end of London, flying one of his collection of models. He once related to George the tale of a model Lancaster Bomber he made whilst on National Service with the Royal Air Force, stationed on Malta in the 1950's. He made this accurate model and experimented with radio control for the first time. He made several flights in private but eventually swayed by pressure from his peers gave in, so came the time when he made a public display for the first time. It took place at T Quale airfield on the south of the Island, and unfortunately timed at six o'clock in the evening and coincided with Radio Libya commencing its evening broadcast. To a delighted audience the Lancaster Bomber taxied into position and went down the runway and made a perfect take off. Once airborne, with sufficient height, *Bas* guided his model through a series of gentle manoeuvres until precisely at six o'clock the Lancaster bomber acted strangely by refusing to comply with his electronic instructions and headed south. No matter how he frantically fiddled the controls, his aircraft headed south and eventually disappeared from sight, despite a frantic search for faults to the control panel. He discovered later that his model aircraft operated on a similar frequency to Radio Libya and became influenced by a more powerful signal.

Bas invested in Premium bonds and it seemed like every month, when Audrey, a very pleasant tea lady, always with a cheery word and a pleasant smile, brought the tea trolley around in the afternoon selling cakes, often took some pleasure in telling everyone some good news.

'This afternoon.' She announced in a raised voice to all and sundry. 'The cakes are on Bas!'

The first few occasions this happened, it was greeted with much enthusiasm and delight, for every draughtsman, draughtswoman and tracer enjoy free cakes. As the months passed by and free cakes became a regular occurrence, the news was greeted by moans or groans for it meant *Bas* had won some money again. For those folk with premium bonds and who were persistent non-winners, it appeared that *Bas* enjoyed a charmed life, with his collection of bond numbers clearly etched in the memory of ERNIE, the computer who allegedly chose the winning numbers at random. One afternoon Audrey greeted everyone with the news that the cakes were on *Bas* again. The following morning *Bas* arrived at work in a two year old Chevrolet Impala. This magnificent monstrosity had a 5 litre V8 engine, air conditioning, electric seats, electric windows, acres of shiny paint and chrome bumpers, all features in keeping with a luxury limousine! With such impeccable credentials, it is not too difficult to appreciate why *Bas* had to be quickly eliminated from his trawl.

George continued through the office a person at a time, being both positive and negative about personalities, suspicions or assumptions he made about a particular person. It is not too difficult to reason why it took about a week to complete this task, to end up with the single name of John Ferguson. His reasons were to say the least spurious and not founded on fact apart from common knowledge that he usually failed to pay his card school bill on time. This is not sufficient reason to suggest John Ferguson was the thief, but his was the only name on a short list of one.

Child by name wandered by one lunchtime. 'Who do you reckon the thief is, George?' He asked in a casual manner, leaning on George's desk.

Adrian Child, to give his proper name, was nicknamed *Child by name, child by nature,* shortened to *Child by name* by many staff who fell foul of his unpredictable tantrums, whenever someone upset him.

*

George had been so deep in thought, he failed to observe him approach. By coincidence he had finally reached the end of his trawl with only the two Ronnies left, namely Ron Waud and Ron Clifton. Both men were very popular and worked on the dunking sonar project, which George worked on for while when work for the Sentinel Project modification contract temporarily dried up. Neither fell into his category of even a near suspect, so he had almost disregarded them. Thinking of Ron Clifton's involvement with the Japanese during the Second World War distracted him from his task. Ron served in the Royal Marines, on a Royal Navy Aircraft Carrier, which island hopped with the Americans and assisted clearing the Japanese from the island yard by yard. He once mentioned that on the first island, which had been shelled continually for several days from the sea, he disembarked from the landing craft with his squad of Marines, in virtually complete silence, fully expecting all the Japanese to be dead. As they ran up the deserted beach, to their surprise a small group of Japanese soldiers started firing at them from the scorched remains of a palm forest. The whole assault group returned fire and killed them all, to find others, quickly replaced those Japanese killed. A deadly fire fight ensued with the Japanese losing many men. Finally some decided to surrender and came out with their hands up, whereupon the Americans in their group immediately opened fire, killing them all, despite the fact that they were clearly unarmed. Ron and some others protested at the inhuman behaviour, only to be told that once they reached the interior of the island and saw what they did to the natives, especially the women before they were murdered, they would not complain again. Ron and Co were not impressed and continued to complain and express their distaste.

A few days later after fierce fighting they reached the burnt out remains of a native village and saw naked native women staked out in the sun, tied to wooden stakes by rope, tied so tightly that it cut into the skin. Most showed signs of being sexually assaulted and some had body parts removed or dismembered. Other bodies had their sexual organs mutilated before being covered with honey, which attracted a particular species of aggressive soldier ant with obvious horrific consequences. The Americans were correct. All Japanese soldiers from that time were shot dead by Ron and Co, no matter the circumstances of their surrender, and until the bombs were dropped on Hiroshima and Nagasaki which heralded the end of the war, did not see a live Japanese soldier except just before they were shot.

Ron felt incensed that the fact that British aircraft carriers operated with the Americans in clearing the islands to ultimate victory was not commonly known, nor was the fact that the American carriers were of inferior design to their British counterparts. The Americans lost so many carriers, solely due to their flight decks being made of wood, whereas the British carriers were metal and did not burn so easily.

*

George came back to reality.

'I am not prepared to say.' He answered truthfully, trying to sound evasive. The question put him on his guard, as he could not possibly name the suspect without some sort of proof. 'I do not have...'

'If you have a name, you must tell me who it is.' He insisted.

'No, I do not have to tell you anything.' George answered simply. 'I have a suspicion only, no proof. When I do have proof, you will be one of the first to know.'

213

'You're not going to tell me, then?'

'At this precise moment in time, most certainly not.' George replied firmly.

To his surprise *Child by name* wandered off, not wishing to persist with his questioning. George received another visitor within a minute. This time it was Doug Watson the Union representative.

'Hello Doug.' He greeted. 'What brings you over this side of the office?'

It was a known fact that Doug did not approve of anyone who was not a member of the Union, with the inappropriate name of TASS, abbreviation for Technical and Supervisory Staff. There seemed to be some irony naming a trades union with the same name as a Russian news agency. It so happened the handful of non union members were accidentally concentrated over this side of the office.

Doug grinned, and looked at George over badly fitting glasses in dire need of a clean. 'I noticed Child by name was here. Was he by chance asking you to name the thief?'

He looked at Doug with some suspicion. For no apparent reason he had been one of his suspects for a while. 'Why do you ask that?' He wondered.

'I think I know who the thief is!' He said in a whisper, peering round in case anyone had overheard.

'So do I!' George boasted. He now paid full attention, as there could be some small detail he had overlooked.

'Tell me your name?' Doug whispered in such a loud voice, George looked around to see if anyone had heard. All those within view sat reading or eating and had not looked up.

'No.' George replied, with some relief.

'Why ever not?'

'I shall say the same to you as I have just told Child by name.' He said. 'I have a suspicion only, but absolutely no proof.'

Doug considered the answer, for a moment. He blinked several times before giving a reply.

'Fair enough, But what if we write down initials on separate papers then swap papers.' He suggested. 'There could be no harm in us doing that, could there?'

It was then George's turn to consider his response. A name was one thing, but initials were of no consequence, for they meant little on their own. If for instance a paper with two letters written on, happened to be found in a wastepaper basket, they could be no repercussions, no matter who discovered it. George quickly made up his mind.

'I agree.' He replied and sought paper, which he tore in half and handed one to Doug. George wrote 'JF' on his piece and when Doug had written on his piece, they swapped papers. George glanced down and was absolutely amazed when he read 'JF' on the paper handed to him. By this time Doug had read his paper and seen the same initials.

Doug looked up and positively beamed. 'Marvellous!' He said with a grin so large, it nearly cut his face in half. 'What do we do now?'

'All we can do is to keep this quiet and watch him.'

'That's it?' Doug stared with disbelief.

'Do you have any actual proof to justify those two letters you have just written down?' George demanded, speaking quietly, trying to make the conversation appear casual, in case were being watched. He glanced up and saw to his horror John Ferguson, seated nearby, and probably by coincidence, looking in their direction.

'Well, actually no...'

215

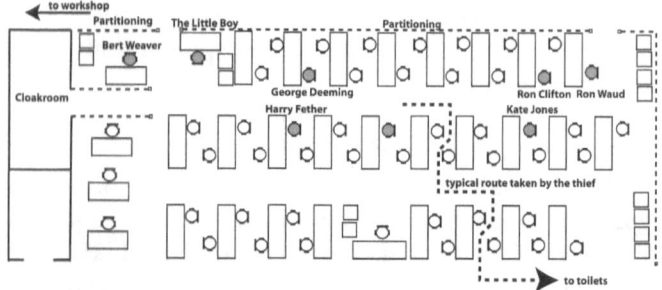

Drawing Office layout (the author)

Included to show a typical route taken by the thief to remove wallets from jackets on the backs of swivel chairs. There were variations depending on his target.

The method: Wallet taken on the way out to the toilets and replaced on the way back.

'You have your answer then.' He replied firmly. 'Until we have actual proof, we must keep quiet. And I mean quiet. This must not be mentioned to anyone.'

Doug stared at him, mentally questioning his wisdom.

'Believe me Doug, we have no choice.'

With a resigned shrug of the shoulders, Doug wandered back over the invisible divide line and returned to his desk. In a way George felt sorry for him. A single man who lived with his mum, George detected a trace of anticipated excitement, a chance for Doug to escape the routine of boredom, which surely encompassed his life.

There were five single people of full age in the drawing office, three men and two women. All shared a common denominator. When George spoke to them, about work or trivial matters they seemed to come alive throughout the time he was in their company. At all other times they withdrew inside an invisible shell to block the outside world out, to sit silent and motionless, never appearing to be happy. The familiarity was uncanny. In a moment of foolishness, George thought of suggesting they all shared a house together, surely this would induce a feeling of great happiness?

Meanwhile the thefts continued from within the drawing office with no apparent pattern. It was as if the thief had abandoned taking money from the male cloakroom in favour of easier pickings. During the day, at odd moments, George pondered over the identity of the thief and the method by which he could, in full view, extract money from wallets, without being observed.

In full view? This was the problem and he would have to unravel the method of thieving in the open, even before he set about identifying the thief.

This was a difficult puzzle to resolve. All the thefts from within the drawing office took place in approximately half of the office only, the half nearest the cloakroom. This did not make sense. Where is the logic of pattern in this? Could it be that the men in the part nearest the cloakroom were more careful? A quick scan of the office whilst undertaking his duties, revealed there appeared to be no obvious difference in either half, but a difference surely existed by the success of the thief. George racked his brains, often giving himself a headache for his trouble.

In full view?

George altered his tack for a change to thrash out a solution, which surely must be staring him in the face. How could the thief, in full view, extract money from wallets, without being observed? Short of being a magician, the skill required to perform such a trick seems beyond comprehension. He resorted to creating a scale drawing of the office and marking on the theft sites, hoping the solution would slap him in the face.

It did not.

The Little Boy even caught him studying his plan during work time, but he realised at once what George was doing and walked away without comment. However it could be described, attempting to trace a thief was definitely not skiving and he knew it!

The thief reached an all time low when one of the youngest drawing office staff, Tom Ribbitts, gained his majority. The drawing office clubbed together and bought him a leather briefcase and also presented him with a card and £30, then a considerable sum of money. This money he left in his coat pocket on the back of his chair. It is worth pointing out that his desk was across the aisle, from John Ferguson and within the half where all the thefts had taken place. After lunch Tom received a summons from the Apprentice Officer in the front office to collect his indentures. When he returned, happy and smiling with his precious indentures, he discovered his wallet on the floor beside the chair, with the money gone. Tom was heartbroken and George seriously considered doing Ferguson some harm after work. Only common sense prevented him from doing a violent act, which later he may regret. *Child by name* called George into his office and with the door closed, placed him under a great deal of pressure to tell him the name, but without proof George was not prepared to reveal the name of his suspect.

'I shall make it known to some of the victims that you have a name.' He threatened. 'They won't be pleased to hear about you.'

'Do what you will, Adrian, but I will not give a name until I have proof.' George replied, knowing full well that he had no intention of carrying out this threat.

He eventually gave up and allowed George to return to his desk.

John Ferguson, now under constant surveillance by Doug and George, did not appear at any time to put a foot wrong. If he did prove to be the thief, his actions did not give him away. George began to have doubts and undertook a trawl of the office again but ended up with the same suspicion. Doug wandered over from time to time across the line at lunchtime whenever the office was quiet, but ultimately the thief, whoever he was, still held the upper hand. For the moment at least.

George even considered the thief to be female and as a side issue justifying the earlier thefts from the cloakroom to have been carried out by someone no longer working at ESR, but studying the women revealed the grand total of absolute zero. Apart from the fact a couple of the tracers had adorable shapely bodies, especially bosoms, which he studied as often as possible, whenever they gave him opportunity, none gave rise to suspicion.

In full view?

One lunchtime whilst listening to the card school discussing a bad call from one of their number, George carefully studied his scale drawing, hoping to be distracted away from the noisy debate. There were six lines of desks in groups of two, each separated by an aisle, and for the first time, he noticed that in the half where thefts occurred, only one had taken place in the row where John Ferguson sat on the side row. Access was not possible because of the half partition separating the office from the print and filing room. Moreover, no thefts had taken place in a point forward from John Fergusons position. He had made some progress without fully appreciating its significance.

For John Ferguson to be the thief, he had to do a magician's trick either on the way from his desk or on the way back.

The only trouble, how?

In full view?

George eventually discovered the method used by the thief by accident, after yet another office change round. These occurred every few months at random for no apparent reason, other than one Section Leader or another thought he could improve the working of his section by dabbling in a simple but necessary reorganisation of his group. In the past there had been some horrendous complicated moves, which caused chaos until everyone became used to the new set-up, or as in one case, the office resumed to its original layout a few weeks later. Invariably someone forgot about the telephone reconnections or the precise location of existing connections in the floor, which made it either impossible for the move to take place as planned, or it made it extremely complicated for Fred Green to get the telephone connections up and running without undue delay.

On this occasion the Sentinel project section were unaffected, but leading up to move day, those around George complained incessantly about the inconvenience and how so and so was getting a better position, and so on! The move of two particular men was the direct cause of George successfully identifying the thief. The two people were John Ferguson and Bert Frost.

Bert was a strange individual, whose facial skin must have in the distant past been affected by spots or boils, or similar. His face was badly pocked marked which gave him an almost hostile appearance, although this initial reaction was not totally justified. He wore heavy black framed glasses with over large lenses and these unfortunately enlarged parts of his pocked face, make him look quite hostile. Shortly after his arrival at ESR, George sat next to a lively character, who went by the name of Les Dale, unfortunately no longer with us, as he died after a massive heart attack a few years ago. John observed the strange habits of Bert Frost and George heard him laughing a couple of times without noting the cause. One morning he heard Les gasp, then laugh making a comment under his breath. 'What a silly stupid bastard!'

'What's up Les?' George asked, not having the faintest idea of the reason for this outburst.

'Look at that silly buggar over there!' Les replied nodding his head in the general direction of the far side of the drawing office. George glanced over but detected nothing obvious.

'Where?' He asked in desperation.

'Look at Bert Frost!'

His eyes were drawn to Bert instantly, since the move now sitting at a desk one position down and across the aisle from John Ferguson. He adopted a strange and most probably uncomfortable pose, by sitting in his chair whilst bending down to grasp the neck of his thermos flask, down on the floor by his feet. Inclined to corpulence, the strain on his stomach whilst sitting in this position, must have been unbearable and quite beyond George's comprehension. Bert was one of the few souls who boycotted the tea trolley in favour of bringing in their own assortment of refreshments. He maintained this strange unnatural position whilst subjecting the unfortunate thermos flask to subtle public masturbation for several minutes, before going into another ritual of placing his palm over the top of the thermos. After giving the thermos manual pleasure, this was to presumably to prevent violent ejaculation, which normally follows a series of stroking hand movements around a rampant object. Bert then alternately tapped the thermos flask top and the desk, inches away, with two fingers in silent rhythmic accompaniment. He moved his hand at a furious speed, resembling a frustrated drummer trying to maintain a tempo kept up by a manic, but unseen and unheard musician, for another few minutes until the Gods were appeased. He then used both hands on his reference table, which creaked under the strain, to haul his large frame upwards and resume a normal sitting position, now with the flask resting on his knee. You could almost hear his compressed stomach, now eased of restriction, give out a great sigh of relief! He went through another strict routine of unscrewing the top, with exaggerated twisting hand movements as if a male dancer performing the tango, or some other equally exotic dance routine. Eventually the top came off and he proceeded pouring out the steaming liquid. Even this simple act could not be undertaken without flourish and repetitive movement. Beside George, virtually silent hysterics overtook Les, to the extent that his whole body shook. Slightly unfair, mocking the afflicted, as anyone could be subjected to trauma, be knocked over the edge and into a whirlpool from which escape required expert help. Surely Bert Frost must be mentally ill to have compulsion to undertake this ritual every day? George failed to appreciate how this routine went generally unnoticed, and for over the coming weeks witnessed the same routine time after time. On one occasion Bert was well into his cycle of offering masturbation to the flask, when George Spicer walked over and spoke to him. Bert remained in a slumped position still grasping the flask and straining his neck to look upwards, spoke to George without interruption to his appeasement of the Gods. From where he stood, slightly stooping in order to speak to Bert, whose head was three feet nearer the floor, *Nutmeg* was unable to see what Bert was doing under the desk. Either way he eventually walked away without suspicion of the suspect sexual activity taking place in work time.

Les continued to shake with laughter.

Eventually Bert managed to pour out the tea and sat actually drinking quietly. With normality resumed, George thought the ritual complete, but he was wrong, very very wrong.

He went back to his work, disturbed five minutes later by a gentle tap on the arm.

'You've seen nothing yet, young Deeming.' Les said with an evil grin appearing on his face. 'You watch this fiasco.'

George glanced towards Bert's desk and found it unoccupied. Where had he gone? He turned his head quickly to look down the office and watched as Bert sauntered along, reaching out touching each desk with a hand as he passed by. Beside him, Les resorted to fits of silent laughter again.

'The best is yet to come.' He assured. 'You watch this!'

After seeing the performance a few moments ago, George wondered what could possibly happen next. As if on cue, Bert suddenly veered right to cut across two vacant rows, an aisle and another vacant row, to emerge in the aisle immediately before the office of *Lumpy Bumps*.

'Frooooooooooooooooooooost! Wait for it! Wait for it!' Les whispered excitedly then paused before saying in an army voice, where the first syllable is five notes higher than the second. 'Frost!   Frost! Scraaaaaaaaaaaaaaaaaaaaaatch elbow!'

As he walked past the door of *Lumpy Bumps*, Bert, right on cue scratched his right elbow with some enthusiasm. He walked onwards, still tapping the office partition on one side and the desks on the other, towards the next office, that of *Child by name*.

'Frooooooooooooooooooost! Wait for it! Wait for it!' Les repeated. 'Frost! Scraaaaaaaaaaaaaaaaatch elbow!'

With great precision without hesitation or breaking step, Bert scratched the elbow on his left hand side. As George stood with mouth agape Bert walked through the door enroute to the toilet.

'There will be a repeat performance on the way back from the toilet.' Les informed George, still with signs of the evil grin lingering on his face. 'It's the same every bloody time.'

George missed the return journey, but the following morning he watched an identical re-run of the thermos masturbation session. Five minutes later Bert went to the toilet but on this occasion was unable to cut across for all desks were occupied, but when he returned he cut across without hesitation. He must have been a mite careless for he managed to knock a coat hung on the back of a chair, as he passed by. The coat owner, Rex Willcox, stood nearby speaking to Ron Waud, witnessed his coat falling to the floor. 'Watch it Bert!' He exclaimed in a raised voice.

Bert stopped dead at hearing his name spoken and turned to face the speaker.

'What?' He demanded with innocence, sounding most indignant, for he clearly had no idea of the cause of the accusation.

'You knocked my new coat onto the floor, you clumsy idiot!' Rex said angrily. 'I hope you're going to pick it up and place it back where it was!'

Bert moved back immediately, when he saw the coat lying on the floor.

'Sorry Rex.' He mumbled as he bent down with obvious difficulty, and then placed the coat back on the chair, followed by a gentle pat on the shoulder pads, before resuming his way back to his desk. Rex, not renown for his sense of humour, stood and glared at the retreating back.

Later during the day George was returning from a visit to the toilet and saw Bert heading towards him, still tapping desks in time to unheard music and scratching his elbows at precisely the correct moment as if obeying the command of Les.

'Frost! Wait for it! Wait for it!' He thought followed by a pause, to say on cue. 'Frost! Scraaaaaaaaaaaaaaaaaaaaaaaatch elbow!'

Someone called George's name. It was Ron Waud. Without thinking he turned and cut across two desks to the middle aisle then repeated crossing two additional desks until he reached him. To achieve this he had walked through four spaces usually occupied by four draughtsmen. The manoeuvre past the swivelled chairs involved a gentle push to get the chair to one side, combined with turning the swivel chair through 180 degrees to aid passage. All chairs were unoccupied as their owners, complete with jackets were out and about somewhere. Had they been nearby but not sitting at their desk, a coat and potential wallet would have been hanging on the back of the chair. It would be easy to pass by once and remove the wallet without observation as the chair was turned, withdraw the wallet, take the one pound note out within the privacy of the toilet and place the wallet back in situ on the return journey. In those few seconds George had become a magician with instant membership of the magic circle!

8

Obscene calls

Sitting in the draughty hospital corridor next to his brother on an uncomfortable rigid black plastic seat, one of those that are joined together in a line of four, George watched his father standing by a window some distance away. Two or three stones overweight dressed in a light green sport jacket, and mid brown coloured trousers and the infuriating scruffy dark green tight fitting sweater he always wore. In keeping with his shabby appearance he wore cheap unpolished mock leather casual shoes. This description may seem unkind, but then Dad only had money for a single purpose and clothes did not even come close. He chose to describe his purchases as *railway ephemera*. Mum always described them in a derogatory fashion. 'His old iron.' This sentence accompanied by a rising of eyebrows.

Dad passed the time by gazing down at the activity in the car park three floors below. He looked no different to normal, and leant with his elbows on the window sill, without a care in the world, outwardly totally unaffected by the traumatic events of the previous evening. Provided he could admire his precious stamp collection and his vast assortment of Great Western Railway memorabilia, both of which constantly preoccupied his mind during his waking hours since his retirement ten years ago, Dad appeared to be thoroughly content. Whenever George visited him, Dad talked incessantly about Penny blacks and plate thirty three, Penny reds, and plate seventy something, halfpenny sidebands, seven foot gauge, and Gauge One Locomotives. At the slightest prompting,

226

especially with a captive audience, Dad spoke of his God, Isambard Kingdom Brunel, the acclaimed Victorian engineer, in loving terms. Builder of the Great Western railway known throughout the world as G.W.R. or by enthusiasts as *Gods Wonderful Railway*, Brunel could command Dad's loyal admiration 120 years after his death. Because of Dad's constant rambling about the subject, George knew a great deal about Brunel who sustained a serious injury whilst helping his father build a railway tunnel under the River Thames at Wapping. During his subsequent recuperation at Bristol, he heard about a project to design a suspension bridge over the River Avon at Clifton. Brunel entered and then won the competition. Dad often said that he was not in the least surprised by this, as he considered Brunel to be a genius, and as such, a worthy prize winner. This award acted as a springboard for Brunel's career although the magnificent bridge was not completed within his lifetime. This is where Brunel and Dad share the only thing they have in common. Throughout his life, Dad started several projects, building a workshop complete with lathe and other engineering machinery, restoration of a live steam locomotive, naturally one of the famous GWR and of course gauge one and to design and enter a frame display in the Thematic Class at Stampex. None of these pipe dreams were completed during his lifetime.

Indeed after he passed away a year later, his stamps were in disarray and not worthy of being sold in proportion to their original purchase cost and the locomotives were in the main incomplete or broken.

During the half an hour car journey to the hospital, Dad casually mentioned that he intended to go to a local stamp fair at Folkestone the following Saturday, no matter what! George found this attitude astonishing, given the likelihood of burying Mum on Friday that is provided they were able to obtain a death certificate this morning and the undertaker had room in his diary. The presumption by George about his Dads mental state as he stood gazing out of the window at the activity below, was most likely accurate, for he usually cared only about himself. By way of confirmation, Dads snoring during the night suggested he was neither unduly concerned nor troubled.

By contrast George felt exhausted and so tired, he could barely keep his eyes open. He had hardly slept a wink, and spent the whole night tossing and turning, his brain refusing to comply with his desire to sleep. It churned away repeating the same angry and frustrating thoughts time and time again, and there was little George could do to divert it from the cycle.

Who was in charge of a body, the person or the brain?

If it's the person why doesn't the brain do as it's told?

If it's the brain it should know when the body is in dire need of sleep.

Perhaps they were one and the same.

Whatever.

Last night his brain won a decisive victory and George now had two good reasons to feel thoroughly miserable.

Mum had passed away peacefully at around eleven o'clock the night before, having over-achieved her three score years and ten, by four months. Now after his restless night's pretence for sleep George was back at the hospital before eight o'clock. The three men waited for the Registrar's Office to open, so they could collect Mums few personal possessions together with a death certificate. George sat with fingers crossed hoping that the doctor had remembered to sign it, given it was late on a Sunday evening when Mum passed away. With that single essential document in their possession, they would be able to proceed with the formalities of probate. At least they were unlikely to undergo the ordeal of an inquest, for her death was hardly unexpected. Mum had collapsed on Thursday lunchtime showing signs of having suffered a massive stroke and died three days later.

A long corridor, a nearly a quarter of a mile long, ran the entire length of the hospital. Even at this early hour, people strolled by in endless stream, mainly in silence, each with a similar expression on their face. It was a look of concern combined with worry, perhaps with the prospect of spending a long stressful day at the bedside of a loved one, or undertaking a variety of tests or examinations. In any event some aspects of the coming day for these folk was likely to be traumatic, some more, some less. The stream came from all walks of life and of all ages, although George noticed one or two children, he noted the majority were over fifty. Amongst the stream of bodies still wearing thick coats, for it was bitterly cold outside, a woman strolled alone, unhurried and without an apparent care in the world. She was typical of a number of hospital employees who are regularly seen wandering along hospital corridors, holding a file or a wad of papers. Their walking has neither apparent purpose nor a common denominator. In every hospital throughout the land, streams of similar workers wander slowly around throughout the hours of daylight. They are rarely seen at night or at weekends. The reasons for this phenomenon are unclear, and you must draw your own conclusions. She was smartly dressed in a red skirt and black wool sweater decorated with an offset multi coloured motif in what appeared to be silver coloured thread, embroidered in the shape of a star. Clutched close to her chest was the inevitable brown folder. She had short, dark brown, neatly combed hair and blinked in a constant and an exaggerated fashion, sure signs of the latest optical fashion accessory -contact lenses. Seen momentarily through the crowd of people, her face somehow seemed vaguely familiar, but George was unable to ascertain whether or not he knew her. Almost upon him now, he scanned his memory banks, positive she was someone he had known in the past, but unable stir his brain into action, to identify the who, the where, the when.

There was a sudden gap in the passing horde and in these lasting seconds George suddenly recognised the face, but still could not recall the name.

For no apparent reason he found himself transported back in time to a stressful period about five years earlier. It was just after the Daniel Tailor incident, recently successful in his undertaking to sue the police for wrongful arrest. Daniel was now the recipient of a considerable sum of money, but everyone at the factory was on edge wondering whether the MoD would continue with the contract or place it elsewhere. The stakes were relatively high and the livelihood of many workers depended entirely on this decision. Senior management at ESR felt obliged, given the high security essential for a top secret project, to keep the MoD fully informed of events and high powered meetings were known to have taken place. Although he refused to reveal what took place, Daniel admitted in a moment of weakness that he had been interviewed at some length during these managerial meetings. The whole factory was buzzing with rumour and counter rumour. Very few people knew the facts and tongues were wagging furiously for no useful purpose. What was known as a fact, was that if the MoD considered that the project had been compromised by the unfortunate incident, the contract would be withdrawn immediately and employment at the factory placed at risk. It could even mean the closure of the factory with disastrous consequence for everyone. Alternatively they could simply request that Daniel Tailor was removed from the project. From past experience George knew that change could happen quickly and without warning.

*

Before he became a full time employee at ESR, he worked there on contract for a few months, as part of a section whose sole purpose was to decide what raw materials or spares were to be held at the main base at Faslane and on Depot ships. The whole group, from the section leader Richard Dickinson, to four men and a woman, took their work seriously. Several times each week there were discussions, often quite heated and argumentative on likely failures rates and for example, whether rubber components could be turned using a lathe from raw material. It was a laborious project with the section inspecting every component drawing, and then adding the material to an ever increasing list. Consideration was given to whether a major part could be repaired at sea, or only replaced at a Naval Base, with some lively discussions taking place on what seemed practical or otherwise. This process went on for months making good progress until one morning, the end of the task could be seen. True it was still months away but a good part of the work had been completed. The parts list consisted of two large red leather bound volumes officially titled Electro-Engineering Spares Schedule but nicknamed E^2S^2 or E squared, S squared, that enjoyed the reputation of being the Sentinel Bible, a constant source of reference to anyone closely

231

associated with the project. The section quickly dispelled this myth by finding endless inaccuracies on a regular basis, to the extent that a reprint was now thought to be necessary. One morning, without notice, Dick, the section leader received a summons from *Lumpy Bumps* and spent half an hour in his office. When he returned he looked stern faced.

'The contract has ceased.' He announced. 'Start packing up.'

The work ceased immediately and they spent the rest of the day, collecting their files and associated paperwork, which was then placed in heavy wooden packing cases to be dispatched to the MoD and the section disbanded. All in the space of an hour! None of them established the reasons to end this project.

Being on contract George was spared the worry shared by the section. It was of little consequence to him whether the Sentinel contract continued or not. If it did, fine. He would get a Christmas bonus, if it did not, his bonus would evaporate and he would go back to base for a paid holiday until the next placement came along. A placement could last for a few days as holiday cover or sickness cover up to a few months. From one day to the next he could not predict what the future held, for that is the routine of contract draughting. In the two years he worked as a contract draughtsman George was sent to all manner of offices throughout the Home Counties, from an engineering company with offices in Crown Street, Reading, to a the office of a petrol-chemical engineering company with their main office in a spectacular high rise office block on Millbank in Westminster, and by coincidence another engineering company in Crown Street, off Chiswick High Street, to Prittlewell, near to Southend-on-Sea, the HQ of a contract draughting company.

*

The Head Office in Prittlewell stood in the High Street of the small but stylish town centre within a four storey building with the grand name of Cavendish Chambers and a grand entrance off the main road The ground floor was occupied by a gentlemen's outfitters with a name, in keeping with the exclusive surroundings, of Cecil Tailoring. A solicitors suite occupied the first floor and the contract office was on the second floor, the side windows overlooking a dress shop, in particular the changing rooms at the back of the premises. Some staff took delight in standing on a table in order to see over the cubicle screens to view women in underwear.

During a previous time back at base, he lazed around most days drinking coffee and playing darts with other draughtsmen and Charlie Garner, manager of the Contract Draughting Office, until a telephone call resulted in one of the dart playing fraternity going away for an unspecified period. Charlie Garner was another one of his former colleagues whose mould had been broken at birth. Charlie was, by his own admission, a man with a roaming eye for the ladies. From some of the women George had seen in his company, for he was not shy in bringing his women to stay overnight in the office, he had an exceptional eye and was probably the reason he could play darts so well. His long suffering wife tolerated his many affairs but eventually even she found some aspect of his behaviour beyond common decency and kicked him out. It was quite a traumatic event apparently with the police being called to the family home in order to keep the peace. Not in the least put out by his sudden change of fortune, Charlie moved his clothes and scant possessions into the office and resorted to sleeping on a put-you-up bed in a small unused office upstairs. Being his own man, he naturally failed to keep the affairs of

233

his former household in order and amongst other items, forgot to keep up with his mortgage payments, and then refused to give his wife an allowance for their three children. Eventually bailiffs threatened to take possession of the house and his agitated wife subjected the office to several visits. Whilst Charlie hid himself away upstairs, those unfortunate to be in the office at the time, did their best to be pleasant, and to get rid of her without revealing the whereabouts of Charlie. When everything was said and done, she was still the wife of the boss. If only half the things she claimed were true, living with Charlie must have been extremely arduous and difficult. One Friday afternoon, they were recently back from the pub and enjoying a novel darts game, which follows the scoring of ten pin bowling, where a score of ten represents a single pin. To claim a strike a player must score over one hundred. There was a sudden knock at the door, now kept locked, with the chain on since the demise of Charlie's marriage. With an uncharacteristic sudden loss of memory, Charlie opened the door himself to be confronted, not by his wife as they all fully expected, but by a well dressed man, holding what appeared to be a summons.

'Mister Charles Garner, my good man please. I am here on County Court matters.' The man announced in clear tones walking forward at once, confident at being able to gain entry. It was apparent he was well versed with this kind of procedure. 'Tell him I wish to speak with him immediately.'

Charlie stood his ground and as he was about sixteen stone and well over six feet six tall, he represented a formidable obstacle. The man wisely chose to abandon his attempt to get by.

'Mister Garner is not here.' Charlie replied, sounding both friendly and polite as he lied to his back teeth. Being as he was face to face with officialdom, this was quite an unusual reaction for him. Those in the office could see that throughout the conversation, Charlie kept both hands behind his back so he could not possibly take possession of a summons, if that was the intention of the court officer. Perhaps, he too had been through this procedure before. 'Can I give him a message, Sir?'

'When are you expecting him to return?' The man demanded.

'No idea Sir.' Charlie stated innocently. 'I only work here.'

'Please inform Mister Garner that David Kennedy from Southend County Court wishes to see him on a most urgent and personal matter.'

'I will most certainly do that for you, Sir!' Charlie said as he shut the door with some relief, realising that he had just experienced the narrowest of escapes.

Charlie's relief was short lived as the man came back later that evening with some heavy duty minders and forced an entry, catching Charlie in bed with one of his girlfriends. Charles spent two uncomfortable nights in Brixton Prison until a relative was persuaded to bail him out.

Whilst Charlie was in prison, Jack Wiggins one of the draughtsman, a high opinionated individual who considered that he could be quite a joker, decided to entertain shoppers in the High Street two floors below. He noticed that the gentleman's outfitters had its name *CECIL* boxed as individual letters lit independently, and this apparently gave him an idea.

One morning he arrived carrying a cardboard box, which contained a large black spider made from painted pipe cleaners. It also had large red eyes. It was the cause of great merriment in the office but Jack refused to say what he intended to do with it.

The office back from the pub, played ten pin bowling on the dart board until it grew dark, then Jack insisted they turned off the lights. Jack retrieved his spider out of the box and tied it onto a ball of string and he quietly opened one of the sash windows before he lowered it onto the box of the middle illuminated letter *C* of the tailors name.

'Not a sound lads.' He advised, as he leant out of the window.

The other windows were opened and the whole office peered downwards upon the heads of shoppers as they walked by and on the roofs of cars in the main road. Passengers on the top deck of buses could see them all looking out of the windows, but not the spider perched on the sign.

Jack kept the spider on the letter looking out for his first victim. After a few minutes he saw two teenaged girls walking together. In a single movement he lowered his spider on to the top of one girls head, then whisked it back behind the protection of the letter. The girl screamed and looked around but not upwards and did not see anything. When it quietened Jack leant out of the window and repeated his search, George saw the girls still giggling, further along the street. Within a minute two women walked along together. Jack repeated his manoeuvre with the same success and response. This happened time and time again until he spied a woman walking alone. In preparation he moved the spider away from the protection of the letter and as the woman passed by underneath, lowered it onto her head. This coincided with the woman reaching up with her hand to adjust her hair and as the spider landed, she grabbed it. One glance of the spider with its red eyes however, turned her into a hysterical wreck. She flailed her arms wildly for a second, slipped off the kerb and fell into the road in a faint. Fortunately there was a gap in the slow moving traffic, but the sight of a body collapsing in the road caused a car driver to brake violently and two cars behind collided first with each other, then ran into the back of the first car. Jack quickly cut the string and withdrew his head. Pandemonium reigned in the street with the car drivers arguing as shoppers dealt with the hysterical woman.

The office had withdrawn back inside the office leaving the windows open, every man leaning up against the outside wall whilst trying to see and hear what was happening below, whilst keeping out of sight. After a while things quietened but then came sounds of an approaching police siren. By the time it arrived all the windows had been surreptitiously closed and fastened.

First one light was turned on, then another and the office resumed playing darts. Jack went downstairs on reconnaissance. He reappeared within a minute.

'They think the spider came from here....' He said sounding breathless.

'Well that comes as no surprise, 'cos it did!' One of the old hands interrupted.

'They are coming up in a tic to investigate!' He exclaimed.' So be careful what you say.'

'I can say what I like, I haven't done anything.' The same voice said. 'You did it, not any of us!'

Outside in the corridor came the sound of banging on the door.

'Please mates!' Jack pleaded. 'Don't drop me in it.'

George went to open the door. Before him stood a uniformed constable of the Essex Police.

'Yes Officer.' He greeted. 'What can I do for you?'

'Good afternoon, Sir.' The constable said politely, trying to peer into the office. 'I am investigating an incident in the High Street, no doubt you heard the commotion a short time ago.'

'No, constable I didn't.' George lied. 'We have been playing darts.'

'We?' Darts?'

'Yes me and my colleagues.' George replied. 'We always play darts on a Friday afternoon.'

'May I come in sir?'

'Certainly.' George said and stood aside.

The constable advanced cautiously and ignoring the group still playing darts walked straight to the windows where he inspected each frame to check if any were open. To his disappointment all were securely fastened. He undid the lock on one, opened the window and peered downward. He look to each side and upwards before shutting the window and left without speaking, nodding to George as he left the room.

After the constable disappeared and they heard front door slam shut, Jack cautiously emerged from his refuge in the stock cupboard looking decidedly white faced. Needless to say he did not attempt that stunt again.

*

Within a few months, the end of George's contract period approached and to his surprise he was offered a permanent position at ESR, which he decided to accept, and became a full member of staff, eventually working on the Sentinel Project again. The main item which helped him decide to accept, was that after the Daniel Tailor affair, the MoD took no action regarding the Sentinel project, except for insisting on a few simple preventative measures designed to ensure the incident could not repeat itself. The minor change was that all employees staying in hotels on a regular basis for business purposes were required to remove the address and other personal details from all documents before their disposal, thus rendering the item useless to any person with evil intentions. Those carrying sensitive documents as part of their remit were issued with portable shredders.

*

The woman was now within arms reach. George suddenly recalled that she caused a great deal of stress and suspicion amongst the male population of ESR. It started with Margaret Paish, the personal assistant and secretary to the Chief Draughtsman. Affectionately known as *Lumpy Bumps*, George Barratt, his real name, suffered from initial symptoms of baldness and through thin greying hair, two bumps, probably cysts, could be clearly seen. Why these were not removed earlier remained a mystery. Strangely enough after George left ESR, he heard through the grapevine that *Lumpy Bumps* had finally undergone the simple surgery procedure to have them removed.

*

Occasionally, usually at inconvenient moments, George had flashes of inspiration, thinking of sentence structure, but with no means of recording his thoughts, until he adopted the habit of having a notebook within reach. Much to the amusement of Carole he carried a small notebook and pencil everywhere.

*

It was a Friday afternoon, and most of those recently returned from the Pub, were in varying stages of wakefulness. In those days it would not be considered uncommon to have a couple of pints on a Friday

239

lunchtime. They were in the main still conscious enough to be able to carefully study a drawing on the desk before them, so as not to cause suspicion amongst the fully alert and ever watchful section leaders. Fully relaxed George rested his head on an upturned palm whilst studying a parts schedule, aware that his section leader Eddie Littleboy – *The Little Boy*, two drawing boards away, was speaking loudly on the telephone. He was speaking to Dennis Flack, their technical support officer from the Admiralty Underwater Weapons Establishment at Portland Naval Base in Dorset. As long as Eddie continued to speak, George knew he could safely remain in a semi-comatose condition.

Eddie's desk was out of view behind drawing boards, and a row of filing cabinets, which was fine because he could not see George. He was the type of sly individual who would creep up to arrive without notice. George was wise to his sneaky regime and developed a tried and tested method of skiving without detection. It comprised of concentrating fully on the task in hand, but with head held upright to remain in full view. The advantage of this stance was that he could easily obtain maximum advantage should the infamous *Little Boy* approach. George had long since renamed Eddie to show his utter contempt for the man. This ploy gained one or two precious seconds, just enough time to secret the object of his attention out of sight, without any unnecessary giveaway movement of the head. He learned to keep an eye out using peripheral vision. The subterfuge could be maintained only if George did not appear to react to this sudden appearance and despite the panic he really felt inside, seemed surprised by this unannounced arrival. Today *Little Boy* spoke for ages on the telephone, his voice gradually becoming fainter without George fully realising it. Perhaps he should have been grateful for the sudden noisy outburst from Margaret.

If Margaret had not screamed loudly and slammed the telephone back with great force onto its cradle, George would have eventually fallen asleep and when the creep *Little Boy* had finished his animated conversation, complete with exaggerated laughter, he would have sneaked quickly down the aisle and caught him dozing. A successful operation of this nature would make his weekend and as an added bonus for everybody, give him the impetuous for a blitz, to purge all potential skivers during the following week, when he would be completely insufferable. It would be fair to describe him as being both pompous and overbearing for most of the time, dispersed with being obnoxious for short periods. He would strut up back and forth enjoying the feeling of power that he relished since his recent promotion from the ranks. He had previously been deputy to the particularly unpleasant Section Leader by the name of Terry Smythe, who ran a small section dedicated to torpedo modifications. To describe what made Terry tick, he often drove to work in a well maintained Morris Minor and it was claimed by the wags that it did twenty miles to the Chamois! He and his wife held regular soirees for the office managers at his bungalow at Wickford, at which it was rumoured, being so house proud they supplied a pair of slippers for every visitor! To add to his false social standing he insisted on being called Mr Smythe, as in Hythe.

Terry Smythe, a combination of physically resembling Bob Hope, but with a bloated face and thick fleshy ears, and sounding similar to the Clitheroe Kid, had a high pitched voice as if it had never broken. The character, a mischievous schoolboy, was both created and played by James Clitheroe, who in real life, was a forty year old adult only four feet three inches tall, whose family originated from the northern town of the same name. During the 1960's he was heard frequently on the wireless each Sunday afternoon, in between the Navy Lark and Beyond my Ken.

On George's first day he was placed in the care of Terry Smythe, who by his unfortunate misdemeanour and high pitched voice, George took him to be the office junior and to his annoyance treated him as such.

One afternoon George, collected a drawing from the print room and walked back to his desk as Mister Smythe seated at his desk, held his right arm skywards as he snapped his fingers and called out.

'Deeming! Deeming!' He snapped. 'Come here at once!'

George ignored this and returned to his desk.

Five minutes later Mister Smythe appeared by his drawing board.

'I was calling your name out.' He complained. 'Why didn't you answer me?'

'If that was you snapping your fingers and calling out my surname, no I will not answer.' George retorted. 'In the first instance I am not a waiter and in the second I will answer to Sir, Mister Deeming or even plain George but *not*, definitely *not* Deeming!'

Mister Smythe stormed off into the office of *Child by name*.

This was not a good start to his employ and Adrian Child, either being told of a potential conflict by the creep Smythe or by noticing it himself, immediately transferred George onto the Sentinel project, out of reach of the squeaky voiced puppet. Give him his due, Terry Smythe never retaliated to this initial reaction, but *The Little Boy* took the incident almost as being a personal attack and when, years later, he obtained promotion, picked on George from the first day, apparently intent on seeking revenge. He was fully aware however, that George was both good at his job and as he was an accomplished skiver, so he found it difficult to make anything stick other than minor misdemeanours. This did not deter him from trying constantly to keep George on his toes. As a direct consequence George was forced to develop a fail-safe early warning system and this kept him in the clear throughout his time at ESR. George suspected *The Little Boy* knew that for most of the time George had been up to something each time he chose to descend on his desk, but he could not catch him doing it.

This warm and sunny afternoon though, George was gradually drifting off to sleep as *The Little Boy*, talked on. Both of them, for entirely different reasons, unaware of a missed opportunity. The explosion from Margaret, when it occurred ten minutes later, brought the whole drawing office into an immediate state of enforced wakefulness, including George and the lunchtime drinkers. Even *The Little Boy* stopped speaking and a great aura of hush spread throughout the drawing office. Everyone stopped whatever they were doing, and for a few seconds stared in the general direction of Margaret. From this distance there was nothing obviously wrong. Lumpy Bumps rushed from his office and was quietly talking to Margaret, offering assurance, a comforting arm wrapped around a shoulder. It was rumoured that Lumpy Bumps was one for attractive secretaries. His previous secretary, Jill, left under strange circumstances without warning and they appeared to enjoy a close relationship. She was a beautiful woman with blond hair and green eyes. She was not too tall, not too slim and she had generous curves that were both pleasant for the eyes and a comfort to the soul.

She was, as George often said on these occasions. 'She is easy on the eye.'

How close a relationship existed, no one actually knew, but everyone presumed the worst. They were well known for going out for walks on a regular basis at lunchtime, but in all fairness it could have been totally innocent. Some wags claimed to have seen them kissing and cuddling in the street but this seemed most unlikely. If they were having an affair it was doubtful they would risk doing anything improper in public, for fear of being seen. Even Henry Reade the chief engineer, who was definitely having an affair with the luscious Mavis Clarke, went out at lunchtime to a secluded spot in his car and did the evil deed in comparative privacy, behaved impeccably, and did nothing in public to arouse suspicion.

Margaret was going out with a young lad, a fitter from the shop floor, and by all accounts it was becoming serious. They were making plans to marry then immigrate to South Africa. Between them they had thought things through most carefully. Margaret with her secretarial skills could kind a position easily, as apparently good shorthand and typing skills were in short supply down south and her young man, being a skilled man would little difficulty obtaining sufficient qualifying points for a working visa or getting employment. She would not welcome close attention from Lumpy Bumps, but needs must, for she appeared to be troubled and was crying, clearly in some distress. Kate Jones, one of the senior tracers wandered over to offer a few words of comfort and a handkerchief, which were gratefully accepted.

Child by name, detecting a sudden subdued hush descend on the office, made an uncharacteristic venture out of his office and saw the sight of everyone inactive and staring in the general direction of the office next to his. 'Right you lot, the show's over!' He shouted in his booming voice. 'Everyone get back to work! Come on! Chop chop!'

By degrees the office resumed normality. *Child by name* first wandered over to firstly talk to *Lumpy Bumps* then speak briefly with Margaret presumably to enquire how she was, then he disappeared back into the depths his office, out of view behind filing cabinets. George felt intrigued as to the cause of the outburst, but unlike some, he remained at his desk. In due course he would find out what there was to know. Others were not so patient and one by one wandered over for a short chat. They found out very little for Margaret was keeping the problem close to herself. It transpired later that she had been subjected to a nasty obscene telephone call, compounded by a threat of violence that included mutilation of her female private parts. Over a period of several months, most secretaries throughout the factory were subjected to obscene calls, some being simply asked the colour of their knickers being worn or were knickers worn at all. These questions although, not that unpleasant, randomly alternated from requests to wank him off, to actual threats of bodily harm. Margaret eventually revealed to one of the married tracers that the caller had asked her to wank him off and when she refused, threatened to be waiting for her after work. Quite naturally every man in the factory, who had easy access to a telephone, came under suspicion. The majority of men in the drawing office only had access to their Section Leaders telephone and adopted a self protection scheme whereas they asked another member of staff to listen as witness to their conversation. A system, which worked, for the obscene calls continued without anyone from the drawing office coming under suspicion.

In due course Margaret received another call when she was again apparently asked to wank him off. This time Margaret retaliated verbally.

'Fuck off you pervert!' She exclaimed in a very loud voice, but this time did not slam the receiver back on the cradle. Most of the office heard this outburst and to her added embarrassment turned to peer in her direction. The pervert however was not deterred by the reaction, and threatened to poke a sharp stick up her fanny unless she complied with his demands. Margaret on her part had learned from the first call and was determined not to be intimidated. 'In that case, I'll get my boyfriend to ram a sharp pointed stick up your arse' She screamed down the telephone. 'So fuck off, you evil lump of shit!'

Fully aware of several pairs of eyes upon her person, she placed the telephone back on its cradle with care and to the sounds of enthusiastic clapping, stood up and curtsied to acknowledge the applause!

From that time, someone from the drawing office escorted Margaret to her car each evening in case the threat was carried out.

One afternoon on his way back from the toilet George was summoned into the office of *Child by name* and invited to sit down. He wondered where this was leading for he was not usually this friendly. *Child by name* sat at his desk looking down with a painful look of concentration on his face, quickly replaced by his usual blank expression. He offered George a polo mint, which he accepted, and *Child by name* looked at George, then asked casually. 'Who do you think the pervert is?'

George sat up in his chair, paying full attention, gave *Child by name* a look of disbelief, for the pervert could be any one of the one hundred and fifty billion male population of the world, whatever the true male population was. How was he supposed to know his identity? The call could originate from anywhere in the country. Given the fact that the caller appeared to know he was talking to a female secretary and not making random calls, suggested to George that the call to be internal, but he doubt whether anyone had checked.

'Why do you think I should know?'

'With your constabulary skills, there must be clues, similar to those which enabled you to identify our thief, which by the way you have still not told me who it was.'

He felt like telling *Child by name* to fuck off, but as he had given him a polo, a particular favourite of his, he decided to be civil and humour him. Instead of being rude, George shrugged his shoulders.

'The pervert could be anyone in the factory, including you and me.' He said with some honesty. 'Anyone with access to a telephone is a potential suspect.'

This observation caused *Child by name* to raise an eyebrow.

'Its true, believe me!' George insisted. 'It could be anyone in the factory.'

The eyebrow resumed its normal position.

George decided to continue, if nothing else he might be offered another Polo mint. 'Surely in the telephone exchange, there is a way in which a listening watch could be kept? The exchange is probably organised in a logical fashion so faults can be easily traced. In that case, all of the telephones within the factory can be tapped, the majority eliminated, narrowed down to a department, then a section and then to an individual telephone. Simple!'

The beginning of a weak smile appeared momentarily on his face then disappeared. 'How could that be done?' *Child by name* asked, crunching on his polo whilst studying George's face. George then realised he was being serious and not asking silly questions. 'You must get to know about these technical techniques in the Specials, then?'

Child by name assumed that because of his part time policing duties, George, in his capacity of a Special Constable at a local Police Station, was expert in all matters regarding crime detection and English Criminal Law, which was not a fact. He knew sufficiently about such matters to be able to conduct his duties and suspected that in some instances with certain individuals a little knowledge could be dangerous. The case of obscene telephone calls may be one such occasion, but he could at the very least think things through, to be able to seek a logical solution to any given problem.

'No, not so you would notice. I have no specific knowledge but I would have thought that the exchange must be arranged in a logical fashion so the engineer can easily trace faults. It should be relatively simple to determine what part of the factory the calls originate, assuming that is, they are internal.' George suggested. 'Also a record should be kept when each call is made to see if it reveals a pattern.'

'Go on.' *Child by name* encouraged, leaning forward on his desk, paying full attention. Thankfully he had crunched his polo to dust and held out his packet to George, who gratefully took two. *Child by name* either did not notice, else chose to ignore it.

What am I supposed to do? Write it all out as a paper for further investigation?

'Well.' George replied, thinking intently, trying not to appear to patronise the naïve person sitting the other side of the desk. These questions left him totally unprepared to go into detail at such short notice. It was particularly worrying as he suspected *Child by name* was likely to depend on his response. 'Think about it, Adrian. If it is you making the calls, it is possible for you do that at any time as you have your own office. With your door closed, there is no one to overhear your conversation. Whereas if it is I, I am only be able to make telephone calls when Eddie Littleboy is away from his desk, or at least gives me permission when he is. In any case there is every likelihood that someone would be able to overhear part if not all of my conversation. There are a lot of folk like you, mainly managers, who have sole use of an office and can easily make calls at random in private. Make a list of all those with an office to themselves and also keep an accurate log of the calls first, to see if a pattern emerges, that's the only sure way to find out. If a pattern does emerge it might be easy to tap those phones in the exchange if you are able to predict the time of a call or can reduce the number of lines to be tapped. Also has anyone checked whether the calls are internal or external, but I am positive that they will be found to be internal, because the caller seems to know in advance he will be speaking to a woman. That's the best I can do at such short notice.'

Child by name leant back on his chair deep in thought, still crunching on his polo, then appeared to make up his mind. 'You have come out with some very good theories George, and thanks for the suggestions.' Quite an admission for someone not normally so charitable. He reached for his telephone before dismissing George most politely. 'Please excuse me, I must make a call.'

'Hope it's not an obscene one!' George joked as he left.

George heard later from *Child by name* that he had made a telephone call to John Digby-Jones, the Managing Director, informing him of their discussion.

To George's amazement *Child by name* revealed to the MD that George had been the source of inspiration and claimed he did not take any credit for it himself. Probably a wise move on his part, for George could have been talking complete rubbish or making legitimate observations. He doubt whether *Child by name* could tell the difference either way. All obscene calls were logged over a period of weeks without a pattern being apparent, other than the fact that every call was made during the afternoon. Until George had mentioned it, none of the secretaries knew whether the calls were internal or external. The fact that it was quickly established that they all appeared to be internal calls, made the whole episode rather sinister. The pervert could not satisfy his needs, whatever they were and as a direct consequence was becoming more violent with his threats as the weeks passed. Almost every secretary in the factory became subjected to his obscene suggestions and threats of physical sexual violence unless they agreed to do as he requested. Despite the threat of getting his victim after work, no woman was actually attacked, otherwise a more determined effort would have been made earlier to catch the pervert red handed. One attractive secretary, the lovely Julie from the front office, repeatedly the unfortunate recipient of particularly harrowing calls, became so incensed, she apparently agreed to do precisely as the caller requested. 'Oh come on then love, I'll wank you off and if you've got a nice big fat cock, and a pair of balls to match, I'll even let you come in my mouth. Name the time and place and I'll be there. I haven't sucked off anyone with a large cock for weeks!'

Quite out of character, the caller, probably surprised by such an unexpected submission, rang off. The calls ceased for some weeks and everyone thought the episode concluded, then without warning, again in the afternoon, they resumed. Of course the attractive secretary was the victim. Julie, a tall leggy blond, but unlike the alleged reputation of dumb blondes, was intelligent and possessed a good sense of humour. She did not replace her receiver and went off to see the telephone engineer in case the call could be traced, which unfortunately it could not. At least she tried.

Those in power did not frighten her so she was not going to be easily intimidated by a pervert on the other end of a telephone line. George recalled the episode of the hot pants.

*

The year before it had been a very hot summer and ESR, not being air conditioned unless opening all available windows counted, was always hot, stuffy and airless, particularly in the afternoons. Julie arrived one morning wearing tight fitting hot pants, which were very revealing and most men, including George, walked around with their tongues on the floor throughout the time she remained in the drawing office. This also applied when she wore a normal dress but this morning the sight was too much for the blood pressure of a normal hot-bloodied male. She used to have regular meetings with Henry Reade much to the dismay of the luscious Mavis, who clearly saw her as a threat, and made her feelings apparent by being totally hostile and openly unfriendly. Julie remained aloof from this approach and continued to show her body off to anyone who cared to look and that was most of the draughtsmen. Julie was by all accounts an accomplished technical writer who ESR valued and allegedly paid her more than the normal rate, but this claim was unfounded and not based on fact. This

251

morning with Julie sitting the other side of the desk, showing acres of leg right up to the knicker line, if she were in fact wearing any, Henry appeared as if he were under severe strain with beads of perspiration virtually dripping off his forehead. The imposing figure of the Managing Director, John Digby-Jones emerged without warning through the swing doors leading to the workshop and breezed with great confidence into Henry's office to be confronted by the magnificent leg display.

A noisy scene developed which everyone heard, but no one was able to decipher a single word. It was never established what he actually said, but the leggy Julie flew out of the office at speed, apparently ordered off the premises, with clear instructions not to return until she wore more respectable clothing, either a skirt or a dress. Later that day she returned and resumed her meeting with Henry. She had complied with the order from the Managing Director and wore a top and a skirt. The skirt left nothing to the imagination and Digby-Jones who was allegedly sent off with his tail between his legs had already confronted her again. From what George could see of her attire it could well have been something other than a tail! After her meeting ended she deliberately went upstairs to the mezzanine floor via the open staircase in full view from the drawing office. If the pervert had been someone in the drawing office he could have determined the colour of her under garments without asking! As Ron Waud boasted afterwards with a good deal of moustache stroking, whose desk, the best seat in the house, lay at the bottom of the open staircase! 'Thank God she wore knickers, otherwise I would have been able to see what she had for breakfast!' Then added. 'As it was I could see what she had for supper!'

*

The obscene calls continued and George was shown the call log in confidence. His opinion was regularly sought from both Digby-Jones and Fred the resident telephone engineer.

He was taken to the exchange and the layout explained in detail. It was a mysterious place, very warm, tending to be stuffy, where dialling mechanisms constantly burst into violent staccato mechanical action. Fred explained that it was organised by department or location and it was comparatively easy to determine from where a call was being made. To monitor and listen simultaneously would be difficult because of the large amount of extensions to be covered, despite the suggestion that George made to isolate or at least identify those extensions in a private office. After some months the call log did appear to have a pattern, but one, which did not make sense. Virtually all of the calls occurred during the afternoon between two and three o'clock, the majority on a Thursday or a Friday, but no one was able to suggest an explanation for this. In short there going to be no obvious solution.

A few days passed.

Then one Thursday morning, George was having to endure his yearly personal assessment meeting with *Child by name*, and *The Little Boy* when the door burst open. The head and shoulders of Digby-Jones appeared briefly around the opened door to the office. 'Hello George, excuse me for interrupting.' He greeted, then looked towards *Child by name*. George noted with a certain amount of pleasure, that he ignored the presence of *The Little Boy*. These two had been in conflict over George's involvement with the obscene telephone call investigation. 'Adrian, my normal Thursday afternoon Senior Managers meeting has been cancelled yet again

253

until tomorrow. Damned inconvenient to keep changing the day! So if you want to have a short or a long round tonight I will be able to make it. Quite by chance I have brought my clubs with me.'

Child by name mumbled a reply, which Digby-Jones seemed to understand. How he understood was beyond George. 'Fine. I'll come by here at five on my way out, then.'

Child by name, The Little Boy and George resumed their assessment meeting, with something nagging around inside George's head. Try as he did, he almost gave himself a headache attempting to extract the information. All in all the assessment went well with George being awarded a merit rise. Only a modest sum but it gave him some satisfaction as he sensed there was a certain amount of resentment by *The Little Boy*, who in all probability had been overruled.

Later that night as he lay asleep, the caterpillar which had been crawling around his brain all evening chose this moment in the still of the bedroom to clump around wearing great hob nailed boots and metamorphose into a fifteen stone town crier.

'HEAR YE! HEAR YE! HEAR YE! HERE IS TODAYS IMPORTANT NEWS! THE PERVERT MAKES HIS CALLS ON THURSDAY AFTERNOON OR FRIDAY AFTERNOON WHEN DIGBY JONES IS AT HIS SENIOR MANAGERS MEETING! HEAR YE! HEAR YE! HEAR YE!'

The caterpillar cum Town Crier yelled with such gusto, George sat bolt upright with shock. He heard and understood the loud message but was still reeling from the bombshell making his head feel that it was likely to explode at any moment. He sat upright for several minutes before he felt inclined to lie down again, and when he did, sleep remained elusive. When the alarm went off at seven thirty, George felt as if he had been awake all night.

With this discovery his problems though were just beginning. Was he supposed to go to *Child by name* with these revelations or was a restrained approach the better option? His realisation was not proof in itself just a possible explanation, probably one out of a few others as Digby-Jones did not attend the meeting on his own. There would be other senior managers present, some from ESR Marine, depending on the interpretation of the title Senior. They were unknown at this time but it would not be too difficult to check other potential unattended telephones where a pervert had opportunity to make his calls.

He eventually decided caution to be the way of things.

By chance he saw Fred the telephone engineer just after start time, who went and retrieved the call log, which he left in George's care without a second thought when he asked to see it. George took it back to his desk and studied it. The Little Boy chose this moment to sneak up and view whatever it was he was carefully studying.

'Put that down George.' He instructed with obvious pleasure given an opportunity to throw his weight about. 'You have more important work to do, and a deadline to keep. Those modifications must be complete by next week.'

'This is just as important!' George said without bothering to glance up. He suspected this made *Little Boy* more determined to get his way. 'There's still plenty of time to complete the mods.'

'I have given you an instruction which you have chosen to ignore and answered me back.' He said sounding pleased. 'In that case I shall have to put you on report.'

'You do that.' George retorted, still not bothering to look up. 'But before you do, mention to John, that's Mister Digby Jones to you, that I have made some progress with the obscene calls and you are now preventing the investigation from continuing. Now go away, there's a good chap, you are beginning to annoy me.'

In retrospect a foolish way to speak to the power crazy section leader. But George was determined not to succumb to power just for the sake of it. He might yet live to regret it if *The Little Boy* chose to proceed with a disciplinary action.

The Little Boy stormed off without another word, straight into the office of *Child by name* and shut the door. George continued to study the call report and it became apparent that his theory had some strength. The majority of calls were still being made on a Thursday or Friday afternoon. All that remained was to arrange a check in the diary of Digby Jones to see if any calls had been made during his absence. If there had been, it would mean good progress now there was finally something to go on. With his study complete, he stood up with the intention of going to see *Child by Name* to reveal his discovery and as he turned, came face to face with him.

'I was just coming to see you.' George said noticing that *Little Boy* was glaring at him from his desk. He resisted the urge to poke his tongue out at him.

'Just as well, for I was on my way to see you.' *Child by Name* responded grim faced. 'You'd better come to my office for a chat.'

Once inside and sitting, he closed the door. 'I have had a complaint from Eddie about your response to his request to get on with your work. If you have deadline to keep it is imperative they are kept, otherwise the MoD may decide not renew the contract. And you know what that'll mean. There have been redundancies before.'

'I was about to explain what I was doing, but he never gave me the opportunity.' George lied, but what the heck. Why should he take stick from *The Little Boy* without due reason. 'From my first day when I had the unfortunate misunderstanding with Terry Smythe, he has taken every opportunity to pick on me. It's gett....'

Child by Name held up a hand saying. 'No, no, no, no!'

George stopped to listen, suspecting in advance that the rug was about to be pulled from under his feet and that management was about to close ranks as they normally did. But he was completely and utterly wrong and doing him an injustice.

Child by Name leant forward on his desk, for once sounding sincere and speaking very softly. 'We are both guilty of failing to tell Eddie anything about your part in the obscene telephone calls investigation. Now I have explained your involvement he is more than happy for you to carry on, but you must appreciate that he is more concerned with his deadlines.'

Cheeky sod. George thought. On one hand he asks me for my opinion, openly encourages me to help to the extent that Digby Jones had visited the drawing office on several occasions in order to speak with him, then says I must also keep to deadlines. *The Little Boy* certainly knew about the investigation for he came over on more than one occasion, to creep and crawl. Digby Jones did not to fall for that trick and sent *Little Boy* packing each time! *Child by Name* then had the audacity to say it was partly Georges fault that *The Little Boy* knew nothing about it. The look on his face must have given George away, for *Child by Name* continued.

'All right, so it was entirely my fault, I admit it. Satisfied?'

George had won a moral victory so there was little to be gained by continuing his stance unless he wanted to risk a big fall out.

'I am now.' He smiled. 'Would you like to hear why I wanted to see you?'

'I am all ears George. Fire away.'

'I think I know where the pervert works!' George said trying not to sound smug. The words came out as a burst of sound, at a moment when the drawing office suddenly went silent. In the quietness his words seemed to echo around the office, which he regretted in case he had been overheard.

The affect was immediate.

Child by Name sat bolt upright, instantly reminding George of his reaction to the caterpillar cum Town Crier during the night. 'Keep your voice down man!' He exclaimed in a whisper whilst waving his arms about in a most agitated manner. 'And tell me what you have found out.'

George quickly explained about Digby Jones and his cancelled meeting yesterday afternoon that led him to suspect the pervert could work in his office. The Managing Director's Suite was situated in a small detached building formerly a house, so in that respect, isolated from the factory. Although George had never visited the Suite, he imagined that the nine or ten people, five men and about four women, who worked there, had an office each, thus presenting a potential pervert with every opportunity once their boss was out on business. *Child by Name* immediately reached for the telephone, but George reached over to stop him dialling. 'What the heck!'

'We have to be cautious.' He advised. 'I have no absolute proof only a suspicion. Why not invite Digby

Jones over here to make arrangement to play in a fictitious golf tournament and get him to bring his diary over. For the purposes of this exercise we must assume he is the pervert, but if you check these dates I have extracted from the call log, you should be able to quickly establish whether my theory has substance or not.'

'Digby Jones is not a pervert George. You are over reacting! You must be suffering from a touch of the dramatics!'

'No I'm not!' George replied. 'The pervert could be anyone, you, me, even Digby Jones!'

Child by name sat shaking his head in disbelief.

George handed over a slip of paper with a selection of dates written down. *Child by Name* appeared to be very excited and sat rubbing his hands with glee. It was apparent he had assumed once again that George's expertise had come to the fore. On his part he was quietly optimistic but with reservations, for he could yet be proved wrong.

Some time later during the morning George heard the double doors from the workshop burst open and spotted Digby Jones, holding what appeared to be a diary, striding along the aisle on the far side to disappear into the office of *Child by Name*. A short time afterwards *Little Boy* appeared by his side. 'Adrian Child would like to see you in his office.' He announced. 'Hope this doesn't mean you will be there for a lengthy period.'

'I will probably have be there for as long as he wants me to be there.' George foolishly retorted, trying not to sound sarcastic. 'I won't have any say in the matter.'

To his surprise Digby Jones was still there when he walked in. 'Good work George and well spotted. I don't know how we all managed to miss the obvious.'

He greeted with great gusto and genuine enthusiasm. 'There is a good possibility that the deviant could work in my suite. Your call list matches with my absence on several occasions and not just a Thursday afternoon. I would appreciate what I am about to day is kept very quiet. I have a communication expert by the name of Tim Stansfield who will assist meto ensure the pervert is caught. I don't want anyone to know what we are up to. I have already sanctioned this with Adrian, so if you are willing, I would be very grateful.'

George glanced at *Child by Name* who nodded, before he said. 'I will clear this with Eddie. Do you know anything about how an exchange works, George?'

'I do actually.' He replied, but deliberately not mentioning that his knowledge consisted of a single flying visit with Fred at the small exchange by the main gate.

'You agree then?' An anxious Digby Jones asked, sounding relieved.

'Yes I do.' George agreed.

'Good! Excellent!' Digby Jones exclaimed slapping George on the back, before making a quick exit.

After he went, *Child by Name* explained that the Managing Director was setting a trap which would be repeated if necessary the following week. 'It's been going on for far too long George.' He said. 'And we, with your valuable assistance will put a stop to it. I should add that this trap must be kept close to our chest, so mum's the word.'

'What about Eddie?'

'You don't miss a trick do you George?'

'I have to be careful when it comes to him and his precious deadlines!'

'Don't concern yourself about him. I shall deal with him without mentioning why. I shall say you are doing a favour for me. That should keep him quiet.'

True to his word *Child by Name* did speak with The *Little Boy* without mentioning the reason for his anticipated prolonged absence. He tried to find out from George what his special deployment was, but George evaded the question.

'What are you doing for Adrian?'

'I don't know.' George for once told the truth. 'I shall find out on Thursday.'

'Come on George, you can tell me.' The Little Boy persisted.

'I don't know.' George repeated. 'They haven't told me yet.'

At lunchtime on the Thursday, he went early to the exchange whilst the office was quiet and most drawing office staff still out to lunch. This way no one would see him disappear into the exchange by the main gate. Making sure he was not observed, he let himself in with a key given to him by Fred. Fred made an early appearance a short time after and quickly explained the method they would be using. The Directors Suite had been isolated and rewired on Saturday overtime so the dialling mechanisms were close together. Initially they would concentrate on them, but so as to make full use of the time, all telephone calls were to be intercepted, whenever calls were not being made from the Directors Suite. When a call was made, the dialling activated a mechanism that sent a series of electronic pulses through the circuits. For internal calls a five digit number was dialled which enabled them to ignore those with a longer number. This saved them a lot of time. They resorted to listen to every call from the Directors suite, so as to be able to identify the sex of the caller and then disregard those from females. Small slips of paper were lightly glued on the mechanism for the male employees. The second and third time they intercepted calls, this plan was abandoned as obscene calls could be made from a telephone, for instance, if an adjacent office became vacant. For the call to be heard, all they had to do, was to touch a red wire on the dialling mechanism positive terminal with a probe and listen through an earpiece. Fred had wired the other connectors up to a common earth to complete the circuit. So they could obtain corroborative evidence their earpieces were wired in parallel so each other's reception could be heard. Should a relevant call be heard, all the other person had to do was to remove his probe from the red wire terminal from the other set.

They settled down.

A mechanism suddenly sprung into activity, so George instantly touched the red wire with his probe. The length of time the mechanism was active should have told him this to be an external call but he ignored this because he was anxious to get started. After a pause, he heard a female voice announce the name of a medical centre and another female voice request an appointment to see the doctor. George removed my probe. One down, several thousand to go. He considered during that first afternoon they heard every type of call. Everything except an obscene type. Some voices were recognised.

Tiaan Schutte, the argumentative wireman, who booked his car in for a service, made one such call.

'....bridge Garage.'

'Want to book my car for service.' Tiaan said abruptly with typically clipped vowels.

'What day Tiann?' A voice asked with a pronounced eastern European accent.

'Do not say my name!' Tiann demanded.

'No way, it is safe. Okay, no worry Tiann.'

'I have a faulty wire to be fixed.'

'Bring it in Tiann.'

The phone went dead.

Both men heard the call, and Fred started to write details on a call log form.

'What garage was that?' He asked.

'Sounded like Longbridge Garage.' George replied. 'With that accent it was difficult to tell.'

'Sure it wasn't Havelock Bridge Garage?'

'I couldn't be sure, not with that accent.'

Fred continued with his writing and George forgot about the incident.

The most amusing was heard within a half an hour of their listening. Henry Reade called his secretary, the luscious Mavis, from his office a few feet away from her desk, giving advance warning of their departure prompt at one o'clock to a rendezvous at a quiet secluded spot in Painters Lane nearby.

'I'm just finishing off my report and almost ready to leave Clarkey.' He announced. 'When we get there I'm going to give you a treat and slip it in backwards. I feel particularly randy today and I know you like it doggy fashion!'

'Take care and make sure you get it in the right hole!' Mavis joked. 'I don't want any mistakes like the last time you tried that! I had trouble walking afterwards!'

George and Fred laughed heartily for several minutes. If the pervert had made a call during this time they would have missed it. After the initial outburst, Fred resorted to laughing intermittently, going back to normal for a few seconds before another thought set him off again. This type of laughter was infectious and so George felt obliged to join in. Every time their eyes met set the pair off again. They eventually quietened to resume their eavesdropping. By five o'clock George had more than a fair share of mundane communications between employee and employee intermixed with a few outside calls.

The two men stayed put when the bell went and listened as from the other side of the door sounds of the factory disgorging its employees. From through the door endless chatter and footsteps continued for about five minutes, then ceased. Fred unlocked the door. After a wait of five or ten minutes, the door opened and there stood *Child by Name* and Digby Jones, looking very excited. Both men were tall and overweight and keen to gain entry. Rather than burst in which would have caused a blockage, they peered around the door frame. They resembled grotesque puppets.

'You heard it then?' They demanded in unison, and looked with great expectation.

The blank expression from Fred and George, a clear indication that they had not.

'Bollocks!' Digby Jones exclaimed with gusto, now visually deflated. 'How come?'

'You claimed it was going to easy George!' *Child by name* chimed in.

George had not made any claim or offered a prediction how long a task this would be, but did not feel inclined to say so.

Fred and George did not have the answer so desperately needed. Despite listening to most of the calls, the pervert had somehow evaded the trawl. With hindsight they made some wild assumptions, but it took several more sessions in the exchange for their mistake to be discovered.

The following afternoon they returned to the exchange, but there were only trivial matters to hear. Henry Reade made the first move to chat up Mavis's sister Evelyn, who worked for the Purchasing Manager in the front office. She was not in the same league in the lecherous stakes as Mavis, but would provide an interesting substitute. Henry was succeeding and needed only to find the last part of the key that would unlock the flimsy padlock on her even more flimsy knickers. Evelyn was certainly going along with the possibility of a sexual liaison and was concerned only with keeping it from her sister, which appeared to be the main stumbling block.

'Lucky dirty bastard!' Fred exclaimed. 'Some blokes have all the luck. Both are cracking bits of stuff!'

Evelyn suggested that Henry send Mavis on a course for few days and whilst away they could develop a relationship without fear of discovery. They ran the risk of someone at the factory babbling to Mavis upon her return, but Evelyn found an easy solution even for this. She suggested that Henry request her to act as substitute secretary during Mavis's absence, so the pair seen together would not be considered as unusual. It is true to say that both Fred and George were too captivated by the conversation to stop listening and George continued with the connection whilst Fred searched for calls. Luckily the exchange was quiet for some time and this allowed them to listen in. For eight long sessions over a period of four weeks, Fred and George endured the heat in the exchange, and finally realised their error and listened in to every call made from the Directors Suite. As things turned out they were completely wrong to exclude the women from their trawl.

Henry Reade finally succeeded in seducing Mavis's sister. Mavis was sent on a value engineering course for a week in central London and Henry shagged Evelyn each lunchtime. After the first week Mavis enlisted into another course, which kept her away from work every Thursday and Friday. Henry managed to secure the services of Evelyn as secretary and lover for the week Mavis was away and for the two days when Mavis was away for shorter periods. They ascertained from their telephone conversations that Evelyn, unlike her older sister, readily indulged in mutual oral sex, much to the delight of the Chief Engineer. They discovered too that the luscious Mavis was also having a bit on the side during this period, an engineer from the main factory, who had attended the same course. They listened in to surreptitious internal calls made presumably when Henry was not in his office. Unfortunately for them their task had been completed before the luscious Mavis finally returned from her course and they were not able to establish the effect of the liaison with her younger sister had on Henry and Mavis combined with her short affair. Outwardly nothing changed, for they continued to go out at lunchtimes to a secluded spot in Painters Lane.

Back to the call interceptions.

For a short time Fred and George wondered whether the pervert worked at the main factory, as all of these calls would be considered to be internal. If this had been the case their task to trap the pervert would have been impossible.

From the first time, Fred and George did not bother to intercept calls from the women in the suite. After two sessions another obscene call was made, followed by two during the third. They endured a severe bollocking from Digby Jones on each occasion and so Fred decided extreme measures were called for, which he would be able to justify if the same measures produced results. Fred used his knowledge of electronics and blocked all outgoing calls from every extension within the factory except the Directors Suite. Within two hours they listened in on an obscene telephone conversation. By this time they had obtained a tape recorder to be used as corroborative evidence. The target on this occasion was a young secretary in Coilwinding who had only been with the company a short time. The caller used Digby Jones extension. George activated the tape recorder. He only hoped it worked else he would be subjected to more abuse from Digby Jones.

'Good afternoon.' A young voice greeted. 'Coilwinding.'

'Is that Pauline?'

'Speaking.'

'When you are winding your coils, what colour are your knickers?'

The young secretary did not grasp the significance of the question. 'Actually I do not do any Coilwinding. I am the secretary to Mister Dowding.' The penny finally dropped. She gave a sharp intake of breath. 'What did you say? You s..'

The voice of the caller changed to a raucous tone, one of aggression combined with almost hatred clearly sounding in the way the person spoke.

'What colour are your knickers darling? The pervert interrupted. 'If they are my kind of colour I will help you take them off. Your nice damp minge and tight arse will soon be mine, so tell me and come out to play. If you....'

'Fuck off you pervert!' The line went dead.

George immediately telephoned *Child by Name* with the good news, who in turn contacted Digby Jones in his hideaway. It must have been nearby for he appeared in the exchange within a few minutes. By the time he arrived they had ascertained that the recorder had worked. What relief!

He listened to the tape three times, and except for an impatient wave of an arm to indicate he wished the tape rewound and played again, he sat without comment.

What colour are your knickers darling? If they are my kind of colour I will help you take them off. Your nice damp minge and tight arse will soon be mine, so tell me and come out to play. If you....

Fuck off you pervert!

He finally sat upright and gave out a big sigh. 'You say that my extension was used?' He asked, to which Fred and George nodded. 'It that case we have a problem?'

'Why's that?' George asked.

'I don't recognise the voice.' He said. 'You'll have to play it to me again.'

What colour are your knickers darling? If they are my kind of colour I will help you take them off. Your nice damp minge and tight arse will soon be mine, so tell me and come out to play. If you....

Fuck off you pervert!

George and Fred sat in disbelief. If Digby Jones could not recognise the voice it meant that either the pervert did not work in his office, or else could disguise their voice. Either scenario made it even more complicated than it was already.

In the first case this would entail a watch on the office but in the second the pervert would have to be caught red handed. George hoped Digby Jones would recognise the caller. They played it again and he listened several times without success. Another way had to be found to catch the pervert red handed. This was not going to be easy. Tim Stansfield borrowed some portable military VHF communication sets from the MoD and a large van from security, which was placed in a carefully selected spot, so as to be able to see desks in the Directors Suite through a ground floor window.

The plan was for George to assist Fred, but at the last moment George was forced to complete the work to meet his deadline. He was furious he missed the final episode, but thoroughly enjoyed the sequence of events related by an animated Tim later in the pub.

On Thursday lunchtime armed with a cumbersome army radio with a six foot aerial and headphones, Tim had slipped into the van without anyone managing to see him. Fred remained in the exchange would try and give advance warning if and when the telephone was used. He was faced with the possibility that another extension was used instead, in which case it was a waste of time. It was a hot day and the van being in direct sunlight, Tim knew that he was going be in for an uncomfortable afternoon. He turned the set on, a faint hum confirming the batteries worked, and once the headphones were in place adjusted a button to reduce the squelch. He pressed the talk button and spoke into the microphone.

'Hello Fred. Hello Fred.' His voice echoed around the van and he hoped he could not be heard outside. 'Are you there, over?'

The headphones hissed for a few seconds, then a loud electronic clunk, followed by Fred's voice.

"Hello Tim. Hello Tim, Receiving you loud and clear with some interference so try and speak up a bit. Over.' Fred sounded as if he were on the moon instead of a mere fifty yards away.

'Will do Fred, I'll speak loudly and I can see the office, Over.'

The hissing continued then came the same clunk. 'Ok Tim I am ready for your signal. Over.'

Within five minutes the van was both hot and stuffy. Tim had placed black material over the back windows, and by cutting a small slit through one, Tim without any fear of being detected could just see a female messenger, with her back to him, busy at her desk. She stood up then left the office for a short time and Tim advised Fred, but no calls were made from elsewhere in the Suite, then she returned. She then acted most suspiciously. She stood up and went to the door and peered around the frame, looking both ways, presumably to see if anyone was nearby at the drink machine. She walked into the MD's office and lifted the receiver. Out of his sight she began to dial. Tim immediately spoke to Fred on the radio, who made the appropriate connection.

'Fred Fred! She's dialling now. Over.'

Tim could see the mouth of the messenger and she was speaking.

His radio sprung into life with a clunk so loud, it hurt both ears. 'It's her!' Fred exclaimed with the excitement clearly noticeable in his voice. 'It's her, a bloody woman! What a pair of idiots we've been!'

'Who is she talking to?'

'Margaret again, and she's giving our pervert a bit of stick, I can tell you. I am recording everything, so off you go.'

It had been agreed that in the event of a call being made and a positive identification, Tim was to attempt to catch the pervert red handed. This could invalidate his testimony as a witness, but Digby Jones considered it of more importance for the calls to cease than to obtain evidence to be later used as criminal evidence. In any case the police had not been informed of previous incidents so a criminal charge seemed unlikely. Tim burst out through the back doors of the van, startling a driver as he strolled by and struggling with his set, ran inside the suite. The woman was caught off guard and was so engrossed in her conversation, did not see him until it was too late. He grabbed the handset out of her hands and deliberately knocked the woman with an aggressive shoulder charge, which sent her sprawling. She fell backwards on her chair, then fell in an untidy heap onto the floor.

'It that you Margaret?' He said quickly, keeping an eye on the woman now brushing her dress down and slowly getting to her feet. 'It's Tim Stansfield here. Were you the recipient of an obscene call immediately before I spoke.'

'Yes I bloody was, who are you and how did you know?' Margaret sounded very angry.

'It is essential that you leave the handset off the hook, and make sure it stays off. Adrian Child will explain later.'

'Ok, thanks.'

Tim eyeing the woman, still paying attention to her crumpled dress, spoke to Fred on the military radio who said that *Child by name* and Digby Jones were both on their way, but was interrupted by a sudden angry outburst from the woman. She had removed the debris from her dress and sat down at the desk. 'I don't know who you are or what you are doing interrupting an important business call!' She said, glaring at Tim whilst she spoke. 'I shall have to inform Mister Digby Jones of your unprofessional and aggressive behaviour when he returns! The unprovoked assault on me is likely to get you the sack!'

'You do as you like, love.' Tim said, having to refrain from smacking her one in the mouth. 'But I suspect it will be you getting the sack and very soon too!'

'I don't know what you mean…..' Her voice trailed off as behind him the door burst opened and in walked Digby Jones, for once quiet and for him subdued. Moments later *Child by name* arrived looking as if he had run all the way. The woman named Alison sat calmly. Her eyes though revealed the turmoil going on inside her head. They flitted back and forth whilst her body outwardly remained calm and impassive. 'Would someone please explain what this untimely interruption is all about?' She demanded in a soft quivering voice as she hung on to the desk for support.

A fierce look of anger appeared briefly on the face of Digby Jones but it quickly disappeared. To Tim's amazement he then smiled. 'My dear Alison.' He said softly and gently. 'You have led us all a merry dance with your obscene calls but now you have been well and truly rumbled, and caught red handed. So consider yourself sacked. I would therefore require you to put on your coat and fuck off, dear!'

A look of horror appeared on the face of Alison, then she composed herself and spoke with great determination. 'You cannot sack me....., for it will make you liable to be sued for wrongful dismissal. I shall be speaking with my solicitor when I....'

Digby Jones bent down to glare at his long serving messenger from a matter of an inch or two. 'Watch my lips Alison.' He hissed with apparent hatred. 'You are sacked! Sue me if you will but you are still sacked and you will be removed from the premises, by force if necessary!'

He picked up the telephone handset and spoke to Margaret briefly to confirm the conversation and then dialled a number. 'Len. It's Digby Jones here. Please come to my office immediately as I have an unwanted guest who should leave the premises without delay.' He replaced the handset with such force Tim was surprised it did not break and then telephoned George, who quickly walked over.

Alison stood up at once, and whilst *Child by name* and Tim stood and stared as onlookers, a contest of wills commenced. She glared back at Digby Jones, and accompanied by a wagging finger spoke with vengeance. These two seemed to be old adversaries. 'I will sue you, mark my word.' She said quietly still wagging a finger, not distracted by the arrival of George. 'It will cost you thousands, believe me, thousands. Yes. Thousands! I shall bankrupt you and make no mistake about it!'

'Do as you wish Alison but as soon as you are off the premises I will be telephoning your father. He will be very pleased, no doubt, about his lovely precious daughter being a pervert. I shall tell him in great detail of your dirty exploits.' He turned to face Tim. 'Did you manage to record the call this afternoon, Tim?'

'Yes, we did.' Tim replied quietly. 'The whole episode is on tape.'

'I shall play it to him, so you sue away, it makes no difference to me. Now get your coat and go or I shall set security on you.'

As George looked on, Alison stood with her lower lip quivering. Slowly, very slowly, she transformed from a confident employee and before their eyes disintegrated into a sobbing blubbering mass of flesh, quite beyond help. The threat of speaking to her father changed her outlook once she had realised her case was beyond recovery. Her six month reign of terror finally over.

*

The unblinking woman carrying a file was inches away, oblivious to his presence. She glanced briefly in his direction and for a moment there was no reaction, but within a milli-second her face showed signs of puzzled recognition. That one look removed the grief from his thoughts and his heart. She thought of speaking, for her mouth opened then closed again in a single movement, as she had second thoughts. George too considered speaking but really there was no point. The event was

273

in the past and there was nothing to be gained by uncovering the dirt again. He relaxed and changed his expression from one of hostility to one of friendliness.

He smiled.

Her reaction changed everything, and George regretted his change of heart, for the monster, which still lurked within a feeble female frame, came to the surface in a trice.

'Bastard!' She hissed under her breath.

The flimsy cotton thread of restraint, snapped. 'Alison, how lovely it is to see you again since you were sacked.' George said in an overloud voice, exaggerated so all of the people within earshot were aware of the conversation. He supposed Alison to be her element, now she had hundreds of potential victims in the form of nurses, to ask them about the colour of their knickers then threatening to get them in the car park.

'Made any good obscene phone calls recently, Alison?'

9

State of minds

Throughout the working world, most people adopt a personal routine on a normal working day, usually at an early hour, many, like George, on autopilot. Some folk deliberately adopt a non-routine routine to avoid getting into a rut, but this in itself is a pattern or trait, likely to be more mentally disruptive than simply getting up and going to work by the easiest or quickest method.

George always tried to keep his life simple.

His work day morning routine remained the same throughout the time he was employed at ESR. As he prepared to leave the flat, he first kissed his wife Carole goodbye, always an enjoyable event as she normally wore only a thin dressing gown, which sometimes gaped upon to reveal an inviting cleavage, as he caressed her buttocks with both hands. Having dragged himself away from the pleasures of the tempting flesh, he picked up his sandwiches, then felt pockets to check that they contained wallet, car keys, front door keys, and the essential ESR security pass. George and his wife then resided in Leyton, conveniently about a ten minute leisurely drive from the factory. No matter how tired he felt, how hung over he remained from a serious drinking session the night before, the main item on his check list each day was the ESR security pass. Without it, entry could not be gained, should assiduous security staff decide to have a purge, which they carried out without warning on a regular basis. Describing it with the grandiose name of security pass, raised expectations for anyone who heard about it, but were immediately disappointed once seen. It was badly printed on cheap card, a vivid shade of yellow, slightly larger than the credit cards of today. It stated full name and status, date of issue, expiry date, essential for those on temporary contract, department, signature of head of department and lastly signature of holder. The crowning glory of the security pass was the photograph of the holder. In his case, the photograph of holder, consisted of a carelessly cut, badly placed Polaroid, taken by a second rate clown, out of costume but still resembling a clown, on his day off, giving a poor impersonation of a professional photographer. The photograph shows George flat faced, red cheeked, overexposed. Because the office chosen for the session was far too small, cramped with a desk, George as the victim, the alleged photographer and his camera, his shadow is clearly visible on the wall behind him. It would be reasonable to assume that ESR having gone to great expense, in order to comply with the MoD contract's requirement for security, they would employ a photographer who could afford proper lights. Instead, this clown relied on a microscopic flash on his cheap looking camera, by its appearance, obtained using green shield stamps. In his case, George was facing the camera but his eyes were diverted to the right as he was trying to suppress a laugh, due to a variety of rude comments aimed in his direction by his fellow employees from the drawing office waiting impatiently in the queue outside in the corridor. The pass was supposed to be completely encased in plastic, a pathetic attempt at encapsulation to a professional standard, which disintegrated after a month. Everyone was forced to repair the damage with cellotape. If the projects designed and manufactured at ESR were similarly constructed, the MoD would have ceased production within a very short space of time! Despite its cheapness, poor quality print, bad photography, bad construction and repair, it held power supreme over every holder.

One Friday morning, George arrived at work with a minute or two to spare before start time, burst through the outer doors of the factory, to be confronted by Allan, resplendent in his security staff uniform, reminiscent of that worn by police.

'Pass please, young man!' He demanded in a loud authoritative voice, but with a large grin on his face. An outstretched hand anticipated the production of a pass. George assumed someone important sat out of view in the security office that Allan was trying to impress.

Allan, with lightly greased black hair going grey, neatly swept back, inclined to be corpulent, his red face caused by many veins close to the surface, indicated to George that Allan enjoyed the sauce, although to be fair, he gave no outward sign of being a heavy drinker. Out of uniform, George could picture a different Allan altogether. He imagined him with longer hair and pony tail, check shirt made of coarse material, black leather waistcoat and faded jeans, and leather cowboy boots embellished with silver, wearing large metal framed sunglasses that rested on cheek bones, astride a Harley Davidson at the head of a chapter similarly dressed, riding down Route 66 in America's Wild West. He fitted the part precisely. In all the years George knew him, the surname of Allan remained a mystery, for everyone called him Allan. It was never Mister This or Mister That, just plain simple Allan.

Allan had allegedly upset the plans of *Lumpy bumps* who had lecherous designs about his former secretary Jill. Rumours abounded about the relationship and everyone assumed that because Jill did not succumb to his advances, he used subterfuge to get rid of her. For those who knew little about the facts, she simply failed to appear for work one morning to be quickly replaced by Margaret. From Jill's point of view, she had some serious thinking to do. On one hand she had the possibility of a long term affair with a man of power, one who could make her working life easy, but one party being married limited the scope of the relationship, which could only revolve around brief moments of passion at lunchtime. At other times, evenings and weekends her life would be spent alone without her lover. Allan on the other hand was single and with whom she could enjoy moments of passion virtually at any time with benefit of his company and security at all times outside of work. Having deliberately eased herself into the position of the boss's plaything, for her own selfish motives, made her vulnerable to retribution by spurning *Lumpy Bumps* advances.

Jill made her choice and sacrificed her career.

In reality, it later transpired that Allan managed to remove her from the clutches of *Lumpy Bumps*, by persuading Jill to become his girl friend. After a whirlwind, passionate romance, with weekend trips to Paris and other exotic cities, they married at Ilford Registry Office and set up house together. In the mean time Margaret obtained the post of secretary and *Lumpy Bumps* set about luring her into his seedy den. Margaret was several leagues higher than her predecessor and easily resisted all advances and kept the relationship to one in keeping with the position.

George quickly came back to reality to look at Allan standing patiently before him, with arms akimbo.

'Pass please.' Allan quietly encouraged, with a merest sign of a grin on his face. 'When you're ready, George!'

George fumbled in his pockets searching for the pass he knew lurked in the depths. George had been out drinking with the *Fairlop Formation Drinking Team* the evening before and his brain was not functioning properly. It is true to say that he had driven on autopilot the whole journey, and even when he noticed he was driving behind Michael Hayne in his chauffeur driven Rolls Royce, for a good part of the journey, did not shake him out of his half awake state. As a consequence his fingers, without clear or proper instructions from his muddled brain were in a world of their own, not doing what he was frantically instructing to them to do. George continued in his desperate search, as more people came in from behind, in a panic to get in before the bell went, and George was pushed and shoved gently out of the way as Allan inspected the passes offered.

'Haven't you managed to find it yet?' Allan asked with impatience, after the last person had passed by. 'What have you got in your pockets, anyway?'

'No, I have not found it!' George replied, frantically searching for the pass hidden in the depth of a pocket. 'If you will insist on making folks brain work first thing in the morning, you have to suffer the consequences. Impatient git!'

'Oh?' Allan laughed with a knowing grin instantly appearing all over his face. 'Of course, it's Friday morning! I might have known! You must have been out drinking with your infamous Drinking Team Formation. I shall have to insist that in future, all pass inspections are done on the morning after just to get your brain in working order before you start work!'

'Git!' George repeated, at last finding the subject of his search, getting his fingers to hold it properly and with some relief handing it over.

'Thank you very much indeed young Sir.' Allan said with fake sarcasm accompanied by a mock bow, after a cursory glance. 'You can now go about your business legitimately. Move along now, young Sir and allow others to gain entry!'

'Bloody Git!' George said with a grin, as he made to move off.

'That's me folks. I will see you later, young George Deeming.'

'Mind how you go Allan. Do it to them before they do it to you!'

'Oh, I will George.' Allan assured in his usual friendly tone, as he reached out to hold George gently by the arm. 'I will, don't you worry your little head about that.'

He came close, then changed his voice to whisper close in Georges right ear, indicating a direction with a nod of his head. 'As you pass the door, make sure you say good morning to the two pathetic clowns that I have already managed to capture during this mornings trawl. They are scowling in the office, poor buggers! I am positive it will cheer you up immensely George. Enjoy!'

'Thanks Allan, I will.' George replied, carefully placing his pass back into a pocket where it could be more easily found. He felt intrigued as to whom Allan had caught and secretly hoped it would be the pair he had caught previously.

He set off, trying to appear casual and as he passed by the security office, happened to glance through the door. Len, the grey haired and bespectacled Head of Security, sat at the desk, filling out what could only be a temporary pass. Standing solemnly beside him stood the forlorn figures of *Lumpy Bumps* and *Child by name*.

'Morning Len!' George greeted casually in a cheerful way as possible as he passed by.

'Morning George.' Len replied without looking up. Len reminded George of his grandad who died when he was only twelve. Grey hair, always carefully combed and tidy, Len always stood bolt upright, a distinct remnant of his long military career in the Army. His uniform boasted a long line of medal ribbons, which Len refused, point blank to talk about. Not being an expert on military decorations, they were a mystery to George, offering no clue as to what Len did during the war. He had asked Allan about the medals on one occasion and his reply made it clear that Len did not speak about the war to anyone. He had a kind face, a typical grandad wearing tortoise shell glasses, one of those faces, which inspired both confidence and friendliness. Because of this, many folks made the mistake when confronted by Len regarding matters of security. His misdemeanour gave out a false message and it hit hard when the true reality of Len's determination came to the front and he followed orders and rules without compassion or regard for seniority. He could quote the security handbook from cover to cover, chapter and verse and would not budge if the object of his attention fell outside of these orders. To Len it was of little consequence of your position or otherwise, he stuck rigidly to the rules regardless. Even John Digby-Jones, the Managing Director had fallen foul of Len when he broke a security regulation and had been forced to comply.

George deliberately walked on past the doorway, then stopped to retrace his steps to peer backwards through the open doorway.

'Oh, good morning Mister Barratt, good morning Adrian!' He greeted in an exaggerated tone of voice attempting to sound very cheerful, looking at each man in turn. Both were furious that their indiscretion now had a witness and his friendly greeting increased the look of daggers aimed in his direction. *Child by name* managed to mumble a reply whilst *Lumpy bumps* stood glaring at him, choosing to ignore his over polite reaction at seeing him in an embarrassing situation. The best part of this exercise was that someone would now have to vouch for their identity and then sign the two managers in. This morning of all mornings, George was destined to be that person.

'George?' Len said over his shoulder, half-turning with an enormous grin on his face, coupled with going cross-eyed, which neither man could see. George managed, just, to keep a straight face. 'Do you recognise either of these two gentlemen?'

'Mister Barratt and Mister Child.' He replied, struggling to suppress his true feelings and not burst into a fit of uncontrollable laughter. George knew that if he started laughing he would not be able to stop easily. In the background he heard the start bell ringing and knew that *The Little Boy* would already be aware of his absence, and would take great delight in confronting him, when he did appear at his desk, demanding an explanation.

'That is their identity?'

'Yes Len. Mister Barratt is standing on the right and Mister Child standing on the left.' George confirmed.

This procedure always appeared pointless to him, until someone pointed out that Security staff could be called in from any ESR establishment without notice, who would neither know nor recognise legitimate members of staff. The carrying of a security pass eliminated all chances of unauthorised entry. From that moment it all made good sense and sound security practice.

'You are absolutely sure it's them?' Len taking full opportunity to make the point.

'It is, Len.' George replied simply, still maintaining some resemblance of seriousness. 'I can vouch for them both.'

'Are you prepared to sign them i....?' Len asked.

'I protest!' *Lumpy Bumps* said immediately, even before Len had completed his sentence. 'I should be signed in by another senior manager not an ordinary member of staff.'

Len, his humour forgotten temporarily, spoke in his official voice. 'Mister Barratt, I have already explained to you. There are no senior managers on the premises at this time. They are all at Head Office for a presentation and likely to remain there for some time yet. You can wait for one to arrive if you wish. Because of these extenuating circumstances, I am prepared in this case, to make an exception and will agree to have you signed in by a member of staff, well known to me.'

The reply was immediate, as it was abrupt. 'I insist that I am signed in by another senior manager.'

'As you wish.' Len said with disbelief clearly sounding in his voice. 'What would you like to do Mister Child?'

'George can sign me in.' He said with reluctance.

'That's not right Adrian!' *Lumpy bumps* retorted, turning to glare at *Child by name*. 'We should not be treated like this.'

'Remember to bring your passes with you each day, then you will not have to go through this procedure.' Len replied, well practised in these matters. To become head of security, tact and diplomacy together with dealing with senior management had to be second nature. 'You have been treated well, despite having arrived without your passes at least three times this year to my knowledge. All I am trying to do is to comply with MoD and standard ESR security requirements and simultaneous to this not to cause either of you undue inconvenience.'

Len spoke with feeling, having said these words to this particular pair several times previously, then turned around giving George a wink, and a screwed up face, as he drew his attention to a spot on the temporary pass with an index finger. 'Sign here George, please.'

George duly signed, succeeding in his attempt not to laugh.

'Thank you, my friend.'

Len tore the signed sheet out of his book and handed it over to Adrian. 'Try not to lose this paper Mister Child, because if you leave these premises at lunchtime without it, you will have great difficulty getting back in again. Tomorrow morning, you should report directly to me. Bring this temporary pass with you. I will expect you to have on your person your official pass, otherwise I shall have to put you on report.'

'Ok, Len, I'll have it with me.'

'Thanks George, I will be seeing you later.' Len said rising to his feet as *Child by name* and George left the office. George raised an arm by means of acknowledgement. As they emerged from the security office, the outer door burst open behind them and in came Frank DeVaal and his co-traveller Bob Champlin. Both men resided on the outskirts of Saffron Walden over forty miles away up the A11 and shared the driving, simply to reduce the cost of travelling to work. They both worked as engineers in the development section and had recently showed signs of dissent, with regard to the procedure taken by security, whenever a member of staff was more than three minutes late. The staff handbook stated that lateness within three minutes was permitted on three occasions within a calendar month. The reason being that it took at least three minutes to reach the main door from the official car park. Being in the car park made staff legally on the premises and therefore not technically absent from their place of work. Outside of this time, a record of lateness would be kept. After the third time, security staff would formally demand to know the name of the perpetrator, whose name would be given to the relevant department head for consideration of punishment, which could include a variety of penalties, including, in extreme cases, instant dismissal. A number of white collar staff who lived some distance from ESR, shared the driving for matters of economy, including three in the drawing office. Inclement weather, a serious accident, road works or even a simple puncture, invariably meant that these groups occasionally ran close to the wind in respect to timekeeping, and as such they had a constant run in with security staff, over the timing of the three minutes. Then Bob Champlin, after months of dispute, arguments and disagreements, noticed that the ESR security clock did not always replicate Greenwich Mean Time within a reasonable tolerance and claimed discrepancy over the three minute period, then demanded that his name be struck from the list.

Bob, who thoroughly enjoyed the reputation of being deliberately controversial, regularly visited Faslane Naval Base, 25 miles north west of Glasgow, and occasionally returned with a Scottish pound note.

'I've been lumbered with one of *these* bloody things again!' He often complained whenever he found one in his wallet.

In the early days of his service, if Bob offered a Scottish Pound note for payment in the works canteen, acceptance was always refused, on the grounds of it being foreign currency. He resorted to plan B and deliberately used the staff canteen, complete with waitress service instead and having eaten prior to payment, the notes were reluctantly accepted, especially when Bob knowingly had no other cash on him! No matter how trivial or petty, any small victory over officialdom always gave him great delight!

The Staff Union eventually became involved in the clock accuracy dispute and by all accounts some lively discussions took place with senior management, which resulted in an unresolved stand off. In reality, the Security Staff were forced to err on the side of caution, checked their clock on a daily basis and unofficially allowed nearer five minutes instead of the regulation three.

Despite this the disagreements continued.

Frank DeVaal, remained outspoken over the pettiness of the way staff were treated and stated openly he would not co-operate with the scheme. When after a third time Security asked for his name, he refused to give it, arguing that as the record of his alleged lateness had been kept without his knowledge or referral to him, he would not be able to challenge the record at a later time. He expressed an opinion to anyone who would listen, that he failed to appreciate how security had the right to take his name, when it had been legally given to him thirty years previously by his parents, around the time of his birth. If security took his name, he complained, by what name should he be known? Further more, what would security do with a name that was of little use to anyone except to the legal owner, namely himself?

Frank was another of George's colleagues whose mould became broken at the time of his birth. Of medium build, around five feet ten inches tall, with dark brown hair showing the first signs of greyness, his crowning glory, his neatly trimmed moustache in his true hair colouring, of which he was extremely proud. He spoke quietly and with intense passion and was inclined to go into unnecessary detail when explaining anything, frowning with concentration throughout the time he spoke. A brilliant engineer, he worked on the Sentinel project and also the Dunking Sonar, developed, designed and manufactured at ESR. He previously served with the Royal Navy as a sonar operator on helicopters. There had been several modifications made to the Dunking Sonar Project because of Frank's intimate knowledge about naval operating procedures at sea, to the extent he could argue with some authority with the MoD on technical matters, who often appeared to be ignorant of reality. George felt positive that the electronic equipment was better designed and more suitable to be used in extreme conditions, as a direct result of Frank's input. Quietly spoken, he could, when the need arose, show dogged determination. The incidents of name taking by security and Frank's response to this came as no surprise to George.

Frank once related a tale, which explained his philosophy to life, and one, which revealed his true character when under duress. Some years earlier he had been taking part in a major exercise in the Pacific and one evening found as part of a crew in a helicopter at the extreme limit of its operating range, which from memory was in the region of one hundred and fifty miles from its home carrier. To increase the tension and difficulty of the operation, if this were possible, the main part of the exercise took place at night. Frank and his crew were using an early version of dunking sonar, trying to locate and identify the presence of an American submarine, also on exercise. They were hovering at a height of sixty feet using their equipment, knowing a submarine was nearby but also with the knowledge that the Commander and his submarine crew would be using all their skill and determination not to be discovered. A simple case of national pride! Frank detected a faint echo on his screen but remained unconvinced of its origin. Attempting to interpret a signal using comparative primitive equipment in its infancy, in tropical warm waters together with unfamiliar underwater wildlife, which could easily interfere with the signal, was an acquired art. Head down, concentrating on the screen, he heard his skipper through headphones, say a series of words every airman dreads. 'Losing oil pressure! Adopt crash positions and prepare for dunking!'

Moments later he heard through his sound proofed headphones a loud bang, followed by a sinking feeling in the pit of his stomach. Because of his intense concentration, he had yet to appreciate the seriousness of the situation until the helicopter crashing into the sea, coincided with his realisation of the skippers' words. The helicopter, fell sixty feet in around two seconds and being undamaged on the hull, by a miracle did not sink immediately and gave precious time for the crew of four and their neutral adjudicator, to make their escape. The radio operator was the last to emerge, as he had been determined and courageous, despite personal risk, to send an emergency message, which to the amazement of everyone, had been received and immediately acknowledged. Frank was alone in the blackened sea for several minutes in a state of panic bordering on hysteria, until his training came into play. He found his torch and in its feeble beam eventually saw other crew members swimming towards him. They were in a tricky situation, fortunately made slightly less dramatic as the carrier now knew their precise location. Finding them in shark invested waters at night seemed an impossible task, given that the flotilla were over a hundred miles away. Their providence lay beneath the waves, in the shape of the friendly American submarine, they had been trying to locate. If the commander followed a normal evasion pattern, he would soon realise that the helicopter was no longer attempting to track then and if he were close by, the Sonar operator may have even heard the crash landing. For over an hour the crew floated in relatively calm seas trying to keep cheerful, whilst skipper concentrated on the adjudicator. The poor chap was quite unused and untrained for this activity. He would have undergone basic escape training in the tank at Portsmouth but this would not prepare anyone sufficiently to being dunked in the Pacific Ocean at night. The crew who were better trained had difficulty in keeping calm, despite a potential threat of a shark attack expected at any moment, which kept everyone on edge. Logic suggested afterwards that noise of the crash would keep any wise shark well away from potential trouble, but sharks were well known for being unpredictable. Suddenly without warning, they found themselves bathed in the beam of a powerful searchlight. The light brought them all into instant panic until the moment they were challenged in a pronounced American accent. They then appreciated its significance.

The American submarine had located them!

The sonar operator had correctly identified a helicopter crash and the exercise had been abandoned and immediately transformed into a rescue mission. They were pulled from the water in a sorry state and entered the submarine through the forward hatch and escorted to cramped quarters, where they remained well fed and watered until the following afternoon, when they rejoined their carrier. Throughout their time on board Frank was quick to notice that they were kept under constant watch by outwardly friendly guards but not permitted to venture from their quarters. To complicate matters, the submarine was quite unable to contact the carrier directly due to some technical difficulty with military frequencies. They sailed towards the fleet, then discovered that with a major rescue underway, the two vessels had somehow missed each other in the darkness. Literally ships that passed in the night! The submarine backtracked at once and some hours later surfaced whilst the carrier was still frantically searching within the area of the last known position, fearing they had lost the whole crew.

Frank had been convinced that he would not last the night and feared above all else the possibility of a shark attack. He felt so relieved at being rescued, he vowed to treat every day as being his last. Every day became important, and events before his enforced dunking in the Pacific, which would have normally been ignored as being irrelevant, were now worth his full consideration. For no apparent reason he now found he tended to challenge unreasonable authority from any quarter.

As *Child by name* and George walked into the drawing office, they became aware of a row developing behind them and seeing *The Little Boy* rise from his seat the moment George appeared, the possibility of another argument developing in the very near future. *Child by name* must have noticed *The Little Boy* react and said.

'Don't concern yourself about him.' He said, for once sounding genuinely concerned. 'If he should ask where you have been, send him over to me. Thanks for being willing to sign me in. Mister Barratt should have let you sign him in also.'

George was so shocked at hearing these rare words of praise, he did not reply.

The Little Boy did enquire in a forceful fashion about his whereabouts, the moment George reached his desk, but George did his best and not react to this over enthusiastic questioning, but give him his due he went over to see *Child by name* when George briefly explained and he gave him no further grief.

Around this time, the prospective thief John Ferguson, handed in his notice. He had decided to move back to Bucksburn in Scotland so he and his wife could be nearer their family. His son Iain had married the previous year and had announced that a baby was expected in six months time. This prompted John to find a job in Aberdeen and this he had accomplished with apparent ease. George did not believe him when he related the tale of apparent desperation of an engineering firm to employ him, but then it could be said that he was biased.

Should John Ferguson decide to make the most of his last four weeks to steal as much money as possible, Doug Watson and George kept a constant vigil. They need not have worried, for his period of notice passed by without incident. John Ferguson left on the last Friday of the month allowing Doug and George to relax for the first time in months.

It must have been a month later, when George walked by the office of *Child by name*. Two months had passed without a theft taking place and he began to feel confident about his assumption concerning John Ferguson. He had contemplated how much time should elapse before he made revelations as to the identity of the thief. *Child by name* looked up at this moment and in that split second George made a decision and stood in the doorway.

'Hello George.' He greeted, laying his pen on the desk, then leaning back in his chair 'What can I do you for?'

George stepped into the office and took a deep breath before answering. 'The thieving will cease!' He announced with confidence.

Relaxed a moment before *Child by name* became instantly alert and attentive, his violent reaction caused him to lose balance but managed, just, to avoid falling backwards.

'What's happened George?' He demanded, after he recovered. 'Have you caught him?'

'No I have not.' George replied. 'You will have to take my word for it, the thieving will cease!'

To his relief it did.

When George arrived back at his desk, the mock-up foreman David King stood leaning on the petitionl ooking along the gangway. George sat down and saw the subject of David's attention. He was looking at Rita, one of the young ladies who worked in the print room. She was crouching down by the shredder with her knees apart and as she wore a short skirt, this allowed anyone who cared to look a good view of inner thigh and at the top of her legs. Her area of fascination enclosed by thin material, was a blessing for devotees of the female form, like David.

'Dirty sod, she's married!' George commented as he approached.

'She should keep it all to herself then!' He retorted, without taking his eyes off his target. David was one of those clear-thinking intellectuals who cared about his fellowman. Always impeccably dressed in a suit, a neatly ironed quality shirt and a flamboyant tie. He was known to have braces, usually bright red, for David was not inclined to wear subdued colours. This eccentric clothing occasionally came into view if his stylish half overalls parted. Clean-shaven with short hair, and being bespectacled, somehow made him appear friendly and approachable, which he was with most people for most of the time. Beware though, if he became upset because of unreasonable behaviour and did not suffer fools lightly. It would not take long for a potential adversary, or a fool to establish that whilst he made a totally reliable and trustworthy friend, he made a terrible enemy. His Achilles heel was a first class honours degree in eyeing up women, especially those who chose to expose their body parts, deliberately or accidentally.

*

At lunchtime George had once been walking back to the office when he met David and they walked in sunshine along a tree-lined avenue. A few yards ahead a young blonde woman wearing a short red dress came out of a house, and approached a car parked outside. She opened the driver's door with the key, knelt on these at to lean over and retrieve something from the glove box.

David gave a short intake of breath with pursed lips.

'Deary me!' He exclaimed under his breath.

The woman leant over still further allowing the dress to ride up as far as her buttocks. David became so excited at the sight of a shapely pair of legs topped by her pert bum enclosed by lacy red coloured material, he grabbed hold of Georges arm.

'Deary me!' He repeated.

Even George was now staring, totally captivated by the unintentional exposure. They were almost upon her now, walking first at the pace of a snail then to a virtual standstill as they continued to peer into the car. Unbeknown to them they had veered off course. George felt something touch his leg at knee level, but before he had the opportunity to react, found he was trapped between something hard and the momentum of David's body.

'What the f....!'

David and George fell over a low garden wall, and most of their bodies ended up in a front garden. The young lady had now retrieved the item from the glove compartment and stood with a hand unashamedly laughing at their predicament, tears rolling down her face.

David was not amused. 'Look what you have made us do!' He complained, peering at a graze on his hand.

The young lady smiled sweetly, wiped away the tears with a hand, then turned to walk smartly into her house and closed the door.

*

Rita stood up and returned to the print room, whereupon David no longer distracted, smiled briefly in his direction. In a flash, the smile disappeared and he became serious.

'I have a worrying reoccurring problem with the Sentinel main display console.' He said. He produced a wad of folded circuit diagrams from behind the partition, which he handed to George. 'Perhaps you would care to help me resolve it?' This sounded like an invitation but from past experience George knew this to be virtually an instruction.

'What loom, David?' George asked, as he began to unfold the first drawing. He noticed it was the first sheet of six. He searched and found the schedule.

'Nineteen.' Came a quick response. ' It's the one between the 128 pin connector to the range dial and the testrig.'

The test rig was a comparatively simple device, developed to enable analysis of the complete system. It provided the emulation necessary to test the ability of the Sentinel project to function normally, without having to rely on actual sensors aboard a submarine. It generated automated test scenarios saving valuable engineering time and fully tested the system prior to its installation on board.

George unfolded three unwieldy prints before he found the one relating to loom nineteen. The two men carefully studied the complicated wiring schedule, trying to locate the correct connector. George always found these loom drawings difficult because of their size and complexity, but to David they appeared to be simple.

Each to his own George supposed.

'Ah, here it is!' George proclaimed pointing to a particular group of wires.

David peered at the wiring diagram and schedule making notes as he went.

'Right young George, I understand the problem, lets go and find the solution!'

The Little Boy was not within sight, so George left a note on his desk before following David into the Assembly area, and on into the mock up area. The display console had two panels removed, and the 128 connector hung down amongst the mirrors and wiring. David reconnected it and made some adjustments to the test rig. The range dial flickered briefly displaying 2,000 yards, changed to 9,999 yards, went out completely, flickered, then resumed to display the original 2,000 yards.

'I have checked, the loom, the test rig and changed the range assembly, so it is most likely the connector.' David explained.' Shall I get Tiann to change it?'

For some unexplained reason George recalled his time in the telephone exchange. 'No, let's do some investigative work ourselves first.' George suggested. 'We will probably do better sorting it out on our own. Especially if we catch him in bad mood.'

'Fine by me.' David replied as he began to inspect the connector.

For over an hour, they compared the loom to the schedule, used a continuity meter, and as a precaution, replaced the range dial assembly. Then George sent David off to borrow an illuminated magnifier and stand. When David arrived back, George manipulated the 128 pin connector to examine the pins. The loom side seemed fine, but when he viewed the connecting pins, he thought he could see a small piece of debris by pin 27.

'What does pin 27 connect to?' He asked.

Beside him David briefly studied the schedule. 'Why that is a surprise, it's the range dial. Why do you ask?'

'There's a small piece of debris by the pins and I suspect it's causing a short.'

'That's impossible. Let me have a dekko!'

George moved aside to let David view the connector. He was silent for several minutes viewing the pin 27 from several angles. Eventually he took his eyes away from the magnifier and with a shrug of his shoulders, turned to look at George. He gave the appearance of being a worried man.

'I do not understand this George, and that's a fact. It looks like solder.' He said shaking his head. 'It is simply not possible for this to happen accidentally. The connecting pins are always shrouded during assembly, and in any case, as a precaution the whole loom receives a thorough inspection prior to assembly, and it is not touched by anyone. One, without a record being kept, and two without me knowing about it.'

'Who made and checked the loom?'

David picked up a card lying on the display unit. 'I have already checked. Tiann made this loom three months ago, and Ivy checked it. It was modified two weeks ago to accommodate the updated lag line units, but it couldn't have occurred then as this connector was not affected by these modifications.'

'All we can do, is to remove the offending debris and tighten the inspection procedures.' George suggested. 'To go down any other route could land us all in the shit!'

'What are you suggesting?'

'I am not suggesting anything.' George lowered his voce. 'If it is a cock up, or a faulty connector, well that can be dealt with. If, on the other hand it's deliberate, then that will have serious consequence for us all'

'It can't be deliberate, can it?'

'Who knows, best keep it to ourselves until we know one way or the other. George whispered. 'Lets first remove the debris, and take it from there.'

David went off in search of tweezers, but the only pair he could locate were far too large. He found an oddment of wire, which he heated with a miniature blowtorch, placed a sheet of paper underneath to catch the solder. He then gently touched the solder with the heated wire. The effect was immediate. The solder melted at once and dripped onto the paper, where it solidified.

'That's not solder, there was not enough heat for that!' David exclaimed. 'That can only be a gravity or drop casting alloy.'

'What the devil is that?' George asked, still reeling over their discovery.

'Used by model makers, mainly.' David replied, continuing to peer at the connector. 'My brother-in-law uses it to make castings for his railway bits.'

'Do we use it here?'

'Possibly, but I've never seen it. The engineers may use it but it is definitely not used on the assembly areas.'

'How could it have got here, then?'

David considered his answer and shook his head before answering. 'As you have already suggested, I don't want to go down that route George, for it means either a serious accident due to faulty inspection procedures or something much more serious!'

'Hells bells!'

'I shall have to make out a damage report.' David replied. 'For the time being shall I shall leave it under lock and key and also undated, so you and I are in the clear if it goes pear shape.'

A week later, within minutes of the going home bell going, David appeared and leaned on the partition. George looked up from packing his briefcase. 'What's new pussy cat?' He greeted cheerfully as he was about to go home.

'It's happened again George!' David said grimly.' Come and look at the damage. We shall have to report it this time.'

'Oh shit!' George exclaimed. 'The balloon will go up with a bang!'

'It will be more than a balloon George!'

The bell went as they reached the mock up area. George inspected the 128 pin connector and saw faint traces of what appeared to be model makers alloy, but this time it had been disguised by some form of paint.

'We should leave it as it is and report it tomorrow.' George suggested.

He went home a worried man dreading the coming day, slept badly and upon arrival at the factory, first told *The Little Boy* where he was going, then went straight to the mock up.

He found Andrew, the Assembly Manager, kneeling on the floor by the main console in discussion with David. He looked up as George walked in through the door, 'You've already seen this George?'

'Yes, last thing yesterday evening just before closing time.' George admitted feeling very uneasy. 'We decided it best left until this morning.......' Out of Andy's vision, David, held a finger up to his lips, hinting at George to say the absolute minimum.

'This will mean a full investigation and if it involves negligence, the police will have to be informed, notwithstanding the MoD. God alone knows how they will react! I must congratulate you both for the courage in coming forward. It could not have been easy decision to make and I admire you for making this known to me.'

'What happens now?'

'I shall have to go to the top. It will mean no discussion with Tiann, Ivy, anyone on the assembly line, or your lot in the drawing office, including Adrian and co, George. We keep this to ourselves unless I say so. Agreed?

Both men nodded.

'Get Tiann to check the connectors we have in stock.' Andrew suggested.

'No can do. Tiann is not in.'

'Where is he?'

'No idea, just not turned up this morning.'

Later on during the week, it was discovered that a few connectors had defective pins, which caused the short. The cause was never established, despite a thorough investigation carried out by the Assembly Manager and the connector manufacturer.

*

The Sentinel project team had two contract draughtsmen working for a three months period and one, a heavy smoker and a heavy drinker if all his claims were true, managed to provoke *The Little Boy* from his first day. George had not the slightest idea what he did to get himself in this sudden and unfortunate situation, not working directly with him, nor being a witness to the first encounter. Suffice to say that their obvious unstable relationship closely resembled a disaster waiting to happen. The contract draughtsman, by the name of Les Fisher, closely resembled Art Garfunkle, of Simon and Garfunkle fame, and claimed to be able to play the guitar to professional standard. Certainly, the nails of his right hand were longish and those on his left clipped short, with hardened skin on fingertips, made it a distinct possibility that he was telling the truth. George had the odd chat during the lunchtime period and he certainly knew a thing or two about guitar playing.

The ultimate act, whatever that was, took place just after lunchtime, when George happened to glance up from his work to see Les and *The Little Boy* seated at his desk in deep discussion. In retrospect the conversation seemed animated, with plenty of arm waving as one or the other, emphasised a point. Then, quite unexpectedly there was a loud outburst from *The Little Boy*. George paid no attention being grateful for once not to be involved with his tantrums. The next time he glanced up, Les was in the process of being ushered into *Lumpy Bumps* office, where after only a short meeting, he saw Les grim faced, standing at his desk packing his things up. He then stormed out of the office without saying goodbye to anyone. Try as he did George could not find out anything about the episode. Short of asking *The Little Boy*, one thing he would not even consider, those who did know were saying little or nothing.

The following morning there was a flurry of activity around the desk where until yesterday Les worked. *Child by Name* and *The Little Boy* assisted by *Lumpy bumps,* were looking at the drawings left on the drawing board, methodically searching every drawer, inspecting every piece of paper contained within, before taking each one out to peer inside the cabinet. They then descended upon each team member in turn and systematically went through all drawers and drawings without revealing either purpose or intent.

This had almost sinister tones, as both Allan and Len, senior members of the Security staff stood nearby in attendance acting as overseers whilst the searches took place. When his turn came, George asked a direct question of *Child by Name*.

'What are you looking for, Adrian?' He enquired.

'Never you mind.' Came a blunt reply. 'Take my advice and just keep out of the way!'

The thorough search conducted involved looking at every piece of paper in his possession, which included all those paper oddments found in every private drawer. A collection of bills, old diaries, business cards and to his embarrassment the dirty magazines that formed part of the book club he managed to joined by default.

George did a favour for Bob Duncan, the Assistant Chief Engineer, known to all as *ACE*. Bob ran a motoring club and asked George to produce artwork for a tulip rally. George thought this something to do with flowers until *ACE* explained that it was a method of showing a route using a simple diagram to show junction or road layout. A dot represented the start point and an arrow the desired route to take. Once on the correct road, a dot on the next diagram represented the start point on the next diagram and so on until the end of the section. When George delivered the artwork one lunchtime, he noticed a collection of assorted magazines on Bob's guest chair. When he enquired, *ACE* explained that he ran a book club, where for a modest monthly sum, little more than the price of a single magazine, a member enjoyed in return about twenty different magazines. George said that it seemed good value and would like to join. *ACE* replied by saying that membership was normally open to engineers only. He paused to consider his request, then said that a vacancy did exist. He was in the process of deciding which magazine to drop, and given the fact that George had done him a favour for his latest car rally, he would make an exception, provided he did not advertise the fact to other members of the Drawing Office fraternity. George duly accepted, and about a week later the first collection of magazines was delivered to his desk.

The security search found the latest delivery of magazines, including the dirty variety, from the book club, but they did not take the slightest interest in them. Instead they were cast aside whilst they concentrated on their more important task of finding the mysterious document, which George had assumed was missing.

*

The security of all activities within the factory and beyond, especially becoming a temporary custodian of documents or drawings, gave cause for concern and took priority even over the purpose of the work itself.

Documents came in four categories. Unclassified, Restricted, Confidential and Secret. Technically there were five categories but the highest level, stamped *Top Secret* in red ink, would not be in normal circulation. Throughout his years at ESR, George did not get a sighting of a single Top Secret document.

Should anyone have custody of a document with the heading, unclassified, or restricted, these could be used freely during the day as any other drawings or papers, but left out of sight under the drawing board cover or in an unlocked drawer, outside of working hours. Those headed confidential or secret, these should be left out of sight during the working day, except when in use, but at all other times, including time spent away from your usual place of work, stored in a nominated lockable cabinet. Each cabinet, usually in the care of a section leader was then locked at the close of every working day and checked in an approved manner. Senior staff, which included George, were on a four week roster for this security check. At precisely ten minutes before going home time, the keys to all the cabinets, were collected a section at a time from section leaders. One of the pair made sure each cabinet was secure with the steel bar placed correctly in its slot and the Chubb padlock fastened to the top clasp, then locked. Virtually every evening, one or other of the section leaders failed to secure a bar correctly and a bad tempered confrontation prevailed each time. To a man, they did not like being reprimanded, even gently and with humour, by someone they viewed as a junior member of staff. These were crossed off a check list and when complete and signed for, the list together with the collection of keys, placed in a wall safe by *Lumpy Bumps* office. At one time an industrial dispute arose and members threatened to boycott the key checking roster. *Lumpy Bumps* called all those affected into his office and pleaded with them, including George who was not a member of the union, to find some other form of protest. He reasoned, probably correctly, that if the MoD found that security was not as it should be, they might decide to close the factory. George had every reason to assume this would happen. The union were forced to comply with this request and chose to ban overtime instead.

*

Everyone assumed that Les Fisher must have had in his possession, a document headed either confidential or secret, which had been posted as missing after his unscheduled departure. Not surprising if his sudden and traumatic exit was not expected. In any event the responsibility to check documents held by individuals on his section was that of *The Little Boy*.

303

It transpired that the document in question was a secret layout, which indicated the sentinel project located inside a nuclear submarine that identified major components, together with their technical names. The consequence of this particular document going missing was considered serious enough for the police to become involved. An arrest warrant was sent to South Wales Police where Les was known to reside, together with a search warrant for his property. In the event Les had been arrested and questioned by Special Branch, whilst his house searched thoroughly. Finding nothing in the house and with little revealed by the intensive questioning, he was eventually released.

About six months later one of the section heads decided to rearrange his section, which quite naturally involved a substantial office move. One of the security cabinets, being full to the brim with documents, the labourers were quite unable to shift it from its position, so its contents had to be emptied prior to it being moved. As one of the drawer contents was being removed, the section clerk noticed a drawing tucked down the back as if it had been caught up when the drawer was closed.

The document found was indeed the secret layout showing the Sentinel project within a nuclear submarine! Poor Les had endured a stressful time with Special Branch for no good reason.

That event turned out to be only part of the problem. Labourers moved an adjacent cabinet, which backed onto the particular cabinet with the document tucked away inside. One side was lifted up and a barrow lip placed underneath. As they struggled with the heavy load being wheeled slowly across the office to its new position, it became apparent that its neighbour did not possess a steel back! To gain entry, all one had to do was to move the cabinet an inch or two away to gain full entry to its contents.

So much for security!

This caused a major panic amongst senior management and as a direct result of high level meetings the contents of every cabinet in the whole factory, was emptied to ascertain whether their contents were correct. Every cabinet was then subjected to close inspection to check that they possessed a back plate and as a consequence one or two cabinets were replaced. This brought to light other misdemeanours, and although mainly accidental, those in the section underwent a gruelling to establish why they had not followed strict security procedures.

Because of his association with the Metropolitan Special Constabulary, and as such presumed trustworthy, mainly by *Child by name*, George was often chosen for a rather unpleasant and difficult task, in the name of security. Usually he worked with Allan Kippin, *Kipper* from the card school, chosen because they considered him especially trustworthy too.

Without warning, members of the Security Staff appeared at the desks of George and *Kipper* then escorted them from their normal place of work, to descend upon another office, without warning, to undertake a full security check on an unsuspecting target. For security to function as decreed by their Lord and Master, the MoD, every holder or keeper of a lockable cabinet kept a record of documents currently in use. He should also ensure that these were correctly signed out and back in, so in the event of a security check, the location and holder of every document or drawing could be accounted.

Well, that was the theory.

In reality George and *Kipper* usually discovered a discrepancy, with the keeper undergoing a period of anxiousness until all documents were found or accounted for. *Kipper* and George were often the ones chosen to perform this unpleasant task, because they did so without becoming involved personally, and carried out to the letter, that required of them, despite the consequences. It invariably meant subjecting a fellow employee, albeit senior to them, to a great deal of stress. Many of the targets were middle managers, who quite naturally resented intrusion to their personal domain, with *Kipper* and George subjected to all manner of hostile or sarcastic remarks and the occasional threat. Each time this was reported and usually the offender afterwards gave a reluctant apology. Most of the time they took these comments in their stride, but every now and then, they reacted, which only added to the bad feeling. It can be successfully argued that if proper account of a relatively simple procedure were taken, the security check could be carried out with the minimum of formality and inconvenience. Most managers took proper care of documents and the check took the minimum of time to complete. In reality many sections were under pressure to comply with a tight schedule and the absence of the odd drawing could be easily missed or simply forgotten.

When things were not particularly busy, *Kipper* and George did other tasks together. A quiet period gave section leaders the opportunity to trawl through their documents and drawings, then dispose of those considered being either obsolete or not required. As a consequence there were a great deal of documents to be shredded. Office Shredders are relatively inexpensive to purchase from stationers, but security shredders are a world apart. The one used at ESR possessed a nasty set of heavy-duty castellated teeth, which caused great vibration as they revolved. These teeth would grip anything once caught in their grasp and the powerful electric motor ensured that the teeth did their work, which included fingers and they always took great care when using it. These teeth had to be regularly lubricated with special oil. Once *Kipper* and George copied a document, then ran the original through the shredder. Afterwards they carefully retrieved the thin slices of paper from the wastebasket and attempted to reinstate it to its original form. They did not succeed, even having the copy document for reference. The paper had been shredded to about half a millimetre wide, leaving a residue of dust in the collection tray, making it impossible to distinguish any trace of original text or lines on the paper.

During another quiet period, *Child by name* gave them the task to declassify a large set of drawings, in a manner, which could not be easily detected by the MoD. Apparently in anticipation of a decision, someone had designated them as unclassified when in reality the MoD classified them as confidential. Every drawing from foolscap (13 $\frac{1}{2}$ x 17 inches) to the Double Imperial -table cloth size variety (30 x 44 inches) had a box of sufficient size for a rubber stamp classification mark to be placed. The drawings given to them were a variety of originals, from virgin linen to poor sepia copies of standard parts, which were modified to suit the particular project. They acquired, borrowed or stole an assortment of types of paper and linen and set about cutting out the appropriate box, then inserting matching material from their collection. They used a tape similar to magic invisible tape to affix new blank paper before using the official rubber stamp. The result was that the drawing would stand up to scrutiny with the repairs not easily detectable.

*

Pressure on individuals was sometimes considerable. Most could soak up stresses and strains of tight deadlines quite easily, and used the weekend to fully recover before the next week when the onslaught resumed. But what about those who carried on regardless until eventually they snapped? There are those who promote superstition, referring to black cats, lucky rabbits feet, and it is considered bad luck to see a single magpie, but two magpies are lucky. Walking or not walking under ladders, four leaf clovers, touching wood, fingers crossed, horseshoe over a doorway and breaking a mirror. Wearing of lucky heather, talisman or a St Christopher medallion in order to ward off evil spirits. It was essential for a bride, in order to avoid bad luck on her marriage, to wear *something old, something new, something borrowed, something blue*, and a variety of other popular beliefs. One well known saying is that bad luck always occurs in threes. Well, that is one aspect that George could be persuaded to believe in, for he had bitter personal experience.

The first of the three concerns his friend Tim Gabriel.

George had known Tim since his apprentice days and over the years grew to know him and his family well. He was a lovely man, who showed concern when things went wrong. He would always be the first to offer help or advice. He too had been in the army and the habit of maintaining a smart appearance from head to toe, drifted over into civilian life. He always wore an immaculate suit, with carefully pressed trousers with creases so sharp, you could almost cut a finger on them. He completed his ensemble by a white shirt, a silk tie, highly polished shoes and walked about as if on a parade ground. His philosophy proved the point that clothes which made the man did not have to be expensive, but rather that with care, cheap clothing properly cared for, did just as well as expensive clothing. They were not close, but their rapport developed over the years to the point where they could socialise without effort, including Tim's wife Ellen and teenaged daughter Linda. Tim spent most of his waking life laughing heartily at every opportunity, but whose constant merriment disguised the misery he must have felt inwardly. He married when still quite young and his equally young wife fell for a child within a very short period after their marriage. Ellen had a difficult pregnancy and she was in labour for forty eight hours. Once Linda was born his wife refused to have sex with him and Tim endured a lasting dilemma. He needed to enjoy the gratification of a female body but her denial forced him to seek pleasure elsewhere and having found a willing female, he battled with his conscience over being unfaithful. In coil winding, there worked an attractive supervisor named Millie, recently widowed, who Tim befriended. George could certainly appreciate why he felt attracted to her. It would not be that difficult for George, even being a few years her junior to feel the same way. She was about the same age as Tim, owned her own house, had a pleasant demeanour and a very ample bosom, which Millie took great delight to display to anybody who cared to look. Whenever she smiled, her radiance reduced every male to having legs like jelly, willing to do anything she asked. Tim once confided, that if he could persuade Ellen to agree to a divorce, he would be free to move in with Millie. In reality he thought there was not the remotest chance that Ellen would ever agree to a divorce. She would refuse point blank, simply to be vindictive.

Tim constantly sought ways of ending the marriage but felt an obligation to his daughter. His mind became trapped inside an unhappy marriage and he found ways for his body to have an opportunity to escape temporarily. The strain of maintaining the deceit gradually wore him down towards despair. In the days leading up to when his daughter married, his mind reached an all time low. George knew this because he possessed a first class honours degree in hindsight. If he had been able to sense Tim's true state of mind, Tim would probably still be alive. As it was, Tim told George of his suicide but George simply did not recognise the warning signs, which should have been obvious to him.

It is one of the few things in his life, George regretted.

Tim frequently stopped to have a chat, as he went about his business of progress chaser. By chance he too worked on the Sentinel project and this gave the two friends opportunity to use the project for social reasons though if necessary they could both justify to *The Little Boy* or other section leader, their reasons for talking. The main obstacle was Tim's constant laughter, always a give away to non work related chat.

Two days before the wedding Tim walked quickly by George's desk without an acknowledgement. This was most unusual. George called out his name. Tim seemed to come out of a dreamlike state, stopped and walk back immediately with reluctance. George detected even before Tim spoke, that he was not his usual jolly self.

'How are things at home, Tim?' He asked, referring to his home situation, for he knew full well how the wedding arrangements were progressing. His daughter and her prospective husband with almost practised ease, organised their wedding down to the finest detail, not leaving much for anyone to do except turn up on the day. Tim understood fully the reason for the question.

Amongst an almost endless list of misdemeanours by Ellen, she had recently taken in a lodger without first asking Tim if he agreed. According to Tim, she was an elderly woman with a particularly annoying parrot, which squawked constantly, and to his obvious annoyance, flew freely about the flat leaving messages wherever it went. Tim described her as *the scatty old cow!*

He tried to summon up courage to tell his wife that he wanted the lodger and her parrot, to leave very soon. George had suggested to Tim, on several occasions that Tim should leave his wife, and sue for divorce, being sure his daughter would, given time, forgive him. When Tim eventually challenged Ellen about the unwanted lodger she gave him a reply, which could not be misunderstood, especially as it was said in front of Linda.

'Fuck off! You are a complete waste of space!' She yelled showing Tim her utter contempt towards him. 'As a husband you are totally useless and as a man you are an utter failure. At least she talks to me!'

Remarks that were literally the last nail in Tim's coffin.

Tim considered the question for a moment, before giving George a reply.

His words haunt George to this day.

'After Linda gets married.' He said with a severe look on his normally happy face. 'I'm off!'

'You're not going anywhere Tim!' George joked, refusing to think that Tim could walk out on his precious Linda, despite his troubled home life.

'You're quite right. George.' Tim replied, unsmiling. 'I am not going anywhere.'

The double meanings of his remarks were pressed home a week later when George arrived at the factory to see the main entrance swarming with security and police. The corridor, which led by the back of the Sentinel Project mock up, had a rope across with a hand drawn sign which read. 'Police –keep out.'

George sat down at his desk and waited for the start bell to ring. Around him several others were doing similarly. *The Little Boy* strolled by on his way to his desk. 'What are the police doing here, Eddie?' he asked.

The question stopped *The Little Boy* dead in his tracks. 'Your mate topped himself, that's why.' He replied grimly, before hurrying off to sit down and drink his tea.

Mate?

What mate?

The Little Boy should not leave him like this. With his brain reeling with dreaded anticipation, George stood up and walked to his desk. *The Little Boy* sat looking at the headlines of the Daily Mirror, and glanced up at his approach.

'What mate?' George asked almost dreading the answer.

'Your mate the progress chaser. You know the one who's knocking off that Millie upstairs in coil winding!'

George almost fainted on the spot. Give him his due, *The Little Boy* recognised the signs immediately. In a single movement, he discarded his paper at lightning speed so it reassembled a screwed up rag immediately he thrust it aside, stood up, and grabbed hold of George as he fell, guiding him into his seat. Luckily the seat held as George crashed down, barely conscious.

Within ten minutes he recovered sufficiently to able to walk back to his desk.

Tim had told George about his suicide. As soon as Linda married Tim went off, not as George anticipated away to a fulfilling life with the luscious Millie, but to a lonely, empty life in eternity. His last words to George saying that he was not going anywhere proved to be so accurate, it sent shivers down his spine every time he thought if it.

At his funeral, a few colleagues from ESR attended, including the delightful Millie. During the short impersonal service at the crematorium, they were forced to witness a charade, as his widow cried and wept throughout the ceremony. It gave the false impression that she cared. Had she shown some compassion and concern when he was alive, Tim would surely have not contemplated suicide. His last hours on this earth were lonely and unfriendly. Tim had visited the toilets in the corridor by the main gate and in a cubicle, took an overdose of tablets. Finally he collapsed and in doing so cracked his skull open on the porcelain furniture and is where Security found him during a routine check during the night. On a more sinister note Ellen, Tim's wife had not even reported him as missing.

*

George paused in his typing before continuing. Reflecting on these events brought back the sadness felt several years previously, and as George typed, the horror came rushing back, as if it were only yesterday. He thought about his friend regularly, not being able to rid himself of guilt he felt over not picking up on Tim's warning.

*

George's second tale of woe concerns a lively character with the nickname *Bill the Brush*. Surprisingly no part of his job as messenger entailed use of a brush, but his nickname originated by his ungainly mop of bright ginger-red hair. Bill spent his working life in the army spending fair amount of time in India. He was a friendly character and when George married and moved to Leyton, Bill asked if George could give him a lift home. His pay was surprisingly low so George declined the offer of petrol money. He paid his way by buying him occasional bottles of his favourite beer. Before he ended his life George knew him well, but he refused to answer any requests to learn of his army life, except to relate the story of the earthquake he survived, and how he had been taught to drive. He explained in great detail of how grand shocks spooked all the animals. The area surrounding his billet stood in the middle of two bird nesting sites. A large colony of Rosy Starlings occupied a nearby clump of trees, always noisy, squawking and kept up a constant stream of noise from dawn to dusk. On the other side, just outside the compound an equally large colony of Ringneck parakeets, squabbling and squawking throughout the hours of daylight, occupied a crumbling and deserted native building, nesting in holes of the crumbling brickwork. The Rosy Starlings were of similar shape and size to starlings at home, but they had a small tuft of feathers on their head and the main body colour was a pleasant shade of orange pink. When the earthquake started the birds were totally silent and hung onto branches on one hand and sat at the entrance to their nests on the other. After a few seconds elapsed a single bird took off, which cause the two colonies to evacuate their nest sites, and they did not return for over an hour. Dogs roamed about

314

everywhere and were a common sight, some inclined to bark at the slightest pretext. The dogs though barked at nothing throughout the eight seconds the shock lasted. Eight seconds does not seem a long period of time, but to have the very ground shaking beneath your feet for such a length of time, was for Bill and is for George, beyond belief.

The tale of how Bill learned to drive was both equally amusing as it is horrific. His sergeant asked for volunteers to learn to drive, and by dubious means contrived to get the men he wanted. Up to this point in time Bill had felt no inclination to drive, but his sergeant had other ideas. Early one morning a few days later he clambered up into the driving seat for the first time, and his instructor gave a rapid guided tour of the gear layout and operation of the pedals. After a few minutes, his short tempered and impatient instructor ordered Bill to put the vehicle in gear and move off for the first time. Bearing in mind Bill was learning to drive in a ten ton truck, it was nothing short of a miracle he that he managed to succeed. He drove slowly about the Indian countryside, as the man beside shouted at him to speed up and showed signs of frustration when Bill, quite inexperienced in the use of controls of the cumbersome lorry, tried his hardest to comply. In the afternoon session Bill still struggled with the controls and managed to upset his instructor. As he drove about through the villages in the afternoon heat, Bill, being a humane person showed consideration to pedestrians and dogs, which habitually lay about anywhere they chose, including the road. He drove carefully around the sleeping dogs and slowed for pedestrians, to the continued annoyance of his instructor.

'Keep going, don't fucking worry about the fucking natives!' He shouted. 'Drive straight over the fucking dogs, they shouldn't be in our fucking way, fucking mangy bastards!'

At his next lesson, the instructor adopted different tactics in to force Bill to drive as he was told. He had just made himself comfortable in the driving seat when the instructor handed him a piece of black cloth, and briefly thought about asking what it was for. The instructor pre-empted his question. 'It's a blindfold!' He said with sarcasm. 'Not seen one before? Put it on man!'

The corporal ordered Bill to put the blindfold over his eyes then drive about the local Indian countryside and through populated areas. Consequently Bill did not have the faintest notion where he drove. During the journey Bill felt the lorry subjected to some heavy knocking, which he attributed to potholes in the road. The reality was more sinister which he did not discover until a few days after his instructor, apparently satisfied with his style of driving, allowed him to remove the blindfold. Today Bill, wearing the blindfold drove slowly out of the compound following instructions and along the road with obvious approval from his corporal.

'Good gear change.'

'Turn sharp right here.'

'Straight on through the village and turn left down by the river and cross the bridge. Try and not touch the parapet.'

Bill could see neither village, river nor bridge, but successfully carried out the manoeuvre.

'Good, double de-clutch down to first.'

'Good, turn sharp right here.'

Driving through the heat of the afternoon sun, dogs generally fell asleep in the shade, liable to be anywhere, including the middle of the road.

'I have killed dozens of dogs!' Bill admitted with a regretful shake of his head whilst telling his story. 'Dozens of them!'

'You didn't drive over them. Surely?' George enquired, considering Bill to be too humane to kill any living thing deliberately, even village dogs.

'Oh no, I would not dream of doing such a wicked thing!' He insisted. 'Oh, no.'

'How did you kill them, then?' George asked, with none of the story making much sense.

In the early days Bill gave a warning toot of the horn each occasion he saw a dog but this annoyed the corporal, so he had to try and find another other way. Bill, under obligation from his corporal to disregard the dogs, chose instead of driving straight over them, deviated as much as he dared to allow the dogs, sprawled out on the road, to pass between the wheels. This did not cause any reaction from the corporal and Bill should have been suspicious. But being naive he thought he was doing the right thing and not causing the dogs harm.

The dogs passed safely between the wheels, disturbed from its slumbers by the engine noise passing just inches above its head. Whilst still under the lorry, the dog awoke and raised its head to investigate what interfered with its lumbers, just in time for the back axle to decapitate it! Bill recognised the sinister sound and realised its significance of the bangs and jolts whilst he drove blindfold. The corporal found pleasure with each incident and once back at the billet, to his disgust, made Bill hose the vehicle down, especially the bloodied back axle differential casing.

He too brought back into civilian life some habits of the military, appearance and behaviour at work, in particular timekeeping and hard work. Unfortunately for him he possessed an over bearing sense of ethics, which caused his brain to get muddled and confused by anger and frustration.

When they heard about *Belgrano* and recovered fully after the initial shock, its sinking, controversial with some, caused a great deal of discussion at ESR. Some were of the opinion that as a state of war existed, the sinking could be justified, whilst a minority expressed grave doubts about the morals of sinking an elderly ship outside of the Total Exclusion Zone, especially when the Americans were going through the motions of negotiating a settlement. *Bill the Brush* was one of those who thought the sinking immoral, especially as no military action had taken place until that point. He held forth about the damage the sinking would do for Britain's cause.

Ron Clifton snapped back at these opinions. 'What the fuck do you expect?' He shouted. 'Are we meant to wait for the fucking Argies to be nasty first, before we can be nasty back?'

Bill the Brush protested and found himself interrupted. 'It is not ethical. We can't go about sinking ships without....'

'If you think that Bill, then you are talking utter bollocks! As an ex army man you should know better and you know it!'

The trouble was that despite being an ex army man did not mean that he had to blindly follow the rules. *Bill the Brush* held views, which in some circles proved to be unpopular. As a direct consequence he found himself ostracised by appearing to be sympathetic to the Argentinean cause, especially by some outspoken folk like Ron Clifton. Had they known of *Bill the Brush's* unsettled state of mind they would have either have protested in a gentle fashion, or not protest at all.

Within a week Bill went absent and news filtered through the grapevine that *Bill the Brush* had been found dead by police at his home. George wondered whether *Bill the Brush* had personal problems. If he did he kept them to himself. The argumentative debate on *Belgrano* could not be reason enough for him to take such drastic steps, and the inquest, which followed, was inconclusive, with the absence of a suicide note. He escaped his unknown dilemma by drinking a deadly combination of paraquat and sulphuric acid. A most painful way to ends ones life. Surely a better way existed if one chose to die by suicide?

*

George's final tale is one of great sadness and proof, if proof is required, of how speedily the human spirit can disintegrate within a short time span. Frank DeVaal committed suicide and hung himself, within a year of the closure of the ESR factory. The announcement of the factory closure came as a great shock to everyone, but most considered what their prospects to be and adjusted their sights accordingly. No one faced compulsory redundancy until all avenues had been fully exploited. This included voluntary redundancy, obtaining a transfer to other factories in the West Country and South Wales, to seeking employment on the open market.

Those with long service or who were approaching the time of natural retirement, chose to volunteer for redundancy. The package offered by ESR seemed generous and to those without a mortgage and other commitments like children, the prospect of unemployment, even as an unwanted situation, could be viewed as being a feasible and acceptable proposition. Combined with the government's old age pension, many looked forward to a reasonably sound financial period of retirement.

Those more adventurous, gave serious consideration to a move to the West Country. One man in particular, James Tripp made it plain that a move to Somerset where he spent six enjoyable and memorable months with his sister on a farm near Wincanton, when evacuated during the war, resembled the prospect of a trip to paradise. If only half the stories he told about his exploits were true, the combination of Wincanton inhabited by James Tripp closely resembled the promise land! The fact that ESR had a large factory on the outskirts of Wincanton made James very excited, and for weeks he spoke of little else! He told and retold all the favourite stories about the farm, the chickens, the cows, pigs and the sheep, and especially the buxom farmer's wife. She never worried about a bra and wore loose fitting dresses, which drooped whenever she leant down, to allow any small boy the opportunity to witness the delights of the female form. Each time he retold the tale, his eyes were aglow with pleasure. Poor James had no idea what bosoms and nipples were until he saw those of the farmer's wife! With such fond memories James looked forward to the prospect of the move. He and his wife travelled down for the weekend and James was successful in obtaining a position in the drawing office.

Others gave serious consideration to a move to South Wales where ESR had another factory. The majority, including George with his wife, a mortgage, children settled at school, did not fit easily into either category and were left with the prospect of seeking employment elsewhere. ESR generously allowed time off for interviews and one by one, most managed to obtain a position, however unsuitable or temporary. George succeeded in obtaining a position in a graphic studio within a Publishing House in the east end of London. Although the work bore little resemblance to his work at ESR, he quickly settled down into his new career and routine.

A few souls, for a variety of reasons did not succeed and were finally forced to accept compulsory redundancy. Some of these unfortunates accepted their fate with philosophical resignation. Others took the situation as an affront or an insult to their status, the worse by far, that of Frank DeVaal. Try as he did he was unsuccessful in obtaining a position which allowed him and family to keep up with his standard of living. George suspected that the seat of the problem lay with Frank's wife who refused point blank to economise or lower her standards. Frank had a variety of menial jobs, from working in a petrol station to selling double-glazing. He could not make ends meet and the final straw came when his wife left him taking their children with her, followed by his mortgage provider issuing a repossession notice on his house, quite an unusual and desperate event for those days. Henry Reade, the Chief Engineer, stayed on to oversee the Sentinel project until closure of the factory. He negotiated a satisfactory settlement figure with ESR, which included him taking up a post at the main factory in Stratford. Here he was to be in charge of a skeleton staff to keep the Sentinel Project going until the end of the two year modification contract. Quite naturally he needed a personal assistant and Mavis was quite content to go with him, if only for the lunchtime loving interlude.

After the factory closure, many ESR-ites began to meet on the first Tuesday of every month in a hostelry in Chigwell. The practice goes on to this day.

At one of these meetings George learnt of the final act of Frank DeVaal.

He finally cracked and went to a field not too far away from the ESR factory, where he hung himself from the branch of an oak tree in full view of the road.

Difficult to come to terms with, given that as an ex navy man, stress and living under near combat conditions must have been almost second nature to him. Despite the public nature of his demise, his body hung there for three weeks before a passing cyclist spotted it.

The secluded roadside spot used by Henry Reade and Mavis Clarke for their daily romantic interlude lay within sight of the tree where Frank's body hung suspended. When they visited the area during this time, they would have been too engrossed with themselves to notice a corpse. Arriving at the secluded spot in a gateway, Henry joined Mavis in the back of the car, and with well practised fumbling, undressed his partner to lust over her body. Mavis unzipped his trousers to bring his hardness into the open. After an interlude of foreplay Mavis moved her body across Henry and eased his hardened member inside her body. As Henry enjoyed the pleasure of Mavis's supple and willing flesh, she squirmed and quietly moaned with equal delight. So preoccupied with their pleasurable activity the unpleasant smell was ignored. Less than fifty feet away on the other side of the hedge, just within range of the overpowering indescribable stench of death, sweet and cloying, hundreds of blowfly maggots feasted on Franks rotting flesh, which bubbled with the movement of prolific larva under the skin. The stench eventually permeated the car and for the first time they were forced to abandon their lunchtime sexual soirée to another more suitable spot.

The tree stands to this day.

To passing motorists it is just another tree, with no significance, historic or otherwise. To those in the know it is a painful reminder of a past event, which took place there.

10

Factory incidents

The Greengage Public House, was the scene of an incident of legendary status, firmly set in the folk lore of ESR history. The episode took place one Christmas Eve when the engineers went there for a traditional celebratory drink. Always a lively and noisy affair, one or two folk from the factory, not officially part of the group, inevitably became involved in the festivities. George happened to be there when they arrived, sitting quietly with the trio he gave a lift home most evenings, namely *Bill the Brush*, then only months away from his suicide, Pauline Fraser and Kate Jones, both tracers. The group of a dozen or so men and the two secretaries, the luscious Mavis and her large bosomed colleague Sally, were already in a jocular mood, and George become subjected to a variety of comments, mainly because of the two women in his company. It is not surprising, for Kate Jones, a blue eyed blond, was one of those middle aged women who could be described as being very easy on the eye. On her last birthday, instead of a standard Happy Birthday cake, she brought into the office a plain white iced home made cake with $\sqrt{2045}$ piped on in shaky red letters. No one understood this until she explained that she was now 45 and wanted to disguise her true age!

Kate typically wore a close fitting dress that showed her well proportioned body, with a hemline several inches above the knee, and left little to the imagination. Whilst she remained seated facing him, George looked forward to the prospect of a good view of inner thigh. At work in the drawing office, Kate could often be seen leaning over her drawing board, pen in hand, concentrating on her tracing. If she happened to be working on the top of the board, being short, Kate was a touch over five feet tall, she had to prop herself over the lower edge of the drawing board and place a knee on her chair in order to reach. This placed her in a most sexual position. If she removed her clothing, a prospective lover only had to approach to find her shapely body readily available. This pose did little to keep George's blood pressure on an even keel. Ron Waud, the section leader in charge of the Dunking Sonar Project, a professional lecher with years of experience, could see Kate from his desk, in the adjacent aisle, legs parted in a provocative pose exposing acres of thigh. When Kate adopted this position, Ron had a permanent leer on his moustachioed face. To ease the tension he must have been subjected to, he constantly stroked the ends of his moustache.

Pauline, the other tracer was a few years older, not quite so shapely, and her legs tended to be oversized from the knees to the ankle. Her saving grace was that she often wore a blouse or a dress, which gaped open at the neck, and she made no attempt to hide her bosoms from view. Pauline did not seem to mind if George glanced down at her cleavage. He often wondered whether she did this deliberately. Both women had a lively personality, so being in their company was always entertaining for one reason or another!

'Jammy beggar, not content with one, you've got two!' One engineer commented as he passed by.

This was true but depended on the numerical subject. 'Can you see them from there?' George retorted.

'You know that I mean about your female company, not those two insignificant grubby spherical objects lurking in your trousers, you daft sod!'

The engineers tarried by the bar, giving the young barmaid a hard but jovial time as she struggled to deal with their orders. They continued to make exaggerated comments amongst themselves until the serious drinking began, when the bar resumed an air of frantic but celebratory enthusiasm. Similar sounds came from the other bars as the festivities drew on.

*

As he sat at his desk, George could see the faces clearly, but if asked, would be able name only one or two. His notebook was crammed full of memories but contained very few names except those who worked in the Drawing Office. With so many former colleagues now passed away, their names were lost for eternity.

*

After an hour, Ron Clifton, accompanied by his wife Isabel, a secretary in the Chemi-lab, burst in though the doors and made to join the engineers. The group had downed a few pints by this time and a fair amount of mickey taking or rather Ron baiting ensued when he arrived. Ron retaliated immediately and gave back as he received, which made him liable to continued abuse. Ron went to the bar and returned with a double scotch for himself and a glass of orange juice for his wife. George continued to be pleasantly distracted by the body parts of his two female companions, but found time to notice that Ron was drinking heavily. Either he had left the car at home or else his wife Isabel was the driver for today. Ron had the reputation of being sober most of the time, but when he decided to push the boat out, generally did so in style and to the extreme. He claimed to have adopted this habit from the Marines who were obliged to be sober throughout their time at sea, but once ashore and on leave, made up for lost time. George had the impression that Ron had decided to treat today as if he were on shore leave!

When the engineers went out for a social event they were always boisterous and invariably well organised. This Christmas proved to be no exception for they had previously ordered trays of assorted sandwiches, pork pies, pickles, crisps and salad. The licensee and his wife enjoyed a justified reputation for good food, although it would be true to say that their appearance failed to make a good impression, and did not show their profitable business in good light. Jim Baker, a short man, always wore an oversized white warehouse coat on his body, white plimsolls on his feet and a permanent scowl on his thin face. For an elderly gentleman who owned a thriving established business, he made little attempt to make himself presentable and often looked as if his hair had not been combed. His wife, by contrast, known to all as *The Painted lady*, they never knew her actual name, looked as if she had been up all night attending to her grooming. Only one trouble, her makeup looked as if she had used emulsion paint, which left her face with the finish of painted rough planed wood. The colours used were bright and gaudy, and this combined with an outrageous hairdo and an unusual dress sense made her the subject of some cruel jokes.

It was possible to criticise her body parts, from head to toe.

The hair.

The Painted Lady must have been approaching the age of retirement, and having lived life to the full, her grey hair, dyed black had thinned to the extent that remains of the hair colouring solution used could be clearly seen on her scalp. George was not an expert you

326

understand, but he was assured by those who knew about these things, that a backcombing technique, used in excess, allowed her hair to resemble the shape of a guardsman's bearskin. Every single hair carefully lacquered into place with utmost precision, stylish, but thirty or more years out of date. George was convinced that if she stood outside in a gale, her hair would remain in place!

Her face.

This also gave clear indication of her living life to the full, being lined and wrinkled. She overcame this affliction by applying layer after layer of foundation, than applying rouge to give her cheeks a rosy colouring. Her lips were dealt with in the same manner and were thick coated with lipstick identical in colour to her cheeks. Eyebrows and eyelashes were coated thick with mascara so as to appear as if they were solid objects. Either she was colour-blind, had bad taste, or both. Either way the appearance was that of crude painted wooden soldier, unblinking, stiff faced and unsmiling.

Her clothing.

Her sleeveless transparent black embroidered dress, worn every day without fail, permitted her underwear to be in view. She clearly had little dress sense and she often could be seen with a white bra, with black knickers or vice versa. By way of variation she wore a blue bra with yellow knickers and onto endless permutations. Once, in a spell of hot weather, thankfully it was only the once, she did not bother wearing a bra, a sight that made the beer taste sour! Despite the horrendous sight, George could not help but look on with total fascination. *The Painted lady* had breasts inclined to sag in keeping with the rest of her body. The one redeeming feature was that she had enormous nipples, which poked through the embroidery.

Her legs and arms.

The sleeveless dress did not hide her upper arms, which had little life in them, for they sagged obscenely, without muscle in any form. Her legs suffered similarly. She topped her ensemble by wearing black carpet slippers, decorated with pink ribbon, no matter the weather or occasion. Her manner of walking became the subject of much hilarity to customers. Imagine attempting to clutch a pencil between your buttocks whilst walking, simultaneous to trying to fight off a severe bout of wind. Your clenched muscles prevent any natural movement except to walk stiffly. Try this method of walking and it will be appreciated how *The Painted Lady* normally walked in the manner of a constipated Penguin!

George once overheard a comment in the bar made by a customer but aimed in her direction 'She looks like lamb dressed as mutton.' He privately disagreed, for George considered her to be a prime case of mutton dressed as mutton!

When *the Painted Lady,* assisted by a couple of young ladies, brought out the plates of food, the engineers descended like vultures and feasted. George's group gave them five minutes until they were totally preoccupied with eating. Hoping no one would notice, the four surreptitiously wandered over one at a time and each helped themselves to a plateful of food. The group easily managed to escape attention of their uninvited participation, but a few moments later, one eagle-eyed engineer spotted Ron quietly taking a few sandwiches. Just as Ron sat down and began to tuck in, someone, by accident or design, called out for Ron from the other bar, so he stood up immediately and went though the connecting door, leaving his plate on the table. At this time Isabel was engaged in quiet animated conversation with Kate concerning personal matters. Eagle eye immediately went to the gents and emerged moments later with a packet of three. He quickly opened the packet, tore open the foil to remove a rubber sheath. This he secreted in the uppermost sandwich and returned to his seat two tables away, without attracting the attention of other engineers. When Ron came through the door, George watched as he returned to his seat and took a mouthful of sandwich. Some of the engineers were in the know by this time and anticipated his return, but outwardly paid Ron little attention. The expression of horror, which appeared on Ron's face seconds later, should have been captured on film, when he bit into the offending rubberised object. He took the sandwich out of his mouth and placed it on the plate for further inspection, to find an unused French letter amongst the lettuce. At this precise moment with impeccable timing, Jim Baker, resplendent in white warehouse coat and plimsolls to match, appeared by the sandwiches. He began, in the way of a professional innkeeper, to rearrange the remaining sandwiches into a presentable appearance and generally tidy up the table previously the subject of attack from a ravenous horde.

The sudden outcry from Ron distracted him momentarily and he looked towards the direction of the sound, to see an enraged Ron heading towards him. In those few seconds it took for Ron to stand beside the white coated innkeeper, George imagined Ron, with his Marines, armed to the teeth, running up a beach of a tropical island under fire, determined to get to safety unharmed. This island had a completely unpronounceable name to most westerners, but ended with *jima, kuku or sagi*. Ron would, quite naturally be under severe stress and probably have a fierce expression on his face, and likely to be yelling at the top of his voice, caused by copious amounts of adrenaline flowing through his veins. This is a good description of Ron in the bar as he hurtled towards the Innkeeper standing by the refreshment table.

Give him his due the Innkeeper stood his ground.

When he reached the licensee, Ron thrust the plate containing sandwich remains complete with torn rubber sheath into the face of the Innkeeper. The Innkeeper did not move an inch. He glanced momentarily down at the plate inches from his face, then up at Ron who towered above him.

'What's the matter Sir?' Innkeeper asked innocently, not having the faintest idea of the reason for the anger of his customer.

'What's the....' Ron replied with a raised voice, not believing that the Innkeeper could not see the offending article in his sandwich.' What the fuck do you think is wrong with it?'

Innkeeper looked down at the plate only inches from his face.

'Can't you see the fucking durex man?' Ron demanded.

'Actually no, I cannot.'

'Why the fuck not? Are you completely blind?'

'Not completely blind, just without my glasses!' Innkeeper said with a smug look on his face, but in a calm manner. 'If there is a durex in the sandwich as you claim, it must have been put there by one of your colleagues. You have been the subject of a silly prank, Sir. I'll take it away and cut you another fresh sandwich of your choice.'

This reaction justified the reputation of the food quality at The Greengage. Typical of Jim Baker, determined to maintain his standard of good food served to customers, no matter the reason, even for a Christmas prank. Innkeeper made to take the plate, but

330

Ron moved at the speed of light and managed to keep it out of his reach. The trouble with this type of manoeuvre undertaken with Ron partially intoxicated, combined with his quick reaction, the plate and contents swung in an arc reaching tremendous speed, simultaneous with his fingers losing their grip. The china plate, now minus the offending sandwich and partly chewed sheath, floated in slow motion and headed at an angle silently across the room over the heads of engineers and towards the bottle laden shelf behind the bar. A few engineers, and George were watching open mouthed waiting for the impending collision between plate and who knows what. As the plate glided graciously over the serving counter, *The Painted Lady* emerged from a side door and stood with her back towards the counter by the till, but directly underneath the flight path of the china missile. The Innkeeper without his glasses could see neither plate nor wife and as such not in a position to utter a shout of warning. The plate now losing speed, dropped into a gentle arc of descent, continued onwards and because of the steep angle crashed into four large brown coloured display bottles, previously safe on a shelf about eight feet above the floor level. Two smashed into tiny fragments immediately on impact and the other two were dislodged off the shelf to descend and land either side of *The Painted Lady*, missing her by a matter of inches. She disappeared from view as she ducked down instinctively and tried desperately hard to escape the inevitable deluge from the liquid contents contained within the four bottles. Two from directly above, two from either side. The shelved area became a temporary waterfall and most customers nearby, hearing the crash, ducked by instinct. When silence ensued, the people nearest the bar, finding themselves in the main unscathed stood up, including *The Painted*

Lady now facing us. She stool forlorn, hair no longer a bearskin but hanging lopsided, limp and dripping. The liquid contents of the bottles washed out her hair colouring, and planted it on her face. It tarried there for a few seconds turning her makeup into a semi liquid state, which ran slowly downward, resembling molten larva as it progressed toward the floor, with the combined mixture of unknown liquid and hair colouring.

Simultaneous with this, those within ten feet of the plate and bottle collision found themselves showered with glass, adding to their confusion. At this stage, no one by the bar was aware of the drama quietly unfolding behind their backs.

The face of *The Painted Lady* resembled a wax doll melted by heat, great streaks of uneven colour descended onto her black dress, transforming her into a masterpiece by Picasso. If she stood there crying no one could tell, probably at this time of the proceedings, to be truthful, no one cared, but in either case it made little difference. *The Painted lady* no longer painted, looked what she really was. A thin elderly, white faced individual who had lived her life to the full and paid the consequences. The painted lady stood and wailed like a demented cat with its tail caught in a vice. With this sad eerie noise the bar went into a state of total silence, so quiet a pin dropping onto the carpet would sound like gunfire. She looked in a sorry state, comical even, but no one laughed.

Behind the spectacle a sober, elderly, five foot tall Innkeeper, minus his glasses, battled with a partially intoxicated six foot six tall ex-marine.

The encounter must be the quickest in history.

The victor hurled his opponent to the floor, hanging onto a single arm and the loser lay on the carpet with a face pressed into the well trodden nap, renown for its contents of twenty-year-old cigarette ash and gallons of spilled beer. No one knew where to look first. The pitiful sight of a drenched unpainted lady or towards her victorious husband seeking retribution on the person responsible of his wife's unfortunate situation.

The bar, still totally silent, waited for a pin to drop, so it could be heard.

'Christmas Eve or no, pal.' Innkeeper hissed at what must been a blurred image of his opponent on the carpet. 'You are banned pal, and do not bother to come back next year!'

In compete silence, Innkeeper twisted the arm gently and as if by magic, Ron, his face and jacket festooned with food remnants, dropped onto the carpet by ravenous engineers, eager to relieve their hunger, rose to his feet and was ever so gently escorted to the door where the two men passed through the swing doors. Moments later one man returned. Innkeeper looked triumphant, rubbing his hands with glee as he walked through the bar to place an arm around his wife to offer comfort.

When Innkeeper and *the painted lady* left, the bar quickly resumed an air of normality.

*

The unfortunate plight of Ron Clifton made George smile, as the episode continued into the New Year. Ron was not inclined to take offence, but rather sought to get even. Several engineers, not involved with the original prank found personal items glued together or found a brick inside a briefcase when they arrived home. Others endured other revenge tactics and found their briefcases locked and permanently glued making it impossible to open. When he eventually discovered the identity of eagle eye, this individual endured a stream of revenge acts for months. George laughed out loud as he typed, which prompted an enquiry from Carole, who wandered in from the lounge to ask about the subject of his merriment.

*

This bar was also the place where George first spoke to and met Wally Durrant. One Friday morning, the peace of the drawing office was disturbed by a gang arriving from the workshop, making a great deal of noise as they battled with the self closing door carrying long ladders and an assortment of equipment. *Child by name* wandered over to enquire why they were there and established they were putting fire detection sensors on the roof. Over the coming three weeks, Wally and his crew of six, on tall ladders trying to keep as quiet as possible, progressed through the office neatly placing their sensors and associated wiring high up upon the roof.

At lunchtime, George wandered over to the Green Gate for a pint and one of their fabulous home-made pork pies. Wally and his crew were already there, attempting to get to grips with bar billiards. None of them had sufficient skill to gently hit the cue ball and thus avoid hitting the toadstools over. Wally recognised George and wandered over to his table.

'Hello mate, I'm Wally.' He greeted, grabbing George's hand to shake it with great enthusiasm. 'You're from the drawing office over the road, aren't you?'

George looked up from his paper and saw the friendly face of the foreman ladder man. 'That's right.' He replied. 'Thought I recognised you.'

Wally, typical of those whose origins lay in the east end of London, dropped aitches like a drunken knitter dropped stitches, spoke with an animated expression whilst talking with plenty of hand movements which made him liable to knock over glasses on the table.

'Do you know how to play this stupid game?' He asked, waving an arm in the general direction of his crew behind him. 'I'm sure we aren't supposed to knock these mushrooms things over.'

'Let me finish my pie and I will come over.'

'Thanks mate.'

'My name is George.'

Thanks, mate. Odd place this, but excellent food!'

'Yes it is!'

'What do you make of that skinny old bird behind the counter?' Said at the precise moment when the bar went very quiet, the remark clearly overheard by *The Painted Lady* standing at the bar.

'She's the landlady.'

'Oh!' Wally replied, glancing towards the woman staring in their direction with an annoyed frown on her forehead. Wally raised his shoulders and hands by way of a visual apology 'Sorry, lady.' He said quietly. *The Painted lady* snorted in his direction to show her contempt, turned and walked into the public bar.

Five minutes later, George was part of the group, attempting to show them the art of bar billiards, and spent the remainder of the lunch hour trying to get them to hit the cue ball gently. At twenty five minutes past one, he made his farewells, leaving them to it, making it back to his drawing board with seconds to spare before the end of lunchtime bell rang. About an hour later the gang returned to the drawing office continuing with their high rise works.

Wally sauntered by. 'I mastered it, George.' He boasted. 'Now I'm rather tasty at it.'

Until their contract ended, around six months later, George played in a knockout competition with the sensor installation crew. Wally had mastered the art as he claimed and described each achievement, as 'Tasty!'

He exclaimed this adverb so many times it became his nickname.

Eventually the contract came to an end and George no longer saw Tasty and crew in the Greengage.

After an absence of four weeks news filtered through the grapevine that Tiann had been arrested. Initially everyone thought for grievous bodily harm or assault, for Tiann was known to drink heavily on a Saturday and it was not too difficult to imagine him being slightly the worse for wear, arguing with a fellow drinker over some minor incident, which then developed into a fight. With his known temper it was very easy to imagine this scenario, especially if the police became involved.

They were all wrong.

Incredibly wrong.

Tiann lived with his wife and three small children in a large house in East Ham. His mother-in-law, who lived on the top floor of his house, infatuated him to the extent that Tiann contrived to get her to sleep with him. By all accounts she was a most attractive woman, with a shapely body and persona of a goddess and Tiann boasted about her desire towards him all the time. She went to a chapel, which practised the type of religion based upon fear of God, a believer of fire and brimstone and eternal retribution for wickedness and sin. Tiann, so desperate was he to sleep with this woman he came up with an outrageous scheme, but one feasible, given the extreme beliefs of his Mother-in-law. Without the knowledge of his wife, he placed a loud speaker system within the loft space above the bed of his victim and recorded messages on a tape recorder. The whole sordid affair became revealed during the subsequent trial.

On the first occasion Tiann gave a live performance in the early hours.

'Alice can you hear me?' He spoke from the spare room and listened by pressing an ear against a small hole drilled previously through the wall.

No reaction from his mother in law.

'Alice!' He spoke louder now into the microphone. 'Can you hear me?'

Alice woke up and eased herself up on her elbows unsure what had disturbed her sleep. She thought someone had entered her room but could not be sure.

'Alice. You have been chosen to save the world from sin.'

'Who is this?' She whispered, almost too petrified to speak. 'Why can't I see you?'

'Alice. You have been chosen to save the world from sin.' Tiaan repeated. 'I am God, speaking to you from heaven.'

'My Lord, I beseech you...'

'Alice, please listen.' Tiaan spoke clearly but quietly so as not to disturb his wife and children. 'You must not speak of this conversation to anyone including your daughter and her husband.'

A pause.

Fully awake now, Alice lay with only the top of her head above the bedclothes. 'How do you know about my daughter?' She asked after she considered the situation. She blinked in the blackness trying to detect the presence of the speaker, who sounded so close, she expected someone to be standing in the room.

'Alice I am all seeing and know of your belief in me, which is why you have been chosen.'

'What do I have to do, my Lord?'

'When the time is right, I will make a visitation here. It will be necessary for you to obtain a baptismal gown and prepare to meet your maker.'

'Yes, my Lord.'

'It will be necessary for you to cover your eyes, for you may not see me on pain of being condemned to hell.' Tiann continued, virtually rubbing his hand with glee that he was believed, despite a heavily disguised strong South African accent. 'When I appear, you will lie naked prostrate before me and it is important for you to remember that my holiness does not permit you to cast your eyes upon my being.'

'My Lord it will be an honour. I already own a white cotton baptismal gown and will pray every day until we meet.'

Tiann knew full well of the baptismal gown owned by his mother in law and grinned at the prospect of seeing her naked, followed very quickly by a willing seduction.

Over a period of weeks he managed to convince her fully that the mysterious voice she heard throughout the hours of darkness was that of God. He persuaded her that he, as God, wished her bear him a son destined to become the saviour of souls in the twentieth century, and she become a modern day Saint, equivalent to Mary, wife of Joseph.

Time passed.

His wife announced that she wanted to go and visit her sister in Brighton and made plans to take the children with her for the weekend. Tiaan set to work making his plans. He gave warning of his planned visitation and on the night before told Alice of his intended visible visitation the following day.

As soon as his wife and children left the house, as a precaution he first disguised himself by dying his hair and beard, then took his clothes off and wore a flowing robe, he bought from Romford market. Within an hour of his wife and children leaving the house, he announced his presence from the other side of Alice's bedroom door.

There was no reply. Then he heard a noise downstairs. He walked downstairs and knocked on the kitchen door.

'Alice I am here.' He announced.

In her enthusiasm, Alice tried to open the door and Tiann had to use all his strength to keep the door closed. When she calmed, he passed a pillowslip through the door, which Joan slipped over her head.

'Is your head fully covered Alice?' He asked.

'Yes my Lord, you may enter.'

Tiann with caution entered the kitchen. Alice stood by the kitchen table wearing her white cotton baptismal gown and the pillowslip over her head.

'My Lord?'

'Alice, let us pray.'

Alice immediately dropped to her knees. Tiann approached and thrust his groin into her face. If Alice objected she did not speak of it.

'I give sister Alice the strength and courage to do my will and command you to remove the baptismal gown so you stand naked before your maker.' Tiann spoke with authority and fervour. He then spoke quietly to emphasise his warning. 'You must not look upon my countenance upon pain of death and eternity in hell.'

To his amazement Alice undid the buttons of her gown and allowed it to fall to the floor. She stood in all her glory still wearing the pillowcase. Tiaan gazed upon her ample bosom and body, which he had been lusting after for months. He reached out and held her right hand, which he placed upon his hardened member.

'My Lord?' Alice seemed puzzled. 'I cannot touch you. It is a sin.'

'I am God.' Tiaan responded still pressing her hand against his body. 'I tell you it not sin, but you must obey the will of your Lord.'

'It is sin....'

'No Alice, it is my will and command.' He removed his hand.

After a moment of hesitation, Alice held him by encircling her hand around him encouraging him into life.

Tiann then touched her breasts and encouraged Alice to place her lips around him. After a minute or two of ecstasy, he pushed her gently backwards so she ended up lying on the table and he placed a hand towards the top of her legs. Once this occurred Alice resembled putty in hands and she willingly did any sexual act he desired.

Tiann almost succeeded with his fantasy.

His wife, whose car had broken down enroute, arrived back home in the middle of the religious encounter. She came in the front door walked through the hall towards the back of the house and caught her naked mother, still wearing the pillowcase *'in flagrante'* with her husband on the kitchen table. The children and the taxi driver who had brought the family home witnessed the spectacular sexual event.

At first his wife did not recognise her husband, but when she did she became very violent and threatened Tiaan with a knife. Once she pulled the pillowcase off her head, Alice looked visibly shaken by how easily Tiann had deceived her. Her daughter still violent with Tiaan, then accused her mother of seducing her husband. When she eventually realised her mother was also a victim, mother and daughter combined to became violent towards Tiann.   Mother and daughter both armed with a knife chased Tiann first around the kitchen, then moved outside to the back garden. In the process all three were injured as Tiaan also had a knife. The children still in the house screamed so much, it alarmed neighbours.

So vocal and violent was the attack, the woman next door, fearing for the safety of the children, called the police. All three adults were badly injured in the brawl. The garden resembled a battlefield with three blooded bodies and blood on the patio. When police arrived, two women armed with knives, intent on attacking a man, also similarly armed, confronted them. They were quite unable to persuade the women to hand over their knives, so instead they arrested Tiann after a brief struggle. Six months later he was convicted and jailed for rape and sexual assault.

*

The more wicked of draughtsmen, the original *Two Ronnies*, Ron Waud and Ron Clifton gave a single unrehearsed performance one lunchtime down Thorns Tavern, speculating on the announcements coming through the ceiling in the still of the night. They did not know the name of Tiann's mother-in-law, so they gave her the name of Joan.

'Joooaan! Are you awake?' A deep male faint voice from the direction of the ceiling. The first Ron perched on the arm of a chair above the other Ron and spoke through cupped hands and attempted to make his voice resemble an echo.

Ron lying back on the chair pretended to be asleep then wake up. 'Who is that talking to me?' A high pitched squeaky voice an octave higher than the voice of the perched Ron. 'Who are you?'

'I aaaaaaaaaaam God, and want to get inside your kniiiiickeeeeeeers!'

'I am not wearing any knickers!'

'I still want to get inside them.'

'That is very rude, I'll tell my vicar!'

'I am your vicars boss.'

'I have not had sex for thirteen years!'

'I am not superstitious!'

'I am not a virgin!'

'Virginity is against procreation.'

'Will you have to see my body naked?'

'I bloody well hope so!'

'My body is not worthy of your attention!'

'You have a lovely body.'

'I am a sinner and not worthy of attention.'

'You have such lovely bosoms!' Said loudly, then repeated softly. 'You have such lovely bosoms!

'Why are you speaking twice?' Ron asked in normal voice looking up at the other Ron.

'I am not, it is an echo, echo.'

'I do not understand.'

'Your bosoms are so big they are like two great mountains in the Drakensberg.'

'I'm not sure I can do what you want. The Zulu's are so big and strong and so heathen, and have such large.....'

At this point Ron fell off the arm of the chair with fits of laughter and they could not continue.

*

Thirty years have passed and driving past the Golden Lion on Tower Hill has changed beyond recognition. The pace of vehicles is frantic, full use of the accelerator pushed to the floor, as if speeding away from the lights and changing lanes in order to press ahead, can save valuable time. Visitors to the Tower of London emerging from the underground no longer have to cross the road. It is considered to be too dangerous, the flow of traffic too fast, and visitors from abroad have the tendency to look left instead of right, before crossing. Instead there is a direct link via a pedestrian tunnel, which leads along a narrow bed of flower and trees resembling a park, adjacent to the former moat, leading directly to the pay kiosks. On the way a visitor get an opportunity to view Roman remains and a short section of Roman Wall which once stretched around the City.

To travel to the site of the former ESR factory can be achieved without too much aggression despite the furious rush of some drivers heading in the same direction.

It is still possible to travel northwards half a mile to the Whitechapel Road and travel on a less adventurous but more direct route. The current traffic calming measures by their very nature, successfully slows the traffic to an average crawl speed, despite the inclination to rush between the many sets of traffic signals, pedestrian crossings, bus lanes and other obstacles encountered along the way.

The neighbourhood of Whitechapel, as it is now called in local government parlance, has entered a third phase of accommodating a minority population. The first phase consisted of persecuted French Protestants called Huguenots, ousted from their land and place of birth, during the latter part of the 16th century by a catholic regime inclined to maintaining a religious status quo. They built a temple in Brick Lane in a style reminiscent of their former places of worship. The second phase came from Europe too, but this time from Russia, an assortment of Baltic States, Poland and Germany. A Jewish population ousted by prejudice and religious intolerance by the Nazi regime. The temple in Brick Lane became known as a synagogue but despite a change of name, still maintained its internal features.

The area remained largely intact, despite many attempts by the Luftwaffe during the Second World War to bomb east London into submission.

The third phase, there may yet be a fourth, but only time will tell, came more recently, this time from the sub-continent of Asia. They were not, in the main persecuted, but rather viewed England as a haven from famine and pestilence. They too brought their religion with them and the meeting place in Brick Lane has resorted back to the name of temple, though in a non-European script. Still visible on the walls are the remains of Hebrew text, proof that religious tolerance can exist to this day.

The Kray twins are long gone, but the name of Jack the Ripper still resounds around his former haunts, as nightly guided tours initiate small groups of tourists into the gruesome horror of a past era, surrounded by blood curdling mystery. An average traveller progressing along Whitechapel Road could still be oblivious to such historic distractions.

A typical journey now is along the improved wide road, still called The Highway. It has been widened and improved at the eastern end, by a long tunnel named the *Limehouse Link*, built to ease congestion, with multi-access portals. This usually prevents drivers from being delayed without due reason, to a variety of destinations. Access to and from the City, access to and from Canary Wharf and access to and from the Blackwall Tunnel northern bore, have all been improved and drivers wishing to travel in and through this area, benefit from its construction. Parts of the former docks have been renamed *Saint Katherines by the Tower*, and transformed into a tourist attraction and a haven for luxury yachts. Other sizeable enclosed areas of water are an attractive feature of prestigious housing developments built around the periphery. The tunnel built by Brunel still exists, but has been successfully refurbished and is now a museum open to the public on alternate Sundays. The tunnel remains out of bounds and is only accessible on a few days of the year simply because of a lack of funds.

It is no longer necessary to deviate from this direct route, for the Limehouse Link tunnel, by the northern bore of the Blackwall Tunnel, avoids all previous congestion. With other road improvements and the building of a new river bridge, it is now easy to traverse the River Lea. The large expanse of open water, still known as *The Royals,* docks no more, the waterside comprises of expensive luxury flats and houses, a large exhibition complex and London City Airport constructed in between the Royal Victoria and King George V Docks. A series of basic manoeuvres leads you northwards onto a section of the North Circular Road and by simple means are able to drive to Manor Park where the ESR factory once stood. In the name of progress this has been demolished, replaced by three modern superstores, each with a large car park.

*

Within hours of the surrender, the islands name resorted back to the Falklands and the inhabitants took the first steps to resume a normal life. Except this was literately impossible. First and foremost of many problems that faced civilians and British troops after the enforced removal of the Argentines, was that of mines. The Argentineans had planted thousands, nearly all of the plastic type, making them virtually impossible to detect. Several British soldiers and a single Argentinean conscript were injured in clearance work in the early days after the war, so London made the decision to suspend minefield clearances until new equipment was developed and produced, capable of detecting plastic mines. An estimated 18,000 remain buried in the sand and soil.

If a minefield is laid correctly, fences and markers help friendly troops and act as a deterrent to the enemy. In the Falklands however, a disastrous combination of undetectable mines, unmarked minefields and a haphazard policy of mine laying was compounded by the setting of booby traps with improvised charges. The fields laid by Argentine Marine or Army Engineers should have followed a simple drill. A cable with metal rings at intervals along its length was laid out on the ground from a known fixed point marked on a map. Mines were then dug where the rings appeared. With an overlay on an Argentinean map it would be possible to plot mines relatively accurately.

In reality however, records were not well kept or not kept at all, and Officers often passed down responsibility for mine laying to junior ranks. It is well documented that a corporal laid minefields at Goose Green and Darwin. Some had been *laid* by soldiers throwing mines from their trenches onto the ground in front of their position. This indiscriminate behaviour led to casualties amongst the Argentinean troops and after their enforced departure, animals wandered into minefields and had limbs blown off or mutilated by anti personnel mines. The British Garrison then had the grim task of dispatching crippled animals. A direct benefit from this unfortunate scenario was that it helped to indicate the presence of minefields, which were then marked and fenced off. Shrouds of barbed wire mark over one hundred plots of abandoned minefields, where ubiquitous red sign warn: *DANGER MINES*. The problem of Falkland minefields with plastic waterproofed mines will still pose problems in 50 years time.

George recalled the thoughts of a tribesman in another war, in another century fought on the other side of the world. He too realised the legacy of minefields laid without proper care. 'You fought your war and went away, but you left these things and now you do not care.'

*

The authorities recognised that the airfield at Stanley was not suited for a normal landing for any aircraft other than a Hercules. Even with a 2,000 yard long runway extension, use of rotary hydraulic arrestor gear was necessary to enable Phantoms to land. A Hercules had to be refuelled several times on a journey from RAF Lyneham in England, and the maximum speed of a Hercules in level flight was less than the safe minimum speed of a Victor tanker. During refuelling, the aircraft had to complete the delicate manoeuvre by maintaining a steady dive, which enabled them to fly at the same speed. The crews nicknamed this as *tobogganing*.

The British Government were committed to defend the islands in a policy referred to as Fortress Falklands. To avoid continuing expenditure and a large permanent garrison, a major airfield and associated installations were constructed near Pleasant Park, an hours drive from Stanley. Mount Pleasant airfield is able to handle large wide-bodied jet transport capable of reinforcing the Falklands at short notice. The flight schedule gets announced each evening on the news, as does a list of passengers booked on each flight. Everyone is kept informed. Tourists visit the island to see the variety of wildlife or visit the battlefields. The war is talked about regularly and even now Argentineans are not allowed to visit.

Port Stanley still comprises typical English houses, from magnificent villas to simple run down cottages, each with its own plot and outhouses, which stand alongside each other in neat rows. The islanders feel isolated and lonely, but at the same time predictably English. Hardly anyone walks or cycles, and the majority of vehicles are Land Rovers. The Islanders form a tight knit community. There is little migration.

Parts of the Falklands still have the feel that military operations are in progress, as if the war never ended. RAF jets scream over Stanley Harbour as a matter of routine, and it is simple to appreciate why the Argentines crouched down at the intense wall of sound. Many places remind islanders of the war in 1982, be it monuments or fenced off terrain with land mines. Throughout the island are several strategically placed and expertly camouflaged Rapier missile sites. The price of vigilance are long frustrating hours of scanning the horizon for intruders. There is one major unanswered question for future Argentinean military intent on reclaiming the Falklands. Will the Rapier crews and RAF pilots actually attack or will they merely warn and escort? Considering the frustration of a five months garrison tour in the Falklands, if a Rapier crew had the chance to engage a live target and were cleared to do so, there would be no hesitation in firing.

*

When Marcelo reached Ushuaia, Argentina's most southern port, he was taken to the Naval Hospital, where his wounds and burns were duly treated. The wounded were looked upon with the greatest regard.

Doctors, nurses, even civilians came to the hospital to visit and everybody did their best to help them recover. Marcelo met several crew members similarly burned, or suffered minor ailments caused by the cold. Rumours abounded about dead bodies found where there were no more than five people manning the raft, and about a couple of capsized rafts, one empty, the other with a pile of dead bodies inside. They heard about cases of trench foot due to freezing bilge water, but fortunately none of them suffered amputation.

From Ushuaia they were flown in a hospital plane to Puerto Belgrano. Unfortunately, on the upper bunk to Marcelo was a first corporal who died during the trip. They all prayed for his soul. The Commander, an old marine, came to see them on the first day. He offered encouragement with phrases like, "Be strong, my boys" or "Come on, marine!" He was an inspiring presence.

When they reached the Puerto Belgrano Naval Hospital, Marcelo was taken to an intensive care room. A Surgeon-Captain entered the room carrying a basin and a bristle-brush of the type used to wash clothes. "What do you like best, chlorinated water or lemon juice?" He asked. Marcelo didn't understand this, but remembered well that when he was a child lemon juice hurt a lot if it touched a cut, so just in case he chose chlorinated water. The Captain filled the basin with liquid, took firmly the brush in his right hand and said matter-of-factly. "Yell as much as you want, but if you touch me, I'll knock you out!" He started to clean up his wounded legs. Marcelo screamed so much he felt sure his cries could be heard in the Antarctic. Once he was finished with the legs he continued with Marcelo's arm and hand. Long before the time brushing was over, Marcelo had passed out. Later the Captain explained that it was the most effective method he knew to avoid infection. He was right. Burn wounds are very painful indeed, not only during treatment but because of the long recovery period required. Marcelo suffered 25% burns with first, second and third degree burns. This notwithstanding, no grafting was ever needed.

After a couple of days, he saw his parents looking at him from the other side of his room window. His mother started to cry and it was not possible to make her stop. His father tried to tell jokes, (they were awful, by the way), to avoid crying himself. They had not received any news since the sinking of the *Belgrano*. They were desperate and had been frantically trying to trace him for days. His Mother surreptitiously entered a corridor when he was being taken to intensive care to be treated and was able to see him face to face. Marcelo realised then that he was probably looking very bad, her face said it clearly, but her eyes also gave him strength. He spent 30 days in the hospital, then went to Buenos Aires to finish his conscription! He was fortunate to be posted to the Northern Dock Naval Station. It was light work. In the remaining four months he spent there, he just did one night watch at the barracks and another at the dockyard. Of course being the quartermaster who prepared the duty lists helped and everybody was friendly towards him. In October 1982 he left the service, and made his way of life, studying, working, raising a family and growing up as a human being.

*

The *Conx* went home to be greeted by a relieved nation united in euphoria at the success of the military operation. At the helm a triumphant Margaret Thatcher riding on the crest of a political wave, taking credit for the success that others earned. Whether she deserved adulation is a matter of opinion, but, had the military failed, she and the nation would have gone through painful period of frustration and anger. In Argentina, a rising tide of civil discontent boiled over into violence on the streets. Conscript soldiers arriving home as prisoners of war, bore the brunt of Argentina's defeat and humiliation. The political inaptitude of the Junta and incompetence of the military became apparent at the time of the surrender. The lies and bluff that Argentina was winning the war then sparked fury, which swept throughout the land.

At Faslane Base, the controversy surrounding the sinking of the *Belgrano* nearly spoiled the party. Those intent on mischief made mileage on whether the *Belgrano* was within the Total Exclusion Zone and whether she was sailing away or towards the Task Force. In reality it was of no importance. The TEZ had no military significance other than to give warning to the enemy and its creation did not imply that ships outside the zone would be safe from attack, disregarding their heading.

Ken and Andy totally ignored the fuss over the controversy. They had carried out orders and knew that as a direct result of the attack, hundreds of British lives had been saved. This was a side issue, as they would have had few regrets over the attack anyway, for they were there to carry out the wishes of politicians no matter how controversial they might be.

*

With few exceptions, most ex *Belgrano* crew members, commanding officers, petty officers and conscripts have never lost their sense of camaraderie. The crew of *Conqueror* dine regularly, for precisely the same reason. It is probable that they have purposely maintained the comradeship they found so many years ago, because that is something precious. Somewhere between the natural suspicions of Falkland islanders,

351

the unpredictable political and military reaction of Argentina and a remote British Government, a way must be found to secure a peaceful future for the Falkland Islands. Perhaps healing wounds will have to start somewhere other than a hospital. Someone should suggest the ex crew of *Belgrano* and *Conqueror* meet, for they share a common bond. They have already settled a dispute where politicians failed. They are enemies no longer and could succeed a second time.

11

Hidden history

The sea has no memory and the history of any stretch of ocean, would have been swept away by the next wave and a succession of waves leaving no trace. The perpetual movement of the sea would eventually disperse any persistent oil slick. The spot where the *Belgrano* sunk beneath the surface appears no different to the water five miles away. Only precise navigation or a GPS system accurately locates it. It is a lonely desolate place even without knowledge of its past. The dead are still the dead, the howling wind from afar, a constant reminder of their state of endless rest.

Those injured by the explosion and trapped when *Belgrano* slipped beneath the waves lie in peace without pain. Many survived the explosion, escaped into a life raft only to die of exposure or were drowned when their life raft capsized. They now sleep, eternal sleep. The only sign of life are passing sea birds and the fish and sea life, which use the rusting superstructure for refuge.

There was one acknowledgement to mark the passing of *Belgrano* when the ship *Lago Lacar* set sail with a small group of Argentinean relatives aboard. They held a ceremony at sea on the first anniversary of the sinking, but where they stopped were miles from the actual place. It is gone, only ghosts remain. It is a buried place. No one to place flowers on graves which do not exist, nor seen by human eyes. Some things cannot be raised. The hull gradually rots beneath the swell, only hope remains.

The history is hidden and will not be seen by human eyes.

History surrounds everyday life even though most folk are in the main unaware of its presence. It is possible to swim in the warm waters of the Mediterranean a few miles west of the Straits of Gibraltar and have your body caressed by microscopic remains of blood from the body of Horatio Nelson, the great English naval commander, who in 1805 lay fatally wounded on the deck on HMS Victory during the battle of Trafalgar. Even as the Admiral lay dying saying his immortal words 'Kiss me Hardy', or the equivalent, a small quantity of his blood gradually seeped along a tarred joint between two great pieces of oak on the gently rolling deck and into a scupper, before draining into the sea. In England to the east of London, a part of Epping Forest called Kingswood, according to local tradition, was felled to build Nelsons Fleet. It would be ironic if oak timber hewed here ended up on the deck of HMS Victory. In this event the swimmer would be totally unaware it had occurred.

Tourists from the four corners of the world wander down The Mall and walk across the junction with Horse Guards Road unaware that they pass by a significant spot. On Saturday 13 June 1981, during the Trooping the Colour Parade to celebrate the Queens Birthday, a man from Kent, fired blanks at Queen Elizabeth II. He found himself promptly disarmed, then arrested by a guardsman on ceremonial duty and a Special Constable. Afterwards there was mention in the popular press that the guardsman was to be charged with disobeying an order as he had moved from the spot where his officer ordered him to stand, but common sense eventually prevailed and all charges were dropped.

The history is there but cannot be seen. How many times has a rural setting been shown on television, when the remains of a magnificent Roman villa are unearthed? The land owner, who together with a local archaeologist are the probable reason for the television company being on site, after finding a few scant pieces of pottery whilst ploughing. The main objective of the programme, the suspected remains, can only be detected by *Geo-psychics*, a process using the technology of radar to locate, that which is below ground. The fact that human eyes cannot see it nevertheless takes nothing away from the fact that it exists.

The history is hidden.

George often walked to a pleasant country park less than a mile from his home near to Claybury Hill Wood. An idyllic setting, the main feature being a large lake where yachts and windsurfs, scurrying back and forth, can be seen virtually every day of the year. The whole site is a nature reserve and bird sanctuary, where at any time of year a large variety of bird species, some in transit urged on by migratory instincts, can be observed with binoculars. Elsewhere, joggers, walkers, some exercising a dog, use the paths for recreation well away from traffic fumes and noise. Near the lake is a public golf course, popular with locals.

Within the site a large Oak tree once stood, situated in the middle of a glade within Hainault Forest in a wooded area known as Kingswood, which legend claimed to have grown for over a thousand years. Part of the great Epping Forest, which once stretched from Epping to Barking a distance of ten miles, the trees were felled to provide the wood for Nelson's fleet. The forest thinned and thinned until the main section south of Chigwell village disappeared altogether apart from the few acres of Claybury Hill Wood, and gradually turned into first farmland and then partial conurbation. The Fairlop Oak survived this onslaught because of its great age and size. It was said that in the midday sun its branches cast a shadow of 300 feet circumference. It was under the branches that a Fair was held from 1725 on the first Friday in July, organised by Daniel Day, a merchant from Wapping. Born in Southwark in 1683 within the parish of St. Mary Overy, south of the River Thames, he later became credited as the founder of Fairlop Fair. He was the son of a brewer, and his trade of Engine, Pump and Block maker took him to Wapping, a north-Thames-side parish in East London.

Daniel Day inherited some property near Fairlop and with some friends travelled there on the first Friday in July to collect annual rents. He arranged for a feast of bacon and beans to be sent from *The Maypole* then he and his friends enjoyed a bean feast under the ancient Fairlop Oak. Over the years other folk joined in and the gathering took on the appearance of a Fair, with sales of gingerbread men, toys, ribbons, together with puppets, circus acrobats, wild beasts and other entertainment. It was said to be most respectable and well regulated, but gaming and illegal sales of liquor took place resulting in the prosecution of several stallholders.

Day who felt most at home on the river, had been involved in several accidents when travelling by horse, mule, and coach, so to give an impression of safety put wheels on a boat. With a team of horses to pull it, he travelled to the Fair in safety and style accompanied by a band of musicians. In the 1750's over 100,000 people attended the Fair from all over London. Day had asked to be buried under the Fairlop Oak but his request was not carried out and he was buried in Barking Churchyard in which parish the Oak was to be found. His headstone can still be seen today. The tree caught alight after being struck by lightning and it burnt for more than 24 hours, despite attempts to put out the fire by local residents. On Fair day in 1813 a gentleman paid a boy 2/6d to climb up and procure the last green sprig. Gales eventually brought the Fairlop Oak crashing down to disappear into the mists of time.

The end of the Oak?

Not quite.

Oak timber was a valuable commodity and part of the Fairlop Oak still exists today. The sounding board at Wanstead Church a few miles away is said to have been made from the great oak.

During the war a fighter station existed at Fairlop with over 1,000 personnel stationed in primitive accommodation, with some irony similar to that in which prisoners of war were housed in Germany. The legendary Spitfires and Hurricanes flew there from 1941. Later came Typhoons and Mustangs. Visiting the site at the present time, it is not too demanding to conjure up with a touch of imagination, the deep throbbing magical sounds of Merlin or Sabre engines combined with rolling clouds and skylarks twittering overhead. Listen to the haunting music of George Butterworth or Vaughan Williams and you will be able to savour the experience.Two Canadian pilots crashed landed after a sortie when their typhoons, both damaged by flak could not make the runway. One crash-landed onto a road by an engineering works and the other into the railway embankment near to Fairlop station. Others set off to war in their Spitfires, Hurricanes and Mustangs and did not return. Nearby in a small churchyard lies the grave of a young Canadian pilot, three thousand miles from his home in Thunder Bay. His gravestone will tell you that he was Jewish, but he was buried within a Church of England churchyard. His gravestone will also tell you, that someone, perhaps a relative, has paid a visit, for in keeping with tradition two pebbles have been left on top of the stone.

The reason for this unusual setting will probably never be established.

The graveyard is tended with care, and a register of graves kept in the Church.

At least a register exists.

George wished there could be a register of the former RAF Station Fairlop site. He also wished there could also be a register in the former ESR factory site.

The history is there but cannot be seen.

Scant moments of history exist as printed paper and in the memories of those who were there and their relatives, who know the stories by heart. Local people in the main are not aware of the past history of their neighbourhood.

It is not commonly known that at the start of hostilities in 1939, 600 Argentine volunteers, of Anglo-Argentine descent, joined the British and Canadian Air Forces, many in the 164 (Argentine-British) RAF fighter squadron, motto *Firmes volamos* (Determined We Fly). Its insignia a British lion in front of a rising sun representing Argentina. Some pilots adorned the side of their aircraft with a picture of a popular Argentine cartoon character called *Patoruzú*, a mythical Indian with incredible strength. In September 1943 the squadron moved to Fairlop, where it was equipped with Hawker Typhoons to begin operations against enemy shipping and coastal targets. After providing support for the landing forces on D-Day the squadron moved to France in July 1944.

Beneath the acres of farmland and the former fighter station site lay tons of aggregate which was extracted in stages and then land filled with rubbish in a similar fashion to Hackney marshes a century before. Initially the ground literally bubbled with escaping methane gas, but this will mean the land remains an open space, or at the very least with limited building opportunities, for the foreseeable future. The fate of the runway was sealed when gravel extraction commenced and it became broken up and dispersed to who knows where. Today no trace of RAF Station Fairlop remains apart from a short section of runway, a handful of tank traps around the perimeter and adjacent to the railway embankment, remains of a gun pit surrounded by trees and bushes. Only the site boundary marks the plot where the airfield stood, but the fact that it cannot be seen does not mean it did not exist.

The same can be said of the ESR factory. The factory no longer exists. Only the site boundary marks the plot where the factory once stood, and even that is difficult to recognise. When the factory closed in 1993 the site stood derelict for months, then construction work commenced by a bulldozer levelling the ground and around the same time a sign appeared erected near to where the original ESR sign stood in Upper Drive. It pronounced in large black lettering. 'Coming soon on this site. Three retail units of electrical, DIY and furniture, with adequate parking.'

The completed buildings retained the trinity.

The first stands on the spot where the drawing office once stood. The second stands on the spot where the telephone exchange, the security office and the corridor to the front office. The third, the largest stands on the spot where the assembly area. used to be.

Three separate units each with its own car parking.

There were 255 Britains killed in the Falklands War, many hundreds more saved by sinking of the *Belgrano*. The sinking is, in some quarters, controversial but not to George and his colleagues. When the *Belgrano* slipped beneath the waves, 323 crew members died. There were three Civilian deaths on the Falklands, all women.

Just to show how history can repeat itself is shown by the original three car parks within the site of the former factory of ESR. The largest contained 320 spaces, about the same number of deaths on the *Belgrano*. The second largest 256 spaces, around the same number as those of the Task Force killed. The final irony were three car spaces in a quiet corner, which visitors passed on the way home, almost hidden from view. The reason for this, if there is one, you will have to draw your own conclusions.

There were other casualties of the war, a few who did not go into battle, heard no guns, but were affected nevertheless. The sinking of the *Belgrano* was their D-Day. As George continued to type it was D-Day plus 10,950 or so and he still felt injured, like an aching back, which will not go away. They, the anonymous go about their lives, with no acknowledgement or gratitude, except that they know that the Sentinel Project and Dunking sonar functioned well despite hostile conditions.

George had few regrets because his work and those of colleagues saved a great number of lives and many were spared the agony of seeing two padres walking up the garden path. They were spared anguish of losing a loved one and the heartache of a funeral. Children grew up knowing their father and doing ordinary things within a complete family. It is for these people that George decided to relate his tale as a reminder of how others helped keep the family intact.

His tale is almost at an end

This text will not be required to be vetted by any authority, nor his previous employer, nor would he claiming that he did anything other than carry out his duties with care. It is perhaps ironic that the purpose of his employment, the Sentinel project was later used by the *Conqueror* in such a publicised manner, in striking contrast to the previous and continuing secrecy surrounding its existence.

*

George once had the opportunity to speak on the radio with a Harrier pilot who flew during the Falklands conflict, when listeners were asked to put questions to him. For George this was too good an opportunity to miss, so he dialled the number at once. He spoke to the producer who asked for his question. 'The Argentineans once showed interest in the Harrier and in 1978 they were given sea trials in the English Channel. For their own reason they concluded it was not suitable.' He said. 'If they had accepted the Harrier and the war commenced as it did, would the air war in the Falklands had a different outcome?'

'Good question George, so I am putting you on first.' A voice crackled through the earpiece. 'When I have finished speaking you will hear the programme live. When you next hear my voice I will be counting you down to you asking your question. Understood?'

'Yes.' George croaked.

This was it, a golden opportunity to speak the unspeakable. There may be a time delay for the broadcast so he may not get away with it, but he was determined to try. He listened to the broadcast continuing, then the producers' voice, quite loud. 'Ok George you will be able to ask your question in the next few seconds. Good luck.'

Good Luck? He was merely asking as question on a local radio station not giving a first night performance of Hamlet on stage.

'We have the first caller. We have on the line, George from Manor Park.'

George found himself shaking

'Good evening George, You are live on London City Radio, what is your question to David?'

'Good evening, David.' He said cautiously.

'Good evening, George'. Came an immediate and confident reply from the Harrier pilot.

He took a deep breath.

'Before I ask my question, I would like to say that it is a great pity that the skill and bravery shown by all members of the Task Force, could not be matched by politicians who caused the conflict in the beginning.' He was about to say more but the interviewer interrupted.

'Thanks for that George, but we are short of time. Your question please.'

His question produced an uncompromising reply, to the effect that the outcome would be the same, as the British equipment, training and the pilots were superior, and in any case the Argentineans were flying far beyond their capability, without good leadership and strategy. George felt disappointed at the negative response to his statement, but the words he spoke were said with sincerity and that is what really matters. It is quite an admission that politicians do not necessarily have adequate skills to carry out the responsibility given to them by the electorate, when they are supreme commanders of a highly skilled workforce and dedicated armed services, prepared and in some cases, required to lay down their lives. It is regretful, but on quiet reflection the British politicians were elected, and as such are accountable, whereas dictators do as they wish without regard of the consequences.

*

George hung onto the fact that the sinking of *Belgrano*, however controversial, saved many British lives by keeping the Argentinean navy in port. The Exocet missile though nearly spoilt the party and the Task Force came close, very close, to disaster. Twenty miles or so that is how close the Task Force came from disaster. Years later George saw video footage taken from *Hermes* showing *Sheffield* ablaze on the horizon. She stayed ablaze for hours before she slowly disappeared from sight beneath the waves. He finally realised just how close the Task Force had been from disaster.

As George typed the last paragraphs, his memories came flooding back.

Regrets?

Yes he had those as well, but his feelings were now under control.

He suffered his anguish back in 1982.

When he heard about the *Belgrano*, George was at home with his family and listened in horror, and managed, just, to keep his feelings hidden. He spent time subsequently agonising over the loss of life, but kept coming back to the saving of British lives. The Argentinean losses were not his concern. Easy to say, but difficult to live with, but he did nothing wrong. The fault lies firmly with the *Junta* who decided to divert attention from a failing economy by invading islands known to them as The Malvinas with an ill equipped, untrained and untried army.

George was still a member of an exclusive club, caught in the Act of the Apostles, but had succeeded in telling his tale, keeping integrity intact, without breaking a trust and most important of all, without revealing a single secret.

A story you now know well.

The secrets you do not and will never hear from his lips.

No certain Members of Parliament, nor a civil servant, a catcher of small burrowing insectivorous animals, nor a housewife, can claim that.

The apostle, still silent, moves onward.

12

Conclusion

Ken completed his service under routine peacetime conditions, retired to Chatham in Kent and went through the motions of easing back into life as a civilian, with strange regular periods of daylight and darkness. He married a local girl but his wife could not cope with the regular bouts of drunkenness and violence, and they divorced within a year.

Unknown to everyone including Ken himself, he harboured a secret reaction to the sinking of the *Belgrano*. Being an outspoken extroverted character, those about him, well used to his forthright manner, tended to ignore what should have been obvious warning signs of mental deterioration. Perhaps unwarranted rudeness hides a deep seated unstable mental condition. His fears dominated his life and manifested itself by an outward resentment to those who showed interest in his life as a submariner. He attended the reunions with great enthusiasm, which successfully masked his anger to most, with one exception.

At one reunion dinner an ex crew member brought with him his brother, a psychiatrist who recognised the signs immediately. During the evening he had opportunity sit at the same table as Ken and used the time to diagnose and suggest a solution to Kens, as yet undeclared mental illness. Eventually Ken realised that his fellow drinker knew all about his condition and fell apart at the seams with relief, knowing help was at hand.

He underwent a period of counselling and has returned to near normal living. He has retained his resentful and outspoken nature, verging on unreasonable rudeness but is able to cope without undue stress. In these enlightened times many folk easily recognise the signs of an unstable personality, especially when they learn of Ken's previous experience.

By contrast Andy felt a loss when Ken retired, but as leading hand concentrated on passing his knowledge and experience to a new generation of submariners. Eventually his period of service came to an end and he left to go to University. He graduated with an engineering degree and went to work for an international engineering company in Germany, a leading manufacturer of pressure sensors.

Andy married and found satisfaction and contentment with his new life but always found time to attend the annual reunions. He detected a deterioration of Ken's health but offers of help were always rejected. Andy was surprised when Ken broke down for he always considered him to be a strong character, when in reality it is not too far short of a miracle Ken managed to get through his service in one piece, without catastrophe.

*

Marcelo went home to his parent's home at Villa Giardino 80 Kilometres north of Cordoba City with the sole intention of picking up the remains of his life again. His physical wounds gave a constant reminder of his near past, subjecting him with a good deal of pain, but the prediction of the Surgeon Captain came true for he remained clear of infection. Then one spring morning his outlook changed dramatically when he met his childhood sweetheart by chance. Marcelo was supposed to be at hospital for a routine check up, but missed the bus. Maria would normally be at work but her mother felt unwell and she had to stay at home and get her medicine. They met on a street corner by the bus stop and a dispensing chemist. There followed a lightning romance during which they were offered unwanted advice from their families against making hasty decisions.

They overcame the reservation of their respective families and married within six months with the blessing of former opposing caring parents turned prospective grandparents.

Maria kept her job as a school teacher whilst Marcelo went to college to emerge as a fully qualified computer programmer. With impeccable timing, around the time Marcelo received his diploma, Maria announced her pregnancy. The grandparents blessed their good fortune, convinced that their advice on caution of the commitment of marriage after a short whirlwind romance was sound, but grateful that it had been ignored. Their first born, a daughter Maria was followed eighteen months later by another, Jude.

Marcelo worked long hours and within five years was promoted to Manager with 15 staff. His career development gave added security and on the first family holiday by the coast he happened to go for a short cruise on a yacht, the first occasion he had been at sea since his service. Despite an initial uneasy feeling, the sight and sound of the sea in good weather conditions rekindled his desire to go back to sea. He overcame his reservations, and the following year the family return to the same resort where he purchased a share in an ocean going yacht.

Around this time he was in communication with George who located him using the Internet. The two men exchanged family photographs as Marcelo related his story of the sinking. After a year of trial day cruises at sea with his co owners, Marcelo revealed his plans to organise a three week trip, which would ultimately end in pilgrimage to the sea above the wreck of the *Belgrano*. Only time will tell whether Marcelo will succeed in realising his dream.

*

After the closure of ESR George quickly adjusted to his new career and routine in the studio and succeeded in the transition and within a year was promoted to graphics designer. Two years later the directors promoted him to Studio Manager.

George faces the prospect of the Fairlop Formation Drinking Team and their reaction to his revelations of his work when his thirty years Official Secrets Act obligations are ended.

When George heard about Marcelo's ambitious plans to visit the *Belgrano* site he felt tempted to ask if he could travel as crew. After much thought he decided against it as he did not feel confident about having to offer an explanation for his presence.

Instead as he approaches his retirement George is taking tentative steps to visit the Falklands *to see the penguins* and is considering travelling to Argentina to meet Marcelo. Only time will tell if George will succeed in realising his dream.